Praise for Donna...
BECAUSE I L...

"In this beautifully rendered, evoca... paints a portrait of star-crossed lovers, brought together by their love of horses and torn apart by tragedy and closely guarded secrets. And yet there is an enduring power to this love that traverses decades and takes many forms, even as their lives take them in different directions. Brown brings her characters from the darkness of loss and betrayal into the light of forgiveness and ultimately peace."

—Mary Morris, award-winning novelist, most recently of *Gateway to the Moon*

"The story is a compelling one, with Leni and Cal's relationship at its core. The two come across as fully realized characters, not just star-crossed lovers. Brown brings both the Texas and New York settings to life, and complex secondary characters, especially Foy and Hank, add to the novel's richness. . . . a page-turning story that will keep readers invested."

—*Kirkus Reviews*

"Cal and Leni first fall in love with horses, then with each other, a love that not even Donnaldson Brown's beautifully rendered North Texas landscapes can contain. Because they've other loves, as well, mathematics for Cal, art for Leni, which conflict with the expectations of their families and their town. There are other secrets, too, one of them buried so deep under Leni's family tree that perhaps it should remain, but it can't, not if Leni is to be free. *Because I Loved You* is deeply affecting, swooningly romantic, hard as diamonds, too: dreams don't always add up, and trouble can sometimes be our friend."

—Bill Roorbach, author of *Lucky Turtle, Life Among Giants,* and *The Remedy for Love*

"The characters in this deeply moving, lushly imagined novel stayed with me long after I turned the last page. A novel of passion and place, ambition and expectation, *Because I Loved You* is a beautifully written story that speaks with equal tenderness to the wild abandon of young love and the awful heartbreak of dreams deferred. A gorgeous debut."

—Amy Brill, author of *The Movement of Stars*

"*Because I Loved You* is a gorgeous book, heartbreaking and joyous, full of love and wisdom. In chiseled prose that evokes a precise sense of place and time, Brown explores the conflicting pulls of love and duty and what a life can be. The novel begins as a slow burn and grows incandescent. You won't want to let go."

—Alexandra Enders, author of *Bride Island*

"As hard as Texan chaparral and encompassing as the night sky, this beautiful debut about two young lovers torn between their life's calling and their desire for one another reads like a saddle you have to get back into, even when it breaks your heart."

—Courtney Maum, author of *The Year of the Horses*

"Expansive and intimate, rural and urban, tragic and romantic, *Because I Loved You* embodies all of the expansiveness and intimacy of a contemporary Western page-turner, and more. Starting in a small town in East Texas and traveling to New York City and beyond, this vivid, riveting narrative will transport you and break your heart at the same time. The vibrant, memorable characters of Leni and Cal will stay with you long after you turn the last page of this beautiful novel."

—S. Kirk Walsh, author of the national bestseller, *The Elephant of Belfast*

"What I love most about Donnaldson Brown's first novel, *Because I Loved You*, isn't the tactile reality of places and times that she so sharply renders—the harsh beauty of East Texas, New York City in the simultaneous throes of guerilla art and AIDS and financial obscenity, the tender urgency of first love—but her ability to feel so deeply into her characters that even as they make shattering mistakes we can believe along with them that their actions are exactly what they need to do in the moment, just as they convince us of who they become in consequence. Brown is a writer with the deepest empathy for imperfect humanity, and her people and their lasting impact on each other is so knowable it makes you ache."

—Kate Moses, author of *Cake Walk, a Memoir, Wintering: a Novel of Sylvia Plath.*

BECAUSE
I LOVED YOU

A NOVEL

DONNALDSON BROWN

SHE WRITES PRESS

Published 2023
Printed in the United States of America
Print ISBN: 978-1-64742-298-1
E-ISBN: 978-1-64742-299-8

Library of Congress Control Number: 2022919482

For information, address:
She Writes Press
1569 Solano Ave #546
Berkeley, CA 94707

Interior Design by Tabitha Lahr

She Writes Press is a division of SparkPoint Studio, LLC.

Michael, this is for you.
Would that you were here to hold it.

And for you, too, Lyle.
You make me so proud.

October 16, 2016

Caleb McGrath

I t is a cool, blustery morning. Caleb McGrath boards a train at Grand Central Station heading north to Wassaic, New York, the last stop on the Harlem River line.

The week before, Caleb saw his brother, Hank, for the first time in forty-two years. Caleb knew Hank had his own well of secrets. It turns out he'd been keeping one of Caleb's, as well. One Caleb didn't even know he had. They are a burden, secrets. Sooner or later we have to leave this world. The fewer secrets we carry, the less bound we are to it.

Sitting upright on the hard, creaking seat, the dog-eared and yellowing diaries and sketchbooks Hank gave him heavy in his lap, he watches the city give way to low-rise suburban houses, clapboard or stucco, and small businesses. Gyms and hair salons, auto repair and lawn mower sales give way to thickets of trees, already yellow and orange, and an occasional bloom of red.

There's no station at Wassaic. Just a platform, not even benches. Though still unaccustomed to it, Caleb's grateful he brought his cane. Something to lean on as he waits and watches the last passenger bounce down the platform steps with her overstuffed knapsack and ukulele and hop into a squat yellow Fiat that barely stops before scampering out and south on Route 22.

Perhaps she's changed her mind. Perhaps she's not coming.

PART ONE:

BETWEEN THE CREEKS

Life is woven out of air by light.
—Jacob Moleschott

CHAPTER ONE

Naples, Texas
August 1972

Leni O'Hare

Her mother's native tongue snaps and spews, skimming after her across the dry goatweed and brush.

"*Madeleine O'Hare!* Come back here. *Reviens! A cet instant! Écoutes-moi! Arrêtes! Arrêtes!*"

But she and Foggy are gone. Galloping beneath the dove-gray sky to the far rise in a frantic waltz—*one-two-three, one-two-three, one-two-three*. She imagines clods of dirt and grass from her dappled mare's hooves, like one of Foy's fastballs, lodging in their mother's throat. That would shut her up. No more talk of selling Leni's prized mare.

At the top of the rise, Leni glares back at the patchwork of paddocks circling their barn, like pieces of the stupid quilt *Maman* makes her work on week after week, scraps of their old clothes and dishtowels, nothing wasted, everything to be used and reused until it's shreds.

Mad all over again, she gives Foggy more rein, urges her on. The mare stretches her neck and lengthens her stride. The saddlebags with grain for Foggy, and the few clothes and whatever else she could grab, jostle behind her. The tall switch-grass passes beneath them like rushing water. Faster and faster, over the crest of the small hill and down toward the river.

But even by the river, with the beating of Foggy's hooves across the dry ground, her mother's shouts seem still trapped between her ears. "*Dieu te vois*. Remember that! God sees you!" Leni tightens her legs around her mare as they jump ditches and dodge one hawthorn bush, then another, desperate to shed her mother's curses, because she'll be as wide and open as this Texas chaparral. Infinite, maybe. Not pockmarked and scarred by her mother's curses, like Evan Holt's face since he came back from Da Nang with shrapnel from his navel to the crown of his head, and now Marguerite—perfect, buxom Marguerite with their mother's dark curls and her always starched blouses and smoothly pressed skirts—won't marry him like she'd promised.

Beyond the bend, across the Old Tram Road, the river widens into a small marsh. Leni pulls Foggy up to a jog, then a walk. Sweat lathers the mare's neck, runs down Leni's neck and back, too. They are both puffing hard.

With the reins loose now, resting on Foggy's neck, the mare picks her way lightly over the dry grasses. Leaves and twigs crunch beneath her hooves as they follow the river north.

Exciting to be on her own. And away—finally—from her foolish mother, in her homemade hats, lace-up shoes, and white socks, insisting Leni give up her horse and barrel racing as though she'd ever be prim and prissy and boy crazy like her sister.

The river winds calmly here, especially lazy now since there's hardly been any rain since spring. Dry as a turkey's gullet, her daddy says. The air, though, is moist and thick today. Foggy's ears spin forward, watching a jackrabbit bounce and weave from a cluster of cottonwood trees into the tall grass.

Clumps of old hardwoods along the shore mark the river's path. Cottonwood and oak mostly, some sumac and scraggly white pines. Leni scans the banks for a place to camp. Here between the creeks, the Sulphur River and the White Oak that dip into Texas at the bottom of the Ozarks, is like nowhere else. These creeks can be nearly dry as spit one day and rise ten feet the next. Along the bottomland, big old boar can spring out, fast and sudden as a pitch hit hard to the outfield. Eagles and osprey hunt over the watering holes. Blue heron and white egret pose, so proud and still, in the tall reeds. There's quail and mourning doves. The white-tailed deer, almost as skittish and muscle-twitched quick as the squirrels. She likes that her daddy and Foy don't hunt, even if some people think that's crazy. There're coyotes and bobcats, of course. Even an occasional, and especially sly, wolf. And she'd need ten minutes to list all the snakes. Most of them you just want to stay away from. The way they flow over the ground, like trickling water so easy and quiet, makes her wonder sometimes if this earth is where she belongs. Except when she's on Foggy.

The day before, Leni was helping her daddy over at the Conyers' big farm on the other side of the creeks. Her daddy's the best vet from Texarkana to Decatur. Everybody says so. They were seeing to one of the Conyers' ewes that had a real bad eye infection. Swollen and pus-filled. The Conyers moved recently from somewhere way over by the hill country. Austin. Or even further maybe. Leni hugged the ewe's nose under her armpit, whispered into the twitching ear, and watched Mrs. Conyer, with her painted nails and twirly skirt, watch her daddy as he worked.

When he finished, Mrs. Conyer looked out across their field and asked, "How can a person get accustomed to so much sameness?"

If a pink sunset, stretched thin like taffy across the entire sky, is the same to a person as a twisting gray funnel cloud swirling through pine woods, then as far as Leni's concerned there's no help for her.

There used to be more people here between the creeks, back when most folks were farming. But the small farms with one or two dairy cows and a few pigs and laying hens gave way to ranches raising beef cattle for the feedlots in Midland or stockyards in St. Louis. The McGraths run the biggest ranch. Her daddy says Mr. McGrath's been buying up land for more than thirty years to run his cattle on, and he's got himself wells pumping out oil from here to Oklahoma, too. Leni sees him on occasion at a rodeo or the feed store. He's built like a tree stump. His older son, Hank Junior, looks just like him—dark-haired and thick all over. Only he'll smile on occasion. At girls, mostly. The younger son, Caleb, is in Foy's grade at Pewitt High, a year ahead of Leni. They'll be seniors this year. Caleb's built like a sapling, tall and smooth. He keeps to himself mostly, from what Leni can tell. Like her.

Leni lets Foggy wade over the rocks into the shallow water. Their hearts beating steady now, calmed by the river and the solitude. The reins slide through Leni's hand as the mare stretches her neck to drink. Leni listens to Foggy's long pulls of water, and wonders what it'd be like to be on her own forever. To follow the sun across the chaparral, bathe in the river, catch a bass for supper, and go back to a shelter she made with her own hands under a grove of hardwoods.

Sometimes you can feel rain in the air and pray for it to fall, but the clouds just slide past, holding on to those precious drops of water until they get to the Gulf. This feels different. Very still.

The sky gray and so close. Leni hadn't thought, and hadn't had time anyway, to fetch a mackinaw or tarp.

Foggy paws at the water. They splash back onto dry land. She was figuring on heading to Billy Drum's place. He's an old friend of her daddy's and retired now. He'd take her in, she's pretty sure. But his old sawmill and barn are another hour's ride north and west. Leni eyes the reeds at the edge of this marsh. She could cut fistfuls of it with Foy's old army knife that she snatched on her way out of the kitchen, find a spot beneath some hardwoods, and make some kind of lean-to. Something to at least keep her saddle and saddlebags dry.

Caleb McGrath

Cal had finished his chores and was waiting out the worst of the August heat in his room, tinkering with the miniature ham radio he kept tucked inside his desk drawer in case someone—namely his father—were to barge in. Hank Senior strictly forbade the radio enterprise. Cal figured it was more because he couldn't understand it than because a ham radio was illegal to operate. Cal built a small one anyway. Using sardine tins for the transmitter and transceiver, hammering the tin lids into shape. Scouring ads in the back of *Popular Mechanics,* he sent away for the coils and tiny transponders, paying with money he earned giving roping lessons to the ranch hands' kids and anyone else who'd ask. The radio operated at about two watts, enough to tune into Mexican operators at night and north into some of Oklahoma most days.

The back door off the kitchen slapped shut.

"Molly!" his father's shout ricocheted through the newly-remodeled kitchen and across the open dining room where the heels of his boots struck the stone floor like matches on flint.

Cal's mother was tall and slender. She wore her hair, which was the pale brown color of winter wheat, in a short bob. Her fingers would often flutter up and smooth strands behind her ears. She was a native to Texas and ranching, but she would fit right in in the suburbs of Dallas or any southern city. There was an elegance about her, and grit. She stood eye to eye with her husband, and had a look—with those pale green eyes—that was about the only thing that could stop him, tightly coiled and ready to spring as he was, in his tracks.

"Where's that boy?" Cal heard his father growl, his ire up. Nothing new about that.

"The one you named?" his mother replied, likely extracting a cigarette from the pocket of the small scalloped apron she wore, over her customary cigarette slacks.

Cal's room and his brother's were just past the living room in the long ranch house. Cal stashed the tray with the radio parts in the desk drawer and pulled toward him the book that lay on his desk, *The Structure of Scientific Revolutions.* He'd read it all, and the parts on Sir Isaac Newton and his theories of light and color two or three times. Such a mystery, light. It marks the very beginning. All life depends on it. It has no mass no substance. It is intangible and perfect. Its particles immaterial and immortal, possessing infinity. The book opened to Niels Bohr, quantum mechanics. Particles and quarks, packets of energy that, in fact, led to the development of transistors, but he flipped back to Sir Isaac Newton. Laws of planetary motion.

Cal listened to the *thwack, thwack* of his father's boots on the slate floor as he marched past the wet bar, toward the sunken living room with the wide stone hearth and the new shag carpet, the color of fresh copper, shipped all the way from Atlanta.

Newton's father, an illiterate farmer, died before baby Isaac was born on Christmas Day, 1642, in Lincolnshire, England, and his mother abandoned him to marry again before he was two, returning when he was eleven to pull her son—one of the most brilliant minds the West has ever known—out of school and plop him on a farm to muck stalls and milk goats. Parents are not always one's allies.

"You set foot on my new carpet with those boots," his mother's warning, "and you are sleeping in the shed. And what are you in such a fuss about?"

"The hay!" his father shouted.

Cal's father was thick all over, with a short neck and barrel chest and thighs like full gallon jugs that brushed against each other when he walked. His work shirts pulled tight across his chest into tiny sharp folds at each button. The silver buckle on his belt, the size of a playing card, wedged just below his gut. His black hair was flecked with gray. But he was still a man one would think more than twice about getting into a fight with. Most men, to avoid saying the wrong thing, just got quiet around him. Except for Hank Junior. His brother liked a dare.

"I'll get Caleb," his mother said. Her voice, made husky from cigarettes, was deeper than one might expect, looking at her.

"We got to get up to the Lacey and get that damned hay in before this storm."

"Where's Hank Junior?" Cal heard the quick *click click* of his mother's shoes on the stone floor, as she approached his room.

"That I do not know."

"We got to be easy on him yet," his mother said.

"Easy, my ass. Call George and Danny. Tell them to meet me at the Lacey."

"Hon?" Cal's mother tapped softly on his bedroom door. "Your daddy and 'em need you to help bring in the hay that's been cut."

Cal looked out his window, west across the driveway toward the horse barn. The house was built on a lot carved out of a sprawling pasture, set a good quarter mile back from the road. A year and a half earlier, Hank Senior had taken down the old two-story clapboard farmhouse with its low-slung eaves and a porch that stretched along two sides and built the one-story brick ranch house that looked like every other house built in east Texas since 1960, only bigger. And with central air and heat. Cal glanced out at a stretch of dusty sky, nothing too ominous.

"You know where your brother's at?" she asked.

"No, ma'am. He doesn't answer to me." More than likely his brother was sitting at the Roadhouse, a couple of empties in front of him, or in town chain-smoking in front of the 7-Eleven with a couple of other vets recently returned from the war. They clung together like burrs.

"Hurry now. Your daddy's waiting on you."

To the east, through the spotless picture windows that ran along the living room and dining room, Cal could see clouds as black as barrels lining the horizon. A herd of white-faced Herefords beyond the fence circling the house grazed and flicked their tails, unaware or resigned.

By the back door, Cal pulled on his boots and grabbed an apple from the counter, his hat from the rack, and headed out to the driveway. But Hank Senior was already halfway to the County Road, dust jetting out behind his shiny red pickup and rippling across the dry grass. Cal had let Hank Junior take his truck earlier that afternoon, because his—so his brother said—was at a friend's, with a flat tire.

On a rise past the driveway, a five-foot steel fence enclosed the horse barn and paddocks. Cal saw to the horses, up early each morning to feed and water them, home before supper each night to feed and water again.

Captain Flint, Cal's big bay, swung his head over the fence and watched Cal approach. For his tenth birthday, Cal's mother convinced their father to let him have the pick of the yearlings. Every day for two weeks, Cal went down to the yearling pen and to the broodmare pasture. His father grumbled, wondered when "the boy" was going to make up his "damned mind." But this was the most important decision Cal had yet faced, and he knew it. He'd go after school, before starting on his chores, sit on the fence, and watch the young horses play and graze. Walter, their steady, trustworthy foreman, went with him the first few days, talked with him about horses. Cal quickly narrowed it down to three: Flint, a strawberry roan, and a bay mare. The next week, he picked Flint because he was strong—he had good straight legs and a wide chest—and because he noticed everything, from a butterfly flying jaggedly through the paddock to a tractor engine starting up in the machine barn a good seventy yards away. Cal reasoned he'd be sensitive and smart. And he thought the horse was pretty with his shiny dark coat, white stockings on his front legs, and a blotch of white on his forehead.

Once he'd decided, Walter laid a sturdy hand on Cal's shoulder. "Good choice, young man," he said, nodding, and went back to work. Cal felt proud. And Walter was right. It was a good choice. At eight years old, Flint had filled out beautifully. Thick round rump, that deep chest. He was tall for a quarter horse, but still agile and quick. Too quick sometimes. A little high-strung. But he and Cal were partners. They understood each other, trusted each other.

As Cal crawled between the lower bars of the fence, Captain Flint's rubbery lips mussed his hair and shirt collar. Cal opened his palm and let Flint have what was left of the apple, one bite, then the last. Juice and seeds slid through his fingers.

The air was getting darker. Not the softness of dusk, but heavy, like metal dust was falling over the chaparral. Cal gave Flint a quick brushing—while the other horses looked on, smug and lazy—and slung the blankets and saddle across his back, cinched him up, and got on.

As he started toward the County Road, his mother hurried out of the house and called after him, the wind yanking her hair loose and flinging it about her face.

"I don't want you riding out with this weather coming," she yelled. "You know better 'an that."

Cal also knew they had to get the hay in before the rain spoiled it.

"You take my car." She held her hair off her face with one hand and pointed to the new blue Buick lurking in the carport with the other, cigarette smoke swirling above her head.

"I'd get stuck soon as I turn off County Road," Cal shouted over the wind, as Flint pranced sideways. "I can make it in fifteen minutes on Flint."

She knew that was so. "All right then," she said as she ground her cigarette out with the toe of her shoe like it was a cockroach. "All right . . ." She waved him on as though tired of the whole lot of them, stubborn men, and started back to the house.

When Hank Junior got drafted and shipped off to the other side of the world, their mother got more edgy. Smoked more. Drank more bourbon come sundown. She told Cal late one night when they were alone that if she had to send another son clear across the globe to some jungle swampland the size of a Texas county, she'd do something drastic. That she was sure of, she said, bourbon sloshing the sides of her glass as she stared him down, leaving Cal to wonder just what his mother was capable of in defense of her sons.

Flint and Cal jogged away from the barn. The branches of the old maple trees by the gate quivered, showing the undersides of their leaves as though asking for rain. Cal and Flint sidled up to the gate, let themselves through under the leery eyes of a couple dozen cows huddled together beneath the trees, their bellies already taut with next spring's calves, and loped north toward the Lacey hay pasture.

CHAPTER TWO

Leni

Behind a grove of thick leafed yaupon hollies on the White Oak's banks, Foggy grazes lazily, pausing now and again to run her nose against her foreleg or shake a stray fly from her face. Leni takes out her daddy's old canteen. It's dented and the stained canvas is fraying, but it doesn't leak. From her saddlebags, she gets the bread and cheese she swiped from the kitchen counter before her mother could stop her, then lays out the blanket—her daddy's from his war—brown and threadbare in places. She unwraps the cheese, pulls a slice of bread from the plastic wrap, and watches the skinny switchgrass and bluestem bend toward her in the wind sweeping over the pasture.

Maman. Damn her. Thinking Foggy was hers to sell. To some Mr. Royce from Tyler. Leni doesn't care how much money he was willing to give. So his little girl can start racing barrels? Leni and Foggy race barrels (when she can earn the entrance fees). And ride the chaparral. And swim in the McPeels' watering hole. Leni tends to her every day. Grooms her, feeds her, beds her stall thick with straw. "No!" she said. Foggy is hers. As much as her arm is hers.

And Leni thought that was that.

When that shiny silver horse trailer came bouncing down the drive, Leni knew. That was no one with a sick animal looking for her daddy. It was that Mr. Royce. Needles ran through her veins.

Leni flew up the stairs, four at a time. Grabbed her diary, sketchpad, pen, and ink.

Cradling them to her chest, she yanked her blue sweater from the drawer, boots from the floor. Ran out through the kitchen. Maman shrieking behind her. She snatched Foy's pocketknife from the table, swept the bread and cheese and two apples (which fell out of her arms by the door) off the counter, and tore toward the barn, as the trailer, a big four-horse one, pulled by a matching double-cab pickup, rattled toward the house.

The goats scattered across the paddock, while Agnes, the milk cow, and Roger, Doc O'Hare's old roan, always laconic, watched. Foggy, head high, jogged to the fence, following Leni to the barn. Kicking the tack room door open, Leni grabbed a saddlebag. She dumped the sweater, pocketknife, pads, pen, and ink into one side, and dashed to the feed room. She sloppily scooped oats into the other side of the saddlebags. Then back to the tack room where she rolled the canteen, halter and lead rope, and food into her father's blanket. Tied the whole mess onto the back of her saddle tight. Flinging Foggy's bridle over her shoulder, she jogged to the paddock and slid the barn door open. Foggy—sensing the emergency this was—was already there.

The trailer began its slow circle in front of the house. The kitchen door snapped shut. Her mother hurried out, waving to Mr. Royce.

Leni slipped the bridle over her mare's head, led her into the barn. In front of the tack room, she smoothed the mare's coat with her forearm—no time to brush—and hoisted the blanket, saddle, then the saddlebags onto her back.

Maman was calling. "*Madeleine! Madeleine! Viens-ici!*"

Leni grabbed the cinch and pulled it tight under Foggy's belly.

"*Madeleine!*" Her mother scurried toward the barn. Her small, plump frame, her quick, tight steps. Her large breasts bouncing. "*Écoutes-moi, Madeleine!*"

The fool Mr. Royce was trying to back the trailer up between the paddocks. But the damned thing was so big—maybe he was figuring on taking every one of their animals. He pulled forward, began all over again. Maman, trying to appear in control (always), waved to Mr. Royce, then dodging the trailer, hurried up between the paddocks toward the barn.

Leni couldn't take Foggy out the front. Their only chance was to slip out through the stall for the goats at the end of the barn, where the eaves slope steeply and the Dutch door's so low, Leni has to duck her head to get through.

"Stay with me, Foggy girl. Stay with me. We can do it . . ." Leni willed herself to speak calmly and low.

"*Madeleine!*" Her mother was in the barn.

"You got to do this, girl," Leni murmured to the mare, and flicked her tongue, *cluck, cluck, cluck.*

Foggy raised her head again and, slinking onto her haunches, backed up. Leni snapped the ends of the reins against the mare's rump hard as she could. Out Foggy bolted—the saddle scraping the stall door—Leni at her heels.

Mr. Royce's pickup revving behind her, her mother screaming her name, Leni—reins in hand—ran to the gate, Foggy jogging beside her. She unclipped the chain from the gate. Foggy sidestepped, eyeing the barn, then jogged forward through the gate. Her mother's yells had become shrieks. The goats bucked and mewed in the paddock behind her. Leni pulled the gate closed, leapt onto Foggy. And off they ran.

Away from the barn and the house, her mother's shrieking,

and up over the rise, into the deep grass and down to the river where Mr. Royce and his big new trailer could never follow.

A bite of cheese. A bite of bread. She can't tell if she's hungry or not. The sun begins to melt over the pine barrens toward Sugar Hill. To the east, thick clouds pulled by the wind from the north are sinking over the chaparral.

Leni watches a young willow tree bow with the wind toward the river. She sets down the bread and cheese and goes to the saddlebags for her sketchpad and pen. Not just any pen. The Rapidograph her daddy got her at a veterinary conference two years back in Galveston. He took Leni with him, thinking the sea air would clear up the bronchitis she'd been fighting for near a month. What did her good, though, was seeing the horizon over the water, so big she could make out the curve of the earth. Something she hadn't known how to imagine before. Not really. Made her wonder about all the things that lay beyond her sight. It opened her mind to possibilities. Doc O'Hare wrapped the pen himself in thick brown paper with a gold ribbon almost as wide as the box.

Leni dips her hand into the saddlebags. Something's damp and mushy. The bottom of her sweater wet as if with blood. She takes it out, opens it wide. A jagged black pattern across the bottom of the sweater. Her fingers now moist and black. The ink jar lost its top. Black has seeped across each page of her sketch-pad, blotting out portraits of Foggy, the goats, and the rooster. Ink crept over sketches of the green and rusted tractor beside the well, smearing the pines and hardwoods that divide their house and barn from the river. Damn. And the composition notebook with its black-and-white mottled cover she uses as a diary? A smudge of ink, like a fat pig, all across the front.

A wind gust leaves the hair on her arms and head prickling like she's been jolted. She stares upriver, into the wind. She has only the clothes on her back. A dollar twenty in her pocket. And a loaf of bread. Still, though, better to be out here, free, with Foggy than without her in that cramped house with Marguerite whimpering and Maman nagging, and Daddy reading in his office with the door closed. She didn't want to think about how, if she were at home, she'd watch the storm with Foy. How they'd crouch by his bedroom window. Listen to the rain splatter the sides of their frail house and wait for lightning to streak across the sky. How they'd sneak down to the kitchen at night for peanut butter and crackers, then go back up to write on his ceiling with flashlights.

Waiting out a storm is a risky business. She knows this. Twisters can touch down and race across the chaparral with little warning. The charred stalks of trees smote by lightning stand barren and eerie in nearly every pasture. She considers again pushing on to Billy Drum's place, but she knows she can't get there before the storm hits.

Back to the blanket to think. Another bite of cheese. The soft white bread sticks to the roof of her mouth. They'll be sitting down to supper in another hour. Marguerite will surely be ruffled, having to clear the table and tend the animals. No one looks after the animals as well as Leni does. Marguerite won't wet down Roger's hay, so he'll likely get his cough back. And she won't make sure the goats, Heidi and Scarlet and Clementine, get the proper table scraps—no meat or grease—if there are any scraps left, that is. Now that football practice has started, Foy's eating like a pair of oxen. And Marguerite won't look over the animals for cuts or scrapes or sadness in their eyes either. All that Leni's learned from their daddy.

Two years ago, her mother sold the pigs, Troy and Sissy, when they were only four months old. That was sudden, but not so unexpected. This time last year, she sold Gracy, the donkey, to Mrs. Burton who wanted a donkey to pull a cart for her grandchildren. Crazy idea. Anybody but her mother knew you couldn't get that donkey to do a damned thing. She was an inordinately lazy animal who could calm down other creatures like some kind of hypnotist—a nervous horse, sheep, or cow that might be there for her daddy's tending. Too bad she couldn't calm down her mother. Leni knew her daddy liked the donkey, too. Foy had broken his arm. Maman declared—not even looking up from shelling peas when Doc O'Hare asked where the donkey had gotten to—that she sold the animal to pay for Foy's doctor's bills. It didn't make any sense to Leni. They'd never gone without doctor's appointments. Or food. Or clothes on their backs, even if they weren't as fancy as Marguerite would pine for. Were things really that hard? World War II's over, she wants to shout, but doesn't.

Foggy, though? Her Foggy? "You spend too much time with 'zht hoss,'" was her mother's refrain. So Leni had fallen behind on her chores around the house. Chores that Marguerite did until she graduated high school and started working at DeWitt's Hardware and Feed. The way Leni sees it, if any little thing doesn't go her mother's way, she casts her disappointment about like a spell. Leni knew her mother thought she was marrying a medical doctor when she left the north of France and landed in forlorn Naples, Texas. Quite a surprise to discover he was an animal doctor. Leni, though, thinks her father's profession—taking care of animals—is the noblest. He's patient and caring. And he works harder than anyone else she knows.

Leni doesn't want to keep thinking of her mother. But she can't stop. What is Maman thinking now? After this, Leni's declaration of independence. How's Maman going to explain this to her daddy? Maybe—finally—Maman will see that she can't just push and mold people into whatever it is she wants them to be. Every person has a purpose. You can detour for only so long before you either get too lost from yourself to ever return or something bursts.

And, yet, she knows she can't stay away forever. Once Foggy's somewhere safe, she'll head home. And get grounded for eternity.

The air is eerily quiet. The soft *rip, rip* of Foggy snatching grass is about the only sound. No birds calling. No flies whirring. She needs to build her shelter. There's a sumac tree next to a fallen oak, two small yaupon hollies next to it. And taller trees nearby to draw any lightning, she hopes. Leni folds the bread over the bit of cheese in her hand, stuffs it in her shirt pocket and begins gathering branches, propping them between the downed oak and the yaupon. With Foy's pocketknife, she cuts long stems of grass by the handful and weaves them in and out of the branches and twigs.

Suddenly, Foggy's head shoots up, stalks of grass jutting from her mouth.

"What is it, girl?" Leni follows the mare's gaze back toward the direction they came from. Nothing. Foggy resumes grazing and Leni resumes weaving, trying as best she can with the tender grasses to tighten the branches and twigs. It's close to futile. The best she can do is a rickety excuse for a covering, barely as wide as the moth-eaten blanket she'd brought. It is nowhere near watertight and even she can smell the rain coming now. She finishes the last bite of bread and cheese and tries to patch a few more gaps and slits. It's ridiculous.

With the lead rope in hand, Leni pulls Foggy's head up from the grass and starts toward the trees. The lower branches of the sumac are just tall enough for Foggy to stand under. Leni brings her tack under the shelter and she and Foggy stand beneath the small trees to wait out whatever's coming.

Foggy begins to fidget. A rumble starts deep in her chest. Her ears strain to hear something behind her. She tries to back out from under the tree, but a lower branch pokes her rump and she scoots forward. Holding the lead rope tight, Leni climbs up on the fallen tree and peers over the rise.

Moving slowly along the low ridge, a half mile away, is a lone horse and rider. Scrambling off the log, Leni takes Foggy down to the river, farther out of sight, and wraps the lead rope around the roots extending off the end of the fallen oak. Was someone sent to look for her? Someone sent by that Mr. Royce? Or maybe it's one of the cattle rustlers her daddy's been talking about—some animals went missing from a neighbor's place just last week, right before their calf sale.

Foggy nickers again. Leni scrambles back up on the log. The rider is calling out. This time, Foggy throws her head up and whinnies loud. Leni leaps down the bank, grabs her saddle. Foggy lets out another whinny. Loud and shrill. Scanning the river for a place to cross, Leni jogs toward her, stumbles and falls, landing on her saddle. Leni tries to hoist the saddle onto Foggy, but the mare scuttles away. Leni yanks on the lead shank. Foggy throws her head and backs up, splashing into the water.

The other horse is answering now, the wind carrying its whinny. A whinny with a curlicue at the end, like a yodel.

Leni sets down the saddle and steps back onto the log. Looks out over the pasture. Damn if it isn't Foy on old Roger. She yells, waving her arms until Foy sees her and waves his baseball cap over his head. He pushes Roger into a trot and finally a slow, rocking lope, which is the most that old horse'll do for anyone.

Foy arrives, one hand gripping the saddle horn tightly. Good thing, too. Roger nearly pulls him out of the saddle to start grazing before he's even come to a full stop.

"Nice riding!" Leni calls out.

"*Madeleine O'Hare, qu'est -ce que tu penses que tu fais?*" he says, eyebrows raised. It always makes Leni laugh to hear Foy with his strong athlete's build and blond wavy hair fall into his Maman-mimicking falsetto.

Leni pulls Roger's head up from the grass.

"Hell, Leni." Roger lunges for more grass. "You're gonna get wetter 'an a rat out here. You're gonna get me wet, too, goddammit."

"Stop whining."

"And that'll blow off faster than a squirrel can scale a tree." He's pointing to the rickety lean-to.

"I am not going back there," Leni says.

"He's gone," Foy answers.

"Who's gone?"

"That Mr. Whoever-he-was from Tyler. I got home from practice not long after you ran off."

"He'll come back."

"He ain't coming back," Foy says, letting Roger snatch a mouthful of grass.

"How d'ya know that?" Leni asks. Foy is a person who thinks life is fair and reliable.

"Because Daddy told him the mare was not for sale."

"How'd Daddy do that? He wasn't home."

"I knew he was up at the Conyers' place again. I called him. And he came on home. So, you can come on home now, too. We got to hurry."

Leni has been holding on so tight to her scheme, half-formed as it may be, she has to reconsider everything now.

"Leni, come on."

"OK. I don't know. Maybe." She's patting her chest. Trying to think. "Have a smoke with me first." She starts toward the saddlebags.

"Where'd you get cigarettes?"

"I know where Daddy stashes them."

Foy swings his leg over Roger's neck and slides to the ground. Everything he does, he does smooth, graceful like, whether he's pitching or batting, running past linebackers, helping their daddy hold a calf, or combing his hair.

Foy lights Leni's cigarette, then his own. They stand side by side and smoke. Roger winds mouthfuls of grass around his bit with his slow, thick tongue, and Foggy—ever the scout—snatches a wad of grass, then head up, peers into the wind, tasting the air. Land floats out all around them, the river softly laps at its banks to their left, sumac and yaupon leaves rustle behind them as the storm clouds suck up the last light.

Then—wham! The first slap of thunder is a doozy! Roger flings his head up. Foy catches the reins as they fly out. Foggy jumps. Leni plants her feet and holds the lead rope with both hands.

"Well, Madeleine Bonet O'Hare, you willful child," mocking their mother again. "Can we get back home now?"

"I am sleeping in the barn, though."

"What?"

"I am not setting foot in that house tonight." She is adamant. "That's all."

"You going to get dressed for church tomorrow in the barn?"

Leni grunts. "I'm not going in the house. Till," how does she get out of this, "I don't know when."

"Suit yourself. Come on."

Foy picks up Leni's saddle and swings it onto Foggy's back while Leni rolls up their daddy's blanket, letting what's left of the now gritty bread and cheese fall to the ground. She lays the saddlebags across the back of her saddle, picks up the ruined sweater and sketchpad, and lifts the flap to put them in.

"What happened there?" Foy nods toward the pad as he tightens Foggy's cinch.

"An accident."

"Lemme see." He reaches for the pad.

"No, Foy. Come on, if we're going to go."

His hand lands on the pad. Leni lets him take it.

"It's nothin'. Come on." Now she's whining.

But Foy is turning the pages, one by one. His eyelashes are so thin and long. She'd never realized there was anything fragile about Foy. Solid, conscientious Foy.

"I'm real sorry, Leni. All this work."

"It's nothin'."

"It's something, Leni."

He flips through the pad until there are no more ruined drawings to look at and hands it to her. She slips it back into the saddlebag.

They mount Roger and Foggy and start off.

"You go on," Foy says. "You can ride home and back three times before Roger and I'll make it."

"I'm not in any hurry."

Riding side by side, they pull up their collars, roll down their sleeves, and hunch their shoulders. Not that any of that will keep them dry. Leni slaps Roger's big rump with the end of her reins. They jog slowly away from the river, back across the long pastures. Thunder rumbles. A strand of lightning sizzles across the sky before them.

Caleb

Truth be told, Cal's father would rather have had his head bent over his ledger books than talk with any person, unless that person was going to buy something from him. He'd worked hard from the time he was twelve, something he liked to remind Cal of often, especially if Cal was doing something useless, in his father's estimation, like reading. From the time Hank Senior was ten or eleven, he had to help make ends meet. It was the Depression. By fourteen, he'd proved himself to be quite a salesman. He sold seeds and tools, things he found, things he found and fixed. He lost part of his left thumb to a welding torch at fifteen. But that didn't deter him.

In 1936, when he was sixteen, his mother, father, and three sisters—one with a husband in tow—left Texas and headed west. He didn't go with them. He had been earning more money than all of them put together, so he struck out on his own. Within a year, he bought his first car off a rancher who'd already lost half his land, a 1926 Ford Model A sport coupe. He lived out of that car, traveling and selling whatever he could to whoever would buy it. He ate one meal a day and allowed himself one beer and one whiskey a week, which didn't save him from a bar fight now and again, like the one in Texarkana when he got his nose broken and nearly lost an eye. A man came up behind him and hit him upside his head with a bottle, left him with a scar across his temple and over his ear, and no peripheral vision in his left eye. He'd never say why that man came up on him like that. Hank Junior would laugh when Cal asked him, like he knew but couldn't tell the likes of Cal. The injury kept their father out of the war, though.

Through the Depression and into the early forties, the oil business needed men to lay pipe and work the rigs. And that's what Hank Senior did. The dust bowl didn't reach down as far as east Texas, but the boll weevil and drought did and drove many families off their farms. In 1939, at nineteen, Hank Senior bought thirty acres in Bowie County. Then twenty more alongside those. In '43, he bought a small farm over the border in Oklahoma. That was the first one they found oil on. It wasn't too long after that he was doing some wildcatting himself. He was no geologist. He didn't even finish ninth grade. But he had guts and luck. By 1946, with the war over, he owned twelve hundred acres and at least a portion of the mineral rights to two dozen wells. By the time he was thirty, he was putting together the ranch on close to 8,000 acres. There were ten wells on the ranch alone, pecking and sucking at the earth like giant robotic chickens day and night.

A t the Lacey meadow, with clouds blanketing the sky over-head, Walter, their foreman, was on a baler that knocked and sputtered across the meadow, raking up the shorn stalks of Bermuda grass, stiff and sun-bleached to a pale, chalky green. The machine bound the bales into tight rectangles and spit them out one at a time, every thirty feet.

Cal's father was on the tractor, pulling the flatbed. Two of the ranch hands, Danny and George, were on either side throwing bales up onto it while Errol, Walter's skinny son, stacked them.

"Tie that damned horse up," his father shouted, "and start throwing bales."

If he'd been his brother, he would have yelled right back, "If you'd have had the sense to wait two and half minutes and let me ride with you, I'd already be here throwing bales." But he wasn't Hank Junior.

Diesel fumes, acrid and oily, seeped over the meadow. Cal led Flint to the one tree—a lone pine, scraggly and awkward as an oversized scarecrow, near the bottom of the meadow—and wrapped a rein around a thick fallen branch at its base, then jogged out to the tractor grinding its way up the field. His father was at the wheel, steady on. Danny, Errol, and George were keeping up. Danny saw Cal and leapt onto the flatbed to help Errol stack; Cal took Danny's place throwing bales. They worked like machines. Lifting a bale, hoisting it onto the flatbed. Ten steps forward. Another bale. Lift, hoist. Over and over. Soon the flatbed was piled high and his father turned the tractor and started for the hay barn.

"Cal!" he yelled. "Load up that pickup." He pointed to the new pickup, a hundred yards away.

It'd be faster for him to help unload the flatbed, so they could get it back out to the meadow, and he told his father so.

"You know better 'an me? Is that it?" his father yelled, as the tractor burped fumes and smoke.

Cal shrugged. He was done shouting over the wind and the knocking and whirring of the machines.

"George! Is it faster that way?"

George looked at Cal, then his father.

"You know he ain't gonna say nothing," Danny yelled.

"When you gonna say something, George? When's he gonna say something, Danny?"

No one answered.

"All right, goddammit. Help with the flatbed."

Errol and Danny unloaded the flatbed, while George and Cal stacked the bales, then jogged back out to start loading it up all over again. Their heads bowed into the wind, they moved, steady and fast, to the rhythm and drone of the engines. As they threw bales, splinters of stiff dried grass worked their way inside their shirts, down their necks and the back of their pants, even inside their boots, where they stuck to the salt and sweat on their skin.

"Come on, come on," Cal's father yelled. "We can get this load in and one more!"

The tractor jerked and groaned across the meadow. The men followed. Hoist, heave. Ten paces. Hoist, heave. Cal's gloves ripped across the palms where the baling twine dug in. The air an eerie green, and too still, tasted like gunmetal.

They were loading the flatbed up for the third time when the first drops of rain—fat as bullets—broke the spell. Minutes later, lightning flashed and thunder shattered the sky.

Cal looked to Flint. He was crouching like he wanted to sit down, his nose pushing skyward again and again, as he tried to yank the rein free from the branch he was tied to. Cal ran toward him, calling his name. The branch bounced closer and closer to the horse's legs.

Lightning again blazed across the sky, pulling down thunder and sheets of rain. Flint flung his head upward again and the tree limb snapped. He skipped backward, rearing up. A jagged piece of branch swung toward his legs, and the rein gave way. Free, Flint careened toward the road and out the open gate, his tail high and straight out behind him.

Cal ran to his father's truck and jumped in. He gunned the new truck, bouncing in and out of ruts, his head hitting the roof of the cab. On the old oiled road, he drove, weaving around tire ruts and potholes like a crazed snake. He knew his father would be screaming and swearing a streak. He didn't care. Not a half-mile down, the road began to narrow. The Sulphur River was close and rising already. Flint could have dodged into the woods, even crossed the river or stayed on the road. Cal had no idea. The rain washed any tracks away. Branches and brush screeched against the sides of the truck like fingernails on a chalkboard as he fish-tailed in the slick mud. He knew he should stop. He knew Flint was past where he could follow in the truck. But he kept going.

Ahead a small ash tree had fallen across the road. Water fell with such force, it blanketed the truck like a shroud, the wipers unable to keep the windshield clear. Cal rocked the truck back and forth, getting enough momentum for the front tires to climb over the tree, which scraped the undercarriage all the way to the rear axle. The back tires scrambled over. Thunder exploded again. He kept on. Around the next bend, the road narrowed further. The river was rising. He couldn't go forward. One mistake had piled on top of another and another as the rain pummeled the truck and mud clutched at the tires.

Leni

Leni and Foy jog slowly alongside County Road. The rain's coming hard and fast. Leni shivers, more from anger than the wet. From being misunderstood.

Foy twists, gives Leni his goofy wide-mouthed grin and lets his broad shoulders and narrow pelvis roll and tumble with Roger's plodding trot like he's a sack of potatoes. Leni smiles.

Watching the wet drip down her brother's arms and back and down Roger's shoulders and haunches, she feels bad. He wouldn't be out here in this, with thunder and lightning closing in, but for her. Her and Maman's fighting.

Foy lifts the drenched baseball cap off his head and combs his hair with his fingers. It's a mystery to Leni how her brother got such fair hair. Their daddy's hair's the color of walnut. Her mother's and Marguerite's is as dark as black coffee. And hers is a red brown like mahogany. Maman says her daddy and her two brothers were blond. Leni doesn't believe her, but there's no way of knowing because they're all dead. And she has no photographs. They died in the war, both of her brothers and her daddy, and cousins and neighbors, whole villages set out along the rocky north coast of France, when it was battered for days and weeks and months on end, over and over, by gunfire and grenades and the sea and rain, until they all nearly drowned in rubble and mud and blood. That's how Leni sees it, at least. From the way her mother told it, that one time, sitting around the kitchen table, waiting out a storm that knocked out the lights and pounded the roof. Maman's eyes fixed on hemming a skirt in the dull light of the kerosene lamp. Her fingers—evenly, methodically—looping the needle through the fabric as she talked. Almost like none of them was even there. Her mother's voice soft, younger-sounding. Foy and Marguerite stopped their game of gin rummy. Leni stopped oiling the bridle in her lap, looked to her daddy. He sat, pipe poised in the corner of his mouth, eyes on their mother. Slowly, he reached a hand toward her. The softest pat on her forearm. She just kept sewing. Kept talking, more and more French weaving in and out of her words. Doc O'Hare retracted his hand. Around the table, in the shadows of the kerosene lamp, they listened.

Maybe, Leni thought, her father married her mother to rescue her. Can't get much farther from Normandy, France, and that drenched, rocky coast than dry, scrappy Morris County, Texas. Leni found it hard to think of two people who seemed more incompatible. Her daddy, unflappable animal lover who could lose himself in thought staring out over the land, and her practical mother, all purpose and routine. Her father had been a medic in the war. He had his own stories, which he kept to himself. Leni looked at her mother that shadowy evening, her fingers working, talking to herself as much as she was talking to them. There was something stunned and small and fragile about her. It made Leni worry. Worry for all of them. What would happen, really, if her mother crumbled? Leni wanted to know more. Before bed that night, though, walking up the stairs with a feeble flashlight, her father said they oughtn't ask their mother for any more stories. When Leni asked why, all he said was some things are better left in darkness.

So Leni's left wondering what her grandfather looked like. If her mother felt the same way about him that Leni feels about her daddy. Wonders if Foy resembles Maman's brothers. Her ghost uncles. Or a lost cousin. Did sports and games come as naturally to them as they do to Foy? Did they poke fun at their little sister, Maman, and make *her* laugh at herself, like Foy does? Foy may not be the smartest boy, at least not at school; nobody can help but like him, though. Every new school year, the teacher will look up that first morning during roll call, smile, and ask Leni, "How's that big brother of yours doing?"

Water is gushing from the sky. The culverts along County Road are filling fast. Leni and Foy turn off and cut across the deep grass behind their barn to come in between the paddock fence and the woods. Lightning flashes over the empty paddocks. The goats and Agatha are in their stalls. The hens in their coop. The house is completely dark.

Thunder so loud it hurts, like being inside a barrel, crashes above them. Foggy's balled up like a spring and sawing on her bit.

"You glad to see the house now?" Foy shouts, rain spilling over the brim of his cap.

"No," she sputters back. Stubborn, as usual. "Did you milk Agatha?"

"Marguerite was supposed to."

Marguerite, Leni thinks, is about as reliable with the animals as I'd be on a boat.

Thunder explodes again. Foggy swings her haunches one way, then the other, trying to get around Leni's hold on her. The sky—purple and gray—seems to be descending on them.

Leni sits deep in the saddle and tightens up again on the reins just as Foggy shies left away from the woods, all four feet off the ground, and nearly lands on the fence. Leni growls at the mare and pulls her up hard.

"Ain't nothing in there for you!" Leni yells over the wind. Foggy almost lost her with that little move. She kicks Foggy hard, urging her forward. The mare keeps snorting, staring into the thick woods.

Then Roger whinnies, high up in his throat. An alarm whinny. Leni looks to Foy. He's staring into the woods, too.

Out trots a big bay horse, knees high, his dark neck white with sweat, a saddle stained brown as mud with the wet and a bridle with only one rein. Seeing Leni and Foy, it darts away from them between the trees and the paddock. But lightning like a spear lands ahead of him. The big horse skids to a stop, rears up, and spins back their way.

"Whoa there, whoa there . . ." The fence on her left, woods to the right. Leni holds her hand out toward the horse. He stops, fidgets in place. She watches his shoulders, trying to decipher which way he is fixing to go. He is blowing hard, his ribs heaving. The veins in his neck and chest pumped full. He's been running hard.

"Don't let him get into the woods," Leni shouts. "Push him to the fence. I'll grab his rein."

The horse slinks onto his haunches, backing away. The wind blows Leni's hat right off her head. The horse freezes, watching the hat somersault across the paddock. Leni presses Foggy closer.

"Whoa there," she says again.

The horse looks back to Leni, stretches his nose in the air. He's quivering.

"Whoa there, boy. You're all right now."

There's red streaming down the horse's front right pastern and hoof.

"He's hurt!" she shouts to Foy.

The big horse rolls his eyes back, peering at Leni. There's a blotch of white on his forehead, shaped like a fist, and a small white stripe between his nostrils that are flared and puffing. Leni moves forward, slowly.

"Come in closer," she yells to Foy.

"Careful, Leni!"

The horse is pressed against the fence, not knowing which way to turn. The rain is falling in sheets. Her clothes feel glued to her skin like papier-mâché, the leather reins soaked and slippery in her hands.

"Handsome boy," Leni repeats softly, "handsome boy . . ." Squeezing and releasing Foggy's reins to keep her paying attention, Leni focuses, on the big horse like a cow pony on a calf.

The horse stamps his hurt leg. Blood and water splatter the grass. She presses toward the strange horse and prays the sky will stay quiet for another minute more.

Leni is not eight feet away from the big horse's head. Foy and Roger come around the horse's rear. The horse eyes Leni and snorts.

"He's got a brand," Foy shouts. "Running M."

"Running M?"

"The McGraths."

"How'd a horse from the McGraths get all the way out here?" She inches Foggy forward, leans slowly over the mare's neck. The big horse watches her. Slow as molasses, no sudden moves, she extends her arm toward—

Wham! Lightning splits the sky. Thunder, sounding straight overhead, explodes. Foggy and the riderless horse spin toward each other. Falling, Leni grabs Foggy's mane. The big horse's rein flies out. Stretched along her mare's neck, Leni catches the rein.

"Let go! Let go!" Foy shouts.

Leni's arm twists in its socket. But she is not letting go. The brown horse actually pulls her back to some balance. She holds Foggy up as short as she can, the wet reins beginning to slide through her hands.

His nose in the air, the strange horse rolls his eyes—the whites showing—from Leni to Foy. Leni to Foy again. His sides heaving, he quiets, lowers his head. The rein in her hand slackens.

CHAPTER THREE

Caleb

Cal followed the Tram Road as far as he could, to a bend in the river where old railroad tracks lay like skeletons askew and exposed by the dirt and mud sliding down to the rising river, all the while batting away visions of Flint—a stirrup caught in a branch or underbrush, water rising around him.

His mother was at the kitchen table, waiting for him. She crushed her cigarette in the ashtray and came to meet him, a towel in hand. He felt dense as steel with rage. Lightning flashed through the house. The lights flickered. She reached up, to dry his hair. He grabbed the towel from her.

"He'll make it home," she said. "I know he will."

The softness in his mother's voice nearly broke whatever was holding him up. Cal bent his head, let his mother take the towel. She gently wiped his forehead and neck, squeezed his dripping hair.

"You dented that new truck, you get it fixed." His father—fresh from a shower and in his stocking feet—landed in the kitchen like a fat horsefly. "You hear me?"

"Not now." His mother's words hung in the air. "He's safe."

"He don't need you getting in between."

"Momma . . .," Cal started.

"You're talking to me now, boy. You hear me? You answer me, when I'm asking you a question."

"Why?" Cal grabbed the wet towel, pulled it across his neck so fast it snapped coming down.

"There's a radio in that truck, ain't there?" His father planted his hands on his hips. "Why didn't you use it? Answer me. Why didn't you use it?"

"Why in hell would I think you'd help me?"

He had never talked back to his father before. That was Hank Junior's purview. And Cal saw where it had gotten him.

"Watch. Your. Mouth." His father stared at him. Challenging. Everything was a challenge with him.

"Why?" Cal looked him straight on. "You answer me."

His mother raised her palms open in front of her as though to stop whatever was coming.

Cal threw the towel on the counter, turned, and started toward the door. His father grabbed his arm, pulled Cal toward him.

"Stop it!" his mother shrieked.

Cal was half a head taller, but his father's hand wrapped around his whole arm. Cal yanked himself free and took a wild swing, just missing his father's chin.

His mother, clenched fists in front of her face, screamed, "Stop it! Stop it! Stop it!"

His father grabbed Cal again, pinned his arm behind his back and leaned in closer, his sour breath on Cal's neck. Cal pushed hard. In his socks, no grip on the floor, his father slid back. Cal kept pushing. His father clutching him tighter and tighter so he wouldn't fall.

"Not with him! Hank!" Cal's mother screamed. "Not with him. Stop it!"

Cal and his father twisted, bouncing off the sharp edge

of the counter. Cal grimaced, trying still to push his father off of him. They fell against the screen door, tearing it down the middle, then regained their balance. Cal shook himself free.

"Yeah, not with me. I'm not Hank Junior," Cal screamed, tugging his shirt down. "You two belong together. Crazy assholes. Leave me the fuck alone."

"Caleb. Please," his mother pleaded.

Cal and his father faced each other, panting.

Slowly, his father said, "you had better listen to what you're saying."

"I know what I'm saying. I don't want to belong to you." Cal wiped spit off his cheek. "I wanted to belong to you when I was a boy. But not now. Not anymore."

His father stared at him, his mouth turned down in hurt, or maybe disgust, and shook his head. "Who'd want you anyway?"

Cal kicked open the screen door. Back out into the storm was better than this. His mother called after him, again and again. He didn't look back.

Leni

The barn's red board-and-batten siding is worn and faded. A few broken boards reveal tar paper beneath that's beginning to peel. Foy puts Foggy and Roger, tack still on, into their stalls. Leni leads the McGrath horse into the barn. Rain blows in as Foy yanks and pulls the barn's big sliding door, creaking along its box rail, closed. The rain sounds frantic on the metal roof. Water trickles down the center post and seeps into the dirt floor. Darkness is settling in.

Standing the McGrath horse in the center aisle, Leni takes off his bridle, slips an old halter over the big horse's ears, and snaps a cross-tie onto the metal ring on each side. The horse turns his head to look one way as far as the cross-ties will let him. Gives a snort. Stretches the other way. Another snort. Maybe he disapproves of the surroundings.

Foy fetches two kerosene lanterns from the tack room and lights them. Black smoke swirls out the tops. He adjusts each flame. Leni checks on the goats. All three inside. Good. Foy heads to the feed room. The hay, thankfully, is dry. Leni grabs bandages and rags from the supply chest inside the tack room, while Foy untacks Foggy and Roger. He hangs the bridles on the hooks outside the stall doors and hauls their saddles to the tack room. Leni gets a water bucket from the feed room. Foy takes it from her.

"You ought to baby that arm some." He pushes the barn door open just enough to slip through. He returns, water sloshing from the bucket against his leg, and sets it down. Then he takes off the big horse's saddle and puts it on top of the brush box against the tack room wall.

The white stocking on the horse's left foreleg is maroon, blood mixed with water and mud. With one hand on his shoulder, Leni dunks a clean rag in the bucket, pulls it out, holds it to the big horse's leg. Squeeze. Cool, clean water runs down the thick cannon bone. He raises his head, picks up the hoof and holds it in the air. Leni stands, lays a hand on the horse's shoulder and takes a breath. Exhaling, she waits to feel the horse's intake of breath, his pulse. He releases his hoof back to the ground. She dunks the rag in the bucket again and presses it to his leg. This time, he lets the water run down his foreleg, the slant of pastern and hoof. Dunk again. Squeeze. Again and again, like a pulse. Flushing mud, blood, bits of grass down into the dirt floor.

The gash starts above the anklebone and runs to the top of

his hoof. It is deep and open like two bloodied lips. No telling how far he'd run on it.

Crack! More thunder. Roger jerks his head up, hay jutting from his mouth. Foggy circles her stall, then settles back, head over the stall door to watch the goings-on.

Leni lays a wad of cotton over the gash. "You gotta go see what Maman and them are doing," she says.

Foy stands behind her. "I will," he says.

"What're you gonna tell her?"

"I'll tell her," he pauses, looks up into one of the lanterns' flames. "I'll tell her you were heading to Billy Drum's. I'm sure you made it before the storm broke. I turned back before the river. 'Cause on old Roger, I didn't have a prayer of catching you."

"That's good," Leni says.

Lightning flashes through the barn. They freeze. The big horse tenses. The thunder cracks.

"What are you gonna say about the horse?" Leni asks.

"Nothing." Foy answers. "She won't come out here. Hell, she doesn't come out here in sunny daylight."

"OK. Well, call the McGraths from Daddy's office. And get Daddy out here. Look at this." She takes the wad of cotton away.

"Ah. Don't show me that!" Foy steps back. "I'll get him. What if I can't get him alone?"

"Say there's a leak. You need help covering the hay. Or moving the tack. I don't know. Think of something."

"Right." He starts for the sliding door.

"And Furacin and more bandages from Daddy's office."

"OK."

"And I need dry clothes."

He stops. "Anything else? A steak dinner, perhaps?"

"Ha, ha." But she smiles. "Just my Lee jeans and my gray sweatshirt."

Foy slaps the Texas Rangers cap back on his head, flashes Leni that wide grin and—elbows out, fists to his chest, like some old vaudeville performer—sidesteps out of the barn and into the drenching rain.

Leni studies the wound. The big horse drops his nose to watch. His breath, warm and steady, fans the small of her back. His veins lie smooth now beneath his coat. She wets another rag and wipes down his back and neck, his thick haunches. Rinsing the sweat away. She takes the long metal scraper between her two hands, drags the edge along his coat, flicking water to the ground. He's well muscled with a wide chest. Clear eyes. He's been well cared for. All this racket and rain and strangeness, and he must be hurting, but he is trusting her. Someone—one of the McGrath's cowboys, she guesses—is pining for this horse. She knows it.

The bleeding has slowed, but it's swelling so, it looks like the skin is turning inside out. She crouches again beside the hurt leg. Gently, she tries with her fingers to close the wound, but the horse snaps up his leg. Leni stands, waits. Slowly, he lets his hoof back down.

Foy, head ducked, huddled over the bundle of clothes and medicines wrapped tightly in an orange sweatshirt like a football, jumps into the barn. He sets everything down on top of the brush box next to the big horse's saddle and slaps his Rangers cap against his thigh, spraying water to the ground.

"Old man McGrath had his cowboys out working in this. Can you believe that?" Leni says.

"Yeah. Who in their right mind would go out in this weather?" Foy smacks Leni lightly on the back of her head.

"Some of us do not have a choice. One of their cowboys could be lying in a ditch somewhere. Did you reach them?"

"The phones are out. Lights, too."

"Crap." She peeks through the open barn door to the dark house, then turns back to the big horse. "What'd you tell Maman?"

"Just what we said. She was relieved." Foy pulls the door closed all the way.

"Yeah, my ass."

"She was, Leni. She went upstairs to lie down."

"Where's Marguerite?"

"Doing her nails—by candlelight—at the kitchen table."

"She's useless," Leni says. "Is Daddy coming?"

"He ain't home."

"You said you called him. He came back from the Conyers'."

"I did. He did. Then he left again."

"Where to?"

"How would I know? I was chasing you. Remember?"

She points to the big horse's leg. Raw skin. Blood oozing from the wound, down the white pastern, over the hoof. "He needs to be stitched up."

"Well, you better do it then."

"*Me?*"

"How many times you watched Daddy?"

"Nah, I can't. Maybe he'll be back soon," she says, not convinced.

"Sure. If the roads haven't washed out wherever it is he went to."

"Crap," Leni says again. "What'd you bring?"

Foy pulls a few items from beneath the orange sweatshirt, careful not to disassemble the whole mess. "Furacin. Betadine. Lidocaine." Foy holds each item up in turn. "Gauze. A needle. Suturing thread. Scissors. Soap."

"Crap."

"You can do it," Foy nods. "You can definitely do it." He hands her his flask.

"You have to help me."

"As long as I don't have to look."

"You're pathetic." She takes the flask. Brings it to her mouth, flings her head back. Takes a gulp. Grimaces. "Crap."

Foy fetches another bucket of water. Leni washes her hands, rinsing them in the bucket. A clean towel on the dirt floor. Still crouching, she bows her head. One, two, three deep breaths. She slaps her thighs. Stands up. Walks a tight circle. Foy holds the flask out to her. She waves it away. Crouches down again.

"OK," she says. "Open the bandages."

Foy tears the stiff paper packaging and hands her a bandage.

Holding out her other hand, "Betadine."

He passes the bottle. The big horse shortens his neck, ears flicking back, alert, waiting. Perfectly still. Holding gauze over his hoof to mop up the extra, Leni squirts the antiseptic down the pastern, over the open wound. He lifts his hoof. She waits. He sets it back down. She squirts the Betadine again. Three times. Four. The white hairs and blond hoof turn a coppery brown with the liquid. Leni stands, pats the horse's shoulder.

"What now, Doc Junior?" Foy asks.

"Um . . . lidocaine. Syringe." Foy fetches them. Leni opens the syringe. Fills it slowly with the lidocaine. "Distract him. Scratch his nose, or something."

Leni hovers the needle above the gash, begins to slowly press it into the flesh. The big horse throws his head. Backs up, pulling the lead ropes taut.

"You got to do it faster," Foy strokes the horse's forehead.

"You do it then!"

"I'm just trying to help."

He's right. She's given shots before. What's so different about this? She frames a spot with her thumb and index finger, brings the needle to it. Jab. Press. The big horse doesn't like it.

But he doesn't back up or stamp his leg. She injects the numbing agent in four places on either side of the cut.

"Is that enough?" Foy asks.

"We'll find out."

"What now?" Foy strokes the big horse's nose.

"We wait a little. Pack it with furacin."

With a square of sterile gauze, she scoops out the yellowy gel and wipes it gently into the wound. Staring at the gash, she thinks, start at the top and stitch down, nice and even. Leave a bit open at the bottom to drain. She pokes with her finger around the wound. The big horse flinches and pins his ears back.

"Shit." Leni stands. "More lidocaine."

She prepares the needle, gives him another shot on either side of the gash.

"OK. Tell him he's a good boy or something," she instructs Foy.

"I'm going to sing to him."

"Oh, God, no."

"*Do not use the Lord's name in vain,*" mimicking their mother again.

In a smooth, rocking voice, Foy sings in the ear of the big horse. "*She'll be coming 'round the mountain when she comes . . .*"

"Foy!"

"You hush. This here is between me and him."

Leni pushes on the skin around the cut again. No flinching. She takes the thread out of its waxed paper wrapping and carefully urges it through the needle.

Holding her breath, Leni stares at the slope of the pastern, stained orange with antiseptic. The dark gash. She imagines piercing the skin, pulling the thread. The next stitch, then the next. She coughs. Stands up.

"I can't do this."

"Yes, you can."

She paces in front of the tack room. Foy watches. Hands her the flask. She takes it.

Back to the big horse. She bends down. She feels hollow inside. Light-headed. She stares at the wound. Picks up the needle.

Foy whispers. "It's OK, fella. You're going to be fine . . ." Keeping up his patter, as much for Leni as for the horse. "Good as new. You'll see . . ."

"Bring one of the lanterns closer."

Foy does.

Starting at the top, by the anklebone, Leni holds closed the two swollen flaps of skin. He flinches, pushes his nose against Foy's chest, knocking him off balance. Foy holds the halter tighter, strokes the horse's nose, and hums.

Another crack of thunder, farther away this time. Leni holds her breath.

She knows she has to do this. Knows this gash is near the joint and close to the bone. Knows the longer it stays open, the greater the chance for infection and the worse the scarring will be.

She rehearses in her mind, again, what she must do. What she's seen her daddy do. She draws her focus in. The sound of the rain clattering on the roof recedes. Foy's patter and singing just a murmur. Leni closes the flaps of skin again between her thumb and forefinger. Hovers the threaded needle just above the cut. Holds her breath and presses the sharp point to the skin. Slight resistance. Then it gives way. The needle slides through the flesh. She angles it, pulls it through the other side. The thread seems endless. Pulling, pulling. More blood. She breathes. Takes the gauze, wipes the blood. Holds her breath again. The next suture.

Eighteen stitches. Finished, Leni wipes Furacin over the

stitches, lays clean gauze on top, and wraps a bandage from below the horse's hoof to his knee.

Foy moves Agatha in with the goats. Leni leads the big horse into Agatha's now empty stall. "Get him some hay."

Foy grabs a flake of hay and tosses it into the stall.

Leni stands beneath the kerosene lamp and looks at her steady hand in the soft light.

"Congratulations." Foy takes the flask from his back pocket and takes a swig, then another.

"Did you get my clothes?"

"Yeah, I got some." He goes to the bundle on top of the brush box. Hands Leni a pair of new, stiff Wranglers. And an orange sweatshirt with the tag still on it.

"I said my other jeans and the gray sweatshirt. I don't even want the goats to see me in that thing—some sale item Maman picked up. I'll look like a traffic cone." She rummages through the few things Foy brought out. A pint of Old Crow Kentucky bourbon among them. She lets them drop on the dusty chest. "Maman's asleep by now. I'm going to go in there."

"I thought you weren't setting foot in the house?"

"I'm not sleeping there. I'll be in and out."

"Just wear this, for Christ's sake." Foy holds up the jeans.

"What's it to you?"

"Don't go in there right now, Leni." He's not joking.

"Why?"

"Just don't."

"What's she done?"

"Come on, Leni. This can all wait till morning."

"What can wait?"

He holds out the flask. She pushes it away. Stares him down.

"She emptied your drawers down the stairs. It was dark. I couldn't see what I was grabbing."

Leni explodes. "She what?" Foggy raises her head. "This proves it. She wants me gone. And I want to be gone." Leni grabs Foggy's bridle from the hook on her stall door.

"What are you doing?"

"I'm leaving." Leni slings Foggy's bridle over her shoulder. Lightning flickers through the barn.

"You can't."

"Watch me."

"Leni . . ." No joking. "Don't be stupid. It's pitch black. There's a goddamned storm out there."

"I know what I'm doing." She opens the brush box, grabs her chaps. The lid slams shut.

"What if Foggy gets hurt?"

Leni starts for the tack room. But Foy is already there. His arm reaching above the doorframe, he grabs a key. Jams it into the rickety door's lock. Twists it. Pockets the key.

"You're not thinking straight," he says.

"Foy! Goddammit, give me the key."

"Leni. Wait till morning. Then decide."

She reaches for Foy's pocket with her right hand. The hurt shoulder. He catches her hand. She winces.

"You can't go out again, Leni. You can't. That'd be fuckin' crazy!"

Lips tight. Eyes piercing his. He holds her gaze.

"I hate you." But she doesn't. Not even close.

She circles the post, fists clenched. Kicks it. Foy watches from in front of the tack room door. Leni goes back to him. Takes the flask. And drinks.

"Come on," Foy opens the tack room, gets two saddle blankets. Closes the door. Locks it and pockets again the key.

"I brought flashlights. And peanut butter. And Saltines." He lays the blankets down in front of Roger's stall.

Leni takes one of the flashlights. Checks first the big horse.

He's nibbling on the flake of hay. That's a good sign. Lazy old Roger's laying down. Foggy nuzzles straw, looking to lie down, too.

Foy sets down the palm-sized transistor radio he bought last month with the money he's made working at Dairy Queen. Leni takes the orange sweatshirt, slips into Foggy's stall, and—gingerly—slides her sore arm through the wet shirt, wriggles out of it, and pulls the ugly sweatshirt over her head.

"You don't have to stay out here, you know." It makes her feel bad when Foy does things like this on account of her being in trouble. Or stubborn.

"Hush. And sit down."

The storm is moving out. The thunder, its tantrum over, grumbles in the distance. Foy begins writing with the beam of the flashlight on the tack room wall.

"You have the worst handwriting." Leni slides down the stall wall and sits on her butt. "OK. Start over."

"Reach Out (I'll Be There)," by the Four Tops, comes through the tiny radio all the way from Houston. Foy aims the flashlight at the wall. The fuzzy beam of light scrapes across the tack room door.

"How come," Leni asks, "the light from a flashlight or a car headlight is white? Have you ever wondered that?"

"No. I can't say as I have. You can ask Mr. Regnier when school starts back up. Which is any day now."

Foggy snorts behind them. "My feelings exactly," Leni says. "Are we doing names?"

"Yes, we are doing names," Foy answers.

Leni scoots down and lays back on the blanket. Breathing in the smell of horse and straw, dried sweat and manure. She watches the big letters Foy writes in light swoop up to the ceiling; the leak near the center post glistens as the light passes over it.

The bottle of Old Crow in hand. The radio plays "Poppa Was a Rolling Stone," in its tinny, faraway way.

It is five-thirty. An hour till sunrise. Foy is stretched out, half covered by an unfolded saddle blanket. Mouth open, throaty breathing. The nearly empty bottle of Old Crow beside him.

Leni checks on the big horse. He stands, his head lowered, dozing. The bandage looks clean. Roger's munching hay. The tack room door is still unlocked from when they got more blanket rolls to curl up on.

Leni fetches a dry blanket, her saddle, and her saddlebags. Sets them outside Foggy's stall. Picking up the bourbon bottle, she hides it inside the supply chest, wedging it beneath bandages and towels.

Foy's jacket is on top of the brush box. Should she? She'll pay him back, somehow. The top left pocket. Eleven dollars. She pushes the bills into her back pocket.

Slowly, slowly, breath held, she slides Foggy's door open enough to slip her gear inside. Foy snorts. Leni freezes. Watches as Foy rolls into a ball, facing the stalls. She stretches her sore arm. It's not too bad. A strain. She gets the saddle on Foggy's back. Tightens the cinch. Then the saddlebags, with the rest of the peanut butter and Saltines, and a flashlight stuffed inside. They'd opened the sliding barn door after the rain stopped. Gently, Leni rolls Foggy's stall door open and leads her out. The only sound the soft thud of her hooves on the dirt floor. Foy, the big dolt, doesn't move. And out they step into the cool dawn beneath the morning stars flickering over the still dark house and the paddocks, and the wide chaparral beyond.

CHAPTER FOUR

Caleb

C al rose before dawn.

His mother was in the kitchen, at the stove, in her house-coat. Coffee burbled in the percolator. Rolls waited in the toaster oven.

"What are you doing up, Momma?"

"I knew you'd be out as soon as the sun got up." She cracked two eggs into the skillet. "Sit down and get something in your belly." She pressed a button and the toaster oven began to glow.

"You didn't have to do this."

She turned, a hand on her hip. "You think I don't know what that horse means to you." She poured two cups of coffee. "Soon as it's a reasonable hour, I'll call Walter. Get him to send out anyone he can spare. I figured I'd drive on out 183, head north at Sugar Hill, and circle back. I can at least put the word out to a few folks."

"Thank you, Momma."

"You'll find him," she said, tending the eggs.

She set a cup of coffee down in front of Cal, buttered the rolls, and slid a fried egg onto each of them. She handed one to Cal, wrapped the other in foil, and placed it inside a pouch to tie onto his saddle.

The ground was saturated. Water dripped off the barn roof. Cal threw a few flakes of hay in each of the horses' stalls and as dawn broke, saddled up Reverie and headed out toward the Lacey pasture. He figured he'd stay east of the river for a good ways, then cross over where he could, veer north-northwest, and come back down by Billy Drum's place. Billy was like an uncle to Cal. Like an uncle to a lot of folks. Retired from his sawmill, he spent his days carving animal sculptures with his chainsaws. He kept his ear to the ground. Knew everyone and what was going on. He might have heard or seen something of Flint.

As the sun rose behind them, Cal and Reverie crossed the swollen creek that fed the watering hole behind their barn, did an easy lope to the far corner of the pasture, flushing two cottontails on the way, and continued on toward the river.

North on the old Tram Road, well past the hay meadow and past where the truck got stuck, Cal was looking for a place to cross when he heard splashing in the river. He'd been chased out of low-lying ground by an angry, screeching boar more than once. He backed away from the river, climbed a low rise, and peered through the few hardwoods and shrubs.

A pretty gray mare, saddled, was grazing by the riverbank. Crouching at the water's edge was a girl in blue jeans, waist-length brown hair draped down her bare back. He watched as she leaned forward, scooping water in cupped hands, her hair slipping over her slim shoulders. Sun shone on each vertebra like a pearl strung from her neck to the top of her jeans. She splashed her face and beneath her arms.

He was on the edge of the Wickams' land. There weren't any pretty girls in that family. Much as he wanted to stare at a half-naked girl, he didn't want to get caught. He turned Reverie to head on north, but the mare saw them and let out a loud whinny. Cal looked back. The girl shot up, her arms clamped across her chest. She grabbed a T-shirt from the ground, turned her back to him, slipped the shirt on, and spun back around.

"Just what are you looking at?" she snapped, peering at him through the low trees.

"I was trying not to look," Cal stammered.

"Try harder." She slipped a denim shirt over her T-shirt, leaving it unbuttoned.

"I was just trying to find a place to cross."

"It's a long river," she said quickly, still staring him down, hands on her hips.

Cal looked upriver. He wanted to ask if she might have seen Flint, but she didn't seem predisposed to help him. "Right. Forget it," Cal mumbled. He gave Reverie a good kick and they loped back up over the rise and north along the river.

A little ways on, Reverie's ears flattened, his back arched, and he started to bolt. Cal looked behind him. The girl and her gray mare were tearing up behind him.

Girls were so confusing.

She came right up alongside him. Reverie tossed his head, wanting to race her mare. It took some doing, but they each pulled their horse to a jog.

"You're Caleb McGrath."

He couldn't place her.

She tipped her hat back on her head. "I'm Foy O'Hare's sister," she pointed at herself. "Leni."

Foy's little sister? The skinny, straight-as-a-board tomboy who used to shoot spitballs from a straw at opposing football teams? Boy, had she grown.

"Hi." He shortened up on Reverie's reins. "I'm sorry I startled you," he said, Reverie walking now.

"You lost a horse?" her voice melted into a question.

"Yeah."

"With the running M brand?"

"Yeah. Have you seen him?"

"That's what I've been trying to tell you." She slapped her thigh.

"What have you been trying to tell me?"

"Didn't you hear me yelling after you?"

"No."

"A big bay, with two white stockings, a star between his eyes."

"You've seen him?"

"No." She shook her head, took a rubber band from her pocket and pulled her hair into a ponytail, then turned to Cal, her green eyes wide. "He's in our barn." She smiled.

His insides softened, like he'd swallowed warm honey.

She told him how she and Foy had found Flint during the storm near their barn and how they had caught him and taken him in. That he had a deep cut that she'd stitched up. That was impressive. And worrisome.

"How far's your barn?" Cal asked. He knew the O'Hares' place was south of the County Road but didn't know how to get there through pastures, as the crow flies.

"Go back down the Tram Road," she started, "at the burned-out tree, you know, the one struck by lightning a ways back?" He nodded. "You veer kind of left, onto the Wickams' place. They hang locks on their gates, but they never use 'em. Past the big osprey nest by the watering hole there . . ."

Osprey nest? Cal had already lost track. "Can I follow you back?"

"No, I'm heading that way," she pointed west, "toward Sugar Hill. But you can ride there. It's easy. And Foy'll trailer your horse back to your place for you."

"Where is it you're headed?" Cal asked.

"Nowhere in particular." She looked around vaguely.

He looked at her full saddlebags. And waited.

"I'm heading to Billy Drum's place," she said.

Everybody's 'uncle.'

"I'm going to ask him if he'll keep Foggy for a bit." She patted her mare's neck.

"I see," Cal said, but he didn't. Billy loved animals, carved everything from rabbits to life size bears out of wood, with a chainsaw. His barn, though, had been a tool shed for as long as Cal knew. "And Billy's expecting you?" he asked.

She looked off into the distance. "Um . . ." She patted her mare again.

"Why are you looking to stable her somewhere else?"

Leni looked Cal straight in the eyes. "I just am."

"Well," he couldn't quite believe he was saying this, "I mean, you were nice enough to stable my horse and all. We've got an extra stall. If we ride back, I can get our trailer, drive you to your place and pick up Flint."

"You'd do that?"

Cal shrugged. He would have done just about anything to have her keep looking at him like that, face soft, eyes wide, like he was a savior, though he didn't know from what.

Leni leaned forward, wrapped both arms around her mare's neck. "Thank you." She sat up. "I've got grain in my saddlebags. And I'll give you hay to take back for her."

"We got feed."

"No, of course you must take that for her. Your folks won't be mad?" she asked, looking concerned.

"My father's always mad."

"He should meet my mother."

They both smiled and started back to the dirt road that ran between the river and down to the McGraths' hay meadow.

As they approached the barn above Cal's house, he pointed out each of the other horses. His mother's fine-boned little mare, Lady Belle, with her three white stockings. Then Hank Junior's dun gelding, Butch, dozing in the sun, swishing his black tail lazily at flies. Hank Junior wasn't riding him. Cal felt badly for the horse, but he had his hands full with summer chores and bringing along Reverie—a thick-muscled chestnut, his coat shiny as a new penny. He had also started to work two three year olds, Chester and Daybreak. But they stayed over in the barn by headquarters with the cowboys' horses.

Cal cleared off a rack in the tack room for Leni's saddle. They sponged and scraped off the horses and put some extra straw and a few flakes of hay down in the stall that would be Foggy's. Cal watched Leni turn the overhead lights in the barn on and off, then the spigot above the water bucket in Foggy's stall. Her chaps were worn smooth along the inside of her thighs and calves and hung straight from her narrow hips. He liked the way her jeans pressed against the small of her back. She took off her hat, wiped her forehead. There were small sweat stains under her arms, and her hair was tangled above the rubber band.

They turned Reverie and Foggy out together in the back paddock. Cal and Leni leaned against the fence and watched the horses jog a few paces to a patch of grass, drop their heads, and start grazing.

Hank Junior's horse began whinnying in the paddock on the other side of the barn. "That's just Butch," Cal said. "He's bored. Hank hasn't been on him once since he's been back. He was overseas."

"How long has he been back?"

"Well." It was a little hard to explain. "He was discharged first week in April. But he didn't come home till middle of June."

"Where'd he go?" Leni smoothed her hair behind her ear.

"We don't know. It about drove Momma crazy. Wondering why he hadn't come straight home. Where he'd gone. Still don't really know."

"Guess I'm not the only one prone to make folks worry." She brushed some strands of hay off her thighs.

"No, I'm guessing not." Cal rested a foot on the bottom fence rail. "So," he took a breath, "you were running away?"

"No," she said, head down. "Well, sort of." She cocked her head and smiled at him.

His stomach did a flip. "You just want to give them a scare?"

"I was trying to find a safe place for Foggy. My momma wants to sell her."

"What? Why?"

"Some man offered us a whole lot of money for her."

He looked at her. "Tell him she's not for sale," he said, eying the small, vertical scar at the edge of her left eyebrow, a mole above her lip.

"I think he's got that message now." She nodded, not taking her eyes off her mare. "You check the fence from time to time?"

"I walked it last week. I'll see she's well-tended. I promise."

"Thank you." Her voice quavered the littlest bit.

She's going to cry, Cal thought, and looked away.

"Want to go get your horse?" She pressed her palms into the rail, extended her suntanned forearms, and stretched her torso long. She seemed as supple as a cat.

Leni

The trailer bounces hard over the potholes and puddles in the O'Hares' long drive. Leni steadies herself with a hand on the dashboard as they circle wide around Marguerite's lime-green

Nova (a ridiculous color) and the brown stock trailer, parked by the paddock fence. No sign of Doc O'Hare's truck. Beyond the copse of hardwoods, out of which Flint emerged the evening before, is a creek that runs off the Sulphur River. The two paddocks in front of the barn slope down to the house. The goats and Agatha graze beside the well pump. The chicken coop that Foy built on a flatbed is at the bottom of the paddock closest to the house, its wheels sinking into mud from last night's rain. It had never mattered to Leni before how dirty the white clapboard of their house is, that the flagstones to the front door are askew or that the paint is worn off the front steps and small porch that faces an unmowed meadow. But it matters to her now.

Foy's transistor radio is perched on a fence post. Bill Withers, "Lean On Me," static-filled, floats out across the paddocks.

Foy looks up from pulling fresh water for the goats and watches Cal turn the truck in a slow circle beside the house. Cal leans out the window to look behind and, first try, backs the trailer straight up between the paddocks to the barn.

Elbows on the paddock fence, Foy peers into the cab of Cal's pickup. "Jesus Christ, Leni. Where the hell did you go?"

"I'm back. Just leave it. OK. And Foggy's safe."

"Foggy ain't going nowhere. I told you."

"Yeah. Well, you can trust Maman. I don't." She scans the paddock. "Agatha needs another flake of hay."

Cal gets out of the truck and stands across the fence from Foy, picks up the transistor radio, examines it.

"Damn." Foy punches Cal on the arm. "You found my sister!"

Cal smiles. "You found my horse." He pops the back off the radio.

"Whoa!" Foy reaches for his radio.

Cal snaps it back together, sets it on the fence post.

Leni scoots across the truck seat, hops out the driver's side door. "Where's Daddy?"

"He didn't get home yet. Must be stuck on the other side of one creek or another."

"And Maman?"

"Upstairs. In her sewing room."

"She might not have heard the trailer then."

"Might not have."

"Marguerite home?"

"Yep."

"Your horse," Foy says to Cal, "is in there." And points to the barn. "I got to move the chickens. They're likely to drown in a puddle down there, they're so damned stupid."

Cal takes his hat off and, holding it to his chest, motions for Leni to lead the way toward the barn. Manners, her mother would say, smooth one's road in life.

They approach the barn. Single, weathered planks nailed to raw studs, patched near about everywhere. Water from a well. Light from dented kerosene lamps. Sorrowful compared to the McGraths' place, shining like new at the end of their winding drive. At least inside, everything is in its place. Brooms and pitchforks upright in a corner. Buckets stacked and feed bins hooked tight. Tack oiled and the saddle blankets hung to dry.

"Where is he?" Cal asks.

At the sound of his voice, Flint stretches his head over the stall door. Ears forward, expectant. Cal goes to him. He holds the horse's head to his chest. His brown hair rushes forward. Leni watches Cal's back swell with each deep breath. The red plaid shirt, neatly tucked in. The smooth black leather of his belt. The faded folds of his jeans at the knee and top of his boots. He strokes the horse's neck. Two thick scabs across the back of his hand.

Cal takes a step back. Wipes hair from his face. Places the hat back on his head.

"We ought to change his bandage," Leni says quickly.

"I can do that back home. You've done enough."

"Put him in the cross-ties and I'll get some fresh bandaging." Before he can protest, Leni's slipped inside the tack room. Cal does what he's told.

Laying a clean towel down beside Flint's hurt leg, Leni kneels and carefully sets out gauze, Betadine, Furacin, and one of her daddy's metal medicine bowls. The big horse nibbles the back of her shirt, drawing it up the small of her back.

"Hey!" she pulls her shirt back down. She can feel Cal's eyes on her. She blushes. But she likes it. She continues her ministrations, her hands shaking. "You got to clean it real good," she says unwinding the bandage from Flint's leg.

"I know."

"If an infection sets in that'd be real bad," she starts.

"I know."

"And don't poultice it, because—"

"I know."

She turns to him. He's smiling. "OK. Well." Why can't she stop talking? "You can take a bottle of Betadine if you need it."

"We got some."

"You sure?" Of course they've got that.

"I'm sure."

"It's just real important is all." Leni passes the bandage back and forth between her hands as she unwinds it from the horse's leg.

"OK. I'll take one," he smiles again. "Thank you."

Leaving the bloodied gauze over the sutures, she sets the clump of bandage down. Cal leans over. Leni's breath stops. He picks up the bandage, stands, and rolls it along the top of his thigh until it's wrapped tight and even, and sets it back down beside Leni. She pours antiseptic into the metal bowl.

"I soak the gauze, like this. She lays a strip of clean gauze in the bowl. Cal leans over.

Foy enters, whistling. Stops and stands behind Cal. "You lecturing Cal, Leni?"

Cal straightens up, takes a step back.

"How come when I got something to say, it's a 'lecture,' but you get to talk as much as you damned well please?"

"Because," Foy pauses for effect, "I am enlightening."

"Is that so?"

"Yep," Cal says to Foy. "It's been pretty near a lecture."

Leni throws another strip of gauze into the bowl and hops up.

"Damn, Leni. Come on," Foy says. "I'm sorry. She knows her way around a horse. That's the God's honest truth," he tells Cal. "Almost as good as Pop."

"You going to be a veterinarian, too?" Cal asks, serious now.

"No." She's still mad. "I'm going to be an artist."

"First time I heard that." Foy says.

"Maybe you ought to pay more attention."

"You mean like a painter?" Cal asks.

It is, actually, the first time she's said it. "Yes, a painter." She is firm.

"Well, I'll be damned," Foy says. "You gonna hitchhike to New York City?"

"I might. It'd do me good to get out of here." Leni wipes her forehead with the back of her hand. She said it first out of spite, to get back at her brother. But the words linger in her ears with some sort of truth. Bringing herself back, "OK," she says, her hand on the gauze that was beneath the bandage covering the sutures, "you ready to take a look at this?"

"Ah, shit," Foy whines. "This kind of thing makes my skin crawl."

"Guess you won't be following in your dad's footsteps."

"I will have to live with that shame," Foy says.

Leni lifts the blood-stained gauze off the wound. Cal steps close to Leni and leans over to get a good look.

"So, you going for running back this year?" Foy interrupts, loudly.

"I suppose so," Cal mumbles, handing Leni a wad of clean gauze. "That looks pretty good to me. At this stage, I mean."

"Because it ain't going to happen," Foy interjecting himself again.

"Well, none of you other assholes—excuse me, Leni—can run. So I'd say it is likely to happen."

"And that's why you don't have to show up for practice?"

"Some of us have to work," Cal said. "I've been mending fences all damned summer, and now we got to bring in hay. Was Coach mad?"

"Yeah." Foy laughs. "Of course. You, my boy, will be made to pay."

The big horse is still; his nostrils flutter as Leni gently mops around the wound. Cal hands her more clean gauze.

"Furacin," she says.

Cal reaches for the ointment. His breath brushes her cheek. He hands her the ointment. She dabs some around the wound.

"You ought to count your blessings, though," Foy continues, avoiding looking at the sutures. "It was hotter 'an hell and Coach made us do sprints like we were balls on a string and he was the goddamned paddle."

Leni wipes her hands on her jeans and stands. Pats Flint. "Football's a stupid game," she says, picking straw off the big horse's back.

"Oh, no. Not this again," Foy sighs.

Leni and Cal both lean over to gather up the medicines. Almost bump heads. They smile. Cal backs away.

"It is a stupid game," he says. "You prefer roping and bull riding?" he asks her.

Foy winces. "Oh, you have just headed down a sorry path."

"No," Leni says. "I do not enjoy watching folks beat up on a helpless animal."

"You want me to bandage him now?" Cal asks.

"I got to get a clean bandage. That one's stained now."

"That's no matter," Cal says.

"We got clean bandages, you know." Leni straightens her shirt. Starting for the tack room, she pauses, peers out the barn doors. Marguerite. Picking her way around the McGraths' trailer, over the still damp grass, in her white blouse, print skirt, and red slip-ons.

"Well, well. Look-a-here." Foy watches their older sister approach. "When's the last time she willingly set foot in this barn? Dolled up. She expecting company?"

Marguerite tiptoes around clustered balls of horse manure and enters the barn.

"Hello," she practically coos. "Oh, you were right, Foy. He is a pretty horse," she says admiringly. "Welcome home, Leni." No mirth there.

Leni ignores her sister and, catching Cal's attention, rolls her eyes.

"You gonna tell Maman you're home?" Marguerite asks.

"No." Leni pushes the tack room door too hard. It slams against the wall. She reemerges. "What if Maman had decided to sell your car? And your clothes? What would you do?"

Marguerite looks at Foy, confused.

"There was a man here yesterday come to take Foggy."

"What? I don't believe that." She looks, again, to Foy.

He nods.

"Oh, my. Well, that is not right." Marguerite crosses her arms and looks at the big horse. "He's going to be all right, isn't he?" she asks the boys.

"Yes. I believe so." Cal answers. "Thanks to your brother and sister. I'm Caleb McGrath," he extends his hand. "Pleased to meet you."

Manners, again.

Marguerite takes his hand. Tosses her head. Several dark curls bounce off her face.

Leni, hugging a bandage and a thick roll of cotton to her chest, watches. Marguerite gives Leni that look, lips pursed ever so slightly. Leni's accustomed to that look, their mother's look, too. A look of disappointment.

"Well, I'm glad to hear he's going to be all right." Marguerite taps Flint gently on his neck.

Don't be fooled, Leni wants to warn Cal. *This one is as sweet as vinegar.*

"And how's your brother getting on? I haven't seen much of him these past couple of weeks."

So that's what this is about.

"I haven't either," Cal tickles the streak of pink on Flint's nose.

"Tell him I asked after him."

"Yes, ma'am, I will."

Ma'am? Leni lets the cotton roll and clean bandage drop onto the towel. "And how's Evan Holt?" she asks, since Marguerite seems to have forgotten she was, until recently, engaged.

Foy coughs.

Hand on hip, Marguerite is about to speak when rattling metal and a loud bang diverts all their attention. A pickup, multicolored like a piebald horse, is coming too fast toward the house. Splashing through the puddles, it leaps right up between the paddocks and jimmies to a stop nose to nose with Caleb's truck. Long piercing notes and wild drumming pour out the windows.

"My brother," Cal sighs. He pushes his hat down on his head and exits the barn, Leni and Foy on his heels.

Cal walks past the trailer to his brother's pickup. "Turn the goddamned radio down."

The wailing stops.

Leni and Foy linger beside Cal's truck. Marguerite, languorous now, brings up the rear.

"I need the trailer." Hank Junior drums on the steering wheel, the music clearly still loud inside his head.

"You can have it when I'm done," Cal answers.

"When'll you be done?" More drumming, silent cymbal crash in the air.

"When I'm done. For Christ's sake."

"How about . . ." Hank Junior pulls off his grease-stained baseball cap, combs his fingers through thick, dark hair that hangs below his ears and seems as unwashed as his once white T-shirt. He slaps the cap back on his head. "How about I take the trailer right now and bring it back when *I'm* done?" He stares at his little brother.

"How about no." Cal leans one hand against the door.

"Hi there, Hank." Marguerite, beside Leni and Cal now, turns the toe of her little red slipper in the grass. Is that one less button buttoned?

"Marguerite." Hank tips his cap. "How you doing?"

"I'm fine. I was just saying I ain't seen much of you since, you know, these past couple weeks."

"I been otherwise occupied."

Leni grins. Take that, Miss Flirt.

Cal, his eyes fixed on his brother, makes fast introductions. "Leni, Foy, this is my brother, Hank. Hank, Leni and Foy. They tended to Flint."

"You're the football player," Hank says to Foy.

"Yep. Quarterback."

"That was my position." Hank Junior smiles again.

"I know," Foy says.

"And he's captain," Marguerite squirms back into the conversation.

"That right?" Hank Junior nods. "You must know how to win friends and influence people."

Foy just shrugs. Leni looks at her brother. It's true, he does. He's good with people. And he's a damned good football player, too, she wants to say.

"Coach Prescott still making y'all do wind sprints till you puke?" Hank Junior asks.

"Yeah, pretty much."

If Cal is as lean as a young horse, his brother is as beefy and muscle-bound as a stud bull. Hank looks at Leni. His smile is halfway between a smirk and a laugh. But she can't look away, somehow, until he does.

Hank Junior tips his cap at Leni. His eyes land—just an instant—on her chest. "Pleased to meet you."

That flush again. Up the spine. "Hi," she says in spite of herself. Then looks quickly away. A nudge of loyalty to Cal comes from where? She would go stand beside him. But she doesn't want to get any closer to Hank Junior. To his sweat-stained shirt. And unwashed hair. And she wishes she were wearing more than just this thin T-shirt. She can smell the cigarettes off him even from where she's standing.

"That why you're taking your sweet time?" Hank smiles at

Cal, head tilted toward Leni as he slides his palm back and forth across the top of the steering wheel.

Foy takes a step closer to Leni.

"I was just explaining to Cal," Hank Junior raises his voice to make sure they all can hear, "that I need the trailer to rescue some heifers done got themselves caught over in the creek bottom. On account of the storm and all."

"You got a horse we can't see in there or you gonna chase 'em out on foot?" Leni asks, emboldened by Foy's nearness.

"Right." That smile leveled at her again. His eyes. It's like they can reach right out and touch a person. Hank releases Leni, turns back to Cal.

"You don't want to go down in any creek bottom alone," Foy says.

"Oh, no." Marguerite adds.

As if she knows anything about rounding up strays. She's a trail rider. At best.

"Any boar down there," Foy scratches his head, "they won't think twice about charging you."

"I'm picking up some guys on the way." Hank Junior lights a cigarette.

"What guys?" Cal's voice is hard. "What guys are you picking up?"

Hank shakes the match and tosses it on the ground. Marguerite takes a step back, as though the ground between the brothers might ignite.

"I need the goddamned trailer, Cal."

"Why? Those strays getting ready to hop a train? Go to headquarters if you need a trailer. The cowboys won't be using them all."

"But," Hank talks real slow, "I am here. Aren't I? I do not want to go get a ranch trailer."

"Come on, Hank. Don't be a dick."

"Why can't Cal use our trailer?" Marguerite says. Hair flip as she points down to the old brown stock trailer at the edge of the drive. "We're not needing it."

"Much obliged." Hank tips his cap to Marguerite. "How about that?"

"No."

Behind them, the two young goats, Heidi and Scarlet, toss their heads and butt each other.

"Listen, listen." Foy tries to smooth the roiling seas. "I ain't got nothing else to do. I don't mind trailering your horse home."

"Thank you, O'Hare. See?" Hank's half-smile, half-smirk leveled this time at Cal.

Before Cal can respond, Hank pokes his elbow and head out the window, and backs down between the paddocks. Spins to a stop beside Marguerite's lime-green Nova. Gets out and slings a backpack over one shoulder. Marguerite, Leni, Foy, and Cal watch him approach. Baggy jeans, T-shirt half tucked in. Boots scuffed and muddy. Everything about him and on him needs a washing. And none of them can take their eyes off him.

He opens Cal's truck door. Hand raised, "Keys."

"No." Cal. Tall, clean, kind. "No." He pushes the pickup door closed.

Hank, hand still outstretched. "Little brother, pick your fights careful now."

"Is that a fucking threat?"

"OK, now." Foy steps toward Cal and his brother. Leni reaches to pull him back, afraid fists may start swinging.

Hank glances at Foy, then at Leni and Marguerite. He stops, brings a hand to either side of his head, bends forward, and squeezes his hands to his head, as if afraid his skull might split open. Teeth clenched, he lets out a grunt, like a penned animal.

Leni knows, she thinks, that feeling. Then he turns, backpack dangling, and slouches back to his truck.

Leni and Foy's eyes meet. They each puff their cheeks and exhale with a ripple of the lips. A gesture, identical and in unison. Shared genes. Shared thought: that was close.

Cal turns back to the barn while Leni, Foy, and Marguerite watch Hank Junior's pickup, its wheels spinning in the mud, rattle out the drive.

Slap. The kitchen door bangs shut.

Maman.

Blue cardigan, buttoned tight around her middle, skirt below her knees, damned lace-up shoes over—of course—those white socks. Their mother pauses, squinting after the patched pickup.

Quick, Leni jumps in Cal's truck. Head low, she slides to the passenger side and crouches down on the floor.

"Marguerite! Foy! Who was that? Did zhey bring Madeleine?"

Tongue-tied, they stare at their mother as she picks her way through the grass to the paddock fence.

"Whose trailer iz thees?" She studies Foy. "*Qu'est-ce qu'il y a?*"

"Last night, Maman," Foy begins. Their mother still peering after the pickup that's gone now. "When I was riding back, I found Caleb McGrath's horse. He'd run off in the storm. And Caleb's come to pick him up."

Maman, brow tight, eyes closed, thinking. "How . . . how does he know the horse is here?" she looks to Foy.

Foy hesitates, remembering their phones are still out. "I went over there earlier this morning." Lying is not natural to him. "I recognized the brand. So, I went over there to see if they were missing a horse."

Leni wishes Foy would shut up. He's just going to make it worse.

"*Alors . . . ?*" Maman is beside the truck now.

"Right." Marguerite picks up the ball. "And they were. So Caleb here has come to fetch his horse."

Cal introduces himself. "Caleb McGrath, ma'am."

"*Bon, alors.* Take the horse," she says. "Maybe you have phones working, yes? Where would she go?" Maman sounds almost pleading. "Maybe you can call the sheriff?"

"Yes, ma'am," Cal answers.

"I just know she's OK, Maman," Marguerite says.

"You cannot know zhat," Maman says sharply.

Leni hears a thud as the trailer tailgate is let down. One of them unhooks the tail bar; it bangs against the side of the trailer. The barn door creaks as it slides open and moments later, the soft syncopated steps of Flint leaving the barn.

"He is hurt?" her mother says. "Who put the wrappings on his leg?"

Foy and Cal speak together. "I—"

"I—" Cal hesitates.

Foy intercepts, "I did last night. He had a little scrape, figured I'd wrap it to be safe. And Cal here rebandaged it this morning."

"I'll return the bandage," Cal offers.

"It's no bother," Foy says. "Let's load him."

Leni listens to the shuffling as they reconfigure themselves and prepare to load Flint in the trailer.

"*Il a peur,*" Maman says to Marguerite. "What scares him?"

"You know horses," Foy says, though his mother doesn't. "Could be anything."

"We're making him nervous," Marguerite says. "Come on, Maman. Let's go inside."

Her sister trying to help again. Leni softens a little bit inside.

"What is your name, again," Maman says.

"Caleb, ma'am."

Why is her mother insisting on hanging around?

"Maman," Marguerite again. "We got any iced tea? I bet the boys would like a drink, wouldn't y'all?"

"You want some sweet tea?" Foy asks Cal, loudly.

"Well, fetch some tea." Maman sounds impatient with the whole lot of them.

"Yes, Maman." Marguerite answers.

Leni, her butt on the floor of the cab, is curled over her knees and staring at her boots. She feels the truck jostle as Cal or Foy tries to lead Flint into the trailer. *Come on, boy*, she thinks, *load up so they can pull out.*

"*Madeleine! Mon Dieu! Viens-ici!*" Her mother is at the driver's side door. A tirade of French, ending with, "Get out this instant."

Leni crawls out the passenger side door and stands opposite her mother, the wide hood of Cal's pickup between them.

"Maman," Foy coming to her side. "Leni's safe. That's the thing. Isn't it?"

"You! Running into the rain and storm. And we not knowing where you are." A sharp inhale through rounded lips, she turns to Foy, "Floyd Guillaume O'Hare!" Her words—half English, half French—sputter out. "You knew *toute la nuit* where she was?" Her hands fly up wildly. "And you!" she turns to Cal. "You, too, know of zhis, yes?"

"Maman . . ." Foy, again.

"She doesn't care that I'm safe." Leni says, hands on the hood of Cal's truck.

"Where is your horse?" Their mother tries to look in the McGraths' trailer.

"Safe!" Leni screams. "Safe from you!"

The goats hop with excitement. Butt heads. Butt the fence.

"Maman," Foy's voice even, calm. "She was scared."

"Scared?" Maman repeats, looking to Leni. "You don't know what scared is."

"The war's over, Maman!" Leni screams.

Flint shies. Cal steadies him.

"She was scared you were going to sell Foggy, Maman."

Maman, frustrated and furious, sweeps her arm in a circle.

Flint throws his head, sidesteps, pushing Cal toward the fence. Quick, Cal palms Foy's transistor radio and turns Flint around. Heads back into the barn.

"Maman," Foy, hands up, surrendering. "Tell Leni that no one's taking Foggy anywhere. Just tell her."

Maman is fixed on Leni. "You do not know what family is. You . . ."

"Leni," Foy tries again. "Foggy's not going anywhere."

Leni's fuming. Lips clenched.

"A family contributes." Maman, hand hammering the air. "You work, you sacrifice, together."

"What do you need so badly that you have to sell what's not even yours? Nothing's ever enough for you!" Leni hates that she's shrieking. "Daddy's never here. All he does is work. But it's never enough."

Leaving Flint in the barn, Cal—head down—steps back out, this time to Leni's side of the truck. She looks away. Shameful, what he's hearing. She can't bear to look at him. What must he be thinking? She and Maman screaming. Marguerite flirting with his brother. Their tattered barn, while Foggy nibbles hay in that pristine box stall with overhead lights and running water, in the middle of who knows how many McGrath acres.

"In the house," Maman shouting again, arm pointing straight as an arrow to the back door. "You go in that house. And," she turns to Cal, "I do not want to see you here again. *Comprends? Understand? Yes?*"

Cal nods. His cheeks reddening.

"He didn't do anything but help!" Leni shouts.

"We don't need that kind of help."

"I can't be here!" It comes out of Leni's mouth like a grunt.

"Maman," Foy, still patient—how does he do that—"we'll help Cal load his horse and . . ."

As Foy continues to reason with Maman, Cal slips closer to Leni. Head lowered. "Eighty-seven point nine," he whispers.

Leni freezes, confused. Has he lost his mind?

"Eighty-seven point nine," he repeats. "FM dial. Ten o'clock." He slides Foy's radio into her palm. His concentration or intensity—whatever it is—makes her feel, for an instant, weightless. She doesn't dare look at him. At any of them.

"Madeleine." Maman starting in again.

"I'm not listening to you." Leni's boots gouge the ground as she storms toward the house, the radio held tight in her hand.

"*Madeleine. Arretes!*"

But Leni doesn't stop.

Marguerite coming out of the house, all smiles, nearly bangs into Leni. Tea sloshes out of a glass pitcher. Her smile changes to a grimace. "What's happening?"

Dinner was as expected. Leni's getting her driver's license was put off for another month. She didn't say a word during the entire meal. She cleared the table, silently. Then slipped out the back door for the final barn check and stayed out there well past dark.

At five minutes before ten, the rest of the house quiet, she taps on Foy's door.

"Enter."

Foy is lying in bed, a *Sports Illustrated* propped on his chest. Elton John's "Tiny Dancer" coming softly from the transistor radio on the bedside table.

"Can I see the radio?"

"Why?"

"Can I see it?"

"Get me some crackers and cheese."

"No." Leni leans across Foy's bed, grabs the radio.

"Hey!"

Gulps and static as she flips the small black dial, the tuner jumping over stations. Eighty-seven point nine.

Static.

"What are you doing?"

"Nothing."

"Leni . . ."

"Cal said to tune in to this station at ten o'clock."

"It's not ten o'clock."

"It's almost ten o'clock."

"Patience is a virtue."

"Patience is a bore." She rolls her eyes at her brother.

"Give it to me." He grabs the radio. "What numbers?"

She tells him.

"We can't get that station." He tunes carefully in to the numbers Cal instructed. Static. Leni reaches for the radio. "Uh-uh." Foy, the quarterback, stretches his arm wide, keeping the radio from her grasp.

Then a muffled "testing, testing . . ." Leni and Foy stare at each other, then at the radio in Foy's outstretched hand.

"Um. Hi. Don't know if you can hear me. This is for you. Um. You know who you are. I can pick you up tomorrow. If you want, I mean. Early. At the end of your drive. Six a.m., I'm thinking. Yeah. And we could, you know, go for a ride. So, I figure you can at least see Foggy. Whatever. OK. So, if you get this. I'll be there tomorrow. Six . . ." Pause.

Flabbergasted, they stare at the plastic radio at the end of Foy's extended arm.

"But, um," the radio squawks again, "I don't want to get you in any more trouble. If that's even possible." *Sigh.* "If you can't, or don't want to, show up. I understand. OK. Well. I'll be there. Right. OK. Good night."

Leni, eyes wide, hand over her mouth.

His outstretched arm frozen still above his head, Foy stares at his sister. "You are so grounded. You know that, right?"

CHAPTER FIVE

Caleb

A simple transistor radio, like Foy's, was easy to modify. All Cal had to do was adjust the tiny copper coils that control the frequency range it could pick up. He was pretty sure that would work. He wasn't so sure Leni would pick up the message. But before dawn, he loaded Reverie and Leni's mare into the trailer and threw the saddles into the back of his pickup.

Just before six, as light began to spread over the fields, Cal neared the O'Hares' farm. He slowed. No sign of Leni. Of course. What a harebrained scheme. He lived too much in his head, in a fantasy world, just like his father always said. His brother, too.

Then in the middle of his chastising himself, up popped Leni from behind a rock. Pink T-shirt over jeans with a tear across one knee, chaps draped over her shoulder. She waved her arms above her head. Just seeing her, the blood drained from his brain to his gut. Light-headed, he slowed to a stop. She ran over, tossed her chaps into the bed of the truck. She peeked in the side window of the trailer, then hopped in.

"How much trouble are you going to be in?"

"Foy will tell them I'm picking up Foggy. So long as I'm back before ten or so to do chores, I won't be in much more trouble than I'm already in. I don't think."

They drove north to the southern end of the McGrath ranch and parked near the broodmare pasture. They let the horses grab a few mouthfuls of grass, then tied them to the side of the trailer. Cal set down a bucket with brushes and hoof picks. The air was powder dry, just a whisper of a breeze. The sun already hot.

Careful not to let his gaze linger, Cal watched Leni press the brush in slow strokes down her mare's neck, the long muscles in her arms and back tensing and releasing.

"School starts in ten days," he said, almost tripping on the brush bucket.

"What a waste of time." Leni smoothed her mare's forelock. "And I've got two more long years."

"It's not that bad. I bet you got lots of friends."

"Me? I don't know why you'd say that."

"It's not an insult."

"Popular with the Christian fellowship? Or the rodeo princesses? No. Thank you very much." Leni took a hoof pick from the bucket, leaned over, and settled one of her mare's rear hooves on her thigh.

"What about you?" she stood up. "Football team," she swished her hand one way, "science and math awards." A swish of her hand the other way.

"Oh, yeah. Physics makes you lots of friends." He swung a saddle blanket over Reverie's back. "And I'm only on the team because I can run. A couple of those guys could snap me in half if they caught me. That keeps me motivated."

Leni lifted her saddle from the back of the truck. Cal could see she was favoring her right arm. He went to her, took the saddle, and brought it to her mare. Leni stepped so close, he could feel the warmth from her bare arm as she smoothed the saddle blanket across her mare's back. Cal lifted the saddle and set it carefully on the blanket.

"Cal?"

He leaned down, gathered the cinch under the mare's belly. "Yes."

"Thank you for taking Foggy. And for bringing her today."

"It's nothing," he said, not looking at her, his cheek against the saddle leather as he tightened the cinch.

"You're wrong. It's definitely something."

Silently, they finished tacking up, mounted, and started down the oiled road toward the pasture gate.

C al watched the tips of Leni's ponytail, bleached flaxen by the sun, brush her back in rhythm with her mare's strides. He pushed Reverie to keep up.

Leni looked over at him. "You and your brother don't look a thing alike," she said.

"I know." Cal didn't want to talk about Hank Junior. About how it seemed he was causing trouble wherever he went. About how he used to know when to stop. When he'd said too much, when an argument was going too far, when he'd had too much to drink. Since he got back, though, whatever it was that stopped him from going too far before had lost its grip. He was drinking every night, getting into one scrape after another. Stitches on the back of his head, a cracked knuckle on his right hand. Pops had already taken the truck keys from him twice.

"Do you two get along?"

"We got along better before he went overseas."

"Was your daddy in the war?" Leni asked.

"No," Cal answered. "He can hardly see out of his left eye. Bar fight when he was nineteen."

"That's not hard to imagine."

"No, it's not." Cal chuckled.

"Maman and Daddy don't talk about their war. Hardly at all."

None of the grown-ups Cal knew did either. But it seemed somehow mixed into the earth beneath them.

"Your daddy must be proud of all your science awards and such," Leni went on.

"I don't think anything I've done interests him all that much."

Leni turned to him, pulled strands of hair from her mouth as she met his eyes. "No?"

Cal looked away. "He'll like it when I sell Reverie here. I've been training two others—Daybreak and Chester. If I make some money. He'd like that."

She shooed a horsefly off Foggy's neck and cocked her head. "Hank Junior looks like he could have sprung from your daddy's brow. That's how it is with Marguerite and Maman, too."

"Yeah. You'd think Pops and Hank Junior hate each other, though, the way they carry on. Always arguing. And fighting."

"You mean like fistfight?" She stood up in her stirrups, twisted to face him.

"Sometimes."

"Does your daddy hit you?"

"Not much."

Leni sat back down in her saddle. No more questions.

He didn't want to tell her this either—especially because she didn't seem scared of anything. He'd been scared of his father his whole life until this week, until he almost lost Flint on account of him. After that, he just stopped caring.

"I hate Marguerite sometimes," Leni said suddenly. "She's so damned perky and perfect."

"I don't know about 'perfect,'" Cal said. "She's a flirt. Is that what you mean?"

Leni mulled this over. She nodded and smiled at him.

"I try to give my brother the benefit of the doubt. On account of the war. I don't know what he saw. You know? What he had to do. How scared he was."

Leni pulled Foggy up. Cal and Reverie stopped alongside her.

"I feel small now," she said. "I'm sorry I said that about Marguerite. She's all right really. We're just different." She tapped her heels into the mare's sides. They slipped back into a walk. "I hope this heat breaks. It's hard enough sitting in that school when it's cool out, it's so damned *ugly*."

Cal laughed.

"I mean it."

"I know you do."

"Beige paint on cinder blocks. It saps a person's soul, sitting there six hours a day for near nine months a year."

A couple dozen white-faced cows stopped grazing to watch them pass. They came up on the White Oak, hardwoods lining its banks.

"So," Leni started, "I figure someone like you will be going off to college next year?"

"Someone like me is quite likely going off to Vietnam or Cambodia next year. That's about the only thing that would get me out of working this ranch."

"Do you want to get out of working on your ranch?"

Cal lifted his hat, wiped his forehead in the crook of his arm. She waited.

"I'd like to go to college," he said. He didn't talk about this with anybody. And, it was curious to him in hindsight, he couldn't remember anyone up till then having asked. "I'd like to study particle physics."

"Particle physics. Well, I don't know what that is." She looked shy for a moment, lips tight, head down. "But if that's what you want, you ought to do it."

"It's not that easy."

"Nothing's easy," she said. "Where can you do that? Particle physics."

"Princeton, New Jersey. Pasadena, California. Cambridge, Massachusetts."

"Can't Hank Junior work the ranch?"

"You mean if he and Pops don't kill each other?"

"Oh, Lord. Don't say that. Doesn't your daddy want you to go to college? My daddy tried to get Marguerite interested in studying anything. She wouldn't have it. Course, she was engaged at the time."

"What about Foy?"

"Foy's thinking of studying journalism. So he can write about sports, or be a sportscaster. Something like that."

"He'd be good."

They walked on for a bit, the horses' hooves rustling the grass and the staccato whistle of a sparrow following them.

"You're going to be an artist?" Cal asked.

"Me?" she sighed. Her waist swaying side to side with her mare's long strides. "Well, I don't see much use for more math or history. Or science." She combed her mare's mane with her fingers. "I just use my eyes to understand things, I guess."

"Go to an art school."

"Art school." She scanned the land. The grasses, the blue-stem and bristle grass. The creosote bush and sage. "I don't want to leave this *place*. You know? I just want to leave an awful lot of the people here." She rubbed Foggy's neck. "Everyone knowing what they're going to do tomorrow and the next day for the rest of their days. Season after season. And their thinking they know all there is to know about you. That's what I want to get away from." She paused. "I don't know. I'm just talking." She reached over and let Reverie's ear slide through her hand.

It was funny, Cal had always thought the O'Hares seemed so settled in the town, the whole county. Marguerite, a class beauty. Foy, the star athlete. Their father, a respected veterinarian. He'd never imagined one of them feeling at odds with anything there. Granted, he didn't know Leni, except from a distance, as Foy's younger sister. Not as much younger as he'd thought, it turns out.

"So, Mr. Physics," Leni pointed her finger in the air. "I have a question. What do you know about light?"

"It travels in waves."

"Really? Like sound vibrations?"

"Sort of. Different colors have different wavelengths. Everything has its own vibration, I think."

"So if light's like music, maybe different colors go together because of how their vibrations match."

"Could be."

"Maybe that's how it works with people, too."

"That's pheromones," Cal said, letting Reverie stop, lower his head to scratch an itch on his leg.

"What?" Leni and Foggy walked several strides ahead.

"A chemical an animal produces and emits that affects the behavior of other animals," he said more loudly.

She stood up in her stirrups again and twisted toward him, her T-shirt stretching tight across her chest. "I like my way better," she said and sat back down.

Cal squeezed Reverie into a jog and came up alongside her. "Your way's interesting, too." He smiled.

They loped across an empty pasture and galloped up a rise at the far end. Cal let them through a gate into another of the hay meadows, where they walked side by side.

"When I was real little," Leni said, "wherever they'd set me down, I'd just walk. I'd keep going until somebody came and picked me up. And if they set me down again, I'd walk in that direction. It rarely mattered. And the bigger I got, the farther I'd walk."

"Where were you trying to go?"

She thought a moment. "The horizon. I wanted to see what was beyond where I was."

"Do you still?" Cal followed the gaze of her green eyes across the pasture.

"I guess this ought to be enough space for a person."

"I don't know." Cal said. "Space isn't just acreage."

Leni looked at him and smiled. They ambled on, past a stand of scraggly maples. Cal pointed out a red-tailed hawk perched on a high branch.

"I brought some rolls and oranges. I figured you wouldn't have eaten any breakfast."

"What kind of rolls?" Leni asked.

"Why? You got something better?"

"No." She laughed.

"Cinnamon," Cal said. "Sara Lee. The kind with icing." No response from Leni. "You don't like Sara Lee?" He didn't know anyone who didn't like Sara Lee.

"I don't know. Maman bakes most things herself. She is *Française.*"

"Do you speak French?"

"*Ah, oui.*"

Cal didn't know anyone who spoke another language. They stopped at a rise, beneath some sycamore trees, above a watering hole. They loosened the horses' cinches and let them graze. Everything was very still, except the water striders skidding across the watering hole, the occasional burble from a fish or a frog.

Leni took a cinnamon roll, her slender wrist twisting as she assessed it. He wanted to touch that wrist and the thin scar that cut across the tip of her left eyebrow. A handful of freckles dotted her tanned cheeks and nose. He wanted to touch those, too. She brought the cinnamon roll to her mouth and took a bite.

"This is delicious." She took another big bite.

This made him happy, watching her relish the cinnamon roll. He wanted her to like everything. The ride, his horse. Him. He had to stop staring at her. Her waist, her thighs, the spiral of her arms.

"Do you like stars?" he asked. What a stupid non sequitur, he thought, as soon as it slipped from his mouth.

"Stars? Um, sure."

"The Milky Way," to keep from staring at Leni, he watched Reverie nip at a fly on his leg and resume ripping mouthfuls of grass, "is so big, it's measured in time. Almost a hundred and twenty thousand light years across."

Leni stopped chewing. "I don't know what that means." Cinnamon crumbs trickled down her chin. She wiped her mouth.

"It means," he said, staring at her lips, "it's six hundred trillion miles wide."

"Is that supposed to help?" she rocked back and sat up again, shaking her head. "I don't think like that. If I can't see something, I can't understand it."

"But you can see it. You see the light from the sun and the stars, don't you?"

"Are you going to eat that?" She pointed at the second cinnamon roll.

"I was going to."

"Oh."

"You go ahead."

"No, no. That's yours," she said.

But his appetite had vanished. "What was happening right here in Titus County a century ago?" he asked.

Foggy and Reverie were working their way through the same patch of grass.

"A century ago?" Leni repeated, swatting at a mosquito on her arm. "Well, the trail drivers were coming through."

"Right," Cal said. "There was the yellow fever outbreak along the Gulf. A century's a long time. No cars. No telephones. No antibiotics." He waited for her to agree. She picked up the last cinnamon roll instead. "Well, our solar system was formed forty-six *million* centuries ago."

She held the cinnamon roll and looked at the sky.

"Are you bored?"

"No!" She turned quickly toward him, her eyes wide. "Are you?"

"No, no." His thoughts were muddled. He didn't know how to read girls. He didn't know whether to believe her or not. But he carried on anyway.

"When you draw, you draw light. Daylight. Shadows. Changing colors. Have you ever thought, how is it we can see color?"

"Yes!" she seemed genuinely enthusiastic. "I asked Foy that the other day. He had no idea."

"Well, the range of light waves that the human eye can see is called the visible light spectrum." She was watching his mouth. "Beyond that," he paused, "at the lower range, is infrared light. And ultraviolet light at the upper range. Anyway, white light ..." he paused, staring at the line of her jaw, the folds of her ear as she bent her head and pressed her hand into the grass.

"Yeah? Go on," she said.

"Really? OK." He never talked about any of this with anybody. No one seemed interested. He just read about it all, alone. "Well, the light visible to the human eye is actually a very narrow band of white light along the electromagnetic spectrum, between infrared frequencies and ultraviolet frequencies. Each color seen by the human eye represents a slightly different wavelength of light within that electromagnetic spectrum. It was Isaac Newton, who used prisms . . ."

"I love prisms."

"I do, too." They smiled at each other. "Newton used prisms to show that white light breaks down into primary colors, colors that can't be broken down any further. It's how white light's filtered that gives things color. Like the sky looks blue because air molecules filter out the wavelengths of red light."

"So the grass is green and Foggy's white and black and gray because . . . ?" she pauses, thinking.

"Because different objects absorb and reflect light waves differently."

"That's amazing."

Her jaw dropped a little bit as she looked out across the pasture. The grass, the red and white cows in the distance, the dense gray-blue surface of the pond.

Foggy ambled over to another clump of grass. Leni got up, pulled Foggy closer, and sat back down cross-legged beside Cal, her knee touching his. He set his hat down on the grass and stretched his legs out, his foot on Reverie's rein, and plucked a thick blade of grass, smoothed it between his thumbs. Leaned his lips to it. A hollow whistle.

Leni fingered the grass beside her like she was looking for something she'd dropped.

"Do you really think you'll stay here?" she asked.

Her gaze elsewhere, he took in the sun-bleached hairs on her forearm. The crease of her hip. "On earth?" he smiled.

"No. Here. On your ranch."

"I know what you meant. That's what's expected." He looked across the pond. "If I have to stay here, though," he said, "I think

I might dry up and die." He turned to her. "What about you? Will you stay?"

"I hope not," she said and shrugged her shoulders.

"Where do you want to go?"

"I don't know," she said. "I'm just talking."

He could feel her pulling back. "That's how anything starts, right?" he said. "You have to imagine it." He stared up into the sky. "I think to be a good scientist, or maybe a good anything, you need imagination and optimism. Imagine what's over your horizon. Remember?"

"Emily Dickinson, the poet, never left her attic," Leni said, following Cal's gaze to the sky.

"*The soul should always stand ajar, ready to welcome the ecstatic experience.*"

Leni turned to him, a look of amazement, or maybe just shock, flashed across her face. "How do you know that?"

"Miss Walker's tenth-grade English. Same as you, I expect."

Ecstatic experience. They stared up at the sun, its hard light on the still water.

"It takes eight minutes for light from the sun to get to earth."

"Does that mean the sun's really over there?" Leni pointed higher in the sky as she, smiling, dipped her shoulder into his, teasing him.

Cal followed that beam of sunlight to her lips. He'd never really kissed a girl before. Only a couple of times. Just pecks, really. He was shy, and he was always working on the ranch, or with the horses.

He touched her hair. It was like dipping his hand in a running stream. She closed her eyes. Her chin lifted ever so slightly and he brushed her lips with his. She didn't kiss him back. But she didn't move away either. He brought his lips to hers again. And she kissed him. He put a hand to her waist. She inhaled sharply. He let go. But she leaned into him, her mouth opening. He held her closer with both hands. She sighed and a current went through him.

She laid her cheek on his shoulder and moved her hand over his back, pressing him closer, moving her hand, then pressing him to her again, like she was looking for something. A heartbeat. A wound. He breathed with the pulsing of her hand. He kissed her neck. Her skin smooth and salty. Delicious. He closed his eyes. Her lashes brushed his cheek. Her lips were so soft. He brushed her hair off her shoulder, followed it down her back. Their tongues touched. Her hand on his ribs made him shudder.

"I like watching you with horses," she whispered.

"I like watching you."

She looked shy again. Pulled back a little bit. They sat still for several moments.

Then, "I'm hot," Leni announced, hopping up.

Not looking at him, she pulled off her boots, shirt, and pants. In just her panties and bra, she ran to the water's edge. Waded into the soft silt of the pond. Cal yanked off his boots and clothes, and followed in just his briefs.

She was a good swimmer. Cal caught up to her. She screamed and laughed. Treading water, their legs scissored and kicked beneath them, sliding against one another's. Cal tried to kiss her as they bounced in the water. Leni swam again. Long strokes. Her arms reaching, legs kicking. She went farther into the pond. Cal followed. Reached for her, grabbed an ankle and pulled her toward him, her head yanked underwater. She came up, sputtering, tried to say something. Cal reached for her, hands on her waist, as his legs kicked hard beneath them, holding both of them up.

"I'm sorry," he said, holding her tight.

"I'm fine." She coughed a little and, wriggling free, swam the backstroke—her eyes on Cal—toward shore.

Almost to land. They could have stood if they'd wanted to, but they stayed submerged. Leni floating. Cal on his knees, one hand sliding along her side. Over her hip. Her thigh. Her calf. Leni stretched her arms out long behind, let her head fall beneath the water. Arching her back, then coming up to kneel in front of Cal.

They kissed. It was so easy. They kept kissing. And tingling. No words. He smoothed her hair. His hand slid down her back. Their tongues looping around each other's. His hand on her breast. Lips so soft. She pressed her belly against his. Skin on slippery skin.

"Ack!" Leni screamed and flopped in the water. Taking a stroke backward toward shore, splashing and laughing. "Something swam over my foot."

Cal followed. Adjusted his BVDs before stepping out of the water.

In the sunlight, his chest so pale and smooth, ribs swaying in and out with his breath. Leni tiptoed over the pebbles and prickly grass. She squeezed her ponytail, fist over fist. Water dripped to the ground. She grabbed the two towels from the grass. Cal combed his fingers through his hair. Wiped his face with the towel, then his arms and legs. Leni did the same. They put their shirts back on and, avoiding dried cow patties, laid the damp towels beneath a sycamore, the single tree beside the pond.

When he touched her arm, she met his gaze and they kissed again. And kept kissing. His hand to her belly and her breast. Her nipple stiffening beneath his touch. Magic. No idea how long, how much time, was passing. Moments strung together with touch.

Until Leni broke away. "What time is it?"

Cal looked at his watch. "Ten forty-five."

"Oh, shit! I've got to go!"

They leapt up, pulled on their shirts and pants. They gathered the horses, tightened the girths, mounted, and loped back across the pasture. Leni stretched her hand back, Cal reached for her. Their fingers grazing as they crossed the chaparral.

C al turned carefully into the O'Hares' driveway. "Drop me and Foggy off here," Leni said.

But Cal wouldn't hear of it. "We'll face the music together." He smiled. Leni grimaced.

They circled the trailer in front of the house. As soon as Cal let the tailgate down, the kitchen screen door shut. Mrs. O'Hare, hands on her round hips, Doc O'Hare towering behind her, stood on the back porch. Doc took the pipe from his mouth and, holding it aloft, glared at Cal.

Cal handed Foggy's reins to Leni, slipped his hat off, held it to his chest, and, faced Leni's parents.

"Young man," Doc O'Hare began, his voice gruff and slow.

"Daddy, he was just bringing Foggy back."

"Madeleine," her father's voice dropped very low. "Running off twice. What in the world have you been thinking?"

"I wasn't running off. I was bringing Foggy home."

"How many hours were you gone?" Her father made a point of looking at his watch.

Leni glanced at the sun high overhead. Sweat dripped down the sides of her face.

"Put your mare up and come inside. As for you, Mr. McGrath . . ."

Cal stood stiff and tall, readying himself for the spear of anger he was certain was coming his way.

"I'd ask you," Doc O'Hare continued in his low steady voice, "to think long and hard about the part you played in all this."

"Yes, sir." Cal mumbled, disarmed. He felt weak and small inside.

"Daddy, he was just helping," Leni whined.

"I'll speak with you later, Madeleine."

"But, Daddy, it was about Foggy."

Her father went inside. Mrs. O'Hare made a sweeping motion with her arm. The message to Cal clear: "Get on your way. And don't come back."

Cal shuffled back to the truck, lifted the tailgate and latched it as Mrs. O'Hare glared at him and Leni and Foggy stood by silently.

"I'm sorry, Leni."

CHAPTER SIX

Caleb

Cal called Leni's house once but was informed by her mother that she had lost phone privileges. It was killing him, not being able even to speak to her. He tried to keep his mind on all the chores he had to finish before school started up, but it was hopeless. He'd go to Monday's football practice. At least there Cal would see Foy. He hoped he could get a little information on Leni from him.

At practice, Foy was his usual bantering self. In the locker room, suiting up, Cal managed to get him alone long enough to ask how much more trouble Leni was in.

"She, my man, is not going to have any ground under her feet but the farm—and this school—for quite some time. And no driver's license until next year. Not that that has ever stopped her from driving. Maman is not talking to her. Which is not necessarily a punishment."

"I can't call her."

"No, you cannot. No phone for a month either."

Coach called Foy over.

One last chance: "I don't expect I'd be very welcome at y'all's place?"

"Now that there is what you call an understatement." Foy punched Cal in the shoulder and, his cleats crunching on the cement floor, headed out to the field with Coach.

That morning, the thermometer in the shade of the bleachers said ninety-two degrees. Billy Hutchens and Rabbit Foster and some others were already on the field. Cal felt like Wile E. Coyote out there. Everyone but Rabbit was a thick farm boy. Cal drank a milkshake, sometimes two, every day that summer. Ice cream, malt, two raw eggs, and chocolate syrup. He gained a pound. He was just going to stay long and lean like his mother. But he could run.

Foy was helping Coach set up. He jogged back and forth from the stands to the field, dragging bags crammed with cones and tires, balls and markers. Sweating under his pads before he even finished tying his cleats, Cal watched Foy. Everything Foy did, he did full on. He'd seen Foy doing homework, his face a foot from the desk, pencil gripped, concentrating so hard if you wanted his attention, you had to rap your knuckles on the desk or poke him in the ribs.

"Come on, men!" Coach always sounded like he'd just swallowed a mouthful of sand. "McGrath, Hutchens. Glad you could make it. Can I count on you this week?"

"Yes, Coach!" Billy looked at Cal sideways.

"We're going to drill this week till you all are running and passing like the Cowboys. Got it?"

"Yes, Coach," they muttered.

"*You got it?!*" he yelled again, the veins in his neck popping like they were earthworms under his skin.

"Yes, Coach!" And they broke into a feeble run out to Foy at midfield, who—sweat spraying out through his face guard— slapped Cal's shoulder pads as he jogged past.

The pads felt as stiff and scratchy as burlap, but sweat would soften them soon enough. And if he hadn't been there, he would have been walking the fence lines somewhere, lugging wire and a sledgehammer.

Coach had them doing footwork drills up and down the half field. Before long, sweat stung Cal's eyes and ran into his ears. Billy, usually the team clown, swore nonstop under his breath. Foy was trying to keep them all together. He was like a general on horseback, galloping ahead of his troops, sword raised, shouting encouragement, showing them that however hard they worked, he'd work twice as hard. It was impossible not to feel loyal to Foy.

Finally, after one more give and go drill across the field, Coach gave them a break.

"McGrath!" he called out.

"Yes, sir!"

"Ladle out the water and ice!"

"Yes, sir."

Cal opened the ice cooler, laid plastic cups out on the bench, and filled each one up. Foy stayed out on the field talking to Coach. Everyone else gathered around as Cal handed out the cups. Sweat ran down every inch of their bodies. Some guys held ice cubes to their necks. Billy dropped some down his pants and pranced in a circle like a saddle horse.

Foy jogged toward the bench. Cal poured two cups of water and held them out, but Foy just grabbed a towel, wiped his face, tossed the towel on the ground, and ran back onto the field. Cal drank his water and tossed the cups into the garbage bag.

"This one's easier, men," Coach yelled, and they all started back out to the field.

"Let's go, let's go," Foy waved his teammates toward him.

"It's all about aim," Coach shouted. Even he was sweating like a horse. "What'd I say, Hutchens?"

"Aim, sir!" Billy yelled back.

"That's right. Start at the first set of cones O'Hare set up. Catchers, hold your hand out where you want the ball. Passers, hit your mark. When you hit your mark, take a giant step back and start again. Understood? First pair to the second set of cones wins."

"What do we win, sir?"

Rabbit never learns.

"Ten pushups, Foster!"

Rabbit hit the ground for his pushups, did a few, then lined up across from Foy. Billy Hutchens and Cal were next to them. Billy had a good arm. He threw hard, straight to Cal's chest. Cal returned it fast and took a step back, skipping over the ball Foy fumbled. "Trying to trip me, asshole," he said. No patter back. Cal tossed Foy his ball to throw to Rabbit. Billy's throw came hard again. Coach paced behind them yelling, "Keep it up. Keep it up!" Cal stared at the number fourteen in the center of Billy's chest and took aim. The ball hit the ground a good six feet in front of him. Billy fielded it, wound up to throw. Out of the corner of his eye, Cal saw Foy teeter. "Works better if you're standing, Foy," he yelled as he caught Billy's pass. Cal took another step back, took aim, and threw the ball back to Billy. Foy was staring at the ground like he couldn't tell how far away it was.

"Foy," Cal called to him. He didn't answer. "Foy!"

Foy began to fall backward. Cal lunged for him, but he was too far away to catch him. Foy's helmet hit the ground with a thud. Cal leaned over him. Foy was blinking like he was trying to clear away a bad dream.

"What's going on over there?" Coach yelled.

Foy's eyes fluttered open and closed. Coach jogged over. Then the others.

"Billy, Rabbit, get a cooler and towels. Bring it over here!"

Billy and Rabbit ran to the bleachers. Coach unsnapped Foy's helmet just as Foy vomited all over himself and went into a spasm of gagging. Coach turned him on his side and scooped out Foy's mouth with his fingers.

"Get me that cooler!" Coach screamed.

Billy and Rabbit were running back as best they could, each holding a handle, the cooler bouncing between them. Coach took a kerchief from his back pocket, plunged it into the icy water, and laid it on Foy's forehead. Grabbed a dirty towel from Billy's hand, dunked it in the water, and put it in Foy's mouth.

"Suck on that, Foy. Suck on it. Get me another towel!" Coach roared.

Rabbit tossed him a towel. Coach threw it at Cal. "Dunk that. Keep it on his head. And keep it cold. Rabbit!"

"Sir!"

"You got your truck?"

"Yes, sir."

"Get it over here. Now."

"On the field?"

"Yes, on the goddamned field! Now!"

They laid Foy on top of the horse blankets in the bed of Rabbit's truck and hoisted the cooler and wet towels up with them. Cal knelt, leaning against the back of the cab, holding Foy's head between his knees. The metal rim of the truck bed dug into his back as Rabbit drove across the field, out the drive, and onto the main road. It was twenty minutes to the Mount Pleasant Medical Clinic. You'd have to go to Texarkana, a good hour away, to get to a full hospital.

Billy and Cal dunked the towels, wrung them out, laid them on Foy, over and over. Icy water splashed onto their thighs and arms. Cal prayed the wet and cold and wind from the truck would help, would cool Foy down. Cal was shivering like he had a fever. He remembered that Foy hadn't been drinking water. When they took breaks, Foy was out on the field with Coach. Cal should have seen that he drank some water. And they should have had salt pills. He'd heard Walter and the cowboys talking about this joker or that getting caught in the summer sun without enough water and heatstroke setting in. They'd laugh, like cowboys do, about whatever misfortunes fell on someone, and there were plenty. But this was Foy. His eyelids stopped fluttering. His breathing was shallow and uneven.

"Come on, Foy," Cal repeated under his breath, his hands shaking as he draped wet towels on Foy's forehead, his chest. "Come on." Foy's lips started to move. Cal leaned down to listen. He couldn't make out what Foy was saying. That's when tears began to fall down Cal's face. Rabbit screamed down the highway, twenty minutes away, fifteen. Billy was mumbling, "Fuck, fuck, fuck . . ." over and over. And they just kept dunking the towels and laying them on Foy, dunking the towels and laying them over him.

Finally, they sped into the lot of the clinic. Billy leapt from the truck, Coach squealed up behind them. The four of them carried Foy through the big doors. Two assistants ran out with a gurney and wheeled Foy across the waiting area, past the reception desk, and through two blue swinging doors to the emergency room, such as it was. Coach talked with the nurse at the reception desk, then went through the swinging doors to the back. Cal, Billy, and Rabbit stayed in the waiting room. Billy kept stomping over to the vending machines in an alcove across from the reception desk trying to coax out a bag of Fritos or peanuts, while Rabbit paced by the windows that looked out on the parking lot. Cal sat on an orange plastic chair against the wall, across from an overweight woman, knitting, and a skinny older man who turned, turned, turned a baseball cap in his knobby hands and went out every ten minutes for a cigarette.

Billy had just given the vending machine a swift kick when Coach lumbered through the double blue doors. Cal, Billy, and Rabbit circled him. Hungry, dirty, and sweat-stained, they looked ghoulish beneath the florescent lights as they waited—fear rising—for Coach, hands on hips, to gather his words.

"OK," he started. "You did good, boys. You all did good. He's in good hands. We have to wait now."

"He's going to be all right, though. Right, Coach?" Rabbit asked.

"Yes, that's what I'm praying for. You ought to pray, too."

The realization that Foy needed their prayers settled over them.

"I'm going to wait on the O'Hares," Coach said. "You boys go on back now. And thank you." He clasped Cal's shoulder briefly, then, head down, started back through the blue doors.

"I'm staying," Cal said.

"Come on. You got to get your truck," Rabbit said.

Cal shook his head, no, and started back to the row of orange chairs. He picked up a magazine and waited for Leni to arrive.

Not long after Billy and Rabbit left, the O'Hares' blue pickup sped into the clinic's lot, Leni driving. She and her mother hurried inside. Neither of them saw Cal as they walked straight to the nurse at the reception desk, who wouldn't let them pass through those damned blue doors. Leni argued, but her mother pulled her to a seat. Mrs. O'Hare, a straw hat with dried flowers on a narrow brim perched awkwardly on her head, returned to the receptionist, trying to get information.

Leni spotted Cal. He put down the *Sports Illustrated* he wasn't reading as she approached. She stood in front of him, her hands on those slim hips. "They won't let us see him. Have you gone back there?"

"No."

"How is he?" she was breathing fast. "I mean, what do you know?"

"Well, he fainted," Cal told her, as the shivering started again. "It was so damned hot. I'm guessing it's heatstroke." He leaned forward, his hands clasped in front of him, hoping Leni wouldn't see his trembling.

She sat down next to Cal, her eyes flashing between her mother and the nurse at the reception desk and the mysterious blue doors. He wanted to touch her. He looked at Mrs. O'Hare, then his dirty, sweat-stained hands, and didn't dare.

"Did you bring him here?" she scanned the parking lot through the window. "Where's your truck?"

"Rabbit drove me and Billy and Foy. Coach followed. Billy and Rabbit went back. I thought I'd wait. To see you." He reached, feebly, for her.

She took his hand. "He's going to be all right, right?"

"Oh, yeah," Cal said. Trying to bat away the image of Foy, unconscious, convulsing and vomiting, his eyes open but unseeing.

"I hope he doesn't have to spend the night here."

"Me, too," Cal said, rubbing her hand with his thumb.

Leni looked to her mother, who before taking a seat across from the reception desk looked to Leni and Cal. She either didn't recognize him or didn't care, and sat perfectly erect, eyes to the floor, her purse clasped to her lap.

Leni stared as a nurse came out of the swinging blue doors, files in hand. They could see the bright, empty corridor behind her.

"Come on," Leni whispered, heading for the cubby with the vending machines. Cal followed.

Standing in front of the machines, as though considering a snack, Leni kept her eyes on those swinging blue doors. The nurse walked swiftly from the waiting room back through the blue doors to the corridor beyond. As soon as the receptionist, files in hand, got up from her desk and—her back to the waiting room—bent over a long row of metal file cabinets, Leni dashed through the blue doors.

Leni

Everything is white. Shiny white corridor walls and a white linoleum floor. On the right side, white curtains hang off bright metal rods. Examining areas behind them. Behind one of the curtains, a man is cursing as a nurse says, "Now, now."

The nurse pushes aside the curtain, leaving the cursing cowboy. Beyond the examining areas, a corridor runs to the right and left. Leni ducks left, presses herself against the wall, and the nurse heads right, poking tweezers at something in a small metal tray, and disappears through another door. The urgent care room is on Leni's left behind two beige swinging doors, each with a small square window at eye height.

Leni inches toward the beige swinging doors. She peers through one of the small square windows into a large room. A clean metal countertop lines the far wall. Glass and metal jars on top. Implements, some just like what her daddy uses: clamps, retractors, syringes. And there are two small TV screens. Rolling metal stands with plastic bags and tubes. And a long, narrow metal table, with spindly legs, two nurses and a doctor around it.

One of the nurses steps back, something like ping-pong paddles in her hands. A black cleat on the floor. A dirty shin laid out on the table. Leni presses her cheek to the window, trying to see more of the room.

They are staring at one of the small screens. The doctor and two nurses.

The doctor turns away from the table. Peels white gloves, like extra skin, off his hands. The nurses step away. They move like they are at the bottom of an ocean.

Leni rams through the doors. A flat tone skids out from the room.

There is no blood. Foy so quiet and still. If he were dying, wouldn't there be blood? Foy's flaxen hair pokes through a clear mask they've put over his face. Leni lunges toward him. The nurses block her. She fades back. Dashes again toward the table. A nurse grabs her arm. She wrenches free. Falls back onto one of the rolling metal stands. It spins and clatters to the floor. The other nurse approaches Leni, hands raised. Trying to corner her. Leni screams, more like a squeal, sharp and high. She reaches again for Foy. Dodging the nurses, she circles the table. An assistant enters. A beefy man. A plastic name tag pinned askew to his green scrub shirt. Then another assistant. Younger, scrawny.

Leni, calling Foy's name, reaches for the mask on his face.

The men grab Leni. One arm each. Nearly lift her off the floor. She wrestles and kicks.

"Let go!" A growl from somewhere deep inside her gut. "Let go!"

Maman, purse clutched to her breast, eyes ablaze, rushes in. Coach and Cal behind her.

"*Madeleine, Madeleine. Calme-toi. Calme-toi . . .*"

Leni, trying still to wrestle free from the men holding her, glares at them. The burly one wraps an arm beneath her armpit and across her chest. Holds her tight. Her legs flail out. The skinny one has a hypodermic raised in front of him. Leni kicks out hard. Prick, push. He retracts the needle from Leni's upper arm and steps back.

Leni kicks again. Misses the men. Again. Softer this time. The next just a shuffle, her foot skimming the floor. Her screams a whimper. Her hand, with the strength of a paper flag, waves at Foy, unmoving on the cold metal table. She scans the room. The two nurses. One draws the back of her hand across her cheek. The doctor. Maman. Coach, his enormous hands on Maman's small round shoulders. Solid shapes against the brightness. And Cal. Sweet Cal, frozen. Mouth agape. Tears or sweat leaving clean lines down his dirt-smudged face.

"Take a breath." Someone intones. "You can do it . . ." Leni tries. Gags. Unable to remember this simplest, automatic thing.

The light, the whiteness, is blinding. And it's so cold. Like they're all encased in metal. Will their tears freeze and rust there?

"Breathe," the voice instructs again. "Inhale. And let it out. That's right. Again, inhale. And let it out . . ."

Will she have to learn everything anew?

PART TWO:

THE RIVER

To put your hands in a river is to feel
The chords that bind the earth together.
—BARRY LOPEZ

CHAPTER SEVEN

September 1972

Caleb

As a child, Caleb learned to respect the Sulphur and the White Oak, the rivers that gave them food, watered the livestock they raised and the animals they hunted. Early on, he reasoned that how successful and fulfilled one was in life depended to a great extent on how like water one was: whether one could reach beyond a discrete self to find and bond with others. It was a sociable substance, water. Hydrogen atoms reaching—like two hands—to grasp the hydrogen atoms of its brethren molecules. The attraction so strong that water can move against gravity, can carry moisture up the stems of plants to sprouting petals, up the trunks of trees, across branches, into the veins of even the farthest leaf. But for these molecules' attraction to and ability to bond with each other, life itself wouldn't be possible. Water comprises seventy percent of the earth's surface and almost seventy percent of the human body. Perhaps this accounts for our attraction to water—to baths, lakes, oceans, and glaciers—and for the movement and migration of people. And for a single person's attraction to another.

What if he'd reached out and just put that cup of water in Foy's hand? What if he had paid attention sooner when his friend's usual banter stopped? When Foy of the fancy footwork stumbled? What if?

Leni

September 12, 1972

Dear Foy,

Folks say it gets better with time. How much time? Each day's darker than the next.

Took Foggy out bareback. Rode to the creek and let her graze. Felt her big heart beating beneath my legs.

Maman and Daddy came back from the Piggly Wiggly. Marguerite got mad at Maman for buying too much butter and bologna. "Who do you think's gonna eat all that now?" she screamed and ran upstairs.

The casseroles Mrs. Foster brought over Monday are gone. Daddy made waffles and bacon last night for dinner when he got home. Maman was in bed early again. I took an extra big slab of butter.

This is where I will talk to you. Here. These pages.

I've got your radio and flashlights. Could you see what I wrote you last night? Out your window? Cal told me why light's white and how far it can travel. Maybe it could even reach you.

I missed two weeks of school. But Monday, Maman told me I had to go back.

Rabbit and Billy. You all were like a three-legged stool. I'm sorry for them. They're all broken up. They want to talk. But I can't seem to hear anything anybody says. I've never been one to talk much anyway. But now words just bounce off.

It was easy to talk with Cal. But he can't come around here. And I couldn't find him at school. He might not want to see me anymore anyway.

I don't know anything anymore.

Last bell rings, finally. Leni ambles down the school drive to wait for Marguerite. Kids stream past, giggling, teasing, conspiring. Eyes straight ahead, arms crossed to her chest, she does not invite companionship.

Rabbit Foster catches up to her, though. A white T-shirt stretched across his thick chest. Books cradled precariously under his arm.

"Leni." He nervously shifts the books to the other arm. Almost drops one. Catches it.

Still walking. "Hi Rabbit."

"You holding up?"

He can see her, can't he?

"Momma's casseroles OK?"

"Yes. Thank you. We all thank you."

"You going to the Tarrant County rodeo?"

"No. No more barrel racing for me this year." Still walking. Why doesn't he get the message?

"Sure." He slows down. Then stops. "I'm . . . I'm just so sorry, Leni," he says after her.

She stops. Tears rising, goddammit. "I know." She turns back, studies the pavement between their feet. "Thank you."

Marguerite's leaning against her damned lime green car, talking to Missy Carver's older brother. Flirting again already.

"Rabbit?"

"Yeah?"

"How did it happen?"

"You don't know?"

She shakes her head. "Not really. It doesn't make sense."

Cars roll out and down the drive alongside them. Leni and Rabbit cut across the grass to the low brick wall in front of the school building and sit, looking down the hill to Route 183. Rabbit leans forward, elbows on his thighs. He rubs his hand over the crown of his head, brushing his dark crew cut with his palm.

"It was 'round about two o'clock. Give or take. Heat of the day." He sits up a little taller. His right foot bounces off the brick wall in steady swings, as he talks. "Coach had been running us like we were quail he was flushing. We had a water break. Right before it happened. Cal McGrath ladled out water to everyone. Except Foy."

Leni looks up.

"He was talking with Coach. Or something. You know how he was. Always setting an example. Trying to please Coach." He shook his head. "Then we were just doing a passing drill. I was throwing with Foy . . ."

"Cal was giving out water?"

"Yeah. So we were passing and catching. Foy stumbled . . ."

Leni can't listen. She just wants him to stop talking.

Marguerite spots Leni and waves.

"I drove like a bat out of hell . . ." Rabbit won't stop. "I just," he stares at his big hands in his lap, "I drove as *fast* as I could, Leni."

Marguerite, one hand on her hip now, waving Leni toward her.

"Rabbit, I've got to go." She slides off the wall.

"Oh. Yeah." He stares at her, mouth open as though more words want to spill out. "Sure." He blinks. "I miss him, too, Leni," he mutters. His face so pale.

He's looking to her for something. "I know." She feels bad for him. She leans toward him. A kiss on his soft cheek.

Cal's blue pickup glides by, down the hill, and heads east at the bottom of the drive.

Caleb

It had rained during the night. Fog hung like wet wool over the barn and the paddocks. Cal, earlier than usual, tossed hay to the horses and filled the grain buckets. The paddock was thick and slippery with mud. Flint pawed at his stall door. His leg was healing well, but Cal was only hand-walking him, not taking any chances yet by letting him out.

Mr. Wilkens, Cal's physics teacher, had asked him to come in early before school. He wanted, he said, to talk to Cal about college. A conversation that made Cal feel excited but nervous, like he was about to get shouted at for trespassing.

College wasn't mentioned in the McGrath household. Hank Junior had no interest in continuing any studies and was drafted right out of high school anyway. It was assumed, an unwritten code so ingrained it didn't need to be made explicit, that Cal and his brother would ascend to the businesses their father had built. Hank Senior, who only finished ninth grade and was still the richest man in the county, had a tightfisted view of family and obligations, and more than a little contempt for higher education, which they were all expected to share.

Cal passed through the empty school corridors, past the science labs and art studio, toward Mr. Wilkens's classroom. On the floor outside Miss Perkins's art room, legs crossed, writing or drawing on a pad in her lap was Leni. Cal's insides clenched at the sight of her. He hadn't been able to talk to her since Foy died. She wasn't at school those first weeks. He saw her once earlier that week sitting—huddled together, really—with Rabbit Foster, an image he'd like to forget.

She looked up from her drawing, caught his eye. He smiled, started toward her. But—no smile, no hello—she looked right back down at her pad.

"Caleb." Mr. Wilkens stepped out of his classroom. "Good. Come in."

Changing course, pulling his gaze from Leni, he entered the classroom. Mr. Wilkens closed the door and Cal settled his books on a desk in the front row. Mr. Wilkens perched on the edge of his imposing metal desk and inspected his tie.

"So. What plans do you have for college, Caleb?"

Cal sat down. "Um," he stammered, trying to shake off Leni's ignoring him. "I don't know, sir." That was the short answer. "I'll probably work with my father, sir."

Mr. Wilkens looked up and asked, "Have you thought about what it is you want to do, as a career?"

No one had ever asked him that. If he avoided the draft, or went overseas and didn't get killed, his path into the future had been assumed.

"I like working with horses."

"Beautiful animals," Mr. Wilkens said, nodding.

Mr. Wilkens didn't seem like much of an outdoorsman in his thick-rimmed glasses, polyester button-down shirt, and pocket protector.

"You seem to enjoy math," he prodded.

"Yes, sir. I do. It comes easy." Cal shrugged.

"You have a talent for it, Caleb."

"Thank you, sir. I've never really thought of it as a career."

He didn't want to insult Mr. Wilkens, but he didn't want to be a high school math teacher.

"Math is critical to many careers, Caleb." Mr. Wilkens smoothed his paisley tie again. "You've grown up on a ranch. You know what it takes to keep engines running."

Most country boys know their way around an engine. But it wasn't anything that particularly drew him. It was dawning on him how remarkably little he knew of the world outside of Naples, Texas. Cal looked blankly at his desk. Wilkens tried another tack.

"Or, have you considered school for petroleum engineering? The oil and gas industry can be very lucrative. And your family has some holdings, yes?"

Cal nodded, tried to look interested. But if the choice was going to be his, he wasn't inclined to follow his father anywhere. He picked up his pencil, fiddled with it nervously.

Wilkens pressed on. He talked about economics and statistics, academia. "And there's finance," he said. "The US stock market is the largest in the world."

Cal knew that. But it had never really seemed remotely relevant.

Wilkens tilted his head to read the titles of the books Cal had set on the desk.

"Newton," he said.

"Yes, sir." Cal looked down at the overdue book.

"Observatories." Mr. Wilkens brightened. "Observatories today can measure and track the stars and planets beyond anything Newton could have imagined."

"I bet we're only just now catching up with Newton's imagination." Cal smiled.

Wilkens laughed.

Cal stopped his fidgeting. "What do you think Newton would be doing if he were alive today?" he asked. He did know one thing outside of Naples, Texas. He knew they studied particle physics in Cambridge and Princeton and Pasadena.

Mr. Wilkens thought for a moment. "Probably work for the jet propulsion lab in Pasadena, California," he said. "That or maybe on computing machines at Xerox or Wang Laboratories. They're going to transform everything we do."

Cal liked the word "propulsion." It nearly exploded in his mouth as he repeated it aloud. Motion, movement, the stars, time, the future. And a jet propulsion lab would be bustling with others who liked to think about such things.

Mr. Wilkens opened his desk drawer, pulled out a handful of brochures, and fanned them across his desk. "I got these for you, Caleb."

Cal leaned forward, peered at the college brochures and pamphlets Mr. Wilkens had laid out.

"Thank you, sir." He sat back. "But my father doesn't see any need for college. He's a 'you learn by doing' kind of guy. He wouldn't pay a dime for any of this."

"Well, I respect all your father's accomplished, Caleb. The world is changing. We need education to keep up. Is college something you'd like to consider for yourself?"

"Yes," he said. "Yes, it is." The truth of it tugged at his chest as he said it.

"As a teacher, Caleb, it's my job to open up possibilities for my students. You, Caleb, could be a contender for any of the top schools. These here," he picked up the handful of flyers and shook them in Cal's direction, "are schools that offer full scholarships for math and physics."

"I don't know." Cal stared at the glossy pamphlets. Something was spiraling inside him. Hope or trepidation.

Mr. Wilkens was not deterred, "Have you signed up for the SAT test?"

Cal shook his head. Wilkens opened the desk drawer again and pulled out a sheaf of practice tests and a registration form. He gathered all the materials, tapped the bottom edges on his desk to make a neat pile, and handed it to Cal.

"You can study with these and just mail in the registration form. If you want."

"I don't know, sir." Cal flipped through the pages in his hand. "If forms start coming back to the house . . ."

"I don't want to interfere, Caleb. This is your choice. But if you want to pursue this, you can use the school address, care of me, as a return address. Just think about it."

"Yes, sir."

Cal slid the pamphlets and forms between his books. His secret safely out of sight. He felt taller and slightly winded as he walked out into the familiar din of voices and locker doors clanging shut.

He scanned the hallway. No Leni.

He headed to class.

CHAPTER EIGHT

Leni

Rain all day. A downpour when Leni checked on the animals. At the kitchen table, she fusses with the sewing machine. Her still wet hair hangs down her neck and back. She sucks on a piece of thread and tries to coax it through the bobbin.

A brand-new white pickup splashes down the drive. Leni takes the thread out of her mouth and peers out the kitchen window. Coach Prescott clambers out of the truck, carrying something, and starts up the walkway to the kitchen door. Isn't it bad enough they have to go to the damned homecoming game Friday night? He has to come to their house, too?

Climbing the steps, he sets down whatever it is he's carrying and looks through the screen door into the kitchen. Leni's hands quiver. She pricks herself with the needle.

"Afternoon," Coach says through the screen. "Your momma home?"

"Maman! There's someone here to see you." A panel of blue gingham slides to the floor. Leni picks it up.

Her mother enters. She unties her apron, lays it across the back of a chair, and, scowling at Leni, rushes to swing the screen door open.

Coach leans over, picks up what he was carrying, and steps inside. A shiny gold football player—its arm extended back nearly to Coach's nose, the stiff hand cradling a football—stares at Leni. The figure is atop a shiny black square, atop another, bigger black square. Like a wedding cake. For the devil. He holds it out toward Leni's mother like she's won some sort of prize.

"Oh," she says, not touching the damned thing. "Look, Leni."

Leni looks.

"It's the Floyd O'Hare trophy for Sportsmanship and Leadership. We'd be honored if you and Doc O'Hare would present the award Friday evening?"

"Oh," her mother stammers. "We do not have to say anything, no?"

"You're welcome to say a few words, if you'd like to."

"*Ah, non.* We couldn't. No."

"That's fine," Coach says. "What we're planning is a short ceremony before kick-off. We thought y'all could come out on the field, center field, and you can present the trophy. This year it's going to Rabbit Foster."

Her mother holds her clasped hands together, the knuckles turning as white as the porcelain sink. "Ah, yes," she says. "Very nice."

"Rabbit and Foy were good friends. And good teammates."

"It's very nice. Thank you. Leni, come look."

Leni looks.

"*Madeleine, viens ici.* Coach *Prescoot* has come all *zhees* way. It's a beautiful . . ."

"Trophy," Coach, ever helpful, interjects.

"Come," Maman looks to Leni, her voice stern.

The chair squeaks, the gingham falls again to the floor. Leni, nearly a head taller than her mother, stands beside her and stares blankly at the static football player.

"Well," Coach nods. "I should get on back and check on my boys."

"You don't have any boys," Leni says.

"*Madeleine!*" Maman whispers. As if Coach couldn't hear.

"You don't have any boys," Leni says again. "You just run ours till they die." She sits back down in front of the sewing machine. Hands steady as the sun.

"Thank you, ma'am." Coach mutters, head bowed deeply as he backs off the stoop. The trophy waving its football at the sky.

Leni retrieves the fabric from the floor and sits up—her face inches from her mother's.

"Life is loss." Her mother's whisper is rough as the bark of a tree. "There is loss. And you go on. *Tu me comprends?*"

"*Oui, Maman. Je comprends bien.*"

September 30, 1972

Dear Foy,

Maman is yelling like she thinks I've taken deaf all of a sudden. "Madeleine! Madeleine! Madeleine! Where is she, William . . . ?" Poor Daddy.

I can't believe they're going to a damned football game. I'm not going. I've got to see these people every day at school. The girls stop talking when they see me. Rabbit and Billy Hutchens try to hide their uniforms from me. As if I don't know they're going to practice. Have they all always been this dim-witted or when you died, did you take all the sense in this town with you?

And if I have to listen to another person talking about how it is only because you were "so perfect that he was just ready to pass on to the next life..." Or, "He had learned all there was to learn here in this life. Yessir. He was that quick

and good and kind…" or my favorite, "We are so sorry your
brother was called away." Like you'd just missed supper.

He's dead. I tell them.

I'm not like you, Foy. I don't coddle people.

Daddy's coming up the stairs. He walks everywhere
now like he's carrying an armful of bucked logs. So slow
and careful.

A quiet knock on Foy's bedroom door. Doc O'Hare steps into the room. Foy's bed neatly tucked in. Comb and brush resting quietly side by side beneath the mirror. No jerseys or T-shirts strewn about.

"Come on now. It's time we go." Her father waits. "Sugar beet? I know you're in there."

"I'm not going. You all go on." Leni answers through the closet door. She closes her diary, rests it on her lap.

"You're making this harder for all of us. Come on now."

"No."

The bedsprings squeak as he sits. "This is for Foy, Leni."

"This ain't going to help Foy any, Daddy. You know that."

"I don't know that. I think he needs to know that we're going to be all right. That we're going to look after one another."

"Madeleine!" Leni winces. Her mother's shout is like a knitting needle jabbed in her ear.

Doc opens the closet door. Leni is cross-legged on the floor of the small closet, her diary in her lap. Foy's shirts grazing her shoulders.

"I can't move, Daddy."

He crouches before her.

"It's for all of *them*, Daddy." She waves her hand out in front of her. "It's so they can feel better."

"You still talking to Foy?" he asks.

"No," she lies. He waits. "Yes."

"Leni, homecoming and the ceremony and all of it is a way for all those people who knew Foy and cared for him to say goodbye. They're important, too. We all have our memories of a person. That's what keeps them alive."

He stands. The closet feels small as a mouse hole with his standing in front of it. He pushes the heel of each hand against his eyes. Can he be crying? He's crying.

"All right, Daddy. I'll come."

He turns for the door, his footfall heavy as a giant's. Leni opens her diary and writes quickly.

It is my duty to remember you, Foy.
I know you best. You can depend on me.

The very last of the day's light lingers in the air as they set out in Marguerite's car, which fits the four of them more easily than the pickups. Parked cars extend a quarter mile along the main road in each direction.

Officer Standish is directing traffic. The school parking lot is jam-packed, but he waves the O'Hares straight up into the Pewitt High driveway. They are waved on over the crest of the hill, where the sprawling cinder block school sits, and all the way down to the ball field where Rabbit Foster's little brother moves an orange cone from the last remaining parking space.

They gather by the trunk of the car. Her mother and Marguerite smooth their skirts. A few stragglers eye them and walk quickly on.

"*Pas de sac.* No backpack, Madeleine." Maman adjusts her hat.

"*Non, Maman. Je le garde.*" She presses the backpack to her chest.

"Madeleine, now is not the time . . ."

"Let her keep it." Doc places an arm around his wife and guides her on. They walk several steps like that before he lets his arm fall to his side. Marguerite follows. Leni brings up the rear. Marguerite looks back, motioning Leni to hurry up.

The stands are buzzing. Everyone from Pewitt High on one side. Everyone from Mount Pleasant on the other. The sun has slipped over the pine barrens to the west.

Principal Culver stands at the edge of the bleachers, watching them approach. Doc O'Hare shakes his hand. Heads turn. The noise in the stands melts around them as they make their way to the seats reserved for them. Center field, six rows up. Leni sidles past her kindergarten teacher, Mrs. Pritchard, and her husband, Mr. Pritchard, and sits.

Maman is poised, as usual. She looks straight ahead. Doc O'Hare looks down, mostly, as still as stone. Marguerite scans the crowd. A tear the size of an apple seed slips down her cheek. A tiny smudge of mascara fans out beneath her eye.

Then the squawking. The band marches to center field. Playing "Always on My Mind." An unbelievable choice that sets Leni's teeth even more on edge. She stands. Maman reaches across Doc O'Hare. Grabs her hand.

"*Assois-toi*," she hisses.

"I have to go to the bathroom."

Doc pats her mother's hand. She lets go. Foy's backpack, looped over Leni's elbow, slaps the Pritchards' knees as she crawls back out.

Caleb

Homecoming was one of the biggest events of the year. This was small town USA. The interstate running east out of Dallas hadn't yet made its way as far as Morris and Titus Counties. De Kalb, Texas wasn't on the way to anywhere. News of the war and social protests, of course, filtered in thanks to Walter Cronkite and Eric Sevareid. And there were young men, like Hank Junior, coming home changed from the war. For the most part, though, people were patriotic, God fearing, and proud of their role in feeding the nation.

While the school band marched out onto the field, fanfare blaring, the team stood in a tight circle in the locker room, built into the small hill above the football field. Coach wrapped up his pep talk and let Rabbit, who had been named captain, finish up. Rabbit had been Foy's wingman since second grade.

"Y'all just call me co-captain," he said, gripping his helmet in his hands. "Because no one can replace Foy. Y'all know that." He paused. "Let's win this for Foy!" he shouted and thrust his fist into the air. The others joined in.

They could hear the crowd whistle and yell as Mount Pleasant took to the field. When it was their turn, they jogged out of the locker room, helmets wedged in the crooks of their arms, onto the brightly lit field. The band stood at the far end, swinging their brass instruments somewhat in unison. Both teams' cheerleaders lined up along the sides, pom-poms shaking.

The whole county was there. In years past, the excitement, the yelling and whistling, the honking horns could nearly lift one off the field. That year, though, Cal felt like a rock was lodged in his gut. No Foy. And little chance of winning without him.

Because of a cup of water.

They jogged onto the field and lined up on the thirty yard line across from the Mount Pleasant team. The band, mercifully, stopped. Coach and Principal Culver walked out to center field. Mr. Patmore, the hapless assistant coach, his thin gray hair squiggling above his head in the evening's breeze, led Doc and Mrs. O'Hare and Marguerite out to midfield between Coach and Principal Culver and next to the three-foot-tall trophy perched on a folding table. No Leni. As soon as the O'Hares stepped onto the field, the crowd quieted. Cal heard a single small child cry out.

In the five weeks since Foy died, Doc O'Hare seemed to have gone from broad-shouldered and solid to narrow and soft. He never lifted his eyes from the ground in front of him. Mrs. O'Hare stood straight-backed, resolute in maroon skirt and jacket and a hat, of course. Marguerite clutched her father's arm, her black skirt fluttered about her knees.

Rabbit saw Leni first. He elbowed Cal and nodded toward the sidelines.

She was wearing Foy's home jersey, blue stripes and the number fifteen on white. The top band of color spilled over her slim shoulders, as though she was carrying a great weight in each arm. She'd painted thick swathes of eye black across her cheeks and chin. She walked the sideline to center field, where she stopped and faced her mother and father and sister. Everything seemed to go still and quiet. The leaves on the trees stopped rustling. The birds stopped flying. All living things seemed to hold their breath.

Principal Culver and Coach waited, expecting Leni to join them. Coach even took a step aside, to make room for her. But she didn't join them. And not one of them—not Doc O'Hare or Mrs. O'Hare or Marguerite—reached out to her or went to her. Leni continued walking, steady and slow, along the sideline in front of the bleachers. And just like that, she drew back a curtain as she went, revealing the hollowness of the pomp at centerfield. A trophy to commemorate Foy's death, like they'd won something, felt perverse. For Cal, the very foundation of the school, the town itself, seemed to crumble before him.

Principal Culver watched Leni continue on past. Then he cleared his throat and began speaking, at first holding the microphone too close. Feedback pierced the air. He persevered, some words in honor of Foy. But Cal couldn't take them in.

He wished as hard as he could that Leni would come to him. That she'd seek him out among everyone there, because she'd see that he was reaching for her, that he understood, and they would leave together. And she did scan the field, quickly. And he swore she did see him. But she rounded the bleachers, walked out of the light cast from the field, onto the darkened path that led up the hill and behind the school.

A figure, a man, stepped out from the shadow of the bleachers and followed Leni as she passed. He crossed into the cone of light at the end of the bleachers. It was Hank Junior.

CHAPTER NINE

Leni

Leni walks off the field, leaving behind the lights and noise and people. People, most of all. Two weeks back in school. She still can't bear to be with any of them. Each glance like a dart. Even Cal. She knows he's looked for her. And she's seen him. In the hall, and in the cafeteria. She doesn't know how to balance what Rabbit told her. He called once, but her daddy was gruff with him and he didn't call again. Even still, she can't stop thinking of him.

She follows the narrow path behind the school, its cinder blocks sprawling like a fungus up over the rise. Someone is calling her name. She steps sideways into the shadows and scuttles along the back side of the building. She passes three Mount Pleasant girls sharing a cigarette, then the brick wall where Rabbit cried, and starts across the grass to the driveway. No idea where she's walking to. Just keeping moving.

Suddenly a shiny new black pickup is on her heels.

Hank Junior, one hand on the steering wheel, leans over and rolls down the passenger side window. "How far you planning on walking?"

"It's none of your business." Leni steps off the asphalt, back onto the grass.

"I don't bite," he calls out the window.

"You can tail my sister. She'd be interested." She stumbles on a clump of grass, rights herself, swings her hair back over her shoulder.

"I'm sorry to hear that. For her sake." The truck slides alongside Leni, hugging the curb.

Cheers and roars roll from the field. Leni walks, eyes fixed firmly over the rise to the main road.

"Come on." He stops the truck. The window all the way down now, his hand resting on the passenger side door. "I'll take you wherever it is you want to go."

She stares into the dark cab of the truck, sees only the white V of a T-shirt beneath a flannel shirt and his thick fingers on the door. "Why would I let the likes of you take me anywhere at all?" And she walks.

"The likes of me?" Something like hurt sounds in his voice. "I am offering to help you. Shit." The truck jimmies as he jams it into park.

Cheers again from the fool crowd. A couple, Leni can't make out who, ducks into the hedges. Coming up behind her, over the rise, she hears her name, again. Getting closer. "Leni! Please come out." It's Marguerite.

Leni steps to the truck, opens the door, and gets in. "I don't want to talk." She slams the door and slouches up against it, an arm's length from him.

"Good. Neither do I."

His dark hair is combed neatly behind his ear. His right hand hangs over the steering wheel. Left elbow resting on the door. Candy wrappers and cassette tapes dot the bench seat. A crumpled Dairy Queen bag, T-shirts, and a pair of jeans lie crumpled on the floor.

"So," his fingers drum the steering wheel. "Where is it you want to go?"

She shrugs. "Just go."

Hands off the steering wheel, they roll slowly down the hill. "Well, when you know, you let me know." He digs a pack of cigarettes from the breast pocket of his shirt. "If you're not talking, you can point." He lights the cigarette.

Almost to the road, still no hand on the steering wheel, Leni points right. He grabs the wheel, turns it hard and they head east. Maybe he'll just keep driving, she thinks. *Maybe we'll go all the way to Arkansas.*

They pass Earl DeWitt's Feed Store. McCelhenny's Country clothes. The Piggly Wiggly supermarket. The Esso station. Not a soul around. Everyone at the homecoming game. The whole damned town lives for football.

Beyond town, fields stretch out in both directions. Leni closes her eyes. Lets the cool evening air wash over her. No memories, she begs, because once they start, they don't stop. But it's no use. They slip through. Foy scrounging for crumpled dollars and coins for gas in the old pickup. Foy loping lazily along a fence line on old Roger. She opens her eyes. Counts trees as they pass.

Hank pulls into the Roadhouse, the bar on the outskirts of town. A honky-tonk, her daddy calls it. No lights out front. If you didn't know it was there behind a stand of scraggly pines, you'd go right on by. There's only a pickup and an old Chevy parked near the door. Hank Junior pulls in, parks off to the side, and turns off the truck.

"You smoke?" he leans across the seat, opens the glove box with a key.

Leni nods.

"OK. You got to stop this mute thing. It irritates a person." He scrounges in the glove box. Some papers fall to the floor. He ignores them.

Leni scratches her cheek. Greasy eye black gets on the tips of her fingers and under her nails. Hank Junior rolls a thin cigarette and lights it. It smells earthy and sweet, like mulch with smoky spices. She's never smoked marijuana before. She'd bet Marguerite hasn't ever touched the stuff. Foy would have told her if he had, wouldn't he? She wonders. He sometimes protected her from things.

She watches Hank Junior closely. The cigarette between his thumb and forefinger, he sucks the smoke in deep—like Foggy's long pulls of water when she drinks—then holds it, lips tight, chest puffed out. And exhales like a cannonball. He brings it to his lips again. Inhales. And holding his breath, hands it to Leni. She hesitates.

He exhales again, loudly. "Try it if you want. It helps with all sorts of pain."

She takes it between her thumb and index finger. Inhales long and deep like he did. And coughs. Coughs hard. Can't stop.

"Whoa there, cowgirl!"

"That's like sandpaper," she barks between hacking coughs.

"Take it slow. Start with a little sip. Hold it for a bit. Then let it go. Nice and easy."

She tries again. A little sip. Nice and easy, like he said.

Nothing feels different.

"I'm real sorry about your brother."

She nods.

His fingers slide along Leni's as he takes the marijuana back. The cab of the truck is thick with smoke. The moonlight through the windshield makes everything inside silver and gray. He hands it to Leni again. She watches the tip brighten as she takes another sip. Holds it in. Still waiting for anything to feel different. Back and forth. The tiny ember a flash of red in the gray light.

"Well," Hank Junior says suddenly. "You better be sure you know what you're asking for. That's all."

"What?"

"I mean before you go either trying to follow him out there or keep him too tight in here," he taps his chest. "You know what I'm saying?"

Leni shakes her head.

"What I mean . . ." He sighs. She waits. Floating in the silvery light and the sweet spicy smoke. "Look. It's hardest when you meet death the first time. You got to figure out how to integrate it."

How many deaths had he seen? How many had he caused? How many sides can you know death from and still be here on earth? Questions swirl in her head like a slow-motion twister. This, she suspects, is what he doesn't want to talk about.

"The fact is," he holds the marijuana aloft as he speaks. The ember turns dark. "People die. Boys, especially, die. We're expendable. Kicked out of the pack, like young male wolves or horses or wild boar. Unless you play football," he chuckles. "But die in a jungle far off with a spear in the back of your skull, then best just be forgotten. Football players," he lights the marijuana cigarette again. "They're our heroes."

Leni winces. Images of bodies in jungles, by roadsides, on ball fields flash before her.

"Can I have the cigarette?" she points.

He laughs. "Joint. It's called a joint." He hands it to her and lights it.

She inhales a sip, slow and deep. They are quiet. Floating. A car whooshes by on the county road behind them.

"How long . . ." she starts, figuring he may have thought about this, considering he's seen more death than anyone else she knows, except maybe Maman (but Leni can't talk to her about these things), "do you think a spirit remembers its body?"

Hank Junior looks at Leni. "You don't have a lot of idle thinking going on in there, do you?" he taps her head lightly with his fingers, then stubs out the joint, drops it in the ashtray, and closes it. "I do not know. What are your thoughts on the matter?"

"I think at first they want to come back, be back. Especially if they died all of a sudden. I think they can remember things and I think they can feel our memories. Some of them, I mean." Thoughts keep coming. Things begin to feel clear and even obvious. "Maybe . . . Well, I think it's like this. I think spirits can still see, maybe can still travel down to earth, on the light beams, the waves of light, from all the stars in the galaxy that travel so far—trillions of miles, light-years—to touch us here on earth." She pauses, remembering Cal, the sun shining on his lean suntanned arms, his shy smile beneath the brim of his hat as he talked about light and Newton and prisms. But she doesn't want to think of him either. "And I think," she goes on quickly, "that's how they can come into our thoughts and dreams. And I think we can share memories with them." The thread of thought begins to fray. She must sound stupid. "For a time. Maybe," she says. Embarrassed, she mumbles, "I don't know." She wishes she could ask Foy.

Hank is looking at her, his arm stretched along the back of the seat. "That's very poetic. No one can say it's *not* like that."

Leni snaps her head up. Stares at the roof of the cab. A terrible thought. "Do you think we can keep spirits here?" she asks. "I mean . . ." Didn't her daddy say the way to keep Foy alive is in our memories? "What if it's like they get trapped here—part of them—with our memories? What if they don't want to stay here?" She turns to Hank Junior, tears—dammit—rising up.

He smooths her hair with his hand. Wipes the eye black beneath her left cheek with his thumb and then his thumb on a Dairy Queen napkin. He stares a moment at her mouth. Her lips tingle beneath his gaze. She is frozen. Frozen in the smoky light that's soft like the underside of a dove. He leans closer. Wipes her other cheek. His thumb on the napkin again. This stops the thoughts. Any thoughts. His face. His smell, cigarettes and the faint odor of liquor, whiskey maybe. His lips part ever so slightly. He is closer still. She can feel his breath on her lips and chin. She doesn't move. He kisses her. A little hard. She feels his teeth beneath his lips. His hand cups her ear, draws her toward him. Her lips part. His tongue, dry, finds hers. His head tilts. He presses her between his hand and his lips and tongue. It is dizzying. His left hand now on her thigh. Then her waist. She arches, just a little, into his hand. Wait. *No*, she thinks. She tilts her head away. Raises her arm. Looks out the windshield.

He leans back. Smiles. "OK. That's OK." He pats her thigh.

Leni takes the napkin. Swipes at each cheek. She didn't like the kiss. But she liked that he wanted to kiss her.

"Shall we?" He opens the truck door.

As they walk toward the Roadhouse, everything does feel different. Nerves reaching out into the air, like she can sense three hundred and sixty degrees around her. Hank holds the door and Leni walks inside.

It isn't anything like she imagined. Not much bigger than their barn, if you opened up the stalls and the feed room. And not much cleaner. The bar stretches halfway along the back wall, bottles of liquor on shelves set around a big mirror with a beer logo in the center and a rack of antlers on top. Two old men on stools in worn work pants blend into the bar. To the left, in front of dirty windows, is a spindly microphone and an old standup piano. A handful of small square tables sit between the bar and the door. Past the bar to the right are two pool tables. Lights with wide, shiny green shades, like the underbelly of a frog, hang low above them, draping the tables in light. Behind the pool tables is a tall rack, lined with pool cues and two or three more small tables.

"Howdy, Lester." Hank Junior greets the bartender, who stops wiping down the bar just long enough to swivel a cigarette from one side of his mouth to the other with his tongue, nod in their direction, and go back to his work.

Leni follows Hank Junior to the pool tables.

"You ever play before?" he asks.

She shakes her head.

"I'd say it's time you learned, don't you?"

She shrugs.

"Are you not speaking again?" He lights a cigarette.

She admires the way the light spreads only to the edges of the green tables, making each one look like a small suspended sea. The balls make a crisp *click, clack, clack* as Hank Junior gathers them inside a white plastic triangle. She follows the smoke from his cigarette as it floats through the beam of light. Taking in the bright colors beneath the white light, she thinks of Cal again. Still in the game. Beneath the bright lights on the field. The chants and the band. Surrounded by players and cheerleaders and the crowd. But she keeps picturing him on that field all alone. Just a thin boy, with those long fingers that tickled the velvet of Foggy's nose.

Hank Junior lays a pool cue on the table. Rolls it left, then right a couple of times. He sets down the solid white ball and takes a shot, the cue sliding easily through his fingers. The white ball smashes into the cluster of balls. The six ball glides into the corner pocket.

"What I find," he says, leaning low over his cue and peering at the table, "is that concentrating on one thing often gets you thinking in a clearer way about other things happening in your life." One ball in the side pocket. He walks to the other end of the table and leans down again, cue resting in the crook of his thumb. "What I keep wondering," he says, "is whose damned life am I living now?" Another shot. Sharp and quick. The four ball knocks another aside and slips into the corner pocket. "I mean," he goes on, his eyes scanning the table, "I dodged fate. There were a whole lot of folks out there trying to kill me. But here I am. So, what do I do now?"

"Well," staring at the table, Leni contemplates the question, "whose life would you like to be living?" She scratches her cheek. Wipes another bit of black on her jeans.

He laughs. "Jimi Hendrix's." He swipes the tip of his cue with the chalk. "I'd like to be living Jimi Hendrix's life." He ricochets the eight ball off the side and into the three ball, which runs out of steam inches before the side pocket he aimed for.

"Why?" Leni asks.

"Why? Well." He takes another pool cue from the rack, lays it on the table, and

rolls it back and forth a few times. "You right-handed?"

Leni nods.

"Put your hand here." He grips the cue to show her. "You got to lean down so you can see the line you want the ball to follow." He demonstrates.

She puts her hands on the cue, like he said. And leans down.

"Farther," he presses on her shoulder.

She tenses. A surge of blood to her head. She closes her eyes. Rests her forearm on the hard, smooth wood of the table. The

Roadhouse. With Hank McGrath. Her mother would kill her if she knew. Her daddy would be silent, disappointed. Grounded again. For sure.

Who cares?

"Come on. Don't think so much," he says.

Trying to hold her left hand steady, the cue cradled between her thumb and forefinger, Leni jerks back her right arm. The stick catches in the armhole of Foy's oversized jersey. The tip of the cue skips twice on the table.

"Oh, damn." Hank rubs the marks on the table with his thumb. "That jersey's in your way. Take it off."

"No." Leni steps back from the table.

He unbuttons the plaid flannel shirt he's wearing. "Here. Take this." He hands Leni the shirt with one hand and tucks in his T-shirt with the other. "Come on. Take it."

The skin of his outstretched arm is as tight and smooth as new leather. Muscles spiral one way around his upper arm and the other way down his forearm like a piece of taffy someone's stretched and twisted. She takes the shirt.

The bathroom marked "fillies" is small and dark. The sink drips. Disinfectant lingers in the air and makes her sinuses tighten. Her eyes water. She pulls Foy's jersey over her head. Hank Junior's shirt smells like cigarettes and the pine of men's deodorant. She gazes into the broken mirror above the sink, turns the faucet, and looks for soap to wash off what's left of the black on her face.

When she comes out, Hank Junior is talking to a skinny guy with stringy dark hair almost to his shoulders. Deep acne scars make his cheeks look like he fell asleep on gravel. Leni lays Foy's jersey on a cocktail table to the side of the pool table.

"So, tomorrow," the guy is saying as Leni walks up, his shoulders bouncing as he talks.

Hank Junior ignores him and hands Leni a beer. "I got you this."

"OK. So, tomorrow . . ." the guy starts up again.

"I told you all right," Hank Junior interrupts. "I'm not talking about it anymore here." He chalks his cue and walks around the end of the table.

The guy holds his hand out to Leni. She reaches for it.

"She doesn't need to know who you are," Hank Junior says, studying the table.

The guy drops his hand and walks out of the Roadhouse, his head twitching like he's still carrying on a conversation.

Hank Junior picks up the white ball, places it back down where it was before Leni scratched the table, and hands her the cue.

"Come on," he says. "Let's play. Lean down. Get comfortable. Get your line of sight, like I showed you."

She pushes the plaid shirt above her elbows and leans down. The scent of pine and stale smoke floats up to her nose. Her mouth tastes sour from the beer and the joint. Her arm stretches long over the green table, the cue balanced in the crook of her thumb. She feels the warmth from the light. Staring the eight ball dead center, she slides the cue back, then forward.

"Whoa. Nice shot, cowgirl," Hank Junior says. "OK, OK." He circles the table. Looks for angles as he taps his cue on the floor. "Seven in the corner. You can do it. Line it up."

She wipes the chalk across the cue, like she saw him do, swigs a gulp of beer—which only makes her thirstier—pushes her hair behind her ear, and leans over. She stares down the length of the cue. Brings it back real slow and smooth, like she's casting a fishing line on their pond back home, and slides the cue forward.

"You are a natural." Hank Junior smiles proudly at her from across the table, his arms open like he could hug her.

Leni grabs the chalk again. She walks to the other side, her eyes fixed on the table. Everything seems more real. The colors more saturated, the balls more solid, shiny, and dense beneath the light. The next shot, the five ball in the side pocket. She misses. By a lot. She steps back into the shadows.

Quick and easy, Hank Junior sinks the last three balls, one after the other. He lights another cigarette and sets up the next game.

Three men, about Hank Junior's age, baseball caps low over their eyes, come in, get beers from the bar, and head to the pool tables. The way they stick together and the upright handshakes and shoulder bumps they give Hank Junior make her think they were overseas, too. They step away and start a game at the other table.

"Break 'em." Hank Junior nods toward the perfect bright triangle of balls in the sea of green.

She tries.

"That sucked." He gathers the balls back into the triangle.

"Where'd you go?" Leni takes another sip of beer. "After you got out, I mean."

Hank Junior jostles the balls, getting them even over the mark on the table. Lifts the triangle straight up. "'Got out?'" he repeats. "You make it sound like prison."

"Got back. From Vietnam."

He sets down the cue ball. Shoots. The sound so clear and sharp. Balls skitter across the table and off the sides.

"Where'd I go? I went to Ohio."

In quick succession, he sinks the four ball in a corner, the one ball in a side pocket, the three ball off the side and into the corner.

"Why?"

"Because there was someone there I needed to see."

"A girl?"

"No, not a girl."

When he concentrates, his face gets narrow and sharp. Like he's homing in on a target. Another ball in a side pocket. He stands back. Plucks the cigarette from his mouth. Exhales. "I needed to see some people." Cigarette back between his lips. He leans down. Peers through the smoke. *Clack*. The nine ball misses the corner pocket. He stands, takes the cigarette from his mouth. Still as a hunter, he looks straight at Leni. "The family of a friend. A friend who died."

She feels challenged. But equal, somehow. "Is that where you stayed?"

"That's where I stayed."

"Why didn't you tell your momma and all?"

"I was not accustomed to checking in with folks." He stubs his cigarette out on the floor. "Find your shot."

She looks. Points her cue at the five ball. He shakes his head, nods at the blue and white ten ball lingering alone in front of them.

"Bank it off here." He taps the opposite side of the table.

She wrinkles her nose, shakes her head.

"It's easy. Physics. Have you even had physics yet?"

She shakes her head.

Physics.

Cal.

Her chest begins to throb. Then her fingers. She stares at the table. The light glinting off the balls like shooting stars.

Hank Junior comes toward her. "Like this." He puts a hand on her hip. Moves her a foot to the right. "Look," he says. "It's not that hard. You aim there," he taps the opposite side of the table with his cue, "and the eight ball comes right back here," he points at a spot in front of them, "and the blue and white ball," which is stagnant in front of them, "will do just like it's told. And, snap, you sink it here." He taps a corner pocket.

Leni swings her hair over her shoulder, leans down, and steadies the cue. Picturing Hank Junior's face, she narrows her eyes. She feels his hand between her shoulder blades.

"Stay steady. That's right." He places his other hand on her hip. Guides her ever so slightly to the right. "Good."

She breathes into his hand, steady and strong on her back. Eyes fixed on the ten ball until the green of the table seems to vibrate. She draws the pool cue slowly back.

"You really are an asshole, aren't you?"

Leni bounces up. Cal is standing on the other side of the table, light flashing off his wet hair. The sight of him makes her cheeks burn. Her blood drops. Light-headed, she uses the cue to steady herself. Cal's still wearing his jersey. But no pads underneath. His mouth is tight. He pushes on the table with both hands, his arms like springs. He's breathing hard, like he ran there. His jersey swings around him; he's just movement and grace.

"No, brother," Hank Junior straightens. "I really am not," he says slowly.

Cal steps back into the shadows and circles the table.

"My guess is the game didn't go so good." Hank Junior twists a square of chalk on the tip of his cue.

"How old are you?" Cal demands, starting around the table toward Leni and his brother.

"Cal. . ." Hank Junior starts.

"Everyone's just someone to play with, with you. You know what she's been through?" Cal points at Leni.

"Leni can take care of herself. Ain't that right?"

He looks to Leni. The same direct, challenging look as before. But this time it feels like a shot between the eyes.

"We're just playing a game," Hank Junior says, the pool cue swinging wide as he spreads his arms.

"You brought her to the Roadhouse?" Cal couldn't sound more disbelieving.

It feels like a snap of the fingers could light the fuse running between the brothers.

"What's wrong with the Roadhouse? I recall you couldn't wait to come here."

Leni follows Cal's eyes as he scans the dimly lit room. A broken stool. A window with tape across the center. The sticky floor. The three guys huddled at the other table, watching. It smells of cigarette smoke and spilled beer, stale and sour. Suddenly she feels woozy. Places a hand on the smooth, hard edge of the table.

Cal steps toward his brother. "And why's she wearing your shirt?"

"Why don't you ask her?"

Cal, both hands to his brother's chest, pushes. Hank Junior is shorter by half a foot, but he's rigid as a post. Doesn't budge. Cal pulls his arm back, fist clenched, nostrils wide.

Quick as a snake, Hank Junior grabs Cal's wrist mid-swing. "You do not want to do that, little brother."

Cal yanks his arm back. Takes a step away. Leni wants to stop him. But her body's turned to lead. She can barely breathe. Cal lunges at his brother.

Hank Junior drops his pool cue and grabs Cal around the chest. Grunting, Hank Junior shoves Cal away. Cal's arms flail as he hits a chair, catches his balance.

"Straighten up over there!" Lester shouts from the bar, clanging a metal ashtray like a gavel.

But Cal won't stop. He leaps on Hank Junior, wraps his arms around him, and twists, like an animal with prey.

"Please!" Leni's voice hoarse, caught in her throat. "Please stop!"

Evan Holt, Marguerite's ex-fiancé, comes through the door—with Earl DeWitt's son, Payne, and the Moore brothers. They see the commotion.

"Hey, hey, hey!" Evan yells. "Hank! Caleb!"

They rush over. Payne pulls Cal back. It takes both Moore brothers to hold Hank Junior. Evan stands between Hank Junior and Cal, his arms outstretched like a traffic cop. "Come on. Settle down now," he looks back and forth between them. "Or does one of you have to leave?"

Evan turns to Leni. "You all right?" The light shines harsh on his scars: the left side of his nose and mouth stretched tight toward a dent in his cheek the size of a nickel.

Leni nods. And looks away.

"You know how many folks are looking for you right now?"

She hadn't thought, hadn't imagined any such thing. Evan looks to Cal, so Leni can see the still-smooth side of him: the dark sideburn in front of a still-perfect ear. The others step away from Hank Junior and Cal.

"She's fine," Hank Junior says, shaking off the Moore brothers.

"Let her answer," Cal spits out.

Leni looks to Cal. Words are buried too deep in her chest to come out.

"Jesus H. Christ, little brother. What are you so worked up about?" Hank Junior reaches out, strokes the side of Leni's turned cheek and neck.

Cal springs forward, lands a punch square on his brother's jaw.

Hank jerks toward his brother. The Moore boys try to grab him again.

"It ain't nothing," they say. "Let it go . . . Y'all need to cool down . . ."

But Hank Junior now has that look of his locked onto Cal like a sniper. Payne faces Cal like he's guarding a basketball player. But Cal, quick, ducks around him. He's like a fine colt going up against a tractor.

"Don't!" Leni cries. "Please!"

"Y'all got to get yourselves under control over there. You hear me?" Lester peers over the bar.

Leni, her pool cue braced in front of her, steps forward. Hank Junior sweeps the cue away like it's a cobweb. Evan pulls her back.

"I told you you didn't want to do that. Didn't I tell you?" Hank Junior moves slow and black as a locomotive, eyes locked on his brother. "You don't listen. That's your problem. You got a lot to learn."

"Please!" Leni cries again. Evan is holding her. "Please!" she leans around Even's shoulder.

Hank Junior is puffed up like a rooster and . . .

Bang!

They all cower. Like they'd been gut punched. All except for Hank Junior.

"I done told you fools to stop!" Lester stands in front of the bar with a long rifle in his hands. He shot a hole in the floor right there at the end of the bar. "Whoever's got a hankering to fight, get on out 'a here. Y'all come back like you're still over there fighting the goddamned Nips. I've had it with you."

Some folks hovering by the door skitter back out.

"Y'all is bad for business. Now I mean it. You want to fight, get the hell out 'a here."

"It's all right now, Lester," Evan says.

"It'd better be."

"I know, Lester. I know," Evan cajoles him.

Lester, still muttering to himself, stomps back behind the bar, striking the butt of the rifle on the floor with each step.

"Can you all behave yourselves now?" Evan asks, looking back and forth between the brothers.

Hank Junior finishes half a beer in a gulp. Picks a pool cue up from the floor. And nods. Cal shrugs off Payne, who still had a hand on his shoulder, and steps away from the table.

"You need a ride home?" Evan asks Leni.

She nods. Swipes tears from her cheek with the sleeve of Hank Junior's shirt.

"I'll take her," Hank Junior finishes a beer and hands the empty bottle to one of the Moore brothers.

"That all right?" Evan asks Leni. She's searching for Caleb.

"Come on then," Hank Junior sets the cue in the rack hard, rattling the others.

Payne DeWitt's in the shadows by the backrooms, a hand on Cal's shoulder, talking to him like you would a spooked horse, his voice low and even. Leni watches. Wanting Cal to look at her, wanting to catch his eye. But he won't take his eyes off the floor.

Hank Junior swaggers toward the door. Folks are already back to yammering and ordering drinks. Someone put money in the jukebox and an old half-yodeling song starts to play. Leni scoops up Foy's jersey and follows Hank Junior out of the Roadhouse and into darkness.

Her brain's a fog from the marijuana and the beer. Thoughts dissolve. She's all sensation. Cheeks tingling. Eyes stinging. Fingers pulsing.

She climbs into Hank Junior's truck. He slams the truck into gear. Swings his arm over the backseat and guns it into the dark. Then, swearing, stands on the brakes. The truck shimmies. Leni slides to the floor. Hank Junior jumps out, slams the door. Leni pushes herself up. Slinks out. Cal is right behind the truck.

"OK. Come on," Hank says, shaking out his hands. "How long you been wanting to fight me? Since I been back? Since I took your train set when you were five? What?"

"I didn't have a train set."

"Well, what the fuck is it you want?"

"I want you to stop running over people." Leni hears the sadness taking over his anger.

"Then don't stand behind my goddamned truck. Jesus!"

It wasn't that words were stuck in Leni's throat; she couldn't find words. Words weren't up to the task. Overwhelmed by everything from the day into the night. The trophy for Foy. The loss of him. The despair in her father's eyes. The dingy Roadhouse. The sight of Cal, the white of his jersey catching the moonlight. So pure.

"I'll take Leni home," Cal says, his voice shaky.

Yes, Leni thinks. She leans into the truck to get her things.

"Ah, stop shitting yourself," Hank says. "I ain't going to do nothing but drive her to her front door. For fuck's sake."

Foy's jersey isn't on the seat. Leni rakes through the clothes and papers on the floor. Can't find it. She climbs into the truck to look. Sweeping her arm across the seat, then reaching to the floor beneath the steering wheel. It's caught on the brake pedal. She frees it. Clambers out of the truck as Hank Junior climbs in. She looks around. But Cal's gone. She calls his name. Feebly. Her throat's so dry. Parched. All that comes out is a chirp. She swallows. Tries again. No answer.

"Get in," Hank Junior says.

She looks into the darkness. No Cal.

She gets back in the truck. Hot tears sting her cheeks. Hank Junior yanks the truck into gear and, spraying gravel behind them, speeds out onto the road.

The empty pastures look silver in the moonlight. Past County Road, a stray dog or maybe a coyote, lopes alongside them for several strides, then splits off into a field.

Hank Junior turns into the O'Hares' drive. Circles slowly in front of the house. The only light on is in the kitchen. Leni mutters a "thank you," gets out and, head down, starts for the porch steps. The driver's side door closes. Hank Junior is beside her at the bottom of the steps. The porch door swings open. Light splashes over the front stoop.

She feels as thick as paste.

Doc O'Hare comes down the steps. Hank Junior slinks back as Doc grabs Leni, wraps his arms around her, and gasps, his breaths deep and jagged, like he's been under water for days. Then he holds her by the shoulders. His eyes roam her face.

"You all right?"

"Yes, Daddy."

"Who's that?"

The truck engine starts.

"Hank McGrath, Daddy. He just drove me home. That's all."

The skin sags on his face. His eyes so deep in their sockets. Absence gnaws at every sinew. Her father's as hollowed out as she is. Longing for Foy is eating them away.

He presses Leni's head to his chest. His heart drums steady against her ear. Releasing her, he bends his face to hers. "Hearts can break twice, you know." He brushes wisps of hair from her forehead and holds her again to his chest.

Her mother is standing in the doorway in her white robe, like a paper figure cut out of the kitchen light. Leni is happy to see her. Happy that she's come to join them.

Maman clutches her robe and starts down the steps. "You," she adjusts a slipper, takes the next step, "are the most selfish of girls."

"No, Ludevigne," her father says.

"Where have you been? Do you think of anyone but yourself?" One more step. "What were you thinking?"

But there are no words. No words to explain any of this.

"You think," her mother reaches the bottom step, "your pain is stronger than anyone else's?"

"Ludevigne, stop." Doc's voice is sharp, like a spear thrown down between Leni and her mother. "Not now."

And she quiets. Jamming her hand in the pocket of her robe, her eyes glistening, Maman turns and climbs the steps back into the house.

Upstairs, quiet as she can, Leni slips into the bathroom. She stuffs Hank Junior's shirt into the hamper and leans over the sink to try—with the cold water they only ever have that time of night—to wash off the smell of beer and smoke.

A strip of light sneaks out from under Marguerite's door. Leni pauses, slowly turns the doorknob and peeks in. But Marguerite is asleep, an *Elle* magazine open on her chest. Leni turns off the bedside light. Passes her own room and enters Foy's.

Laying down, she pulls the patchwork quilt up to her chest. The thin curtain flutters in the open window.

Caleb

Cal pulled up under the magnolia tree in front of the house. His mother was in the kitchen, a coffee cup in hand, turning pages of the *County Gazette*.

"I'm sorry, sweetheart. It was a tough game. Y'all have had so much on your minds. You hungry?"

Cal grunted something and walked out of the kitchen. He took a long shower and laid on his bed, in the dark, an arm cradling his head, which hurt. Leni leaving with Hank; the game, which they lost badly; two cups of water; Leni in Hank's shirt at the Roadhouse; the fight that could have been, maybe should have been. It all spun in his brain until he heard his brother tromp down the hall. The doorknob turned, and Hank Junior pushed Cal's bedroom door open with his foot.

"She's home." He leaned against the doorjamb.

"Good. You waiting for me to thank you or something?"

Hank rolled his back across the edge of the doorjamb like he had some hard-to-scratch itch. "She's all safe and sound."

"Yeah, I bet," Cal said.

"You think I fucked her?"

"Fuck you, Hank." His fists clenched.

Hank turned to go, then paused, his stubby hand on the door. "Look, I didn't know you two were a thing."

"We're not 'a thing.'"

"Life's too fuckin' short for bullshit, Cal." He yanked a cigarette from his shirt pocket. "Truly it is." He lit the cigarette. "What's all that?" One of the college brochures laid on Cal's desk.

"Nothing."

The last thing Cal wanted was Hank Junior in his face about what a waste college would be and getting their father all riled up about it. But his brother reached in, grabbed the Princeton brochure, scanned it front and back: the prim students, impossibly green lawns and ivy-covered brick buildings. Watching him, Cal knew he was reaching for Oz.

"Put it back, Hank."

"Is there anything you're straight about?" Hank asked somberly. He put the brochure down and turned to leave.

"Close my goddamned door."

"Close your own goddamned door."

Leni

In her dream, Foy is running toward her. She smiles, waiting for him to get closer. As he does, she can see how hard he's running, as hard as he can, like he's running with all the energy he had stored up for the fifty or sixty years he was denied. She waves to him. Wanting him to stop. But he runs right past her. Slows up, looks back. He has a haunted, almost hunted, look on his face as he turns away and keeps on running.

When she wakes, her face is buried in the pillow, damp with tears. She is cold all over, like she's been plunged in ice.

Has it, she thinks, been painful for him to be remembered? Is she keeping him here? Some part of him. Yanking him back when maybe he needs to go on. Go somewhere else now.

And she wonders if ghosts have weight. Because she swears she can feel him right there. Sitting beside her. She opens her eyes.

"You were having a dream." Her mother reaches for her hand. "I heard something. I think maybe—for one moment," she holds up a finger, "it is him." She smiles. It's a sad smile, but a smile. And she pushes Leni's tangled hair off her face. Her mother looks so tired.

Still holding Leni's hand, her mother strokes her arm. "It is very hard. I know what you feel. You don't think I know. But I do." Her mother squeezes Leni's hand. "There is—I am thinking tonight, thinking about you—there is something that was easier about the war. Yes. And it is that everyone— everyone I knew—had lost someone they adored. It didn't make the pain leave. No. But it made you less alone. I know you feel alone." She pats Leni's hand. "I know you feel very alone." Tears swell under the dark circles beneath her mother's eyes. "And that," she is whispering now, leaning closer, "makes me so sad for you."

Her mother lets go of Leni's hand and opens her arms. Leni sits up. Her mother wraps her arms around her. She can't remember her mother holding her before. She can't remember climbing into her mother's lap if she was hurt or sick. Her mother had to have held her when she was very small. Before she could remember. Before she had words to remember with.

She does feel alone. Separate. And no words, nothing anyone says, helps. In fact, people try, but everything they say makes it worse.

"Parles-moi en Français, Maman."

"Ma cherie, tout va bien. Tu verra. Je te promets. Tu es forte. Encore plus forte que les autres. Reposes maintenant. You must rest, my dear."

CHAPTER TEN

Leni

Leni rounds the newel post at the bottom of the stairs and steps gingerly into the kitchen. Sunlight streams across the kitchen table where Maman is mending one of Doc O'Hare's shirts. Marguerite stares at the toaster.

"Madeleine," Maman not looking up. *"Tu as besoin de quelque chemises et peut-etre une jupe, aussi. Vous deux."* She gestures to Leni and her sister. "Marguerite, take your sister to Wolcott's. Madeleine needs a nice skirt and," she pauses, waves her hand, *"quelque chose,* for school."

"Oui, Maman."

Marguerite grimaces at her sister. "You're not going to argue and run off?"

Leni ignores her. The toaster pops. Marguerite pinches one piece of hot toast and drops it onto a plate, then the other.

She won't try this time to convince Maman that jeans and T-shirts and denim shirts are perfectly fine for school. That she doesn't have to wear "proper" blouses and skirts, especially since she has little chest to boast about, and her knees are permanently scraped and bruised, mostly from barrel riding.

Marguerite dangles a piece of dry toast to Leni. Leni knows that look. Her sister's silent treatment. She takes the toast, gets a knife, and scrapes butter across the top.

"Do you need anything from Wolcott's, Maman?" Leni asks.

"*Non,*" concentrating on her sewing. "*Rien de tout. Merci.*"

It is gentler between them, at least for now. Maman watches, without a reprimand, crumbs drop from Leni's toast to the floor. Leni takes a sponge, wipes the crumbs. Pours herself a glass of orange juice.

Marguerite puts her dish in the sink with a loud *clack*, grabs her red purse from the counter, and marches out, letting the back door slam behind her. Leni gulps her juice and follows.

One hand on the roof of her green Nova, the other on her hip. "That was some stunt you pulled last night," Marguerite blurts, lips pursed.

"It wasn't a 'stunt.'"

"What would you call it?" One eyebrow raised.

"You can stand up there, smile at the crowd—"

"No one was 'smiling at the crowd.'"

"—And get a trophy for Foy dying, if you want. I want nothing to do with it. With Coach, with football. With any of it."

Leni flings what's left of her toast to the goats and stomps to the barn. She hates shopping anyway. Heading straight to the tack room, she picks up a tin of saddle soap and a sponge. Turns.

"Blaming Coach—" Marguerite is in her face.

"—He should have known," Leni shouts. "He should have watched. He should have done better."

Marguerite shakes her head. "Leni. Blaming Coach or anyone for what happened, that's just going to eat you up. Coach is broken up over what happened."

"He should be broken up."

"You aren't the only one who lost him, you know. Don't make it harder on Maman and Daddy."

Leni drops her head. Her nose and eyes sting.

"And what about me?" Her sister's voice has grown softer.

Leni opens her eyes. Marguerite's cheeks are red. Tears about to spill.

Leni looks away.

Slowly, Marguerite opens her arms. Leni steps closer, closes her eyes. Her cheek against her sister's soft dark curls.

"I don't know what to do."

"None of us does." Marguerite strokes Leni's hair. "One foot in front of the other. That's all we can do."

"Yesterday," Leni swipes her cheek, "I felt black as tar."

"I know." Marguerite continues to hold her, to stroke her hair.

"I feel different today. Maybe some of it got squeezed out. I don't know."

"Come on," Marguerite steps back, holds out her hand.

"To Texarkana?" Leni takes her sister's hand.

"To Texarkana. We'll take a drive. Maman gave me money to buy you a skirt or blouse. Surely you can find something, if only to please her. Come on." Marguerite's floral skirt and red purse swing as she turns.

Sunlight sneaks through the open barn door, making a slanted sheet of dust particles suspended in the air glisten. They walk out into the bright day.

Driving east and north, they pass the edge of the McGrath ranch, where a few of its oil wells peck and pull at the earth. Saturday morning in town is busy. For De Kalb, at least. Payne DeWitt and his father are unloading a flatbed of grain sacks. A horse trailer and a couple of pickups are waiting for the pumps at the Esso station. Once out of town, breezes comb the tops of the winter grasses, already a foot and a half tall. Further on, cattle graze alongside the road. A horse or two here and there.

Leni tries to tune in a radio station, gives up, turns the radio off, and stares out at the passing fields.

"OK," Marguerite glances at Leni, "let's let the elephant out of the room. What happened with you and Hank Junior last night?"

"Nothing. We drove around." Leni watches a baler chug across a field, spitting out rectangles of straw as it goes.

"You drove around for four hours?"

"Yeah. Pretty much."

"What'd you talk about?"

"Nothing much."

"That's a long bit of time to talk about nothing."

Leni stares out the window. They pass pastures so large, the far fence line is out of sight. Cows gather beneath the shade trees.

Finally, Marguerite sighs. "Let's be friends again, Leni."

"Why?"

"'Why?' Why are you mad at me?"

"I'm not mad at you."

"Yes, you are."

"I'm just mad. All right? Can I be mad?"

"Yes. Yes, you can be mad."

"When I get mad, I want everyone to know it. And I want everyone else to be mad, too. If they aren't going to be as mad as I am, I've got no use for them."

"Well, I guess you and Hank McGrath have that in common."

"I guess so." Leni smiles an inward smile. "OK. We went to the Roadhouse."

"You what?"

"We went to the Roadhouse?"

"You're lucky no fights broke out."

"One did."

"Are you kidding?! Who?"

It's been a long time since she had her sister's attention like this. "Yeah. Hank Junior and I smoked a joint. In his truck."

"No!"

Leni smiles, her face feeling warm. Maybe she's one up on her big sister. "Yeah, we did. Have you ever? Smoked pot?"

Marguerite, mouth hanging open, looks at her sister. Then back to the road. "Yes," she says slowly. "Once or twice." She smiles, looks to Leni. "Maybe more. Did you like it?"

"I'm not sure. So much was happening."

"Tell me about the fight. Lester hates that."

"Oh, my God, Greet" (the nickname Leni gave Marguerite as a toddler when that was as much of her name as she could pronounce). She feels a little jittery, talking with her sister like this. She would have told Foy first chance she got. But for the past year, she and Marguerite have been like cats vying for territory. "Lester took an old rifle—I've never seen a barrel so long—and shot a hole right in the floor."

Marguerite laughs. Leni had almost forgotten the dimple in her sister's right cheek. Not the left, just the right. "Who was fighting?"

"Well, Hank Junior was teaching me how to play pool. And Caleb came in. And . . ."

"And . . .," Marguerite eggs her on with a wide smile.

Leni's choking back words or tears, she's not even sure.

Marguerite looks to Leni. Her smile fades, and she looks back to the road. Most everyone around here knows better than to press a person. Better to let the sky, the fields, the space do their work.

Leni tries again. "Caleb came in and he thought . . ." Marguerite reaches her hand out. Leni takes it. "He thought

Hank and I were . . . I don't know what he thought. But I wasn't. I wasn't doing anything with Hank Junior!"

"Did you tell him?"

"It all happened so fast." She can't speak again. Doesn't want Marguerite's attention any more. The whole evening—from the fool ceremony, to the Roadhouse, to Daddy, then the dreams, and Maman holding her—spins in her head.

"Did he get hurt? Cal?" Marguerite prompts Leni.

"No." She reminds herself to breathe. "No. Evan and Payne DeWitt and the Moore brothers came in. They broke it up."

"That's good. I wouldn't put money on Caleb in that matchup."

Leni turns to Marguerite, wants to defend Cal. But her sister's right.

"Then Hank Junior drove you home?"

"Yeah. I didn't even want him to drive me home. Evan offered, but I thought you wouldn't want to see him. Then Hank Junior said he'd take me. I looked for Caleb, but he'd gone."

"Hank didn't try anything, did he?" Marguerite asked again.

"No. I told you." She wasn't going to tell her sister about the kiss.

"What's he like?"

"Cal?"

"No." Marguerite laughs. "Hank Junior!"

"You're not his type."

"Don't be ornery."

"You're not."

"Oh, OK. So, he likes skinny tomboys."

"Right. No way," Leni says, remembering the kiss again—the liking it and not liking it. "I don't know," Leni mulls it over. "He doesn't like bullshit or games. He's real straight. But he's got secrets. That's for sure."

"What kind of secrets?" Marguerite hands Leni a pack of gum.

"Well, they wouldn't be that secret if I knew, would they?"

Where did Hank Junior go when he got back from Vietnam? Who was the skinny, greasy-haired guy at the Roadhouse? What were they cooking up? She won't say anything about that either. It feels like they have some sort of pact, Leni and Hank Junior. And she's scared of him. A little. Scared of what he knows. Scared of what she imagines he's done, and what he might do.

As they approach Texarkana, the houses get closer together. Small brick ranch houses, with picket fences out front, and a few older clapboard homes with front porches and low-slung eaves. Soon, they come to the stores on the main drag.

Entering Wolcott's, they pass a woman staring into the makeup counter display case. A saleswoman looks up, says "hi" to Leni and Marguerite, then turns her attention back to the customer. Past the makeup counter, before the escalators, several women mill about the displays of scarves and gloves. Getting ready for winter. Not one of them stops what she's doing as Leni and Marguerite walk by.

No one knows them.

Leni follows Marguerite up the escalator to the second floor, where racks of skirts and dresses and shoes fan out before them. Marguerite goes straight to the skirts and rakes through them like she's looking for something she thinks she left there.

A saleswoman, not much older than Marguerite, stands beside Leni. Her hair flips up evenly all around her head, not a strand out of place. Her name tag says "Jean."

"I'm just here with my sister." Leni nods in Marguerite's direction.

Marguerite, holding up half a dozen skirts, passes on her way to the fitting rooms. "Blouses. Over there," she points, then disappears behind a curtain.

"Why, now, don't you want to get yourself something, too?" Jean, the young saleswoman asks. "You've got a cute figure."

Leni studies the blue eye shadow beneath Jean's eyebrows and the eyelashes that are too black and too long. Two girls—Marguerite's age—step off the escalator, each with a baby on her hip. They stand across from each other, a rack of skirts between them, chatting nonstop and bouncing their round babies. Leni watches them.

Jean steps back to get a better look at Leni. "A lot of men like tall girls." She nods, agreeing with herself, and smiles at Leni.

"I'm supposed to find a tie for our daddy," Leni fibs, and heads down the escalator.

The saleswomen downstairs are friendly, too, in an easy way like you'd be to anybody. No sad eyes. No "How y'all doing, really?" Marguerite may like the attention. But it makes Leni feel like she's got a sorry-looking chicken tied to her leg.

Leni ambles alongside the makeup counter. The plump, middle-aged woman behind the display case has a rosy face and very thin blond hair teased up and hair-sprayed till it looks like lace. Leni tries to place what it is she smells like. Her mother is good at placing smells. Daddy used to say it's in her blood because she's French, which would make Maman smile.

"And what are you looking for today, young lady?" The saleswoman cocks her head. Her plucked eyebrows rise. Her name tag says "Betty Anne."

Gardenias and oranges. That's what she smells like.

"Anything I can help you with?" Betty Anne asks again.

"Ah," Leni pauses. An idea takes shape. "*Non*. Zhank yoo. I am joos looking."

"Now where are you from?" A smile widens Betty Anne's round face.

"France." Leni says. This feels so easy.

"No fooling? France."

Leni is fooling. But she feels the excitement of an opportunity opening up. She sidesteps further down the makeup counter.

"Paris?" Betty Anne asks, following. Eyebrows raised again.

"*Ah, non,*" Leni smiles shyly. "A smull town in zhe nort. Near zhe sea."

Betty Anne looks around. The other saleswoman is busy with two customers. She leans forward, as though conspiring with Leni on something. "How do you say 'lipstick' in French?"

"*Rouge à lèvres,*" Leni answers. Betty Anne mimics her. Leni corrects her.

"And," Betty Anne thinks for a moment, "I like your dress."

"*J'aime votre robe.*"

"This is really something." Betty Anne looks around again, preparing to tell Leni a secret. "I have always wanted to go to France. Can I ask you something silly? What do y'all eat for breakfast?"

"Ah," Leni exhales through a slightly puckered mouth, like her mother does when she's thinking. "French toast," Leni says. She has no idea what they eat in France for breakfast.

Marguerite is coming down the escalator, only her red purse dangling by her side. Leni quickly bids *adieu* to Betty Anne and hurries to Marguerite.

"You didn't see anything you liked?" she asks Leni.

"*Non. Et tu n'as pas aimé aucune jupe?*" Leni asks.

"No. They all looked horrid on." They pass the makeup counter. "I think that saleswoman's waving at you?"

Marguerite throws her purse into the car, rests her arms on the roof.

"Nothing's the same, is it?" Marguerite sighs. Leni looks up at the clouds stretched thin high overhead. "What are you thinking on?"

"*Que le ciel est si grand,*" Leni whispers, looking up.

"Careful." Marguerite rests her chin on her hands. "You can get lost looking up there too long."

That's what Leni wants. To get away. To be lost. To be somewhere where she can keep her thoughts and her secrets to herself.

CHAPTER ELEVEN

Leni

October 10, 1972

Dear Foy,

Greet's not hogging the bathroom. Amazing, right? And she's smoked pot. Did you know that?

I've gotten two after-school detentions—thank you very much—for speaking French in class. But no one here knows because Marguerite picks me up late, after she finishes work at DeWitt's and after I've finished detention.

If Maman and Daddy do find out, I'll be grounded again. I'm not going anywhere anyway. Not invited to any parties. Which is fine. Because I can't stand the gossip and the worrying over makeup and who's made out with who, or whatever. So childish. I'd rather have time with my thoughts. I've been thinking a lot. Like about how everything dies. We'll all die. But sometimes there's so much precision to death. Things coming together in just the right way. At just the right time. Like a car spinning into a ditch—how fast was it going, what's the angle of the ditch, how close to the tree does it land? Same for the bobcat waiting for a hare to trip by, or the cottonmouth and the mouse, at just the right spot with the wind blowing the scents in the right direction. What if you'd had that drink of water? Or took off your helmet? Or if you just didn't try so damned hard?

I understand, I think, Maman wanting to get to a place where she could ignore death again. Like most people do.

Didn't cry today.

Caleb

Cal quit the football team after the homecoming game. He spent his time after school working with the two young horses, Chester and Daybreak. He wasn't sure what to do about the scholarship and college test applications, which seemed to be vibrating in his desk drawer beneath the miniature ham radio. Thankfully his brother hadn't brought the matter up again.

And no matter how tired he was when he finally laid down, he couldn't get Leni out of his mind either.

Taking a day off from working the horses, Cal went to the library after school let out. He found a desk along the back wall between the stacks, and slid the scholarship applications from his backpack. He ran his hand over the glossy photograph on the cover of Princeton's, smiling students in V-neck sweaters and pressed pants with books tucked under their arms.

He did want to go to college. His heart beat a little faster just looking at the list of subjects one could study.

Footsteps. He looked up. Leni was beside him. Her back-pack on one shoulder, a couple of books held to her chest. He'd gone a whole half hour without thinking about her. Without wondering why she was so scarce.

"*Bonjour.*"

"Bun jure," he answered.

She corrected his pronunciation. He tried again.

"*C'est mieux,*" she said.

"What are you doing here?" His heart was fluttering in his chest.

She held up her sketch pad.

"What are you drawing?"

"*Un portrait.*"

"Are you speaking only in French?"

She nodded.

"I can't speak French," he said.

She nodded again.

"What about in class?" he asked.

She nodded a third time.

"Even with Miss Perkins?" The art teacher.

She hesitated, shook her head, "No."

She wrote something on a piece of paper and handed it to him. "Detention," it said. She took the paper back, wrote something more, laid it on the table so he could read it. "For speaking French in English class." She turned the paper over, wrote something more, showed it to him.

"He's doing well," Cal answered. "I think I can start to ride him next week."

She smiled. Turned the paper and leaned down to write again. Her hair brushed his shoulder. He closed his eyes.

"He's a beauty," she wrote.

"Yeah, he is. Thank you." So was she. "How's Foggy?"

Mrs. Calhoun, the librarian, waddled by, cradling a stack of books in her arms, and hushed them. Leni took the paper back to write again. With her standing in front of him, the smell of her, he got muddled. He'd thought she was mad at him. Or was it that he felt in some way guilty, implicated in Foy's death? Couldn't he have done more? Did she think that?

"Do you want to sit outside?" the next note asked.

Cal tried to clear his thoughts. The pages of scholarship applications and test registrations, each with its own deadline, in front of him.

"I just got here," he mumbled.

She snatched the piece of paper and he watched the tips of her hair stroke the small of her long back as she strode away.

Leni

She plops down on the cool cement curb in front of the school. The pen gripped hard in her hand, she opens her diary.

> *OK. Fine. He's got plans. Obviously. Doesn't want to give me the time of day. I don't need to waste any more time on some lanky boy. Those damned eyes, soft as a calf's. And where the hell is Marguerite anyway? Am I going to have to walk home? What do we have in common, Caleb McGrath and I? Horses. We have horses in common. I've got one and he's got a herd . . .*

The school's metal entry doors snap open behind her. She looks up. Truck keys in hand, head down, Cal strides past her toward the parking lot. She picks up a small stone and rubs it nervously in her hand.

"Why won't you talk to me?" Leni shouts.

Cal turns—books and catalogs under his arm—mouth agape. "Why won't *I* talk to *you*? In what language? Or maybe I should just pass notes."

"We were in the library!"

"*You've* been avoiding *me* for," he has to think, "weeks."

Leni opens her mouth for a comeback. He waits. But it's true. She has avoided him. After talking to Rabbit. And then after the game and the Roadhouse.

"Guess things didn't work out with my brother." Cal tosses his keys up, snatches them out of the air. "Could have told you that." He turns and starts for the parking lot.

Leni throws the stone, hitting Cal right between the shoulder blades.

He spins around. "What was that for?"

"I am not up to anything with your brother."

"My brother's always up to something these days."

His eyes on her are like fingers pressing on her sternum.

"Why are you angry with me?" he asks, finally.

She shakes her head. "I don't know," she mumbles.

He turns, starts again to his truck.

"Rabbit said—"

"Oh, right." Cal stops, swings his arm toward the brick wall at the top of the rise. "I saw you two—"

"No!" Leni whines. Knees to her chest, she begins rocking back and forth. "There's nothing with Rabbit. Or Hank Junior."

"Well, something's going on."

Can she say this to him? "Rabbit said . . ." Deep breath. She shakes her head.

"What?" He takes two steps toward her.

"Rabbit said you were giving out water that day." Wincing, she looks to Cal. "Why," her face twists, "didn't you give Foy water?"

She tries to stop them. but the sobs come so fast and strong she thinks her ribs might crack. She gasps for air. Mucus fills her sinuses. Panicked, she pins her eyes on Cal.

He rushes to kneel beside her and wraps his arms around her. "I'm sorry. I'm sorry," he moans. Her head pressed to his chest, his fingers tangled in her hair. "I'm sorry." He rocks with her. "Every day, I think Foy would have made sure everybody got water before they got back out on the field."

Her breathing ragged, Leni wipes her face. Foy's problem, she knew, was that he always wanted to make things easier for everybody else. Easygoing, where Leni could be intolerant. Forgiving, where Leni didn't like to let things go. Accepting of people, where Leni questioned everyone. She takes a deep, segmented inhale. "He loved me, you know, even though I'm a little shit."

"Don't say that, Leni."

"But I am."

A flash of lime green. Marguerite speeds up in front of the school, pulls a tight, impatient circle, and stops in front of them. She gets out of her car, flouncy peasant shirt, brow furled. Leni wasn't at the appointed pickup spot at the bottom of the drive. But seeing her sister's tear-stained face, she turns off the car, hurries over, and crouches before Leni.

"What is it? What happened?"

Leni can't speak. Cal lets her go. He stands up and takes a step away.

Marguerite slips an arm around her sister. "It won't always hurt this much. I promise it won't," she whispers. Leni buries her head in her sister's shoulder.

Cal wipes the back of his hand across one cheek, then the other. Marguerite sits on the curb. She looks to Cal. "Thank you," she mouths and turns back to her sister, her cheek next to Leni's, whispering in her ear.

Cal gathers up his books, the catalogs, and his keys and walks to his truck.

As he rolls slowly past Leni and Marguerite, Leni releases her sister's hand, springs up, and runs out. Cal stops. She swings open the passenger side door, steps onto the running board, and leans inside the cab.

"It wasn't your fault." Holding his soft brown eyes with her own, "It wasn't," she repeats. She steps down and gently closes the door.

CHAPTER TWELVE

Leni

The following week, Marguerite begins working late several afternoons, helping the DeWitts with their books. This gives Leni and Cal time together after school. If her sister knows, she's keeping it to herself. Really, though, their parents ought to be happy because being with Cal has gotten Leni to stop speaking French in class and racking up detentions.

They go to Dairy Queen to get swirly soft ice cream cones and drive down the long county roads and find isolated places to make out. One day, a mile before the McGrath ranch headquarters, Cal pulls off. They bounce down a dirt road and stop in front of the broodmare pasture. A dozen mares, with their six- or seven-month-old foals, graze in the tall grass.

Sitting side by side atop the metal gate, they admire the young foals. Still a little gawky, big-kneed, their manes standing straight up off their necks. Cal points out Flint's dam. And Reverie's. Then Chester's and Daybreak's as Rumsey, the quarter horse stud, tears up from the bottom of the pasture, nostrils flared, eyes on the two intruders.

The stallion bounces to a halt, lifts his nose in the air, turns his head to look at them sideways, then, deciding they're no threat, snorts and drops his head to graze.

"He's beautiful!"

"You're beautiful," he says.

She stretches toward him. They kiss. She sidles closer. They kiss again. Cal takes her hand. They climb down off the gate and get back in his truck, where they kiss more. And more deeply. They slide out of their shirts and Leni, giggling, slips out of her bra. Elbows hitting the windows. She lays down on the bench seat. They are both long and taut. Their skin hot, pressing into each other. His fingers hum across her collar bones, the pale skin of her belly and breasts, the crest of her hip. She sighs and smiles. She likes his touch. Likes pressing against him. His weight on her. It's the first time. For each of them. They are too amazed to be too scared.

"Are you all right?"

"I think so." She holds on to him tighter, just below his rib cage.

He straightens his elbows, arching his chest up, away from her, breathing hard. "You should be sure."

They slow down. Still belly to belly. Still kissing, deeper and deeper. "I don't have anything," he whispers. "Are you on the pill?"

How would she get the pill? Maman still sitting in on her checkups with the same pediatrician she's had since she was sucking her thumb.

"Marguerite has them."

"You have some of hers?" he asks.

She pauses and nods.

He is strong and supple. Their bodies find a rhythm. In a moment, they are breathless again.

"I'm sure," she whispers, draped in front of him, her hair spilling over the seat. She unzips her jeans. He pulls them off. Then his, awkwardly. Head hitting the roof, knee into the gear shift.

They are all dampness and rhythm, desire and wonder overtaking any trepidation.

Then they lie in each other's arms, feet pressing against the armrest. Stunned. He smooths her hair off her face. Smiles.

They sit up and watch the mares graze. Leni holds her shirt to her chest. Cal slides his arm around her. Their fingers find again each other's skin, tracing soft curves, the path of muscle and sinew. Lips melting again into one another's.

They slip on their shirts, still naked below. And they talk. Leisurely. Ambling from one topic to the next, like the mares amble from one patch of grass to another, telling each other not so much who they are, because they don't know yet. Not really. But who they want to be.

Miss Perkins had lent Leni a book on Georgia O'Keefe. Leni pored over the images. Paintings from O'Keefe's time in New York City, then from the Southwest. Leni nestles against Cal's chest as he muses about colleges back east. About the science and philosophy and math courses he could take. About the professors from all over the world. Mathematicians who'd cracked codes in World War II. And physicists studying galaxies.

Then it's time. Can't keep Marguerite waiting.

Still dreamy, moving as though through liquid, they put on the rest of their clothes. Kiss.

"I love you, Leni."

"I love you, Caleb McGrath."

Leni snuggles up close to Cal. His arm drapes across her shoulder as they drive back to town. The world has changed. It looks older, somehow. Objects more defined. Has it always been like this, Leni wonders—the browns and greens of the grasses so perfect, the arc of the branches against the sky, the gentle roll of the hills so mesmerizing—and she hadn't noticed?

"Can I call you?" Cal asks, as they pull up the school drive. Marguerite's already there, hip leaning against her car, arms crossed. "I don't want you to get in more trouble. I just want to say good night."

"I have Foy's radio." She tucks her hair behind her ears, smooths her shirt. "Send me a message. Ten o'clock."

Her lips brush his cheek, their fingers touching until she slips from his truck to the ground.

October 29

> *Touching him is like the moon rising inside me*
> *Looked through Marguerite's cabinet. Couldn't find*
> *any. She must have them.*

CHAPTER THIRTEEN

Caleb

The McGrath ranch headquarters was a five-acre compound of offices and barns, paddocks and pens. A wide dirt road ran through the middle. Cal had planned on selling Daybreak and Chester—the two three-year-olds—the following summer, when they would be further along and he could ask more money for them. Money he now hoped to use to help him get to college, if he got in. But their foreman, Walter, got a call from the head wrangler at the nearby Moores' ranch, a Mexican named Jesus. The Moores needed to add some young horses to their string. Walter told Cal it was a good opportunity. Cal agreed that Jesus could come by that Saturday to see the horses.

The next day, after school, Cal went to headquarters to work with the horses. He passed the cavernous, metal machine barn where a couple of guys were repairing a baler, country music from an old radio blaring behind them, drove on past the main horse barn, where the cowboys kept their horses, and the pens where they worked the cattle—separating the calves in the spring for dehorning, castrating, and vaccinating amid a lot of mewing and braying. Beyond the hay barn was a small horse barn with half a dozen stalls and two paddocks, which was used for yearlings getting accustomed to being handled, or for horses that were laid up, for whatever reason. This was where Cal kept Chester and Daybreak.

Cal pulled up in front of the small barn. The horses weren't in either of the paddocks, which was odd. He got out of the truck and checked the barn. The stalls were empty.

He got back in his truck and drove up to the main horse barn. He knew they wouldn't be there, and they weren't. No one would ride them without Walter's OK and Walter wouldn't give anybody else his OK.

Silent George was working on his pickup outside of the machine barn.

"You seen the two three-year-olds I been keeping at the little barn?" Cal asked.

George shook his head. "That barn was empty when I come in this morning and did barn check." He spit out a string of tobacco. "Figured you'd moved them to y'all's place."

"You seen my brother?"

"No. Can't say I've seen him today neither."

Cal jumped back in his truck, spun around, and tore onto the main road. He stopped first at the Roadhouse. Hank's truck wasn't there. He slammed his palm against the steering wheel. It was pointless to drive all over the county. Hank would be back home at some point and until then Cal would wait for him.

He pulled out of the Roadhouse, back down County Road, turned into their drive. He crossed the cattle guard in front of the house and there was Hank Junior's new black truck, parked under the carport.

Cal flung open his brother's bedroom door so hard, the knob stuck in the drywall. Hank Junior was on his bed beneath the window, facing the wall.

"What the . . .?"

Cal picked up a bronzed baseball from its stand on the dresser just inside the door. Tossed it once and set it back down, hard. "Get up."

Hank Junior pushed himself up onto his elbow. "Fuck you," he mumbled and rolled back down onto his side.

"Don't play your fucking games with me, Hank." Cal flipped on the overhead light. Hank covered his eyes with his arm. "I know what you're doing."

"Yeah, well, I don't know what the fuck you're doing. I'm sleeping." He took his arm down. "For fuck's sake!" he screamed.

"Get up!" Cal hated him right then. He hated his swagger, his callousness. He hated him for wanting to make everyone else hurt as much as he did.

Hank squinted in the light. "No!" He waved his arms, like he could sweep Cal out of the room.

"Where are the horses, Hank?"

Hank's arm fell over his eyes again.

"Answer me, Hank."

"Calm down, little brother." He rubbed his eyes.

"No. I'm not going to fucking calm down. Answer me."

Hank sat up slowly, his feet tumbled to the floor. "What horses might we be talking about?"

"Are you kidding me? When will you stop?" Cal went to his brother and leaned in so close he could count the streaks of red in his brother's eyes.

"Stop what?!"

"Stop stealing—"

"Whoa, whoa, whoa . . ." Hank stood, took two unsteady steps toward Cal. Cal backed up.

"Stop lying!"

Hank held onto the edge of his desk to steady himself. "Who's fucking with who now?" he screamed, shaking his head. "Huh? So help me God, don't start this!"

"I didn't start this!" Cal thumped his own chest.

"Don't start something you can't finish." Hank wagged his forefinger.

"What the fuck does that mean?"

Hank grabbed the bronzed baseball from its plastic stand and started to wind up. Cal got a hold of his arm. Hank pulled away. Winding up again, he hurled the baseball, which barely missed Cal's head and careened through the window, shattering the glass. Thin jagged shards landed on the bed. The two of them, clasping each other, spun in a circle and fell on the bed, dragging the blanket to the floor.

Suddenly, "Stop!" Their mother was at the door. "Stop it! Stop it! What is this?"

Cal let go. One of Hank's hands still clenched Cal's shirt. "He—" Cal started.

"—It's a misunderstanding," Hank shouted.

"A misunderstanding?" their mother repeated, her face contorted. "About what?"

"It's not a misunderstanding." Cal shook off Hank's hand, scrambled to his feet. "He's stolen—"

Hank Junior, standing upright, grabbed Cal's shoulder. A sliver of broken window glass pushed into his skin. He winced.

"It is a misunderstanding," Hank repeated. "And it can be corrected." He looked at Cal. "I can put it right."

"What in heaven's name?" Their mother was at a loss. "What misunderstanding? Is it over a girl?"

"No."

"Yes," Hank Junior said simultaneously.

"That O'Hare girl?"

Cal glared at Hank. "That O'Hare girl has a name, Momma."

Hank Junior, his back against the wall, slid down until he was sitting on the floor, his legs straight out in front of him. "I gave Cal cause to worry, Momma. But I can put things right."

"Can you?" Cal asked.

"I can." Hank said, staring at his hands.

"Look at you." Their mother came toward Cal, her hand reaching for his face. He shied away, glanced in the mirror above the dresser. A long bloody scratch ran down his cheek. "Caleb, honey, you heard your brother. Whatever's happened—"

"You have no idea what's happened, what's happening, Momma."

"I done told you," Hank Junior shouted, "I can put it right."

"You heard your brother, Caleb. Honey? Right?" Momma cajoled. "Can you give your brother a chance to make whatever it is right?"

Cal wanted with all his might to tell her everything he knew, that Hank Junior was rustling and stealing and if he knew, others did, too, and it wouldn't be long before the sheriff did. But he didn't. She looked so fragile. She could go up against their father and stay solid and strong. But when it came to Hank Junior, worry and love and having come so close to losing him once already made her as unsteady as a new foal.

"You two are brothers." Their mother was an only child. "And I won't have it." The emergency averted, her backbone strengthened. "I won't have any fighting between the two of you. You have a sacred bond, as brothers. A lifelong bond. Don't ever forget that."

"Yes, Momma," Hank Junior said.

"I don't know what I'm going to tell your father," she pointed to the shattered window, the curtain tearing as it fluttered across the broken glass. "You both clean that up now." And she started down the hallway.

Hank Junior reached out his hand. Cal took it, helped him to stand. Hank brushed off his shirt and tucked it in.

"They'll be back before sunrise."

His brother wasn't home for dinner that night. But later, after studying, Cal went to get a bowl of cereal and light slipped out beneath Hank Junior's door. Cal knocked. No answer. He pressed his ear to the door. He wanted to tell his brother what he must have already known: that he was going to get caught.

He tapped his knuckles again on the door and slowly pushed it open. His brother lay on top of his covers fully clothed and sound asleep, knees curled to his chest, as though trying to climb back into the womb to start all over.

The next day, Chester and Daybreak were back in their stalls. Cal had two more days to work with them and fuss over them, and give them Friday off before the Moore's head wrangler would come see them.

Friday after school, Leni and Cal went to the McGrath's for a ride. The chaparral glistened in the sun, grasses waving in the breeze. Cottontails bounced out of a scrub brush, a hawk floated on an air current above them. It had been almost ten weeks, and Flint was pretty well recovered. Cal saddled him up. Leni rode Mrs. McGrath's little mare, Lady Belle. They started out, side by side, through a meadow of knee-high winter wheat and oat grass, down toward the White Oak, Leni complaining about her algebra class.

"What's the point?" Leni moaned.

"It's about finding patterns," Cal told her.

"Why do I want to do that?"

"To make sense of the world."

"Algebra does not make sense of anything."

She sounded kind of mad, but Cal was sure he could persuade her. "Yes, it does. People used to explain things with elves or trolls or gods—"

"Are you talking down to me?"

"No!" Lady Belle was a good hand shorter than Flint; Cal tried not to look down at her. "I'm not. I'm just saying people have different ways of explaining things and they used to explain things with magic."

"You're all about laws and strata and sub-strata. I just don't think that way."

"I'm not all about laws." He knew he sounded defensive. "And strata is in biology." He took a breath and started over. "Math takes imagination. You take what you know, that the earth revolves around the sun, say. And you imagine what else that means, about the other planets, orbits, gravity. You posit your thesis. Then you test it out. With math."

"I can't test it out with math."

"You could if you tried."

"No, I couldn't. I hate math."

Then she kicked Lady Belle hard and took off at a gallop. But Cal didn't want to run Flint yet. "Leni!"

Flint tossed his head, eager for the chase. Cal let him go just until he was alongside Leni, then reached over, grabbed Lady Belle's rein close to the bit, and pulled the mare and Flint up hard.

"Don't do that!" He was angry.

"What?" She was angrier.

"Don't run off from me like that. What's wrong?"

"Nothing." She wrenched the rein from his hand and stared at him, dumbfounded. "You are so smart, and so stupid some-times." The mare stamped her hoof to emphasize the point.

He had no idea what she was talking about.

"You're going to Princeton, Cal."

"You don't know that."

"Yes, I do! Princeton or wherever. It doesn't matter. You'll be there where Einstein taught, right? With all those famous thinkers. You'll never come back here."

"I will if you're here."

"No, you won't."

"Of course, I will."

"You're gonna meet fancy girls. Brainiacs, like you. You won't care a whit about me, some hayseed in this..." She flicked her hand as though the chaparral was nothing but a fetid swamp.

How could she not know? "Leni, I love you."

"Cal . . ."

"All I do is think about you. All day, all night."

"Your future's not here. Don't you see that?" She slapped her thigh. "Foy's gone. All Marguerite talks about now is going to California. When you go, I'll die here."

"Leni," he slid off Flint and stood beside her, both hands on her thigh. "Don't say that."

"I hate it here."

"I won't leave you. Ever."

"You don't know that."

"But I do." He dropped Flint's reins, held his arms out to her.

She swung her leg over Lady Belle's neck and slid off into his arms. They kissed, as though missing each other already. And they sank into the tall, soft grass—the horses grazing beside them. Soon they were skin to warm, soft skin.

After, they laid in the grass on the blanket roll, catching their breath, warm in the afternoon sun. The horses grazing nearby.

"Cal?"

"Yes." He couldn't stop running his hand over her ribs, across the top of her hip bone, down the top of her thigh. He kissed her smooth belly.

"Don't you want to go to one of those colleges?"

"Well, yes. I do." He kissed her again. He pushed himself up. "Come with me."

Leni

Saturday morning, the last clouds from the night's rain unfurl and clear out, layer by layer, leaving clear skies for the weekend. Marguerite dropped their mother off at church for some sewing circle and her father—having taken longer than usual—finally left on his rounds. Leni finishes feeding the animals as Cal pulls up. He gets out and goes to her. She takes his hand and leads him into the barn, away from the door, and kisses him.

"I missed you." She smiles.

"You saw me yesterday at school." He kisses her neck.

"School doesn't count." She tilts her chin, raising her lips to his.

He runs his hand down her ponytail, squeezes her toward him, and kisses her again.

"Daddy was late leaving. You had to have passed him. He's on his way to the McPeels, up past your place." She kisses his neck.

Cal shakes his head.

"You must not have been looking. He had to go by y'all's place." Leni waits for an answer. Cal shakes his head again. "Well, come on. Let's go make Chester and Daybreak all pretty."

Foggy and Roger are in the large paddock. Foggy nickers and walks the fence, following them to Cal's truck.

"I'll be back, girl," Leni says. "I'll never leave you."

They arrive at the small barn at the McGrath ranch head-quarters; Cal takes off his hat to smooth his hair down for the umpteenth time.

"You needn't be so nervous," she says. He ignores her. "Walter knows you can handle this."

"Walter would be here if his daughter hadn't gone into labor two weeks early."

Leni puts Chester, a cute steel gray with a slightly dished face and big fluttery nostrils, in the cross-ties and grabs a hoof pick from a bucket Cal sets down. Cal brings Daybreak, a chestnut with three white stockings, into his stall.

"What are you going to do with the money?" Leni asks as she leans her shoulder against Chester's, lifts up his hoof, and circles the metal pick inside the shoe.

"Not count it before I get it."

Cal's so practical. "You mean you haven't given it any thought?"

"Of course I've thought about it."

"Well?"

"I'm going to save it." With one hand on Daybreak's chin, he takes the other with a soft brush and follows the swirl of fur around the horse's forehead and ears. "So if I get any of these scholarships Mr. Wilkens thinks I've got a chance at, I can bring you with me." Silence. "If you want to come."

"You talking to me or Daybreak?"

"I prefer not to go anywhere without you." He doesn't look at her.

Is it possible? Could she leave here with Cal?

She circles the currycomb over Chester's back, trying to sound nonchalant. "What would I do where you're going?"

"Study art."

How is it he always seems to know what she wants before she does? She steadies the currycomb. With him, this sounds possible. Perfect. Terrifying.

She brushes Chester until he shines, then paints hoof black on his hooves, making them glisten, finishing just as a pickup with the Moore's brand on the side pulls in front of the barn.

Cal wipes his hands on his chaps. "Wish me luck." He steps out of the barn. Leni follows.

Jesus is a good six inches shorter than Cal, and stocky. Black bangs beneath a Texas Rangers cap. A button-down shirt tucked neatly into his jeans. Brown western boots scuffed but clean.

"Leni," Cal says, "this is Jesus. Jesus, this is Leni."

Jesus takes Leni's hand. His face is as unlined as a river stone, with dark eyes that look almost solid until he smiles.

Leni smiles back.

Jesus goes to Chester. Strokes his nose, pats his neck. And runs his hand down the length of each of Chester's legs.

He wants to see the horses lunged.

"I haven't lunged them since they were two-year-olds," Cal says.

"They'll remember," Jesus says. "And we will see if it is a happy memory." He heads to his truck for equipment.

Cal and Leni meet eyes. Who is this guy?

Jesus returns with a coiled lunge line and a long skinny whip at his side. Leni unhooks the crossties and attaches the lunge line to Chester's halter. Cal opens the gate to the paddock. Jesus takes the horse, and Cal and Leni step back to the fence.

Jesus, hand on Chester's halter, walks in a big circle, talking to the horse the whole time.

"What's he saying?" Leni whispers.

"I only took two years of Spanish," Cal whispers back.

Jesus lets go of the halter and backs up toward the center of the circle. Chester follows him. Cal starts out toward Chester.

"He doesn't need you, Pappi." Jesus waves Cal back. "He's a big boy now. Aren't you?"

Jesus walks Chester back to the outside of the circle they'd just walked. He lets go of the halter. Still walking beside Chester. Still talking to him. Then pointing the long whip on the ground at Chester's front hoof, he keeps Chester on the outer edge of the circle as he slowly lets out the lunge line and walks to the center of the circle. Confused at first, Chester walks haltingly. Jesus clucks to him. Waves the whip on the ground, making squiggles in the dirt. Chester gives a little kick and breaks into a trot.

In barely any time at all, Chester trots calmly in a big round circle. With a soft snap of the whip on the ground and a cluck, Chester breaks into a gentle lope. Jesus puts him through his paces in the other direction.

When he's seen enough, Jesus winds the lunge line around his arm, bringing Chester to him. He rubs the horse's forehead. Reaches into his pocket and pulls out a handful of sugar cubes.

"He's still talking to him," Leni whispers to Cal.

Cal nods and smiles. You learn a lot about a person watching them with an animal.

Jesus walks Chester over to Leni and Cal. He taps his own temple, then Chester's forehead. "Smart," he smiles. "We had very good conversation."

Jesus goes through nearly the same routine with Daybreak while Cal saddles Chester. Leni takes Daybreak when Jesus finishes lunging him and puts him in the crossties to tack him up. Cal mounts each of the horses in turn and puts them through their paces. Cal's a quiet rider. Steady hand. His long legs snug against the saddle.

When Cal finishes riding Daybreak, Leni steps forward to take him.

"They are good horses," Jesus says.

"Yes." Cal pats Daybreak's rump as Leni leads him into the barn.

Leni wipes Daybreak down and puts him in his stall. She approaches Cal and Jesus.

"So," Jesus begins, "eighteen hundred for the gray and twelve hundred for the chestnut?"

"Yes, sir." Cal nods, eyes fixed on the ground.

"That's what you're asking?"

"Yes, sir," he answers softly.

Leni listens, barely breathing.

Jesus is quiet, no chattering now. He looks across the paddock, gazes out across the sprawling pasture for what seems forever. Cal fills in the space. He offers to take Jesus to the broodmare pasture, to show him the horses' dams. He talks about their temperaments, Chester's steadiness and Daybreak's quickness. Jesus listens.

"I'd take fifteen hundred for the gray and a thousand for the chestnut," Cal offers. "Not too many horses around here speak Spanish, you know." Leni smiles when she hears this.

Jesus laughs. "All right," he says. "Yes." They shake hands.

Cal walks Jesus to his truck. Once the pickup's out of sight, Leni runs to him. "You were amazing!"

"I could have gotten eighteen for Chester."

"Don't be greedy." Leni slaps his arm.

"And I'll get much more for Reverie," he says. "For us."

Caleb

After Cal sold Daybreak and Chester—and for a good price—Hank Senior's attention began to drift from his brother and circle Cal. The next week, he took Cal with him to some of the oil and gas properties. Even at four dollars a barrel back then, the wells were profitable, wildly profitable. His father instructed Cal about working interests versus royalty interests. About which operators he'd work with and which ones he wouldn't go near with a ten-foot pole and why. He told Cal stories about his starting out. Stories where he didn't always come out ahead. He was funny, even self-deprecating. Focused and smart. An entrepreneur.

At dinner that night, his father offered Cal seconds before he took his own. He asked Cal's opinion about local politics, as though once he could talk with Cal about business interests, Cal became a viable human being. Whereas a child was a dependent, something Hank Senior almost resented, not having had a childhood of his own.

One afternoon, in the ranch office, the ceiling fan whirring above them, Cal and his father sat at a long table below a framed map of the ranch that showed every pasture and watering hole, hay barn, pen, cowboy's house, and oil well. Cal watched his father retrieve one ledger book, then another, from a jam-packed bookshelf, its shelves sagging. Standing beside Cal, Hank Senior ran his finger down the tight columns and narrow rows of the dog-eared, light green pages. Expenses, starting with salaries, then machinery and equipment. Feed costs, vaccinations. Advertising for the calf sales. Transportation of the young steers to feed lots. Everything itemized meticulously in his father's strong pencil strokes.

Cal may not have had the vocabulary he later gained, but it was easy to assess the variables of the operation, see which parts were most capital intensive and which yielded the highest return. Also how returns deviated from one year to the next. Weather, feed prices, fuel prices. Inputs that were hard to control and impossible to predict. It was a crazy business, ranching. For most, there was something about it that they loved, because pretty much the best you could hope for, year over year, was to break even. And pray the land appreciated. Cal's father didn't love animals or ranching. What he loved was acquiring things, land and resources. He might have loved the oil wells.

Another bookshelf held the ledgers for the oil holdings, clustered by lease. Each book six inches thick with dozens of plastic dividers.

"You know what's in all those?" his father asked.

"No," Cal answered. "Do you?"

"I'd better know what all's in there. My signature's on every lease." The books showed combined returns and expenses for each well. "Don't look so gobsmacked." His father hauled another book from the shelves and set it on the table with a thud. "You got the brain power to handle this. And this business isn't done. Not by a long shot. There's enough out there for a young man to make his own mark." He slapped one book shut and opened another. "You know what I'm saying to you, Caleb? Yes or no?"

"Yes, sir."

He smiled. "That's good, son. That's good."

Cal watched his father closely as he explained billing statements and work orders. He seemed engaged, amused. Proud. Almost lighthearted surrounded by the ten-pound tomes on the table and shelves. Cal wondered how he hadn't appreciated this before. His father's ambition and perseverance. Where had he gotten the confidence and courage to accomplish what he had, given his upbringing, or lack of an upbringing? It didn't mean he couldn't be a self-centered bastard. But Cal began to understand his father's bravado.

But the more and faster his father talked, the more he joked and told stories, the heavier Cal felt. This wasn't his dream: to amass land and oil. He didn't share his father's ambition or have his confidence. His guts.

At dinner that night, his father stood at the head of the table, carving knife and fork poised over the roast. They waited.

"You try your hand at this, son." He handed the knife and fork to Cal as Hank Junior looked on.

The next evening, after dinner, Cal took a break from homework and headed to the kitchen for a snack. His father was at the wet bar in his stocking feet, pouring himself a bourbon.

"Caleb," he barked.

"Yes, sir."

"Get yourself a drink."

Cal hesitated.

"Something wrong with your ears?"

"No, sir. I was going to get a soda."

His father laughed. "That's not a drink." He settled into the sofa in front of the hearth.

Cal, thinking better of pointing out that he had more homework to do, got a beer and sat in the leather armchair next to the sofa.

"You did good with those young horses."

"Yes, sir."

"You going to take on more?"

"I'm not certain."

Generally his father talked at a person. Cal wasn't accustomed to conversing with him.

"What about that four-year-old you been riding?"

"Reverie? He's getting to be a good cutting horse."

"He ready to sell?"

"Just about. Yes, sir."

"What do you expect to get for him?" his father finished his drink and got up to pour himself another.

"Judging by what I got for Chester and Daybreak, who aren't nearly as far along," Cal paused. "Maybe twenty-five hundred?"

"Don't ask me. Tell me. If that's what the horse is worth, that's what the horse is worth." He looked at Cal hard. "Right?"

"Yes, sir."

"And what about your bay?"

"Flint?"

"What's he worth?"

"He's not for sale."

"That's not what I asked. What's he worth?"

Cal didn't like where this was heading. "I haven't thought about it. Five thousand. At least."

"That's a lot of money for a young man."

"But he's not for sale." His father was back to looking for prey. Like a big cat.

"You're too attached to the animal." His father set his empty glass down on the coffee table. "You got to learn to let go of the things you love. Or you'll never get to where you want to go."

CHAPTER FOURTEEN

November

Leni

What would you say? My getting out of Naples. With Cal. To study art.

When I'm not with him, I feel like I've left half of myself somewhere.

And what would you say about Marguerite? She comes into the kitchen, wearing blue jeans so low they're practically falling off her backside. Maman frets and nags her. They get into a row. "A woman ought to dress for herself," Marguerite says, "not for some man." And out she prances. A big flouncy shirt. And no bra!

Before dinner last night, Maman finished one of her hats. A straw one with a cluster of dried Indian Paint petals and three eastern bluebird feathers tucked into the ribbon around the base. Marguerite gets home. Maman holds the hat out to her, like a peace offering. Marguerite said she wouldn't be caught dead in one of Maman's hats and walked out. I could have spit at her.

So Maman packed up her sewing boxes, the threads and ribbons and feathers and dried flowers, and stuffed the boxes on the highest shelf in the pantry cupboard. It was a sad thing.

Succotash, again. Warming on the stove. Maman pulls a pie from the oven. Leni clears the table. Moving first a pile of Doc's work clothes Maman was mending. Marguerite comes downstairs with wet hair, jeans, a T-shirt. And no bra, again. She grabs an apple from the bowl on the counter and watches their mother and Leni scurry about the kitchen.

"Set the table, please, Marguerite," Maman says. Finally. Leni grimaces at her sister.

"Why can't Daddy do something around here?"

Leni stops midstep on her way to the sink, an empty cup and saucer in her hand.

"He is working all day." Maman stirs the succotash. Clangs the wooden spoon on the edge of the pot and sets it down.

"I worked all day," Marguerite says. "Looks like you worked all day, too. What'd you do today, Leni?"

Oh, no. Leni shakes her head. She's not getting dragged into this. She's only just gotten on their mother's semi-good side.

Marguerite's new attitude is a puzzle. Most especially to Maman. Marguerite, who used to be so neat and pretty. Dressed like a girl. Cooked and baked and sewed.

Leni lays out the placemats their mother made. Silverware, napkins. A trivet for the succotash. A pitcher of milk. She sets the hot pad holders on the counter next to her mother.

"Evening, girls." Doc O'Hare ducks his head slightly to enter the kitchen. He seems to dwarf the room as he enters. The sweet, earthy smell of his pipe tobacco trails after him. He moves a dirty pot from the sink to wash his hands.

"Hi, Daddy." Leni goes to him to get a squeeze. "How was your day?"

"Can't complain." He takes the pipe from his mouth. Kisses Leni on the top of her head.

Maman retrieves a platter of cutlets from the oven's warming drawer, sets it down on the table, and sits. Leni brings over the succotash and sits.

Doc bows his head. "Bless this food that it may nourish our bodies and may we always be grateful for your bounty. Amen."

Grace has gotten shorter recently. Her mother ladles food onto plates.

Leni lifts a forkful of succotash. And sets it back down as Maman hops up to get the salt and pepper. Maman sits. Leni and Marguerite wait for her to settle.

"Hot sauce," Maman says, getting up again.

Doc puts a piece of cutlet in his mouth.

"Aren't you gonna wait on Maman?" Marguerite plants an elbow on the table.

Doc examines Marguerite as he chews.

"She cooks and mends your clothes and cleans your mess. And you can't wait for her before you start eating the food she's cooked?"

Her round, flirtatious sister has honed a hard edge these last months. Leni looks back and forth between her Daddy and Maman. What are they going to do?

"Marguerite," Maman says. "*Arrêtes.*" She sets the hot sauce down. Doc O'Hare sprinkles some on his succotash and prepares another bite.

"Aren't you going to say 'Thank you'?" Marguerite stares at their father.

Leni can't stand it anymore. "What are you on about?"

"Common courtesy," Marguerite answers. "And respect for the work women do."

"Quite right," Doc says.

Leni sizes up Marguerite, then Maman, then Daddy.

"Thank you, Ludevigne," he nods in her direction. "Respect your parents, as well." He gives Marguerite a look. "And that holds true whether you are grown, a girl, a boy, or—"

"A goat!" Leni jumps in. No one laughs. She's never been the smoother over-er.

"Some don't deserve it," Marguerite says, shuffling food around on her plate.

"That's enough," Doc says.

Something's afoot. Leni is beginning to think she may be the only one who doesn't know what. Doc's staring at his plate. Maman's hands are folded in her lap, her head bowed like she's praying. Marguerite's stabbing at her food.

"Daddy's been carrying on with Mrs. Conyers for," Marguerite turns to her father, "how long has it been, Daddy?"

Doc throws his fork on his plate; it bounces off onto the table.

"Well?" Marguerite prods.

Maman shrinks in her chair.

Doc grabs the table with both hands and pushes his chair back so hard milk splashes out of the pitcher. "You," he points at Marguerite, "are out of line. You don't know what you're saying or what you're doing."

Doc marches to his office. Slams the door. Maman gets up. No words. Leaves the kitchen. Pads softly up the stairs.

Leni, mouth agape, stares at her sister, who—startlingly—begins to eat.

"It's the truth, Leni. I'm sorry. But it's the truth." Not looking at Leni, she shovels a spoonful of succotash into her mouth. "Everyone else knows it."

Skinny Mrs. Conyers from the hill country, who can't even put drops in her ewe's eye? That Mrs. Conyers? And "everybody" who?

Leni starts for her father's office. But he brushes past her. Climbs the stairs, three at a time. A moment later, she hears her mother crying.

"English, Ludevigne," Leni hears her father plead. "I can't understand you."

Maman shrieks, "*You* cannot understand *me?*"

Leni goes back in the kitchen. Marguerite's still eating! Leni grabs her sister's purse from the chair by the back door. Dumps it out onto the counter.

"What do you think you're doing?"

Leni grabs the keys to the damned green bug of a car. Throws open the back door.

"Leni!" Marguerite follows down the porch stairs.

Leni slams the car into gear and speeds down the drive. Hitting every pothole.

L eni pulls off County Road and, heading too fast down the McGraths' drive, rattles over the cattle guard, dust trailing behind. A dozen calves scatter in her wake. Having seen her coming, Cal's standing in the driveway when she comes to a halt. Leni gets out of the car. Her face blotched from tears. Quite an entrance.

Cal goes to her. "What is it?"

"It's Daddy," she cries. She eyes his mother hanging back by the front door.

"Where is he? What's happened?"

Leni can't answer. "It's all wrong," she says. "Everything's all wrong."

"Leni, tell me."

She steps back, opens her mouth, and retches at Cal's feet.

Leni sits at the edge of the sofa in front of a crackling fire. Cal beside her. Cal's mother sets down a small tray with a glass pitcher of iced tea, crackers, and a damp washcloth, which she hands to Leni.

"Lay this on your forehead, dear. If you need anything, just holler."

"Thank you, ma'am," Leni mumbles, embarrassed.

"Thank you, Momma."

They watch Mrs. McGrath walk back to the kitchen. This is not how she imagined meeting Cal's mother.

"Daddy's having an affair," Leni whispers. She's ashamed. Ashamed for her daddy. Or her mother. Or herself. Or all of them. She doesn't know. She just feels shame. "With Mrs. Conyers." She presses the cool cloth to her forehead and takes a breath. She sets the cloth down on the tray. "Why would he do that? Did he just wake up one day and think, 'I don't love her'? Is that what happens? I mean, what?" she looks to Cal.

"I don't know," he says softly.

"And Marguerite! I mean, now she looks half the time like she's jumping freight cars. You know what she did with her curlers and makeup? She didn't just throw them out. Oh, no. She crushed and torched them in a midnight, moonlit ceremony at the bottom of the porch steps. The grass is still singed. And she says anything that comes into her mind. No matter the fallout."

"I'm sorry, Leni." Cal rubs Leni's back. She sways slightly beneath his hand.

"She announced last week she's a vegetarian now. What's she thinking? This is Texas."

"Did you ask your daddy if this is true?"

"No. But he didn't deny it." She stares at her hands. "All those times I thought he was working all day, into the evenings. Saturdays and Sundays. I'd straighten his office. Unpack the medicines and bandages for him. Polish his boots. Any little thing I could. Thinking I was making his days a little easier. Where was he really?"

The phone rings. Leni freezes. After several moments, Cal's mother's crosses the stone floor.

"I let your daddy know you're here," she says. "He wants to hear from you."

"Thank you, ma'am." She looks at Cal. "I can't talk to him right now. I don't know what to say."

Cal puts his arm around Leni and looks to his mother.

"Well, at least they know where you are and that you're safe."

"If they say it's all right, Momma, can Leni stay here tonight? In the guest room."

"Oh, honey." She takes a deep breath.

"I don't think," Cal presses on, "she ought to be driving like this." He gestures to Leni, her tear-stained face staring at the floor.

His mother sighs, "*If* they say that's all right. You hear me?"

"Yes, ma'am," he says.

"For tonight. In the guest room."

"Thank you, ma'am." Leni meets Cal's mother's eyes for the first time.

Leni closes her eyes. Her stomach's flopping against her ribs. She takes three deep breaths and, vowing to stay calm, dials. Marguerite answers.

"You took my car."

"I know that," Leni snaps. "You blew up everything."

"Me? No, you have Bill to thank for that."

"'Bill?' You're calling Daddy 'Bill' now?" No answer. "Tell Maman—"

"Maman's locked herself in her room."

"Then tell 'Bill' I'm staying at the McGraths' tonight."

"I need my car!"

"Too bad."

"Leni, you cannot—"

Leni hangs up.

"I can stay," she tells Cal.

S ide by side on the top rail of the paddock fence, the metal cool beneath their jeans, they look out over the pasture down to the watering hole. The gentle curve of Flint's and Reverie's backs and their long sloping necks are silhouetted in the evening light as they graze.

"Talk to me."

Too many words. They jam her throat. Leni shakes her head and stares at the stars.

Cal takes her hand. "When you're ready, you can talk."

"I may not ever be ready."

He gives Leni's hand a squeeze. "You don't have to have anything figured out. You don't even need to make sense. But you need to get it out. And I'm not going anywhere."

The quarter moon is low in the sky. A breeze carries the scent of alfalfa and timothy from a nearby meadow that's been cut.

It may not be Marguerite who's carrying on with Mrs. Conyers. But Leni is furious with her all the same. And Foy's not here. He'd make it better somehow. Just by putting his hand on Maman's shoulder. Nothing soothed Maman like a word or a touch from Foy. No point in being jealous of that anymore. It's just the way it was. Something like rippling silk flowed invisibly between the two of them. Nothing like the jagged static that runs so often between Leni and her mother.

"What's going to happen now?" she looks at Cal. Suddenly

her heart lurches for Maman. "When Lissy Reynolds' parents split up," Leni struggles to think of anyone else she's known who divorced, "Mrs. Reynolds had no money, couldn't get a job. Lissy had to move back to her daddy's house." And he's about the meanest drunk son of a bitch anyone knows. "Maman's never had a job. If Daddy leaves, will we have to sell the farm? Where am I going to keep Foggy? And who'd take Agnes? She hardly even gives milk anymore—"

"Shhhh. You're jumping oceans ahead. That's fear talking. You don't know any of that's going to happen."

He opens his arm. She slides closer. The moon's lifted higher.

"As for Foggy," Cal says, "Foggy'll always have a home here. I promise."

Leni rests against Cal—her head rises and falls with his chest, their breaths becoming like one. They watch the horses amble slowly across the pasture, noses to the ground as though whispering to the grass.

Caleb

Cal was running almost ragged for the whole month of November. The horses, applications, keeping his grades up. And snatching any moment he could to be with Leni. The Monday before Thanksgiving, he dashed into town during his lunch period to fill up his truck. He pulled into the Esso station and glided up to the pump, across from an aging beige and white Volkswagen bus—dented, half a front bumper.

He hopped out of the truck and saw Marguerite standing beside the beat-up bus, jeans hugging her hips, billowy shirt hanging off one shoulder. She was talking with a tall guy, unkempt hair dangling down his back. There was a girl in the front seat with a little black and white dog on her lap. Another guy, fair-haired, squirrelly and small, leaned against the front of the bus, assessing his fingernails.

"I've got a paycheck right here," Marguerite said, as the tall guy scrounged in his pockets.

"Marguerite," Cal called, startling her. Was she being kidnapped? He set the pump handle back.

"Cal. What are you doing here?"

"Same as you all, I suspect." He surveyed the VW bus again. "Who are these guys?"

"Hey now," the taller guy said. "She doesn't have to answer to you."

Everything about this seemed all wrong. He stepped closer. "Marguerite, are you OK?"

"I am A-OK, Cal. I'm heading west. Going all the way to California!"

"With these guys?"

"Opportunity just knocked, Cal. And I'm taking it."

"Your folks know?"

She smiled and leaned a hand on the grimy window of the van. The little dog barked.

Cal pictured Mrs. O'Hare, standing on that porch, looking for another lost child. "So, they don't know. Marguerite, come on . . ."

The girl leaned out the window. Straight brown hair, parted in the middle, framed her round face. She rested her chin on the little dog's head. "You ought to tell your momma and poppa. Jeremy," the tall guy turned, "we drive to her folks." She pulled her head back inside the van.

Cal couldn't place her accent. Missouri plates on the bus.

"If she says so," the tall guy said.

"Marguerite, you can't just leave."

Marguerite looked to the sky, tilted her head this way and that, thinking.

"Marguerite!" Cal shouted. The squirrelly guy stopped chewing his fingernails and looked up. "What has gotten into you?"

"Right, right. I'll tell them." she sighed. "Leni can have my car." She chirped, as though this would solve everything. "It's at DeWitts', which is where I met these fine folks. Oh, and I owe your brother some money."

"What for?"

"He'll know. Tell him I'll send it once I get settled." She stepped up and gave Cal kiss on the cheek. A sideways glance and a smile as she shook her index finger at him. "You take care of Leni now." A glimpse of the old flirtatious Marguerite. "I'm counting on you," she said, smiling as she held his gaze.

C al sped back to school, waved Leni out of her art class. They tore to the O'Hares'. Sure enough, the VW bus was there. The girl, in torn blue jeans, was calling the little black and white dog back from chasing the goats. Leni jumped out of the truck and burst into the kitchen. Cal followed. Mrs. O'Hare stood by the sink, drying a plate.

"Maman!" Leni ran to her.

Mrs. O'Hare continued drying the plate, barely registering Leni and Cal. Leni hugged her. Her mother set down the dried plate and picked up another from the dish rack.

Marguerite came downstairs, a bulging cloth bag slung over her shoulder.

"I can't believe you're doing this!" Leni shouted.

"Believe, Leni. Believe."

"Maman . . . Stop her!"

Her mother just shook her head.

"Why has everyone gone crazy!" Leni screamed.

"Never saner." Marguerite stuffed a banana and some apples into her bag.

Mrs. O'Hare set a dried plate on the counter. Leni snatched it and smashed it on the floor. Her mother wrapped her hand around Leni's wrist. She didn't appear angry. She didn't say a word. She simply waited until Leni met her eyes, and she gave the gentlest shake of her head. Whether it was acceptance or giving up, Cal didn't know.

Marguerite was, after all, the same age Leni's mother was when she sailed across the Atlantic, leaving behind the remains of her family, with an American soldier, who was nearly as much of a stranger as the three in that van.

Marguerite set down her bag. Leni sank onto a chair. Marguerite went to her mother and kissed her on the cheek. Then to Leni. A kiss on the forehead. Then Cal.

"Remember what I said," she told him, serious this time. She picked up her bag and headed out the back door.

Leni rushed to the porch and watched them drive off.

CHAPTER FIFTEEN

December

Caleb

Scholarship acceptances were expected the first week in December. That Monday, ten minutes before the first bell, Cal went by Mr. Wilkens's room. Mr. Wilkens waved him in, closed the door, and sat on the edge of his gray metal desk. He smoothed his tie and handed Cal two unopened envelopes. One with the crimson MIT insignia at the top, and the other postmarked Princeton, New Jersey.

Cal tore open the MIT letter first, unfolded the thickest paper he'd ever felt. "We regret to inform you blah, blah, blah, this year's extraordinary candidates, etc., etc., etc."

Cal took a deep breath. MIT, he reminded himself, was not his first choice. He set down the rejection letter and picked up the second envelope. He paused.

"Go on, Cal," Mr. Wilkens prodded. "Whatever this one says, there are two other schools to hear from after this."

But Princeton was where Einstein had taught. And Princeton, New Jersey had horse farms nearby. Lots of them. Where he was certain Leni could find work. And there'd be art classes somewhere there. He took a breath and slid his finger into the opening of the envelope, and pulled out the folded letter.

"We are pleased to inform you that you are this year's recipient of the Howard J. Bowerman Scholarship for the study of mathematics and theoretical physics."

Cal's face said it all.

"Well done, young man. This is a fine thing." Mr. Wilkens grabbed Cal's hand, shook it hard, and patted him on the back. "You are looking a mite like a deer in headlights."

Cal waited by Leni's locker. As she came down the hall, he held up the envelope. She maneuvered in front of a group of girls and hurried toward Cal.

"Princeton," he whispered.

"Oh, Cal!" She threw her arms around his neck. It was really happening. Her hands covered her face. He held her close, her head against his chest, as they walked down the hall, everyone's eyes on them, making up their own stories about what was unfolding. Outside, they sat on the grass.

"I'm so happy for you."

"For us," he said. "Right?" Getting nervous. "What's the matter?"

"I don't know." She tried to look at him, tried to smile. "Cal. I have no money."

"I've got money," he said, relieved that was all. "I've got money from the horses. Tom Shirley at Dairy Queen will give you a job after school. He'd do it for Foy, if for no other reason. I've thought this through. If you save twenty-five dollars a week, say fifty during the summer, you'd have twelve hundred dollars by the end of the summer."

"Leave school after this year?"

"Get a GED."

"Hannah Floyd did that."

"And Trey Hunter. And Buck Tilson," Cal added.

Leni kissed Cal.

They had a plan. He knew it would work.

Leni

The morning light lands softly on the kitchen table. Leni gets a light peck on the cheek from her father before he slips out. Maman sets down a perfectly browned omelet. Buttered toast. Leni pulls her chair closer.

"*Merci*, Maman."

"*De rien.*"

After Marguerite burst out with news of his affair, her father walked with Leni down to the creek. He'd always been beyond reproach in her eyes. She listened as he apologized and swore it was over, not knowing how she felt or what to say. He and Maman are nearly silent around one another now. Except for the night Marguerite left, when he stayed in their old bedroom with Maman, her father has slept in Foy's room. Maman, really, barely speaks these days to anyone. Common courtesies. A request for clarification. She's wrapped so tightly inside herself, it's a wonder she can exhale.

Leni slides easily into the silence, into her own thoughts. Eats quickly. Scrapes her plate and washes it. Sets it in the dish rack. Grabs her knapsack and the keys to Marguerite's car.

"*A bientôt*, Maman." A kiss on her cheek. "I'm having dinner at the McGraths' tonight, remember?"

Her mother nods.

Leni still doesn't have a license. But no one's going to stop her. She's been driving tractors since she was eleven, her father's pickup on lonely back roads since she was fourteen. She likes the rush of air on her face, the propulsion into space all around her. Even if she's driving a car the color of a grasshopper.

"It's just meatloaf tonight, Leni. I hope you don't mind."

"No, ma'am. Thank you for having me."

Cal and Leni hang their jackets on the hook inside the front door. Leni squeezes Cal's hand. She's there for support. Tonight Cal will tell his parents about the scholarship.

In the kitchen, Cal takes a spoon from the drawer, scoops out a spoonful of mashed potatoes.

"Wash your hands, young man."

"Yes, ma'am." He tosses the spoon in the sink. He and Leni, side by side, wash their hands, then set the table. Leni sits where Hank Junior would, were he there.

"To what do we owe the pleasure of your company this evening?" Mr. McGrath tucks his napkin into his shirt.

Leni smiles.

"Cat got your tongue?"

"No, sir."

"All right." He digs into the pile of potatoes on his plate. "I got some news. Got the lease to a new tract in Oklahoma. I could use your help this weekend, Cal. We got some numbers to go over."

"Yes, sir."

Eyes down, the muffled syncopated clatter of knives and forks on the plates.

"Cat got everybody's tongue this evening?"

Leni looks at Cal, widening her eyes, urging him to speak.

"Well," Cal says, then pauses. "I've got some news, too." Cal sets his fork down. Rubs his palms on his thighs.

"You gonna make us guess?"

"Let Caleb speak, Hank." Mrs. McGrath takes a bite of meatloaf not much larger than a pea.

"You know Mr. Wilkens."

Mr. McGrath looks confused. Mrs. McGrath nods. "Your math teacher."

"Yes. Well, he's been talking to me about my studies—"

"You in some kind of trouble?"

"No. I mean he's been talking with me about studying math, and what I might want to do, you know, for work, I mean."

"What's he got to say about your work plans?"

"Hank." Mrs. McGrath stares at her husband.

"He was just talking with me about all the, you know, different careers that use math."

Leni's stomach flips.

"Like?" His father jabs his fork again into the mound of potatoes on his plate.

"Not just adding numbers and tracking receipts."

Hank Senior studies his son, his mouth making small, slow circles as he chews, then sets his knife and fork down slowly, carefully. Elbows on the table, chin raised as he peers at his son.

"There's engineering and computing and physics."

"Where would you use that?"

"At NASA, at the jet propulsion labs."

"You going to send another man to the moon?"

"I don't know, Pop."

Leni watches Cal deflate, his voice receding. Why can't they give him his head instead of keeping the reins so damned tight? Surely Mrs. McGrath will be proud of him.

"What's the news, Caleb?" Mrs. McGrath asks. "You had some news to tell us?"

No one's eating now. Leni stares at her plate. The potatoes look stiff and glassy beneath the light.

"Cal is so smart," Leni looks to Cal's mother, then his father. "You don't know how smart he is."

"I think I know my own son." Mr. McGrath waits.

She's not helping.

"I've gotten a scholarship," Cal said.

"How'd that happen?"

"Congratulations, Caleb," Mrs. McGrath sneaks in.

"How'd you just get a scholarship?"

"I applied. All right? I applied. I want to go to college."

"All right, now, honey . . ." Mrs. McGrath smooths the table with her hands.

"I applied and I got in."

Mr. McGrath is breathing in short bursts.

"Where did you get in, Caleb?" Mrs. McGrath's voice is steady, controlled. Surely she'll accept this and support him. "University of Texas?"

"No, Momma. Not UT." Cal takes a deep breath, still not looking up.

"Well? Where, honey? Caleb?" His mother prods.

All the hairs on Leni's body stand on end, the tension making her prickle all over.

"Princeton." Leni blurts out.

"Princeton?" Mr. and Mrs. McGrath say together.

"What you have right here isn't good enough for you?" Mr. McGrath says.

"It's not that, Pops."

"Mr. McGrath, forgive my speaking up. But it's his dream. And isn't this something you should be proud of?" Leni interjected.

"I have dreams, too." He stares at Leni. "Did you know about this?" he turns to his wife.

"Pop—"

"I don't want to hear from you yet. You didn't breathe a word of this. Not a word until now. Until it's done?"

"Because I knew how you'd react." Cal's composure gone. "I knew you'd want to stop me!"

"That's not right, Caleb. Secrets like this. It's not right."

"I'm sorry, Pop. But—"

His father's fist comes down fast and hard on the table. Leni flinches.

"Hank!" Mrs. McGrath shouts.

Cal raises his head. The look on his face has gone from remorse to contempt. He folds his napkin, sets it on the table, gets up, and walks away.

"Good for you, son!" Mr. McGrath calls after him. "But you'll get nothing from me."

Leni gets up and follows Cal.

"I don't need anything from you," Cal yells. He grabs his and Leni's coats from the rack. "It's a FULL SCHOLARSHIP!" he screams.

Leni follows Cal across the driveway, gravel crunching beneath their boots. At the barn, the horses' heads bounce up from their hay and watch them approach—ears forward, their round eyes pinned on the two of them.

Cal leans his arms on the metal fencing, bows his head. Leni goes to the tack room, returns with a bucket of brushes. She brings Captain Flint into the crossties. She knows this will help. Long strokes down the animal's neck and across his back. Letting the warmth of his large body soften their own bodies. Letting the beat of their hearts slow to match that of the horse.

"Come August," Cal says after some time, his hand on Flint's back, "we're leaving here. We're going to New Jersey. You want to go, too. I know you do."

"Yes," she says. "I do."

"I'll take care of you, Leni. And you'll find your place there. I know you will."

Leni wakes in a sweat from a dream. All she remembers from it is newborn animals—a whole array, chipmunks and goats and a calf, each still slippery from birth—peeking out from a den, looking for their mommas.

Her eyes still closed, Leni thinks of the babies she's helped her daddy deliver. Foals and lambs mostly, a couple of calves if they were breached, and one time floppy-eared goat triplets at the McPeels'. After each birth, her daddy would bow his head in a silent sort of prayer and give thanks, to God, Leni supposed. Her father didn't seem a religious man at other times, though he'd go to church with them unless there was a veterinary emergency, but in the presence of new life, he'd pause, humbled. And he lost a few, of course. Leni was with him when the McPeels again lost a young heifer and her calf. She watched her father pray then, too. And she prayed alongside him that the gentle spirit of those animals would return to the earth stronger next time.

December 15th

It's been two months.

What do I tell Cal? How do I tell him?

What could I do in Princeton? With a baby on my chest. Most everyone here's got a baby before they're twenty. But that's not what I want.

Can there be a place for me there?

I don't know.

But Leni does know this: Cal wouldn't leave her. If she tells him, he'll stay in Naples, Texas. The smartest boy to walk through this town, stuck here, like glue. Scholarship to Princeton gone. He'd work with his daddy, and he'd hate it. Then he'd hate her.

Her heart beats harder the more she thinks about it. A big day out: going to the Piggly Wiggly. Chattering about Pampers and teething. With girls she's never liked.

She feels sick to her stomach, again.

Marguerite's gone for good. That's for sure. Post card from San Diego saying they're heading north in the rusted piece of junk.

Foy, Foy, Foy . . . What should I do? What would you say? That I messed up. Big time. You're the one who always said Cal could be anything he wanted. Anything at all. And me? I don't want to stay here, Foy. Not without you. Life is loss. Right? Isn't that what Maman says? You lose the people you love. And you go on. Just got to be ready for that, I suppose.

Saturday chores are finished. The animals fed and watered. Leni sits on the porch, feet dangling, as Cal pulls into the O'Hares' drive. He's got some holiday plan for the two of them that he's not letting on about. He leans across the wide seat of his truck and flings the passenger side door open with a wide smile.

Leni slips off the porch and goes to Cal's truck. She climbs over a stuffed paper grocery bag on the floor and sits next to Cal.

"What's wrong?" he asks before she's even settled.

"Nothing."

"You look sad or tired or something." He strokes her cheek.

"What's that?" She nods toward the paper bag on the floor.

"That? Oh, nothing." Cal kisses her. "You taste good."

"I taste like toast."

"You taste like you." He pulls the truck around and starts toward the County Road.

"Where're we going?"

"Well," he draws the word out. "Today is Christmas."

"Christmas is six days away."

"So you get two Christmases, then. And one of your presents," he lays his arm around Leni's shoulders, "is a visit to the Dallas Art Museum."

"Cal!"

"You've been poring over those books Miss Perkins lends you—I figured you'd want to see some of the real thing."

She's about to cry again. Her feelings pop up these days like prairie dogs.

"You sure you're OK?"

"Yes. It's just . . . amazing. You're amazing."

Leni rests her head on Cal's shoulder. Jim Croce on the radio, "Time in a Bottle." The window open just enough for the breeze to ruffle her hair. Cal's steady breath on her cheek. His smooth, long limbs. His kindness. Maybe above all, his kindness. How could she get by without him?

She'd never imagined a day in her life without Foy before he was gone. That he wouldn't share the world with her. He'd always been there. Bound by blood and time. Every day, every meal, how many nights watching TV or the stars. How few arguments. Marguerite, yes. There were tussles and irritations, competition, and resentment sometimes. Never Foy. Regardless, they're both gone. She was helpless to keep either of them here. And she was wholly unprepared for Foy's absence. Ripped raw by that surprise. How could one go through that again?

Leni sits up. Cal's arm falls behind her. "I can't be gone all day," she says. "I didn't tell Maman."

She knows she's disappointed him, saddened him. Her insides clench. It's intolerable, this feeling. She wants to hide. Ashamed of the secret brewing inside her. Suddenly, she's certain that she has to take a stand.

"If you'd told me where we were going . . . Maman's going to worry. And the animals need tending this afternoon." Leni frowns. "You should've told me what you were planning."

"I'm sorry. I wanted it to be a surprise."

"I don't much like surprises." She sits up straighter, indignation strengthening her backbone. It's easier to be angry. Angry she's familiar with. It has propulsion, Cal might even say. Energy to run. "She's going to worry, Cal."

"I heard you. We can call. From the gas station."

"What if she doesn't pick up?"

Cal swings into the Esso station. "Call her, Leni." He fishes a dime out of his pocket.

"I don't need your dime." She slides across the seat to open the door.

"If you don't want to go, just tell me." He sounds uncharacteristically stern.

"Yes, I want to go." She feels cornered. "I already told you that."

"Then why are you so agitated?"

"You make all these big plans. You always think everything's so simple."

"I don't think anything's simple. And I sure as hell don't think you're simple. I just wanted to do something special, Leni."

Leni looks out the windshield smeared with bugs. Her fingers on the door handle, she watches the busy Saturday morning. The chime of another car driving up to the pump. A cowboy coming out of the store tearing a package of beef jerky open with his teeth. She knows Cal is watching her.

"I'm not making big plans without you, Leni."

"Cal—" Her stomach lurches. She feels sick again.

"I'm making big plans with you."

She doesn't know how to not be cruel to Cal. And she doesn't know how to save herself. "How could I leave?"

"You can't save your momma and daddy. You'll suffocate here. You know you would."

"I don't have a scholarship, Cal."

"I'll take care of you, Leni."

"I'm not feeling well." Her voice sounds so small. "I think I should go home."

"Leni. There's something you're not telling me."

"No, there's not!" She hates that she's whining.

"OK, OK. I'll take you home."

They pass the Roadhouse. It's not even eleven in the morning, but Hank Junior's isn't the only truck in the parking lot. Leni pins her eyes on his truck as they pass like it's a fulcrum.

"His home away from home," Cal says, shrugging.

Cal pulls over at the top of the O'Hares' driveway.

"What are you doing?" Leni scans the empty road in front of them and behind.

"I'm giving you the rest of your Christmas present." He leans over Leni, picks up the wrinkled brown paper bag at her feet, and hands it to her.

Leni peers inside. Something awkwardly wrapped in newspaper with a pre-tied gold bow stuck on the top. She pulls the bow off and peels back the layers of newspaper until one of Billy

Drum's beautifully carved wolf pups stares up at her. She pushes the crumpled newspaper to the floor of the truck and balances the carved seated pup on her lap.

"Oh, Cal . . ." She strokes its chiseled wooden fur.

"Do you like it?"

"I love it."

"I love you, Leni."

"I love you, Caleb McGrath."

Caleb

Back home, hungry and worried, Cal had just unwrapped a loaf of bread when his brother came in.

"Hello, Caleb." He belched, already drunk at one o'clock on a Saturday. "What's up with you?" Hank Junior opened the refrigerator and stared into it.

"Nothing." Cal grabbed a plate, tossed two pieces of bread on it.

"Right." Hank took a swig of orange juice from the carton. "Fight with the girlfriend?"

"Maybe." Cal slapped some ham on the bread and headed to his room to mull over his options in peace.

He lay on his bed, a sandwich raised halfway to his mouth, when his bedroom door swung open.

Hank Junior leaned against the doorjamb. "Hey," he said.

Cal set his sandwich down and waited.

"Whatever's going on with her . . . you get the fuck out of here come September. OK?"

"What do you care?"

Hank Junior tipped a hat he wasn't wearing and backed out.

Cal finished his sandwich, went into the kitchen, pulled the phonebook from the cupboard drawer, and called the Moore ranch. Jesus agreed to come out the next day.

It was a cool day. A layer of high clouds skimmed the sky. Flint grazed at the far end of the large paddock, by the watering hole. Butch and Lady Belle nibbled on the same flake of hay in the smaller paddock, alternately stamping a hoof at an occasional fly.

Cal nestled blankets and a saddle onto Reverie's back. With just a little more work, Cal was sure he could place high in a roping competition or two. But it would be more profitable to sell Reverie now and free up time to bring along another young horse.

Cal came out of the tack room with Reverie's bridle, just as Jesus pulled up beside the horse trailer at the top of the small paddock.

"Thank you for coming out." Cal gave Reverie a pat. "I'm sure you don't usually work Sundays." They shook hands.

"I am always working." Jesus planted his hands on his hips. "Who is this?"

"This is Reverie."

Cal slipped the bridle over Reverie's ears and, holding the reins slack in his hand, took a step back, letting Jesus get a good look at the horse. Reverie stretched his nose toward Cal. He had a nice top line, a strong, pretty neck, a well-rounded rump.

Cal mounted and took Reverie past the horse trailer to a good-sized flat spot in the pasture near the top of the paddock. Jesus climbed the paddock fence to watch as Cal took Reverie through his paces. When he finished, he brought Reverie to a halt in front of Jesus, and with one hand on his hip, he let the reins loosen in his other.

"You are asking how much?" Jesus asked.

Cal wanted to talk about Reverie's dam, about his temperament, about how easy he'd been to train. But he didn't. He just answered the question. As his father would have. A declaratory sentence. Don't explain or persuade. No place for attachment or affection.

"Four thousand." Until the day before Cal would have happily taken three.

Jesus raised his eyebrows. *Just tell me what he's worth*, Cal could hear his father say.

"Thirty-five," Jesus said, as Cal dismounted in front of him.

Leni's worry and reluctance were planted in Cal's mind. "I have someone coming to look at him later this week," he lied. "I can get back to you." He gathered up the reins.

Jesus nodded, said nothing. Maybe he knew Cal was bluffing.

"Thirty-eight hundred," Jesus said firmly.

Cal paused a moment, then nodded and extended his hand.

Jesus took Cal's hand and holding on, said, "He's a fine horse. And you are a good horseman."

CHAPTER SIXTEEN

December 22nd

Leni

Christmas break. Finally. Leni's mother is upstairs, resting or tatting. Doc's making rounds. The animals doze in the warm noon sun. Leni hasn't seen Cal for a few days. He's been working with the ranch crew. Leni makes two ham and cheese sandwiches, grabs some chips from the cupboard and one of her father's orange Fanta sodas, and takes Marguerite's car to meet Cal for lunch.

On a hay bale behind the big horse barn at the McGrath ranch headquarters, they sit and watch the two-year-olds graze. Leni eats a few chips. Hardly any words pass between them. Leni's thoughts, like her body, taken over by the pregnancy, by this thing that sits invisible and solid between them that can determine the course of their lives.

Walter has asked Cal to pick up some creosote and propane. When they finish eating, they drive to DeWitts'.

Three old-timers are standing at the counter, gossiping with old man DeWitt, when Leni and Cal enter. Jeb Peel, who owns the Ford dealership outside De Kalb, leans against the counter, fingering an unlit cigar. Foster Hickson, a son-of-a-bitch and terrible rancher, who lives by selling off his wife's family's land (Leni's daddy says), is there. And Trey Johnson, a hay farmer, out past the McGraths' ranch.

"What was his name again?" Jeb Peel asks, with a laugh at the end.

"Jesus," Mr. Johnson answers.

"I thought that's what you said."

"Now we don't do that," Foster Hickson says. "Go naming folks after God. That's not right."

"Still don't mean he should've got shot," Earl says.

"No, it don't," Jeb readily agrees.

"He must've heard something. That gate lock was snapped right off," Earl DeWitt says.

"How many head they get?" Hickson asks.

"I don't know. You know Joe Moore, though, he's mad as hell. He's determined to find 'em."

"Those calves'll be branded."

"Yes. They ought to be."

"They'll sell 'em across the border. They don't care none down there if an animal's got a brand on it or not."

"Um, um. It's a shame," Trey Johnson says, clucking and shaking his head.

Leni catches Cal's eye.

"What happened?" Leni asks casually.

"Oh, there's been more rustling again. The Moores' place this time," Earl says. "They were loading some of his Angus steers and his man, you know, the Mexican—"

"*Jesus*," Cal says.

"Is that how you say it?" Jeb Peel takes the unlit cigar out of his mouth for the umpteenth time.

"Yeah, him," Earl goes on. "He got shot. Last night. Joe come in here early this morning straight from the hospital."

"Is he dead?" Leni blurts out. Cal shoots her a look.

"No, he ain't dead. He's a lucky son-of-a-gun."

"If'n you call getting shot in the middle of the night a lucky thing," Jeb Peel says.

"He and his wife's house is that first one off the road toward the lake. And these rustlers were taking those calves from the pasture right there. He must have heard 'em. Went out and got shot in the shoulder. Right here." Earl puts his hand on the soft spot below his collarbone. "Made it back to his house. His wife can't drive. She called Joe himself. He came and drove the man to Mount Pleasant. By then he'd lost a lot of blood."

"Did he see them? The rustlers?" Cal asks.

"I don't know. The police haven't finished questioning him. Now what can I do y'all for?" Earl asks, clearing some space on the counter.

Leni waits for Cal. No answer.

"Creosote," she pipes up.

"Yes, ma'am. You hear from your sister?"

"Only that she's in California."

"Crazy place, from the sound of it."

"Yes, sir. And propane. Right, Cal?"

Cal nods. Holds up two fingers.

"You know where to get the propane from." Earl nods outside and goes to fetch the creosote.

Cal pays without saying a word. He and Leni walk out, squinting in the daylight. Leni sidles close to Cal. His body's tense as coiled steel.

"Does Hank Junior have a gun?" she asks.

"Everybody's got a gun."

B ack at headquarters, some of the machine crew are changing a tire on a tractor. Cal sets down the propane canisters. The fence crew is back out checking the fence line in another pasture.

"Even if Hank Junior is rustling, it's not like he's the only rustler in Texas," Leni says.

"You sure do defend him a lot."

"I do not. I'm just saying, we don't know anything for certain yet."

Silent George is eating a sandwich in the shade of the barn. Cal goes to him. They exchange a few words.

"He know anything?" Leni asks.

"No."

They get in Cal's truck. Leni rests her arm out the window on the warm metal.

Cal looks out, squinting in the bright sun. "Nothing seems steady or right, right now," he says. "It's like I'm standing on the edge of a mudslide. I'm looking and looking, trying to figure how to keep everything from slipping out from under me."

Leni knows then and there that she must tell him. And they will figure it out. Somehow. Figure out a way for him to still go east to college. As he must. A way for them both to leave there and be together. Despite everything. She doesn't know how to start. Only that she must.

"Let's take a drive," Leni says.

Cal starts the truck and they begin to roll out toward the County Road. She takes a deep breath. How to begin?

Just then, dust spraying out behind it, Mr. McGrath's red pickup roars toward them. Mr. McGrath stops, nose to nose, in front of Cal's truck. Dust washes over them.

"Where's your brother?" he yells, jumping out of his truck.

"You think he answers to me?" Cal shouts back. "I don't know."

"When's the last time you seen him?"

Cal shakes his head and shrugs his shoulders. The machine crew and cowboys stop what they're doing to watch.

"Goddammit," Cal's father's walking a tight circle. "Goddammit! Get back to work!" he shouts at the crew. But most keep watching.

Cal's father presses both hands against the hood of Cal's truck. The muscles in his arms and back swell beneath his denim shirt.

"Dad." Cal starts toward his father.

His father holds up his hand. Cal stops. His father leans his head to the hood of Cal's truck. He rolls his forehead side to side on the warm metal. Cal stares at his father, who's begun muttering to himself.

Cal goes to his father. "Dad." He lays a hand on his back.

His father shoots up. Turns to Cal and grabs him. Cal winces. Leni screams—she can't help it—and clambers out of the truck. But his father pulls Cal in to his chest and holds him. Holds him hard. Leni backs away.

"It was all for you," he mutters, pushing Cal off his chest, still gripping his shoulders. "You and your brother." His eyes bore into Cal's. "It's you now. It's only you. You understand that, don't you? All of it. Everything." He looks about him, across the barns, the pastures. His eyes look lost. "Don't go." His voice cracks. "Don't go. You understand, don't you?"

Cal meets his father's gaze. Slowly, he nods.

His father pulls him into his arms again, Cal limp in his father's grasp. His father releases him and gets back in his truck. He heads out slowly onto the County Road, then speeds east, back toward their house.

Cal, pale and drawn, mutters something Leni can't quite make out.

"What?" she rests her hand on his arm. He feels cold.

"I have to stay," he says quietly.

"It's Hank Junior's mistake. Not yours."

"You saw Pops." He shakes his head. "I don't know . . ."

Nausea grips her belly. She sits down on the running board of the truck. "You're not the one who messed up, Cal," she says, shaking her head.

"I don't know," he repeats softly.

At the McGraths', there's no sign of Hank Junior. Leni and Cal go out to the horses. She carries flakes of hay to the paddock. Cal stands in front of Flint's stall, staring at his horse, pitchfork in hand. Leni approaches.

"I'll work and save up," he says. "I'll stay until you can leave. It's better this way." He lays the pitchfork against the stall door and plants his hands on his hips. "That's what's most important to me," he says. "You."

"Cal . . ." What can she say now? "But you can't defer the scholarship. That's what Mr. Wilkens said. Remember?"

"I'll apply again for the scholarship. And you'll be ready to leave, right? When you're ready to leave, I'll leave. And in the meantime, I'll stay and help Pop. And Momma." He picks the pitchfork back up, still nodding. "Yeah," he says, talking himself into his plan. "That's what I'll do."

Leni watches his shoulders round with the slow scoops of the pitchfork. They won't be more ready to go. They'll be more stuck. She'll be especially stuck.

"It's just a year," he says over his shoulder.

"I ought to get home for supper," Leni says.

"You can stay again. Momma doesn't mind. She likes you," he says.

"I told Maman I'd be home tonight," she says.

Cal takes Leni back to headquarters to get the green Nova. Driving home, she detours to the Roadhouse. Sure enough, he's there. She pulls in.

J ust past midnight, Leni leads Foggy around the back of the barn to the road. They wait in the night's gray light, reflected one-point-three seconds ago off the moon, two hundred and thirty-nine thousand miles away. She doesn't let herself look back to the sleeping house, its blinds drawn like eyes softly shut, Maman and her daddy in their separate rooms. Or to the paddock with Agatha's sloping shadow. Or the barn where Roger and the goats are asleep.

From behind the big rock at the end of the drive, she pulls out the pink suitcase with big round flowers—the only one she has—and the food she'd stashed after supper. Foggy grazes. The rustling in the underbrush gets louder and louder the longer she sits. The night animals. The armadillos and foxes and moccasins foraging, hunting and escaping. Her muscles begin to twitch, like a trapped rabbit.

She can only balance this moment. On this cool rock. She can't think forward or back. She waits.

When the moon crests and starts to fall toward Sugar Hill, she knows he's not coming. She's only a tag-along. She'd only slow him down.

She looks at the knapsack at her feet with her diary, sketch-pads and pencils and the pen her daddy gave her, at the soft pink suitcase she's had since she was nine stuffed with as many clothes as would fit. At the Piggly Wiggly plastic bag with pretzels and bread and jelly, all she's been able to stomach. She clutches the paper bag with the carved wolf pup perched on her lap and thinks of her mother waiting to cross the ocean, at nineteen years old, with her one stained leather suitcase.

Leni's ready to turn back when she hears a trailer rattling toward her on the dark road. She looks. The headlights cut out. The trailer slows and rolls to a stop.

Hank Junior gets out and starts toward the back of the trailer. He lets down the tailgate, stumbling as he backs away.

"You didn't tell him, did you?" he asks.

"No," she mumbles, positioning Foggy to get a straight line to the trailer.

"You promise? Say it."

"I didn't tell Cal I'm pregnant."

Hank takes a piss into the dark, as Leni leads Foggy into the trailer and latches the tailgate.

Neither of them speaks. Leni stares straight ahead, knapsack and suitcase on the floor between her feet, the Piggly Wiggly bag beside her and the wolf pup on her lap. They pull slowly away. Leni looks ahead, concentrating hard on the road. As though this will help Hank Junior stay on it.

When they cross the Oklahoma border, he lets out a big sigh and, reaching under the seat, pulls out a beer. Leni takes it from him. He lets her, and starts talking.

He talks about his time overseas. About Rory Ingraham. The best friend he'd ever had. Will ever have, he says, eyeing the unopened beer in Leni's hand. He talks on and on, without any response or encouragement from Leni. Telling his story to her or maybe just to the dark road ahead of them. She's not sure. But she knows it's the story his family doesn't know.

He talks about the ambush in the high jungle near the eastern Cambodian border that he and Rory were in. About how Rory's leg was nearly severed. How Hank stayed with him as he bled out and for thirty-six hours afterwards until Hank could scramble out from where he was hiding, at one point fighting off a Viet Cong soldier scouting for bodies to loot. It was on account of Hank Junior that Dolly and Ham Ingraham got the body of their youngest son back. And that's where he went when he returned, to bring the few effects he had of Rory's. The ones he didn't trust the army with—a gold cross and chain, Rory's high school ring from varsity track, and a camo kerchief.

Hank Junior is a hero to Dolly and Ham. Even Leni knew he didn't feel much of a hero anyplace else. He told the Ingrahams that as fast as Rory was, he hadn't tried to run off when the fighting started, like a lot of their platoon had. He stayed and fought. He told them Rory died quickly, with little pain. And he assured them that Rory had not died alone, that he'd stayed with Rory. Only the last bit was true.

"What I didn't tell them," Hank Junior lights a cigarette off the dying tip of the one he'd just finished, "was that Rory had been tripping almost every day. LSD, mescaline, whatever was making its way through. That'd he'd lost thirty pounds, couldn't sleep or stand still, but could scale trees like a squirrel, which is what he was trying to do when he was shot."

Only a story this gruesome could shake Leni from her own thoughts.

"I arrived at the Ingrahams' last spring, and Dolly and Ham took me in." It isn't hard for Leni to feel how sad and angry and lost Hank Junior must have been. "I slept for four days," he goes on. "Woke up and stayed for two months. Built a chicken coup. Shingled a side of the barn. Repaired the roof. Then one day, after breakfast, I knew it was time to leave. I came back to Naples."

"Is that where you're taking me? To Dolly and Ham's?"

"Yes, it is. Chillicothe, Ohio." He lights another cigarette. "It's a lot safer than running away. Especially in your condition."

"What makes you think they'll take me in?"

Caleb

It was, for those first moments, an early morning like any other. High clouds over the chaparral made the winter sky as white as paper. Cal grabbed a plum from the counter and headed to the barn.

Lady Belle and Flint nickered as he approached. Flint swung his head over the high fence, eyeing him. Butch next.

Then Foggy.

In those split seconds, he thought—though it didn't make any sense—*she's come to stay with me.* Everything falling apart at her house. It will work. She'll finish school, paint and draw. Soon enough, they'll be free. They'll be together. His heart raced. He jogged to the barn.

At the fence, he called for her. First, whispering. "Leni?" Then louder. He looked in each stall for her long shape, asleep on clean straw. The tack room. The feed room. Flint watching as Cal raced from one stall, then one nook or cranny, to the next.

The horse trailer was parked askew on the grass by the paddock. The tailgate open. He ran to it. Empty.

He looked back toward the house. That was when he saw the empty space under the carport where Hank Junior's truck should have been.

The horses were pacing and nickering, confused by his rushing back and forth, wanting their breakfast. Butch nipped Lady Belle on the rump, and she scooted away.

Cal hurried to the feed room. Grabbed flakes of hay and flung them into the paddock. Back in the feed room, he snatched a bucket and lifted the lid of the grain bin.

Stuffed inside the metal grain scoop was a thick envelope with his name scrawled in black marker. His hands were shaking so he could hardly open it. When he did, he found a fistful of one hundred dollar bills with an index card clipped on top.

"*For college*," it said. "*Go.*" His brother's name was scrawled at the bottom.

Cal raked through the grain bin. No other note. He scoured the hay bales.

Nothing.

In the tack room, propped up in the corner were Leni's saddle, two blankets, and Foggy's bridle. Wedged in one of the saddle's flaps was a piece of paper.

"*Please*," it said, "*take care of Foggy. She'll be happy next to Captain Flint. I am forever grateful. And forever and ever sorry. Leni.*"

He searched for more, another note, anything. He looked under the saddle, shook out the blanket. Nothing. Nothing with the brushes or bridles. Nothing on top of the hay bales. Nothing in Flint's stall, in his feed bucket. Nothing in the trailer.

Nothing but a cold clank in his chest like a blacksmith's hammer.

She was gone.

CHAPTER SEVENTEEN

Chillicothe, Ohio

Leni

D olly and Ham Ingraham do take Leni in, as a favor to Hank Junior, and because that's who they are.

Hank Junior gives them something for Leni's keep, she doesn't know how much, doesn't ask. And he gives her a hundred dollars to buy winter clothes and whatever else she might need. She doesn't want to take it, but he tells her not to be stupid, kisses her hard on the forehead, and leaves. Except for that first day when she overheard Ham worry aloud what folks would say about their having a white girl staying with them, Leni never feels unwelcome.

Ham is as tall and as slim as Dolly is short and stout. He has square shoulders and a square jaw, a neatly trimmed mustache. He never goes outside without his tweed cap. Leni doesn't know how old they are. Some age shows on his face, in the lines around his eyes and across his neck; Dolly's skin, though, is as smooth as butter.

The Ingrahams' three-story clapboard farmhouse is smack in the middle of a ten-acre lot, surrounded by corn and soybeans.

There's a small red barn for their goats and rabbits and chickens. Dolly sells the eggs and chicks and poulets, the rabbits for meat mostly, and sometimes for pets. Leni likes helping tend the animals and right away learns how to help Dolly make the goat's milk soap she sells to a pharmacist in Chillicothe.

She sleeps in the attic room, at the top of a narrow winding staircase, that had been Rory's. Marvel comic books still stacked on the bureau. Gym shoes lined up neatly below the bed frame, their scuffed heels poking out.

One morning, only a week or so after Leni's arrival, while she's watering the goats, Dolly comes out to the barn. She chases the prettiest of the hens, one that wasn't laying well, snatches it up and twirls it over her head, wringing its neck until it goes limp. The other hens screech and scatter, running for their lives. Dolly stomps into the barn, her big chest pumping up and down, the limp bird swaying at her side.

Leni sets down her bucket and follows Dolly into the barn.

"I'll be leaving now," she announces, pulling the dirty work gloves off her hands.

"You most certainly will not." Dolly swings the bird onto a wooden table. "Because of this?" she points to the bird with the cleaver in her hand. "What've you been eating all these years?" Thwack. "She was well-fed. She had a warm coop. She lived good."

Leni stares into Dolly's broad, round face. And though Dolly doesn't say it, *And where would you go?* rattles through her head. It's not as though Leni doesn't know where meat comes from. The rusty, metallic smell of blood filling her nostrils is nauseating.

Leni leaves the barn and finishes her chores.

In the kitchen most evenings, fixing supper, Dolly keeps up a patter. Talking about the weather or chores or a neighbor. After supper, though, her thoughts seem to grab hold of her and she goes quiet. She'll sit in the rocking chair by the window in their small living room, swaying back and forth. Hands on her thick thighs, stockings rolled up and tied in a knot just below her knees. Leni wants to know if she was like that before their son died. Or if, like Maman, sinking into silence came with their son's passing. She wonders if Dolly wants to talk about Rory. She doesn't ask. And she doesn't want to talk about Foy. But she likes sitting near Dolly these evenings, each in her own silence. It's enough to imagine their longing bridging the distance between them and the boys they lost.

PART THREE:

NOTHINGNESS

CHAPTER EIGHTEEN

June 1973
Chillicothe, Ohio

Leni

Her belly can't get any bigger. Leni's pretty sure of that.
She has stopped going into town with Dolly, but continues
with most of her chores. Neither Dolly nor Ham lets her lift
anything heavier than ten pounds, though. That's their rule.

One evening, the sun hanging soft and orange in the
summer sky, her belly starts cramping way down low. Dolly
tells her it's just her body warming up, and sends her in to rest.
Leni and Ham sit together in the living room, Leni drawing
goats and cows in her diary. Ham reads the newspaper.

He sets the paper in his lap. "You talk to your folks this week?"

"Yes, sir," Leni answers.

"They still don't know."

"No, sir."

"And you're still figuring on giving the baby up."

"Yes, sir."

"OK, then," he sighs. "We'll go meet with the agency this week."

Leni can tell he has something more to say. But she keeps her eyes on her drawing, the lines getting thicker and thicker until they're carving into the page.

"I know it seems hard," Ham says. "But you got to think of your future. Your future after this baby business is taken care of."

Leni has tried to think about the future. She can't find a way to it. First she's got to get past the unimaginable: birthing this baby, which looking at her belly is going to split her in half. When she was twelve, she fell off Foggy and got a compound fracture in her right forearm. It hurt so much she threw up. Leni figures this'll be something like that. And that right there is nothing she wants to think about. So, she slips backward. But there's no solid footing there either. Foy, gone. Marguerite, gone. Maman and her Daddy going separate ways. And Cal. She left him before he could be gone, too. There all thinking stops.

"You're a smart girl," Ham prods, peering at her over his reading glasses.

Leni keeps doodling until Ham pushes his glasses back on his nose and raises the newspaper in front of his face.

Three weeks later, Leni watches a crying baby girl calm as the nurses swaddle her in a white and pink cotton blanket. They tuck the edge of the blanket in just beneath her tiny round chin, and stretch a pink cap, barely wider than a sock, over the tan peach fuzz on her head.

"Do you want to name her?" a nurse asks, her hand resting on Leni's shoulder.

"Heather," Leni answers, looking at the baby, then at her belly, in disbelief.

And they take baby Heather away.

The next day, Dolly and Ham drive Leni back to the house. The night she and Hank Junior arrived, Dolly asked Leni what her favorite things to eat were. Chicken and dumplings, fried catfish, fat griddle cakes and hushpuppies, Leni told her. These are not her favorite things. Not one of them something her mother would cook. She doesn't want what were her favorite things. Maman's paper-thin pancakes sprinkled with lemon and sugar, quiches with ham and onion, chicken braised in red wine or sautéed with tarragon gravy—tarragon seeds sent from her cousin in France.

Dolly makes chicken and dumplings for supper. Leni doesn't eat. She thanks them and slowly climbs the narrow stairs to her attic room, blood leaking into the pad between her legs.

She wants to be swaddled, too. She wants around her only enough space to breathe. No more than that. No wide sky. No horizons. No far fields. No birds in flight. No stretching in any direction. Everything contained. Tight. Precise.

The small attic room suddenly feels too big.

The closet smells of sawdust and pine, too much like Foy's closet.

She misses now the cold Ohio winter when she would layer clothes over herself, even indoors. She would lay a lead blanket over herself if she had one. Anything to strap her in, as though binding her body would bind her thoughts.

Leni hears Dolly's plodding steps come up the stairs. She enters, sits on the edge of the bed, and talks to the back of Leni's head. What she tells her is: love is always good.

How she knows there was love, Leni doesn't know.

"It doesn't matter the circumstances," Dolly goes on, softly rubbing Leni's back, between her shoulder blades. "The memory of love will give you courage when you need it most."

What, Leni wants to ask as her silent tears drench the pillow, *if you betray love?*

The next morning, Leni watches Dolly mix batter for thick griddle cakes, her flowered housecoat tied where her waist would be.

In a little over a week, Leni's back in her jeans as though no baby had ever been inside her. Putting the last dinner dish away, she knows, without turning around, that Dolly's watching her.

"How about we learn you to play canasta tonight?" she asks Leni. "Or come sit and watch Ed Sullivan with us."

Leni lays the damp dishtowel over the sink to dry.

"The Lord's got a plan for you, girl. Ain't nobody too lost, no sin too big for the Lord to work his miracles on."

"Leave her be, Dolly," Ham says softly.

And Dolly does.

July 23, 1973

It's the best thing. For the baby.

For Heather. A name soft like the grasslands where she came from.

They wrapped her up safe and tight, then I closed my eyes.

I won't let anything in that deep ever again. Not ever.

Some see the world as atoms. Waves or particles. Numbers or dollars. I see light and dark. All I want now is darkness.

Next to the bedroom at the top of the house—where the ceiling is pitched so steep only in the doorway can she stand upright—is a bathroom with an old claw-foot tub and a square, mottled mirror above a stained sink. She gazes into the mirror, waiting to recognize herself.

She lets the water run till the rust has gone out of it. And in the tub—in the white and the blankness, in the shadowless light of the bare hanging bulb—water as hot as she can stand inches up, over the length and flatness of her belly, over her shrinking breasts to her neck, lapping at the lobes of her ears. Stinging ripples of water move with her breath, scorching her skin pink. Beads of sweat sprout from her scalp.

Will this suck out the hurt? And the sin. What could be more of a sin than hurting the ones who love us? And the ones we love. Is there forgiveness for that?

The water prickles her nose, makes her sputter and sneeze. She swirls it, hot and silky, in her mouth. Spits it back out. She can't stay under. She doesn't know why. But she can't.

The water laps gently at her chin. Goes from hot to lukewarm, cool to cold. Her skin from pink to paste-colored and puckered like chicken flesh. She stares at the flat light on the water. At the blue walls, pale as an August sky, melting into the beige water stain on the ceiling.

She pulls the plug, closes her eyes, waits for the water to drain.

I n August, Leni takes the GED exam at the high school on the far side of town. Two weeks later, her results arrive in the mail. She's done well, very well. Dolly bakes a cake to commemorate.

A week later, Leni climbs into Ham's shiny red Ford pickup with its rounded fenders and they drive into Athens. They park at a diner near the university where Ham buys both local newspapers, sets them down in front of Leni, and hands her a pen.

"Circle every job advertised," he instructs, "that you can possibly stand."

They order, and he asks to borrow the phone book.

Over eggs and bacon and flapjacks and coffee, Leni pores through the classifieds while Ham flips through the yellow pages, jotting down addresses for boardinghouses and the YWCA.

Leni thinks the next stop will be one of the boardinghouses. But Ham pulls up to the red brick registration building of the University of Ohio.

He turns off the car, stretches his arm across the back of the seat. "Well," he says, "what do you want to study?"

"I need a job first." She adjusts the tone of her voice. "I'll get a job, then I'll—"

"No," Ham interrupts. "You start studying something from the get-go. Otherwise life takes over. You'll get fooled into thinking time isn't your own. So, come on. What'll it be? To get started. Come on."

The mid-morning sun beats down on the truck's roof. "I don't know, Ham," she says She'd like to do better for this man who has done so much for her. She can feel his impatience.

"Well," he flips his palm up as though she's missing the answer to the easiest question in the world. "Art," he says. "For starters. Drawing, or something like that. Now what else? There's got to be something that's got your attention."

"Physics," she says.

"All right then," he opens the truck door. "Let's see what they got for the fall."

L eni sits cross-legged on the bed and tears two blank pages from her diary. She rests the pages on her thigh and writes a letter, only her second, home. She lets them know that she's OK, that she'll soon begin classes at the university. She tells them what she can to allay some little bit of their worry. Then she sets the letter aside, gets up, opens the closet, and slips the diaries and sketchpads up onto the top shelf, under a thick pile of Rory Ingraham's old sweaters, and shuts the door.

CHAPTER NINETEEN

January 1974
Princeton, New Jersey

Caleb

I t is irresistible to try to imagine a scene before the Big Bang. And easy to think that summoning up darkness will put one there. But there was no light or dark. No before or after. No self, no other. There was nothing.

Nothingness cannot be known by the senses. For that one needs a soul.

I t would have been easier had she died.

He hated his brother first.

He tried to hate Leni. But it just turned into hating himself. For not knowing, for not seeing what was happening. For being duped.

For a time, his ambition vanished. Nothing made any sense. Even, or maybe especially, staying in Naples, Texas. His father may have thought he needed him, but Cal knew that wasn't really true. The ranch was in good hands. He had Walter and George and all the others.

So, in late August, Cal left for college.

He arrived at Princeton by train, toting one suitcase of clothes, one of books, and a box of linens. His roommate was Robert Milston III, fourth-generation Princeton. He and Cal had a symbiotic relationship from the start, though Cal didn't see it that way at first. He introduced Cal—with equal parts pride and cynicism—to the East Coast, taught him lacrosse, actually accompanied Cal to buy a blue blazer, and coaxed him into growing his hair long to look mildly rakish for the girls. Cal felt sometimes like a pet or like *The Great Gatsby*'s Nick Carraway, accepting Rob's invitations, accompanying him to football and soccer games and parties at the girls' dorms. Rob was only a freshman, too, but he could fit into any group. Jocks, hippies, girls. Cal was a straitlaced cowboy, who didn't fit in anywhere. He was an observer, who made—or so he figured—an exotic sidekick. For his part, he coached Rob in economics, physics, and logic and kept him from failing out of college, which would have humiliated his family, though not Rob.

Many weekends, the two went to Rob's home in Chester Springs, on Philadelphia's Main Line. "It's just an old farm-house," Rob said the first time they rumbled up in his green MGB. An old farmhouse with half a dozen Persian rugs, an eighteenth-century grandfather clock, mahogany tables with inlay, and a Steinway baby grand. To Rob's relief, Cal diverted his father's attention from Rob. While his father bored Rob to distraction, Cal was intrigued. He took note of Mr. Milston's pressed khakis, loafers, and pale button-down shirts, even the way he'd stand, a folded newspaper tucked under his arm, a cocktail in hand. He was masculine and assured, in a deliberate, soft-spoken way.

The country, at the time, was reeling from the war, the oil crisis, and Watergate. The economy was tanking. It would take twenty years for the U.S. stock market to recover. Two students down the hall from Rob and Cal didn't return for spring semester; their families were said to have lost everything. While Rob smoked joints upstairs in his childhood bedroom or watched *Bonanza* and *Perry Mason* reruns in the study, Mr. Milston would pour Cal a bourbon on the rocks, with a splash of water, and lecture him on power and economics, banking and infrastructure. America's withdrawal from the Bretton Woods monetary system was a favorite topic. Something about these afternoons and early evenings with Mr. Milston—his sonorous voice discussing the forces that pulled the strings in the country, often well-greased by generous pours of bourbon—pressed pause on the chatter, the imagined conversations with Leni and his brother, the imploring and recriminations that otherwise ran through Cal's mind.

Then late at night, in Rob's enormous bedroom overlooking Mrs. Milston's garden, Cal would listen to Rob's rambling stories about his family: his older brother, a Phi Beta Kappa studying applied mathematics at MIT, and his younger brother, who was being scouted by every college basketball coach in the country. Sandwiched by high achievers, Rob was sly. He kept his talents to himself. He was smart, but barely an average student. He was good looking, but not too good looking. Neither short nor tall. Dark wavy hair, small chin and nose. He was friendly, easy-going. Nothing about him appeared exceptional or threatening. What he excelled at was making people feel comfortable and like him; only later would he take them by surprise with his shrewdness, a skill he honed running sports betting pools at school, and put to use later as a real estate developer.

It was late January of his freshman year, back at Princeton only a week from winter break, when Cal saw both snow and the sea for the first time. Rob brought a small group of friends to his family's beach house on Cape May. Like the Grand Canyon or heartbreak, as much as one may try, the ocean is beyond imagining. As evening descended, and while the others drank beer and played ping-pong, Cal drank Mr. Milston's Old Granddad and peered through the drifting snow, taking in the arc of the sea as it rolled lethargically over the ends of the earth, infinite and weary.

"Come play, Tex," Rob called to him as the guys started another game of ping-pong.

"Yeah, come on, Tex. Play the winner."

"Nah." Cal leaned against the peach-colored wall between framed watercolors of seashells and kept score.

"He's in love with loneliness," he overheard one of them say.

Cal detested his accent from his very first day at Princeton. It only got thicker with bourbon, closing in like brush in the bottomlands with each fresh finger-full. He kept score for a bit, until he couldn't stand the sound of his own voice any longer, then went out into the snow and down to the water. There he listened to the ocean push and tug at the shore.

The wind was sharp. Salty and cold. It sliced the air like an angry horse swishing its tail. A fuzzy pale light from the moon stretched away from shore. Cal took off his shoes and socks, walked through the wet snow and cold sand toward the sea. He watched the water roll over his feet and skid back out. It was so cold, painfully cold at first, then no feeling at all as the snow was washed away and sand buried first his toes, then his arches, his ankles. Maybe, if he stayed there long enough, he thought, he'd disappear into the green and salt. Maybe he'd find her there, her eyes and tears.

He didn't know how long it took, but the water rose up his shins. His entire body was numb, kneaded by the push and pull of the sea. There was a stillness there, inside the rhythm of the water and the cold. He knew Rob's parents' house, lit and pulsing with music, was behind him. He knew the others were inside yelling and drinking. His body began to waver with the water's movement. He heard shouting and the punch of laughter. But his place, he believed, was there, staring down the wrinkled moonlit path on the water. More shouting: points scored and lost. The shouts grew faint and feeble as he was drawn farther into the pulsing cold and gray of the water. Drawn beyond where he'd ever been. Where he'd yearned to go, just beyond. The shouts behind him so far away now. With no feeling in his body, he floated. There was a lightness then. The water filled his jacket, the pockets of his pants. He was buoyant. And beyond cold, beyond language and speech and thought, beyond feeling, best of all. Carried by the water, its rhythm, its rich smell, like minerals and air together, all he needed. Just keep following the moon, he thought, float on its reflection, out and out . . .

Then a yank. Hard. His left arm wrenched back behind him. There was splashing and suddenly he was cold again. Frigid. Afraid and fighting. Though he didn't know what he was fighting.

"Jesus Christ, Tex! Didn't you hear me?" More splashing and pulling and pushing. In the gray light, he didn't recognize Rob—fear and anger had contorted his face. "I couldn't see you," Rob shouted. Still yelling, he held Cal's jacket with both hands, wouldn't let go. They pushed and pulled each other. The water over their waists.

"Fuck, man!" Rob slapped him. "What the fuck were you doing?" He slapped the water with his open hand. Salt water sliced Cal's eyes.

Like climbing a mountain, they trudged—Rob pulling on Cal's jacket—out of the water. Every muscle of Cal's body tight as iron against the cold. Once on shore, several strides from the water's edge, Rob let go. Cal fell to the sand. Frozen. Gritty and stinging. Vomiting and shaking.

The next thing Cal remembered was bright sunlight stream-ing in through a wide plate glass window. A nurse pressed his wrist while looking at the watch on hers.

"Try this on for size," the nurse placed his wrist carefully inside the metal railing of the bed: "'I am a very lucky son-of-a-gun.'"

He didn't feel lucky. He hurt, from his nose to his knees, every muscle and sinew. Fatigue pinned him to the thin mattress as if the sheet over him was lead.

A chair squeaked along the floor in the corner, and Rob stood beside him. "Hey, Tex," he cleared his throat. "How're you feeling?"

Cal's tongue lay like a pillow in his mouth. "I hurt," he whispered.

"You nearly drowned." As Rob went on, Cal processed only intermittent words. "Hypothermia . . . Stomach pumped . . . Sedated . . ."

The nurse ushered Rob out, admonishing him that Cal needed rest. The next day, they moved Cal to the psychiatric ward for observation. Several days later, after an hour sitting in a circle on a too-small wooden chair in a group counseling session, Cal returned to his room and his mother was there. She hugged him, gently at first, then tighter and tighter, her thin arms clasping him to her. She smelled of cigarettes and a shampoo like over-ripe apples. She took a step back to look at him; Cal stared at the floor. She covered her mouth with both hands and burst into tears.

Two torturously slow weeks later he sat on the edge of the hospital bed, hands on his knees, in the new clothes his mother had bought him—new sneakers tied tight, new neatly creased khakis, a button-down shirt, and V-neck sweater, just like in the school brochures—and waited for Rob to pick him up.

Cal saw him before he saw Cal. Head down, Rob paused outside the open door, tucked in his shirt, took a deep breath, then strode in, head held high.

"Hey, Tex. Ready to blow this fire trap?"

"My name isn't 'Tex,'" Cal said.

Rob jammed his hands in his pockets, and nodded.

"I'm not Tex."

"OK. Relax." Rob picked up the plastic bag with Cal's few belongings. "Caleb McGrath," he said. "You're coming with me."

Princeton assigned Cal a psychiatrist, Frederick P. Ames. He was a short man, gray-haired, who rocked when he walked because of an injury he'd suffered in the war. His office was lined with books. He'd brew a pot of oolong tea at the start of every session. Cal would sit silently for long stretches, sipping the smoky tea.

"What do you think about love?" Frederick Ames asked Cal one day. Cal figured Ames was just bored with his recalcitrance.

Slumped in the large wing-backed chair, holding a teacup with both hands. "I think it's lethal," Cal said.

"Not life-giving, as well? F. Scott Fitzgerald said the sign of genius is the ability to hold two mutually exclusive truths in one's mind at the same time."

"I'm not a genius," Cal answered, cradling the teacup.

Dr. Ames stretched his mouth into a kind of frown, tilted his head slightly. "Do you trust me, Caleb?"

Cal shrugged, trying to suss out where this was going.

"I know hearts can break," Dr. Ames said. "I also know they can heal." He poured himself more tea. "I wouldn't ever lie about a thing like that."

Cal sat motionless. His mother must have told Ames about Leni.

"We tend to not understand time is our friend until it's too late, and time is no longer a friend." He chuckled. "You're a very long way from that, however. You have plenty of time." He leaned back, resting his arms on the burnished brown leather of his chair. "Tell me about her."

Rob continued to take Cal to his family's for Sunday suppers, to frat parties and hippie parties alike. The frat parties were full of keg-drinking young Republicans and jocks. The hippie parties were full of philosophy and physics majors, smoking joints. They both had lots of pretty girls—the ones at the hippie parties generally didn't wear bras or shave their legs.

"How come you still take me to parties?" Cal asked Rob one day.

"How come you come along?"

Cal shrugged.

Rob thought about it for a moment and said, "I trust you."

By the time freshman year ended, Cal had laid down his interest in distant galaxies, in concepts like infinity and perpetual motion. All that felt enmeshed in the past, and no longer capacious. Newton's light waves and particles became merely facts.

The weekends he'd visit Rob's family, Mr. Milston's discussions of industry and banking, dividends, debt, and growth continued to interest Cal. He seemed to set before Cal a plan. Rungs up a ladder to green manicured lawns, tasteful rooms in a freshly painted clapboard house on the edge of a wood, neat stacks of French wines in a clean cellar. Light years away from the dry, dusty summers and muddy winters of the Texas chaparral between the creeks. And a buffer to heartbreak, among other things.

Come summer Mr. Milston offered Cal an internship at his investment firm in Philadelphia. The next year, Cal enrolled in economics classes. Second semester sophomore year, Professor Brottwein—an irascible man with thick, round glasses, an indecipherable accent, and a future Nobel Prize—began to single

Cal out. In some classes, he'd call only on Cal, goading him on through one concept or another. One day he stopped Cal in the halls, stood too close, his eyes blinking behind the thick lenses of his glasses, and demanded in his squeaky tenor to know what Cal wanted to do with the rest of his life.

"Finance," Cal blurted.

And that was that. His new course was set.

PART FOUR:

FRACTALS

CHAPTER TWENTY

July 1986
Saint-Brieuc, France

Ludevigne

She walks early each morning to the water's edge, where she can breathe, where the rich, salty air coats her throat and nostrils. Here, on the northernmost coast of France, the air has weight and body—many bodies still, she thinks. Wet sand, the color of gray pavement, spreads wide, giving way to the dense, rolling sea and thick sky. Here, depending on the season and the moon, the water's lace-trimmed edge can sweep in or out a full kilometer in the time it takes to compose a shopping list.

It wasn't the expanse of east Texas that had unnerved her. She knew of her own insignificance. It had been the light. The brightness. Days on end of sun. And heat. There, she used to wish for rain and storms, not just for the crops as the Texans did, but—especially after her boy's death—as something to hold her to the earth.

Fifty meters out, a young family crosses the sand. A girl, five or six, and a little boy waddling behind her. Their parents, arms resting on one another's waist, follow. It is here—with the sea before her, the heavy sky above, and a past to rest on—that she can think of her son with some ease. It is a relief. A relief to imagine him, strapping and strong, with his easy smile. He was the most beautiful thing. He was all that was good. She believes this still, fourteen years on from his death. His strength, his kindness, his confidence. She used to, sometimes, when she knew he was unaware, watch him at the kitchen table, concentrating on his homework, the light shining on his fair hair as he absent-mindedly reached for the cookies or sliced fruit she would have set down for him. Or when he was on the phone with a girl, twisting the phone cord around one finger, then two, as he listened and grinned, hopeful and open.

It could have been Foy walking the beach, a young father with his family, her grandchildren. He'd never been to France. Madeleine or Marguerite either. Her daughters, so far away now. California and New York.

When she left this drenched coast, running from the dreck of the war, she swore she'd never come back. She had made the perfect escape, she'd thought, from loss and mourning, from the heavy churning sea and the deep green of the place, not knowing then that we're born into patterns we cannot alter. They have to unfold, even if they contain unimaginable violence and loss.

A dozen years earlier, she came for a visit. Her aunt's ninetieth birthday. Once there, it was as though the damp earth sucked her in and wouldn't let go. Without the children, what did she have in Texas to return to? William? Their marriage had become a string of habits. Whatever else they may have had twisted by his affair. Nothing straight or strong enough to sustain them through the loss of the children. So she stayed in France.

She has begun attending services at the church she went to as a child. Not that she believes. She doesn't anymore. Not in a god, his benevolence or mercy. But because the ritual holds a kind of assurance. Not quite redemption. But perpetuity.

She settles herself onto a bench overlooking the sea and extracts from her pocket the most recent letter from Madeleine, who writes only in English now. She unfolds the letter, straightens her glasses, and commences to read.

CHAPTER TWENTY-ONE

October 1986
New York, New York

Leni

Leni's Lower East Side apartment is a long and narrow railroad apartment. A salvaged wood door laid atop two sawhorses is both work table and dining table. One half piled high with sketch pads, pens, and pencils. A plate, crumpled paper napkin, and coffee mug rest on the other end, next to magazines: *Art Forum, Art in America*, the Sunday *New York Times* crossword puzzle. Two not-matching folded chairs are pushed up against the table.

The morning sun filters through the cross-hatched metal security gates and fire escape that strap the old tenement's brick wall and rests on Leni's paintings, finished and unfinished (mostly). Once she glimpsed the tail of a black jacket, someone scrambling soundlessly across her fire escape toward Allen Street, chased by whom or what she never knew. She pauses, a small fine-bristled brush in hand, studying the canvas before her. Another hushed landscape. Dreamlike. Wisps of winter grass—snatched from an autumnal flower arrangement at a catering job she worked the week before—are gessoed over. The blades, their texture and long delicate shapes, whisper the prairie.

She checks the time. Wipes her hands on soft, faded-to-beige work pants, turns to a small utility table behind her, and dips the brush in a clear glass jar of paint thinner. Dips and wipes until it's clean and returns it carefully to a coffee can on the bottom shelf with other brushes of varying sizes, their bristles reaching into the air. She turns off the clip-on work lights.

Leni washes her hands in the kitchen sink, which is the only sink. A claw-foot bathtub rests obtrusively in front of a former closet, now a loo. She opens the fridge, takes a swig from a plastic bottle of orange juice. An almost translucent sheet of blue paper—an aerogram from her mother in France—secured by a round magnet flutters and rests back against the fridge door as it closes.

She's going to be late meeting Eric. Her first and best friend in New York. They met in a drawing class at the Art Students League the week Leni arrived in the City and got on immediately. Leni stayed at his place on St. Marks Place for several months just after she arrived. He even helped her get a job waiting tables at the restaurant where he worked in Tribeca. They know little about one another's past, just that they each come from the prairie—Leni from Texas and Eric from South Dakota—and they fled. They don't talk about, don't need to talk about, what they fled. What is important and immediate is that they'd come—with intent—to New York. They have the same restlessness, the same reluctance to accept what anyone else says or does. They respect each other's need to find their own meaning in whatever they do, to find something that can't be taken away.

Eric makes frames for a crazy guy from Berlin who gets jobs from a host of uptown galleries. He spends the rest of his time curating small shows downtown, displaying work of his friends and others, anything that catches his eye. He was soon kicked out of the apartment on St. Marks, the landlord forbidding what he said was commercial activity. That was a stretch; little ever sold. Money wasn't the point. Eric moved, nonetheless, eventually finding a bare loft on Bleecker Street. He stages shows there and wherever else he can. Several months ago, he rented a limousine, had it park outside an opening at a SoHo gallery he found particularly obnoxious, and displayed small sculptures and miniatures. It upstaged the gallery's highfalutin opening.

The show tomorrow night is in the freight elevator shaft of an empty building off Lafayette. Two dancers, more like rock climbers or aerial artists, will be belayed on ropes from above. Light will cast their shadows on the jagged brick walls as they dangle and encounter one another, play-fight, and play-love. Eric refuses to market. Word of his shows and happenings spreads by word of mouth through the downtown scene, makes its way uptown, across Canal and Houston, and now knocks on the doors of Fifty-Seventh Street.

After using the toilet, Leni sidles past the long table, ignoring the thick envelope that's been there unopened for a day and a half. She pushes aside the shoji screen that surrounds her bed—which she's decorated with leaves, pressed flowers, and seedpods—and undresses. She tosses her work pants and paint-strewn T-shirt on the bed beside Abyssinia, who yawns and extends one delicate leg, then another, high in the air. Leni pulls out a clean T-shirt and jeans, slides six inches of bangle bracelets onto each arm, and sits to put on her black, thick-soled boots.

Quickly pouring kibble into Abyssinia's bowl—and ignoring several that skid across the unmopped floor—she grabs her short-waisted black leather jacket off the back of a chair. The envelope stares at her. Her name and address in sloppy handwriting she doesn't recognize. She starts for the door. Stops. Returns to the table and snatches the envelope. It's been carefully sealed, no space even for a fingernail to slide in and pry open. She really should get going. Eric will be waiting. They still have pieces to hang. She can read it tonight. Or tomorrow.

Then, laying the envelope on the kitchen counter, she picks up a knife and carefully slices open the thick envelope. Inside is another envelope, less tightly sealed. She tears it open and extracts two sheets of paper, each folded once.

It is, as she guessed it would be, from Hank Junior, passed from who knows how many consiglieres between wherever he is (still hiding, she presumes, from US law enforcement) to her fourth floor walk-up in the Bowery.

The last letter that made it to her, almost two years ago, bore the news of Ham Ingraham's passing. She had written Dolly, wanted to do more. To visit or send flowers, at least. But she'd lost her job as a carriage driver in the park and was living pretty much hand to mouth. This time, though, she does have extra money. More than she's ever had. Catering jobs are good money. Six hundred dollars, in a coffee tin, pushed into the dark far corner of the cupboard above the few plates and glasses she has. Six hundred dollars. She could, this time, get a bus, maybe a train, probably not a flight, back to Ohio. Back to Dolly, whose kindness is lodged in her heart. Whose kindness sometimes makes her palms sweat as she recalls it, never knowing how to repay it.

Dear Leni, the letter begins. Hank's jagged but legible writing slanting across the page. *I hope this finds you.* Leni checks the date, September 5th, six weeks past. She reads on. *I want to let you know that Dolly passed. In her sleep. July 18th.* Leni slumps into a chair and reads the rest of the letter.

Rory's brothers sent Hank Junior some items they believed belonged to her that they found in Rory's room. He wants to know what to do with them. Leni knows what was there. Some clothes she wore when she was pregnant. Sketchbooks and journals. Pages and pages of sketches, drawings, and words. Pages that seemed important enough to the girl she was then that she lugged them from Naples, Texas, to Ohio. She wasn't that girl now, though. Nothing that was part of her life then is a part of her life still. And nothing there, without Dolly and Ham, is worth going back for. She folds the letter, stuffs it back in the envelope, and tosses it on the table.

Eric wears his usual uniform: slim-fitting black leather pants, a billowing silk shirt, this one purple, unbuttoned to reveal the plume of dark hair on his chest, and a denim jacket over his arm. He leans against a lamppost, a cigarette dangling from his mouth, James Dean style. He flutters his fingers in a wave as Leni approaches. He is not a demonstrative person. As he twists to stamp out the cigarette with his boot, Leni watches the skin skim his collarbone. She's never noticed that before. Or, before he slips on his sunglasses, how dark the circles are beneath his eyes. He won't want her to ask.

Instead, as they head east, into the blare of an ambulance siren moving slowly (as sirens do here) up Lafayette, she asks, "What's left to do before tomorrow night?"

"Clean up. Sweep out the foyer. Windex the door. And hammer in the hooks to hang some paintings in the foyer. We're hanging one of yours."

"No, we're not," Leni protests. Her pieces don't have the edge, the brashness of the other work. She can be sometimes brash, but her paintings aren't.

"You've got to start showing sometime." He pulls another cigarette from his jacket pocket.

"Says who?"

"Otherwise you're just masturbating."

"Fuck you."

"I've brought down the one you gave me—"

"That was a gift, Eric!"

"—To hang so the world can see it."

"The world may not want to see it."

He ignores her, pauses to light his cigarette. "Come with me afterwards to Broome Street."

CHAPTER TWENTY-TWO

Caleb

After getting an MBA from Penn, Cal spent three years at a Philadelphia investment firm doing quantitative analysis, devising formulas and algorithms intended to help their stock traders beat the equity markets. It was less than inspiring. When his old friend and Princeton roommate, Rob Milston, asked him to come to New York and help him at his real estate development start-up, Cal agreed. Manhattan seemed intriguing and Rob was the closest thing Cal had to a best friend. So, during the fall of 1980, he moved to the City. Wall Street was aflutter, anticipating Ronald Reagan's win. It was a lively time.

Cal helped set up partnerships and structure deals for the company and was paid very well. His real worth, he sometimes thought, was his ability to (usually) rein Rob in, keep him focused and approaching disciplined, something their growing list of limited partners appreciated.

Analyzing numbers, attracting the right investors, boosting partners' equity share. What did Cal appreciate about it? The lifestyle, he supposed. A nice apartment on the Upper West Side, dining at fine restaurants, summer shares with Rob in the Hamptons (though Cal preferred the Berkshires). And being on track to make as much or more money as his father. And beyond that? He'd begun to reminisce lately, to wonder what happened to his dream to follow in Newton's footsteps. To do work that helped further man's understanding of life here on the planet. In quiet moments when his thoughts were less constrained by tasks at hand, he felt harnessed to a smaller purpose than he'd once imagined. Those old aspirations for an expansive life of the mind, days spent peering into infinity, were an adolescent's dreams, a teenager's yearning for grandeur, he told himself. Perhaps. In any event, it had all came crumbling down, as though—he sometimes thought—Leni had been his keystone. These nagging thoughts had begun to slip through cracks in the bulwark he'd built up. Whatever it was that was holding up what his life had become couldn't come loose now.

Cal was engaged. In two and a half months, he'd marry Darla. Darla—petite, with a heart-shaped face, that sweet tapered chin, thick lustrous hair the color of burnished cherry, and a self-assurance that often startled Cal—very much counted on the life they now led. Uptown parties, weekends at friends' homes in the Hamptons or Fire Island (Darla always scanning real-estate flyers on their drive or train rides back to the City), and the occasional gala.

They met "across a crowded room" was how she liked to announce it, at a wedding in Cambridge the year before. In the wee hours of the morning, she was seated at the piano in the living room of a Beacon Hill inn taken over by wedding guests, playing "Some Enchanted Evening." One of the bridesmaids was drunk enough to sing a torch song in front of friends and strangers, though a little too drunk to stay precisely on key. Cal leaned against the wood-paneled wall of the inn's living room, watching the performance. When the song finished, there were calls for more. Darla, though, stood, bowed almost demurely, looked straight at Cal for a long second, and exited the room as friends kissed her cheek and stroked her bare shoulders. He followed.

Several months later, coming out of the bathroom in her Boston apartment, wrapping a towel around his waist, he overheard her say into the phone, "I've found myself a Princeton and Penn man." For a split second he was jealous, then realized she was talking about him.

He supposed if he'd talked about his life before Princeton to Darla, she could have said any number of other things. That she'd found herself "a cowboy" or "a Texas boy" or "a math whiz." But he didn't talk about his life before and she rarely asked anything beyond the perfunctory. When she did, she didn't persist, which allowed him to keep that swath of his life embedded and allowed Darla to hold him squarely on the East Coast, Ivy League terrain she knew so well.

The spring they met, Darla was finishing a master's in arts management at Northeastern University and confident that with her parent's connections—her mother was on the board of the Isabella Stewart Gardner Museum in Boston—she could land a job in New York, where Cal was living and working. And, of course, she did. Darla's family provided her with solid ground beneath her feet. It would be hard for her to fathom how afloat Cal sometimes felt.

She was an only child and essentially a happy and grateful person, though she had a tendency to sulk. She loved her mother and loved her father, whom she still called "Daddy," even more. And they loved her. They were accustomed to life rolling along pretty much as they'd planned and worked hard for. There were no visible fractures in their lives, nor did they expect any in others. This wasn't to say they were shallow. Undoubtedly they'd weathered many trials of life, some small, others not. They were just exceedingly secure. Paths were laid out, if they played by the rules, which they were well schooled in. Darla's father, a corporate attorney, and her mother, a realtor in a wealthy Boston suburb, sent Darla to some of the very best schools. Cal, a real estate developer with that Ivy League education, six years older than Darla (not too old), was established enough that her parents felt assured he knew the rules, too, and could take care of their twenty-six-year-old daughter in the manner they sought for her. In the manner Darla, too, expected.

"Is it a good fantasy?"

Startled, Cal swiveled his chair around to find Rob standing at the door to his office. Cal checked his watch. They were due at a shareholder's meeting in Williamsburg. A family-owned company that had several warehouses on the Brooklyn waterfront, which Rob was keen to buy. Cal stood, buttoned his jacket, and straightened his tie. Rob held two yarmulkes in his outstretched hand, which Cal took and tossed onto one of the armchairs in front of his desk.

"Why'd you do that?"

"Are they having the shareholder meeting in a synagogue?" Rob shook his head. "Then we don't need yarmulkes. You can't impersonate a Jew, Rob."

On their way out, Theresa, their secretary, handed Cal a pink message slip. "Darla called. She said to meet her this evening at some event downtown after work. The address is there." Theresa pointed to the slip of paper. "I would have patched her through, but she said not to disturb you." Cal knew that was actually code for, "This is not up for discussion."

Cal scanned the Lower East Side address. Darla worked in fundraising at the Whitney Museum. What she wanted, though, was to have her own gallery. The next step was to get a job with one of the galleries downtown that were shaking up the whole art scene, spotting new talent and bringing to bear marketing prowess akin to that of Upper East Side realtors to work with collectors from California and Japan, the UK, and Berlin. This event, Cal knew, was important to her networking plans.

"Someone's going to spot the next Basquiat," she had explained to Cal during dinner.

"The next young artist who'll kill himself," Cal replied.

She slapped his arm.

The taxi pulled to a stop on the narrow cobblestone street. Cal double-checked the address on the pink slip of paper that Theresa had given him, as a black town car pulled around them and stopped at the curb.

"This must be the place," Cal told the driver, who grunted and took Cal's five dollar bill.

Light and chatter and people spilled from the sturdy three-story brick building two blocks from the river, built originally—Cal surmised—for light manufacturing. The other buildings on the block were dark, a couple were boarded up. As Cal stepped out into the damp air, a plastic bag wrapped itself around his shoe. He kicked it off and scanned the twenty- and thirty-somethings, plastic cups of wine in hand, loitering in front of the building, smoking and talking. A tall rail-thin woman in a long black coat had a baby bound to her chest with a swath of red fabric. Baby and mother wore matching black berets. Pretentious, Cal thought. And immediately reminded himself to keep his opinions to himself. A few by the door eyed Cal, expressionless or maybe reproachful, sizing up his charcoal gray suit, Italian leather shoes, and Clark Kent haircut. Cal nodded—respect the natives, he thought—and entered.

The building's ground floor foyer had become a crowded, makeshift gallery. The ceiling was quite high, ten feet. Paintings were hung on the bare brick walls. At the end of the foyer was a large, empty and well-lit freight elevator shaft. People were clustered, three or four thick, around the elevator opening, gazing up. Cal spotted Darla in her well-tailored black pants, her black boots with high stiletto heels, and a sweater with a thin fur trim around the deeply cut collar. Uptown had come downtown. A guy in a kilt was talking to her, leaning in very close. His balance appeared precarious. Another seemed to be impersonating Bruce Springsteen, leather pants, denim jacket, short hair, and long sideburns. Cal began to make his way through the crowd to Darla, when he noticed a painting, about three feet wide and maybe four feet high. Cal usually dismissed most of the art at the events Darla dragged him to. He knew he was no expert, but so much of it just seemed like purging. Impulsive. Not thought out. Something drew him to this painting, though. It was quiet, the colors muted. When he looked closely he could see that there were in fact layers of color. Depth and texture. He thought he could make out stalks of tall grasses, the merest impression of wheat heads beneath the paint. As he scanned the canvas, he sensed a vast landscape with horizon, space.

Cal stepped closer, scoured the lower right corner for the artist's name, *M. Bonet* or maybe, *Bonnet*.

Resuming his attempt to reach Darla, Cal was thwarted by several people waiting to greet a small, gaunt man in a fluttering silk shirt. There was a smattering of middle-aged attendees, expensive jewelry on the two women, expensive eyewear on the men. Gallery owners or collectors, Cal assumed. Rounding one group of well-wishers, he noticed a willowy woman, black leather motorcycle jacket over billowing blue harem pants, her shorn hair dyed like a jaguar's coat—platinum blonde with brown spots circled in black. How did she do that? As she leaned her head close to hear her companion above the hum of the crowd, light bounced off a ladder of small gold hoops climbing her ear, a small vertical scar at the edge of her eyebrow. There appeared to be a brand in the shape of an orthodox Greek cross on her companion's cheek. Why the hell would one do that, Cal couldn't help thinking just as Darla spotted him. Her eyebrows arched. She smiled and waved. The off-kilter, kilted guy kept his eyes on her chest—for balance, no doubt.

"Sweetheart," Darla threaded her arm through Cal's as he approached. "How was your day? Not too dreadful, I hope?" she looked up at him.

"No," Cal smiled and kissed her forehead, as he got the once-over from Mr. Kilt before he ambled off.

"That's Eric Wyckoff," Darla said, nodding toward the gaunt man in the flowing silk shirt. "Prince of the underground art scene." She was obviously impressed. "He curated this show."

Just then, Cal saw what people had been staring at in the elevator shaft. A woman in a skin-toned leotard, harness around her pelvis, holding the shape of an archer, was lowered into view, as the slumped body of a man, also in a leotard and harness, was lowered, swinging almost imperceptibly.

Cal averted his eyes from the faux-naked suspended archer. "Keep networking," he winked and nudged her gently. She smiled up at him and scanned the room.

For something to do, Cal made his way to a table with jugs of cheap wine, crackers, and pale cheese. He asked for a seltzer, stepped away from the table, and pretended to look at a piece that seemed made of driftwood, snatches of fabric, and barbed wire. "Cast-offs," he whispered. Maybe he was beginning to get this. He wanted to try his luck and stepped over to the next piece. The woman with jaguar hair was behind him. In front of him was a painting, long black and brown shapes, vertical and slanted, on a white background. It reminded him of the bare branches of a young ash or walnut tree near the Texas creeks in winter. He doubted this is what the artist intended.

Just then, an accent—one that smoothed the hard edges of consonants and lingered, stretching one-syllable words into two—cut through the buzz and hum of the makeshift gallery. It was as though someone had grabbed him by the collar.

"I would sa-ay you'd be courtin' trouble . . ."

Cal couldn't tell where the voice came from in the crowd; sounds bounced off the brick and metal. He scanned the room. He must have looked alarmed, because a young woman standing next to him backed away. He strained to isolate particular voices in the crowd but couldn't find that one again. He gave up, gulped his seltzer, and tried to focus on another of the paintings hanging on the wall. On his way to getting a refill, he passed the jaguar, who had made her way to Eric Wyckoff, the prince of the underground art world, who clasped her arm. She leaned in close to him.

"Ye-es, ye-es," she drawled, "I'll be seein' you tomorrow. Promise."

Cal stared at her. The straight nose, green eyes. His attention before had been drawn to the hair and the sparkling ladder of earrings. Could it be her? No. He chastised himself. His thoughts had been running to nostalgia lately. It couldn't be. He watched as more pierced and tattooed attendees encircled Eric and the jaguar.

Then she turned, her left profile to Cal. A scar cut across the tip of her left eyebrow. He froze, stopped breathing, heard nothing.

Suddenly Darla was at his side. "Cal? Cal?"

"Sorry." He wrenched his attention away and toward Darla. "I can't hear anything in here."

"We're deciding where we want to grab a bite," Darla said. "I'm starving. What are you in the mood for?"

He watched the prince of the underground art world kiss the jaguar on the cheek. She took a ring of keys from her pocket and started for the door.

"Me? What am I in the mood for?" He watched a woman stop the jaguar, or Leni—was it Leni—on her way out.

"Yes, you." Darla took Cal's hand, swung it once. "Your palm's sweaty."

"No, it's not." He retracted his hand.

"Are you feeling OK?"

"Yes." Then correcting course, "I'm actually tired. It's been a long day. And not very hungry."

"You're working too hard." She gave him a little pout.

"Why don't you go on? I think I'll just head home. Is that OK?"

"I'll miss you." That sweet heart of a face tilted toward his.

Cal leaned down, a quick kiss on the lips.

"We won't be too late." Darla's eyes imploring, "Are you sure?"

The jaguar was close to the door. The off-kilter kilted guy staggered toward her. She brushed him off.

"I've got another big day tomorrow," Cal said.

"You do? What's happening?"

"Oh, you know. Just another deal."

"I don't really know," Darla said, a sliver of a smile accentuating that tapered chin. "You could talk with me more about your work, you know. I am interested."

"Well, not here," Cal answered.

"No, you're right. Not here." She frowned, slight disappointment. "OK, well. I won't be late. You get a bite and get to bed."

"Yes, ma'am," Cal answered.

They kissed, chastely.

Cal scanned the heads between him and the door. No jaguar.

The drizzle had become rain. Cal, hand to his forehead, like a scout, peered up and down the street, not sure which way to turn. Couples continued walking in and out of the makeshift gallery. At the corner, a figure moved from the shadows into the dim light of a street lamp and swung a leg over a bicycle. Pants billowed behind as the cyclist headed up Orchard Street.

Cal jogged to the corner and watched the cyclist, already a block ahead, turn north toward Houston.

He flagged a cab.

"See that bicycle," he closed the door and pointed across Houston Street, "follow it."

The driver, a crusty old guy with a Bronx accent, hit the brakes. "Uh-uh. No way. I ain't going to be any part of that."

"No, no," Cal intoned. "That's my girlfriend. I was late meeting her. She's going to be pissed at me."

"Mend that fence on your own time, buddy."

Cal scrambled, swearing, out of the cab. The traffic light was against him. Cars rolled east and west on Houston, head and tail lights blurry against the dark, wet street as Leni—he thought, but what if he was wrong?—stood up, pumping west, then north on First Avenue. Finally the light changed, traffic stopped. Cal crossed the four lanes of traffic, wiping rain from his face, and ran up First Ave.

At First Street, Cal stopped. She was nowhere in sight. He listened—trying to pierce the slurping wet tires, the sirens in the distance, and the huffing of his own breath—for the squeak of a bike brake.

Jogging north, he shouted at the rain, at the absurdity. "Leni!"

Nothing.

Two teenagers walked toward him, heads down, long stringy hair slanted sharply across each of their faces.

"Have you seen a bicycle?" Cal asked, slowing.

"I've seen like a thousand," one of them said, and turned to the other, "how about you?"

"No, never." The other one—no eye contact—shook his head.

Very funny. "Heading this way." Cal pointed up First Avenue. They shook their heads again.

Cal kept going. An old man in too many coats wasn't any help either.

At East Second Street, with no bicycle in view, he looked both ways, picked west, and jogged down the middle of the street, the asphalt shiny with rain, toward Second Avenue. Barely half the streetlights worked. He scoured the dark sidewalk. She wouldn't have headed south. He crossed Bowery. There was movement halfway down the block. Someone or something pulled off the street, sidling between parked cars. He sprinted to the spot. Nothing.

Winded, he bent over to catch his breath. What was he doing? Chasing a ghost. And he'd lied to Darla.

"Who are you?"

He couldn't see anybody. "Leni?"

The woman stepped out of the shadows beneath a fire escape, gripping a bike in front of her like a shield.

"My God. I can't believe it's you." Cal hands on his knees, still catching his breath. "I heard your voice. At first, I thought I imagined it. Imagined you, that is . . ." Energy surged through him. He couldn't really make out her face. He couldn't catch his breath, but he couldn't stop talking. "And the hair. Can I see your hair?" he looked up.

She was still and silent, the bike catching what little light there was from the streetlight.

"I'm sorry," he mumbled. "Have I made a mistake?"

"No one calls me Leni."

"What do they call you?"

She considered the question. "Em. For Madeleine. Don't use O'Hare anymore either."

"What do you use?"

"My middle name. Bonet." She didn't move from the shadows.

"I was at the opening. Or whatever it was."

"I know," she said. Her voice was even. Cold or stunned, Cal couldn't tell.

"You recognized me?" he took a step toward her. She took a step back. He stopped.

"No. Maybe. I'm not sure."

Everything between that moment and the last time he'd seen her suddenly felt like a time-out, like life on pause, suspended, or as though he'd become a fractal of himself, reduced in size, subordinate.

She stood very erect. Her head tipped ever so slightly back, her gaze sliding down her straight nose. The rain receded to a drizzle.

Her recalcitrance blistered him. What reason did she have to be angry with him? "Well," Cal pushed wet hair from his forehead. "Apparently you have nothing to say to me?"

"How are you?" Her tone was flat.

"Wet."

She nodded.

"How have you been, Leni?" He tried not to sound as indignant as he felt. "Can I call you Leni?"

She nodded. "Look. This is a shock."

"You're telling me."

"Well, not so much for you. You're the one who tracked me down."

"'Tracked you down.' You think I've been hunting you?"

"Well, I don't know what you've been doing." She studied the ring of keys in her hand. "But there's too much ground to cover. I know that." She turned toward the door.

"Yet here we are," Cal motioned to each of them, "and—"

"I don't want to go back." She turned to face him, fumbling with her keys. "I can't imagine you much want to either."

He didn't know what to say.

"No, I didn't think so." The keys clanked against the metal door. She pushed the door open and looked back. "Good night, Caleb. You look," she paused, "prosperous."

"I thought maybe you'd left the country," he blurted.

She tried to haul the bike inside. An unsteady fluorescent light leaked out from the foyer. One side of the handlebars caught her jacket, the other the doorframe.

"So, tell me," Cal said, watching her struggle with the door and the bike, "where did you go? You can at least tell me that now."

She yanked on the handlebars, trying to free the bike.

"The two of you," Cal added. "On the run. It must have been exciting," sarcasm snaking between his words. "With my brother?" he prompted. "Remember?" Every pause, every pulse of his heart, made him angrier. "So, how long were you two on the run?"

He watched her beneath the gray fluorescent light in the misty air as though seeing her through ash, the residue of memory. Her back still to him, he kept on.

"Is that why you changed your name?" he prodded.

"No," she mumbled.

"I never mentioned you to the FBI. When they'd come to see me."

"Oh, my God." She turned and almost laughed.

"I didn't think that'd be funny. They'd ask who I thought Hank might be with—"

"You have it so wrong."

"Do I? Really?"

"Yes."

"You didn't leave in the middle of the night with my brother? Or maybe you don't remember."

"Of course I remember!" she shouted. "Please stop."

"Then tell me, what do I have so wrong here?"

She jerked her bike free with both hands like she was about to throw it onto the sidewalk. The door slammed shut behind her.

"You don't know anything and you don't understand. I had to leave. For both of us. You have to believe that. And Hank helped me. That's all." She sliced the air with her hand, cutting the past from her life just like that.

"You had to leave. And Hank helped you. Oh. This is getting much clearer."

"If I'd stayed, it would have been worse for you. Hank knew that, too."

"Well, there's the grandiosity of youth." Cal gestured toward her with an outstretched hand.

She took a step forward. Light shone down through the bars of the fire escape above her like a cage. She swiped the cap off her head. "It would have been worse for me, too."

"Why did you have to leave?" would have been the logical question. He was either too angry to think of it or too scared to ask. Rather than continuing the sarcasm, though, he was quiet. They each stared at the ground at their feet.

"I liked your painting." he said.

She nodded.

Cal took a breath, felt the cool drizzle on his face. "How'd you do that to your hair?"

"You kind of paint the dye on." She rubbed the side of her head. "Are you a physicist?"

"No."

"No?"

"I'm in finance. Real estate," he mumbled. Saying this to her embarrassed him. He looked away, then, to change the subject asked how long she'd been in the City. Six years, she told him.

"Me, too." Cal combed wet hair back from his face again, took another deep breath. "So, how are you?"

"What do you mean?" She was ready to retreat again.

"I mean," he started, wondering if that was it for the thaw. "I mean, are you well?"

"Yes."

"And you live here?" he gestured to the building behind her. She nodded.

"Are you married? Kids?" he asked.

"No," she answered sharply.

"All right," he said, backing off. "I get it. You didn't want to be found. I didn't mean to find you, you know."

"Right. I forgot. You didn't hunt me down." Her turn to be sarcastic.

"Our paths crossed." Cal took a step back, hands raised where she could see them.

"I'm sorry," she said quickly. "I mean, I'm fine. And, yes, I live here," she gestured behind her, "in this palatial tenement. And, no, I am not married." She adjusted her bike. "How are you?"

For the first time, she really looked at Cal. And he could see what she meant. It was a hard question to answer.

"I live uptown, on the West Side," he said, somewhat ducking the question.

"Married?"

"Engaged."

"Good, good. That's good," she said.

"Yes, it's great."

They both looked in the direction of Bowery.

"OK, well . . ." She reached for her keys.

As awkward as it was to stand across from her in the rain, Cal didn't want to let her go. "I'm glad you're still painting," he said.

"Why?" She stopped, looked at him again. "You don't know if I'm any good."

"I don't think that's what really matters." What mattered to him was that she'd stuck with it. "I was trying to compliment you."

"Thank you. Well. Finance and real estate." She mulled it over. "That's the big stage," she said, nodding her head. "Where all the strings get pulled." She waved her hand as though it were a magic wand.

"You're contemptuous of what I do," he said, recognizing how defensive they each were.

"Of what you do? I don't know what you do. No, I'm only contemptuous of people who feel sorry for themselves."

"You think I feel sorry for myself?" That stung.

"I think you're wearing expensive shoes—in the rain. You're married—"

"Engaged."

"Right, engaged to be married. And you're tracking down an old girlfriend."

"Hold on. I didn't . . ." He needed a moment to think back, gather his thoughts. "You're attacking me because I complimented you for doing what you've always wanted."

"Teenagers try all sorts of stupid things," she said.

That was a slap across the face. "I didn't think we were stupid, Leni."

"That's not what I meant," she started.

"Right." His turn to back up.

"When you're seventeen or eighteen—maybe however old you are—you think you know more than you do. It's worth remembering."

"Good night, Leni." The rain started up again.

"And don't tell me you've been living your life thinking about me," she said loudly as she pushed the door open. "I don't believe it."

The door clanged shut behind her.

Cal jammed his fists in his jacket pockets and stared at the scarred, dented metal door. Rain dribbled down the back of his neck. She was right. He hadn't lived the last dozen years or more thinking about her. What he had done, and hadn't realized it until that moment, was live terrified of the feelings he'd had for her.

He'd rolled up tight all that he had loved most—Leni, his horses, the land, the sky, science, theories, and wonder—along with all he had to escape: his father's narcissism and violence, the ignorance and isolation. He'd acted as though it was all tainted, and he walked away from all of it.

He flung whatever was in his pocket—loose change, business cards, a pack of gum—at the door and, head bowed into the rain, started uptown.

Leni

Leni unwinds the bicycle lock from her waist, chest heaving like she's just run four blocks, and peels off her damp jacket.

Double-breasted suit. Cologne. And that Wall Street hair. Probably gets manicures.

Abyssinia perched on the counter beside a coffee can full of clean brushes, observes Leni pace.

"What are you looking at?" Leni snaps.

Well, he's obviously made it. No surprise there. Princeton. Uptown. And engaged. Real estate banking. Or whatever the hell he said. She can hardly remember a thing he said, actually.

She stops pacing. Sits. Abyssinia approaches, nonchalant and stiff-legged. Leni strokes her thick fur. The cat settles on her lap, purring.

She's glad he got away, though. That's what he wanted. And needed. She believes that. And it's what she wanted for him, too. To get away from Naples, Texas. A place too small for his talents. And away from that father of his, the son-of-a-bitch. And even his beautiful, chain-smoking mother.

And he was right. She is doing what she's always wanted. She's not the local misfit with a baby on her hip, making ends meet assisting the Pewitt High art teacher, tiredly explaining why she's not in church Sunday mornings.

A price was paid, though. Like skinning her own arm to get out of a trap. She may not have landed in the Ivy League, but she did it. She took a stand, got out. And made it to New York. Just the place for her. Somehow she always knew this. Even during those first few disastrous, fantastic months when she was held up at knifepoint, had art supplies stolen, had to move out of the apartment she was sharing with a psycho girl from Kansas in the dead of night. Even after all that, she knew New York was where she wanted to be. Because art pervades everything here, and there are no boundaries. Theater and dance in lofts and parking lots and basements. Artists act. Actors make paintings. Audiences are part of the plays. And everyone makes music. Everyone's a poet. And everyone has come from someplace else. As much running from something as running to something. No one asks where you're from or why you're there. Thank God. It doesn't matter. What matters is what you do, what you're making. There are exhibitionists, for sure. A lot of rage and fear. And drugs. But for Leni, there's no explaining to do. They're all misfits and everyone fits in.

Finding out that Cal has been here too, though, has shaken her. Makes her feel that in some way she hasn't gotten all the way away. The distance between Naples and New York has conflated. Maybe she's been fooling herself. Maybe there's no such thing as a fresh start.

She slumps into the chair, Abyssinia still on her lap. And his thinking she'd left the country with his brother. Like they were having some madcap affair.

It was the not telling him. She knows this. Can she tell him now why she left the way she did? Tell him that she'd had about only hours to make her decision? That had she stayed, they'd have had a baby. He wouldn't have gotten out. They wouldn't have gotten out. She knows this, too. And Hank Junior knew it. No east coast college, no study at the great museums of Europe, no—living hand to mouth sometimes, yes but—making and seeing and living art, all because of her mistake? Can she tell him now, now that he's engaged probably to some wholesome girl from the toniest side of the tracks, that somewhere he has a daughter? That they have a daughter. Wouldn't revealing that now blow up his life? Again.

She puts Abyssinia on the table and fills the kettle for tea.

And what if he wants to find her, the daughter they had? Heather. Though her name may be anything now. She cut those lines, set her sails. It wasn't easy. Not by a long shot. But she's made a life that's her own. Selfish? Maybe. Some might say. But so long as she's got only herself to answer to, what matter is that? And the baby—a teenager now—has parents, a family.

She's through justifying it.

Abyssinia jumps onto the counter. Leni picks her up. The tips of her claws prick Leni's shirt sleeve. She unsnags the cat's claws and snuggles her. The gentle, thrumming purrs against her ribs slows her heart. Her thoughts begin to settle.

The next morning is blustery, the sidewalks and street still wet from the night's rain. Leni steps out, watches clouds skim across the narrow piece of sky above her and zips up her jacket. A fresh can of Folger's coffee and a yoghurt on her mind, she starts toward the corner bodega. Head down, bracing herself against the wind off the river, she sees plastered to the sidewalk in front of her building a business card.

CALEB D. MCGRATH
Milston Investment Co., Inc.
570 Lexington Avenue
New York, NY 10022

She peels the card off the sidewalk. Holds it by a damp corner. Two feet away, there's another one. Loose change scattered about, too. And a soggy pack of gum. She picks up the second business card and places them both carefully—so as not to tear them—in her jacket pocket.

CHAPTER TWENTY-THREE

Caleb

The next day was windy and colder. Everyone was muttering about getting ready for winter.

Cal left work early, telling his assistant, Theresa, he was meeting Darla to go over something or other for the wedding. Instead, though, he walked.

The movie theater on East Sixty-Fourth Street was showing *Platoon*. He was a few minutes late but got a ticket anyway and sat down beneath the staccato beating of helicopter blades. He left as the credits began to roll, with every intention of grabbing a cab across the park. He'd be at the apartment by seven, pretty much the usual time.

Instead, though, he kept walking.

From a dingy Irish bar on Eighty-Second Street, he called Darla to tell her he had a dinner meeting.

"Oh, sweetheart. You've been working so hard." He knew her mouth was turning down at the corners. "I have a surprise for you when you get home," she cooed.

Even the thought of voluptuous Darla in their bed didn't shake his thoughts free.

"I got us," Darla continued, and paused for dramatic effect, which only made Cal more uneasy, "tickets to Montreal this weekend." Her voice rose in glee. "A hotel in old town, dinner and nightclub reservations."

"That's wonderful," he told her.

Cal stepped out of the phone booth, looked down the long bar past a couple of old guys peering into their beers, and left—without having a drink. He walked to Fifth Avenue and north along Central Park, past the Met and the Guggenheim, and headed west on 110th Street. He stopped at another hole-in-the-wall bar on Amsterdam.

He ordered a beer.

And left before drinking it.

He was thankful for the chill in the air, as he walked, hands jammed in his pockets. The cold held some bit of his attention back from the crowded opening the night before, from the chase in the rain. It was obvious, from the first moment they stood across from one another, that they were never meant to see one another again. Never meant to revisit the hot Texas summers, the wide barren plains, all that they'd wanted to escape.

He walked and walked, until he arrived at Lincoln Center. He sat at the edge of the fountain, looking up at the swooping reds and yellows of Chagall's enormous murals until both the opera and ballet let out.

From there, he went, finally, home. He pushed open the heavy, groaning door at the top of the brownstone stoop on West Sixty-Fourth Street and entered the apartment, crowded now with Darla's things, her books and clothes. Darla was in bed, pillows propped behind her, *Lake Wobegon Days* balanced on her chest. She reached for him. He went to her, took her hand, and leaned down to give her a kiss.

"You're freezing," she said, shuddering. "How was dinner?"

"Delicious."

"Where'd you go?"

"Kean's." The lie slipped off his tongue.

"What'd you have?" she asked, in a singsong voice.

"Uh ... the porterhouse."

"Oh, yum. Any leftovers?"

"No, sorry."

"You ate all of it?"

"I let Rob take the leftovers for Muffin."

"That's one spoiled pooch." She picked her book back up.

Two days later, they left for Montreal. Everything in the hotel room looked expectant. The enormous, carefully turned down bed, with a gold satin duvet plumped just so at its foot. A champagne bottle, its cork peeking out of the ice bucket like a bulging eye. A bud vase with a single red rose. It all felt like an attempt to rekindle something before their marriage had even started.

Darla was girlish, taking Cal's hand wherever they went. The first morning, they walked around the old town, down the cobblestone streets, past the squat three-hundred-year-old buildings, to the Saint Lawrence. They went to the famous Jean-Talon food market and tried everything from maple candies to pickles. And to Parc du Mont-Royal. They walked around McGill. Had lunch at a restaurant in the ground floor of a townhouse while a jazz trio played. Moose steaks for dinner in a quiet restaurant in the old quarter. They went to the art museum and St. Catherine's church. Everything just as Darla planned.

Nothing was wrong with any of it. Except Cal felt inert.

Back at the hotel, Darla lay on the bed, sinking into the satin duvet, her arms open for him. She was pretty and smart.

She knew where she'd come from and where she wanted to go, her life appeared seamless. And Cal had slipped right in. Their last night, they quietly made love before dinner.

Darla ordered a chocolate mousse for them to share. She reached her hand across the table. Cal took her slender fingers in his.

"Let's go dancing," she said, her eyes sparkling.

He demurred.

"Oh, come on," she prodded. "There's a club just a few blocks from here. It'll be fun."

"I don't dance," Cal said, scooping up a spoonful of rich chocolate.

"Everyone can dance," she answered.

"I didn't say I can't dance. I said I don't. I don't want to."

"Right. Sorry." She retracted her hand, straightened her engagement ring. Then waved to the waiter for the check.

As they walked back to the hotel, Cal reached for her hand and, wanting to want her, held it firmly in his own.

CHAPTER TWENTY-FOUR

Leni

Caleb D. McGrath is like a fish bone caught in her throat. For five days, Leni mulls over what to say, what not to say, were she to find him and say anything at all. She imagines countless conversations, eventually landing on ways to preserve the integrity of a decision she made back when she was a girl. What did she know? Other than to stay was untenable. She was a farm girl. Tough in some ways. She's gotten tougher still since then. It's not that she hadn't thought of Cal, and worried, and regretted. It was that thinking of him, of what she'd done, had been unbearable.

But then he stood, in the rain, at her door. Forcing her to resolve this in her mind again. At the end of five days, she sees something anew. In some ineffable, inevitable way, she did what was in her blood. What her mother had done. What Marguerite did. Hell, what Foy did. (But, no, that was different.) She left.

She doesn't resent the baby. Or regret the adoption. Because whatever she's done since then and whatever she has now is her very own.

There is something that nags at her, like she can't clear her throat. She can't let Cal think that she and Hank betrayed him.

Leni arrives at 570 Lexington Avenue at five-thirty on a Tuesday. Waves of dark suits, black pumps, and gray coats emerge from three large elevators, cross the smooth lobby, and pour out the revolving doors. Leni tightens the belt around her red plaid jacket and, like a salmon battling its way upstream, makes it through the spinning doors, slithers to the side, and rests against the cold marble wall, gathering her courage. She could have just made an appointment. But she doubts he would have agreed to see her. And she might well have lost her nerve waiting. She could have called. But this is a conversation she can barely envision having in person, and not at all on the phone.

She takes a deep breath, makes a dash for the closest elevator, when there he is. He sees her. Of course. White hair with spots, red coat. She knows he does. But he keeps walking. She crosses the lobby, dodging and weaving the scrum making its way to the doors.

The sinewy young cowboy she knew is gone. Well-fitting dark suit. Silk tie. It's not just the clothes and neat haircut. He has filled out. Maybe even grown an inch or two. Everything about him looks substantial. She catches up to him.

"Hi."

He threads his way into one of the revolving doors. She struggles through, and on the sidewalk pushes her way beside him again.

"Can we talk?"

He grimaces.

She just wants to explain what little she can. Then she'll go. They'll leave each other in peace. "Can I walk you to the subway, or something?"

He points across the street. She looks. A green number six subway sign stares back at her.

"I can't talk that fast," she says, sashaying beside him to keep up. "I'm from the South, remember?"

"I thought you were the one trying not to remember." His jaw tightens. He won't look at her.

They're swept south on Lexington Avenue. She can feel it now, how hard he's become, how much what she did hurt him.

"So," she matches his stride. "How's it going keeping the world safe for banking?"

"I'm not a banker."

"Right. Look." She's not one to give up, once she's decided on something. "I'm sorry about the other night." She stops in the middle of the sidewalk, forcing annoyed pedestrians to step aside.

Cal keeps walking.

"That's pretty much what I came here to say," she shouts after him, though that's not the half of what she came to say.

He looks back to her. "That was pretty fast." She catches up to him again. "You're sorry about the other night?" he says. "The other night was nothing."

A cab swerves in front of an uptown bus. Air brakes gasp. The bus's exhausted horn bleats like a goat.

He stops, finally. Looks at her. "Some things are unforgivable until you ask for forgiveness. That would have made a difference, you know."

"You're right." She's both nodding and shaking her head at the same time.

"I looked every day for a month for something, anything, from you. A note." He throws his hands up in the air, shakes his head, and starts walking again. "You're right. It doesn't matter."

"I didn't say it doesn't matter."

"Yes, you did."

Did she? "Of course it matters," she shouts. Then beside him again, "I don't know where to start, Cal."

"How about not falling in love with my brother?"

Leni clutches his coat sleeve and pulls him left, off Lexington Avenue, onto the less crowded cross street.

"You see. That's it. That's what I want to tell you. There was nothing between me and your brother. He helped me get out of town. That's all."

"Why did you have to get out of town?" He's looking not at her, but over her head.

"Because," she starts. Stops. Steps aside for a couple to pass. "Because. . ." She thought she'd rehearsed this enough to say it all straight up. She had to get away, from the town, from her crumbling family. She couldn't have gone with him, would only have held him back. Better that he hate her and have his life. And she'd have her life, too. But the way he's looking at her now—staring, actually, waiting, the whir and horns of traffic and the harried pedestrians pressing against her—she loses her way, knows what she'd rehearsed wouldn't be enough. What bubbles up is an untruth, of sorts. A factual untruth, but true at its core. Something that will—she hopes—set the real gist of it right: "I needed an abortion."

Cal's head rolls back as if he'd been punched in the jaw. "You were pregnant?"

Leni nods.

"You were on the pill."

She looks away. "That's what I told you. But I wasn't."

"Why didn't you tell me?"

Tears, old tears, sting her eyes. Her stomach tightens. She clenches her face hard, turning the tears back. "Because it would have kept you there. It would have kept both of us there."

"I would have done anything for you."

"Exactly." Her eyes lock onto his. "I know that. Knew that. You would have lost your scholarship. And I couldn't have stayed there." She shakes her head. Has to make him understand. "Alone with Maman? I couldn't."

"You got an illegal abortion?"

Leni looks away and nods.

"Hank helped you?"

She nods again.

"Was the baby his?"

"No!" She stares him square in the eyes. "He had to leave that night, remember? And he knew a place. And a place where I could stay, I mean could go."

"Where?"

"In Ohio." She feels back on some sort of solid ground. "He was the only person I knew who would know how to help."

"Ohio?"

She wants this to make sense, to answer something for him. "He took me to the couple he stayed with when he got out of the army."

"You and Hank stayed there." Cal resumes walking.

She senses the beginning of a softening in him. "No," she corrects him. "Hank gave me money and left first thing the next day. He wouldn't tell anyone where he was going. I never saw him again."

"You should have told me."

"I'm sorry."

"I'm sorry you went through that, Leni. Alone." He sounds disappointed. "You should have told me."

Knowing he would have stayed by her side no matter what presses against her heart.

They turn south on Third Avenue, walking side by side. The current of rush hour foot traffic carrying them toward Grand Central Station.

At Forty-Second Street, Leni pauses. "Are you heading home?" She points to the subway.

The light changes. He crosses Forty-Second Street and continues south. Leni follows.

Once through midtown, the skyscrapers give way to brick row houses. Small businesses—hardware stores, a doll hospital, delis and diners.

"Thank you for taking care of Foggy."

"My mother looked after her. Then Walter, after she died."

She was quiet, taking that in. "I'm sorry you lost your mother."

"Cancer," Cal said. "No surprise there, I guess." Hands in his pockets. "I sold Flint."

"You sold Flint?" Of course that makes sense, though it was hard to imagine Cal or Captain Flint without the other.

He nods. "Did Marguerite ever come back?"

"To Naples? Hell no. She landed in a commune in the hills east of San Diego. She's got two daughters. Lives near the coast now."

"She married?"

"No. Different dads. Do you know where Hank is?"

"Canada, I think. I don't know. It's better that I don't know. I heard your mother went back to France."

"Yeah, she did. Without giving my dad a divorce. Catholic, you know. She went to visit her cousin and aunt in Normandy and never came back."

"And your dad?"

"He sold the farm." The shame she felt during that time welled up. "You must have thought it was so ramshackle." She looked down, shaking her head.

"No, I didn't."

And she knew that was true. He wouldn't have judged her, or her family, over their modest house and barn. "He lives in town now. Still working." She last saw her father five years ago.

He was attending a conference in DC and she took the train down to meet him. They talk every couple of months, and on birthdays and Christmas.

"How'd you get to New York?" Cal asks, looking at her now.

She tells him about the scholarship from the University of Ohio, to study in Italy for six months, after which she came to New York.

"Is that when you changed your name?"

"No. Before. When I started school in Ohio."

As they walk, Leni lists the jobs she's had in New York—singing telegrams, waiting tables, cleaning stalls at the stables in Central Park—all the while painting and taking classes when she could afford to. She was even a carriage driver, taking tourists and couples, who mostly wanted to have sex undisturbed, through Central Park.

"I took that job actually thinking I could help the carriage horses. Make those poor animals a bit happier some little how. You can laugh, it's OK." Only she knew he wouldn't.

As evening falls around them, they walk like they're in their own column of air, their strides perfectly matched. They come to Gramercy Park, an island extracted from the rush of the City. Grand nineteenth century townhouses overlooking the wrought iron fence and the lush green park inside. She can feel how closely Cal is listening.

"If I had money," Leni says, "do you know what I'd do?" He waits. "I'd buy a hundred acres. I don't care where, so long as it's got good grass. And I'd rescue horses."

Cal smiles. His watching her walk makes her legs feel long and free.

"I still count strides," she says. "Like to that lamp pole. How many strides to round it."

"And sprint toward East Seventeenth Street."

"Exactly. To that red station wagon."

"Yeah. That's about where your second barrel would be." He smiles.

They walk on. A young mother, struggling with a double stroller, approaches. They move closer together, to give her room. Their shoulders meet. The touch makes clear again how much time has passed. He's a man.

"Tell me about your paintings." he says.

"Oh." She looks down, self-conscious suddenly. "I paint landscapes, kind of. Or dreamscapes, really. Landscapes the way I see them in my head. That's the best I can describe them." She doesn't want to say what he's made her see is also true. That she paints the past. "What about you? Tell me about you."

He doesn't answer right away. She glances at him, sideways. She thinks she sees a hollowness in him. Remembers that about him. The sense that he's still searching for something makes her sad. She'd thought, hoped, that getting out would set him on his course and fill that. Maybe always thinking like Cal did, and seems to do still, is bottomless.

"Well, I've been in New York for six years," he begins.

"I know that," Leni prods.

"I structure private real estate deals."

"More math than science, I guess?" Leni watches his face.

"Yes." He looks straight ahead. "Basically," he adds, his tone flat, "I'm the anchor to a visionary's balloon."

"What does that mean?" She wants to laugh, to bring some buoyancy, but she can't.

"It means I make sure my boss, who's a friend from college, keeps his feet on the ground, doesn't lie too much to clients or regulators, and makes money for us and our investors."

Leni nods, trying to understand. "I always thought you were a poet. A physicist. And a poet."

"This would be a very circuitous route to poetry." He smiles.

Anger or frustration thumps against her ribs. Hadn't she made sure that he had his chance? "Do you like it, what you're doing?" she asks, her tone a little sharp.

"I'm good at it," he says, hands diving into his pockets.

She wants to press. Doesn't know if she should. "That's not the same thing."

"Well, I like it enough to have majored in economics and gotten an MBA at Wharton," he says after a time.

She doesn't know where Wharton is. Doesn't ask.

They turn to Union Square Park, walk over its cracked cobblestones, past the bent and rusted metal fencing and the thirsty-looking linden trees. They pause at Fourteenth Street as buses grind past, and continue south onto Broadway where it bends east. Under the awning of the Strand Bookstore, they stop briefly to scan the racks spilling over with dollar paperbacks, and amble again south.

"Looks like I'm walking you home."

"You're still chivalrous," she says, smiling, reluctant to meet his eyes.

She wouldn't have chosen to see him again. If she were on a park bench and someone said, "Hey, look over there. It's Caleb McGrath," she would have caught her breath. Then stood and walked the other way.

Yet here he is standing in front of an old tenement house with its grimy fire escape, and dented metal door. She breathes in the spice of his cologne.

"Would you like to come up?"

Caleb

He followed Leni up four flights of stairs, watched her unlock three locks, nudge the door open with her shoulder, and flip a switch. Light from a bulb shaded by a pink and orange parasol casts a soft light on walls that were the gold of wildflower honey. The apartment wasn't more than eight paces wide and maybe fifty feet long. A third of the way in was a fabric screen, with leaves, pressed flowers and seedpods, shielding a full-sized mattress on a plywood platform. Just past the bed, were shelves with wire baskets of clothes. Beyond the shelves, two canvases hung on the white and paint-splattered wall, her studio space. Leni tossed her keys on a long table resting on sawhorses alongside the small kitchen.

Cal had never been in a space like this. Despite the wood floors, stained and scuffed, and the baseboard and trim that were patched and chipped, seemingly held together by a century of paint, the apartment glimmered. Carefully chosen objects arranged just so. Postcards on the wall above the kitchen counter like a large collage. Flimsy blue aerograms affixed with magnets to the squat, 1950s fridge. On the long table, a wooden carving of a hand; an assortment of old small bottles; a nest with bird's eggs; and a pile of sketchbooks.

And the paintings. Two, in progress, hung near one of the two windows. Cal walked closer and stood on the strip of plastic drop cloth tacked to the floor beneath her workspace.

She excused herself to the toilet, which was behind a bath-tub, and literally in a closet, near the other window that was largely obscured by metal grating. A makeshift shower curtain hung over the tub, painted in vertical bands of color: sage green, taupe, and heather blue. He thought he saw the soft shadow of a cow and her calf grazing in the foreground.

Leni reemerged, hung her jacket over one of the two metal chairs at the long table.

"I have some wine?"

"I don't drink." He watched her, gauging her reaction. A nod.

She turned to the sink, spun the squeaky faucet, let the water run across her wrist, then grabbed a kettle from the smallest stove Cal had ever seen, filled it, and set it back on one of the two burners. She pulled out a quart of milk, smelled it, and set it down on the counter that was crowded with coffee cans sprouting utensils, flatware, and paintbrushes.

"What's your fiancée's name?"

"Darla."

"Tell me about Darla." She struck a match and lit the burner.

"No." He eyed the sketchpads and books on the long table.

"Well," she turned to face him, hand on the counter. Challenging and apprehensive, both. "Where are we if we can't talk about the present?"

Maybe she had sewn back up whatever had torn way back then, any frayed edges now folded into the smooth contours of a life she'd made her own. But standing near her, Cal could feel again the gaping wound.

Leni went to the baskets of clothes near the bed, pulled out several items, and stepped behind the screen. Cal opened one of the sketchbooks on the table. Ink drawings. Still lifes. Fire escapes. Street corners. He closed that one, opened another. A series of pencil drawings. Most looked unfinished. A man. From the back. Sweatshirt. Short hair. Then several pages of quarter profiles, mostly the back of his head. Unfinished. He flipped through more pages. A three-quarter face now. A young man. Eyes cast slightly away. The beginnings of a smile. He turned the page. Another and another. An entire book of the same face. Unmistakable. Different angles. Different clothes. Altered expressions. In pencil or charcoal.

Foy.

She stepped out from behind the screen. He closed the book, pushed it back beneath the others.

The kettle whistled. Leni, long bare-footed strides to the stove, flipped the burner off.

"Coffee or tea?" she asked.

She'd changed into a white T-shirt, loose-fitting argyle cardigan, and black pants that swirled around her ankles as she moved.

"Um, tea."

"I have—" She opened one of the two cupboards above the sink.

"Anything's fine."

"OK. Mint it is." She grabbed a mug from the drying rack.

Cal walked around the table to the area where she painted. "Do you show your work often?" he asked.

She set the kettle back down.

"No." She turned around. "I mean, sometimes. I don't know. Not really."

Cal surveyed her work area, the two canvases hung on the wall. There was a small rolling cabinet with two drawers and a shelf with cans of brushes and paint cleaner. There were the other paintings leaning against the wall. And between the windows was a wide cabinet with shallow drawers for storing drawings.

She handed Cal the mug of tea.

"How do you know if something's a painting or a drawing?" he asked.

"Oh. Well." She rubbed a jaguar spot, thinking. "For me, painting is when you know something. Drawing is for when you're still figuring it out. Does that make sense?"

He nodded, blew on the tea.

"Mostly I'm still trying to figure things out, I guess." She gathered some small, misshaped tubes of paint and tossed them in the top drawer of the rolling cabinet. "I do a lot of site-specific pieces, a performance or exhibit here and there," she said, still tidying up. Pencils in a Campbell's soup can on the bottom shelf, an eraser and box cutter in the second drawer.

"I rarely have people to the studio," she said with some finality.

"Why not?" he asked.

"Because I don't like to be judged."

"It's a harsh world."

"Yes, it is."

"Can't escape that," he said.

"Yes, you can. Sometimes." She looked back at him.

Those green eyes still so liquid and deep. He had gone, he realized, with barely a thought of Darla in the two hours they'd been together.

"Why am I here?" he asked.

She studied him. "I think," she said carefully, "to bring us, the past, into the present." She resumed straightening up. Brought a glass and plate from the long table to the sink, put away the glasses from the dish rack, snatched a sweater from the back of a chair and folded it, haphazardly, in the air as she walked over to put it away.

"Into the present how?" he asked.

She shrugged her shoulders and crouched down to pick up a pencil from the floor.

"There you are," she said happily. Leni stretched her arms under the table and pulled out a short-haired tabby cat, who took one look at Cal, jumped from Leni's arms, and scooted behind the screen onto the bed.

"I'm a little offended." He gestured toward the vanished cat.

"I'd stick with horses, if I were you." She smiled.

He couldn't tell in that moment, beneath the gaze of her green eyes, snippets of chaparral floating about them, to what extent she'd always been with him. Steering choices he'd made in some subterranean way.

Leni went to the stack of canvases leaning against the wall, flipped through a couple, gazed at one, then another. Finally she pulled out a fourth, went to the wall, and balanced the wood stretcher on an available hook.

"Well?" she asked.

He'd been looking at her, not the painting. He took a step closer. He didn't know how to assess art, something Darla wasn't shy about reminding him. But he looked, took in its dreamy sense of space. He liked the lighter mix of colors above darker, denser colors below. It was quiet. Cool. Pleasing. He took another step closer, and he could see there were layers of color—blues over strata of greens over browns along the bottom, the remnants or shadow of words etched beneath brushstrokes of color. He didn't ask what the words said. Reading them clearly wasn't her intent.

She removed one painting from the wall, took another from the stack and hung it. The brushstrokes were more apparent. A band of darker color lay across the top like clouds rolling in.

It was Texas. Between the creeks. The chaparral. The wide sky and approaching storms.

"They're beautiful, Leni."

"You don't have to say that."

He continued to gaze at the canvas. Something in him softened, as though something in him that had been foundering had found a place to rest.

"So," she clapped her hands, tossing Cal back into whatever the moment was. "I've got a thing downtown."

"Aren't we downtown?"

"More downtown." She laughed. "I'm helping a friend. I worked on sort of a mural. A couple of banners, really. Captions," she mumbled.

He didn't want to say goodbye. Not yet. "Captions. Like Barbara Kruger?"

"Look at you! Mr. Uptown."

He'd picked up a few names from Darla.

She swept crumbs off the kitchen counter into her palm, dropped them in the sink. "You can come. If you want." She twirled a scarf around her neck.

He wasn't sure she meant it. But he accepted the offer. "Can I borrow your phone?"

She pointed to a phone on the wall near the fridge and tactfully stepped away.

Something's come up, he told Darla. No need to wait up.

Leni

Leni locks the metal door behind them, takes two swift strides, stops and rakes through her bag, making sure the sewing kit's there in case she needs it, and starts off again.

"Where are we going exactly?" Cal asks, keeping up.

"SoHo. Broome and Centre Street."

"What's there?"

"An empty lot."

"You're being a little cryptic," he prods.

"Sorry."

She's not keen on sharing more information. And not sure why. Maybe she shouldn't have asked him to come along.

"That's all right. This is kind of like a vacation." He walks sprightly on.

"I don't know about that."

"I'm used to planning for every possible outcome. This will be just having an experience." He pauses. "I like it."

SoHo east of Broadway is deserted after dark. Leni leads them down Broadway, then back over to Broome. A block or two out of the way, but a safer route at night. The storefronts are dark, but most of the streetlights are still working.

The vacant lot at Broome Street is bounded on two sides by five-story brick warehouses. Their aging windowless walls give the asphalt lot a prison yard feel. A red Chevy is parked, or abandoned, alongside one wall. A corner street lamp lights a cone-shaped path into the lot, reaching a raised plywood platform.

A couple dozen people have gathered on the sidewalk watching Eric and a few others hurriedly unfurl cables and secure speakers the size of armchairs on each end of the platform. Leni quickly introduces Cal to Tamara, who wears a bodice-gripping lime green dress and stiletto heels, and Leonard, who is indeed wearing a kaleidoscopic-patterned parachute-cloth jumpsuit (Leni thought he was joking about that). Tamara and Leonard struggle to attach enormous rolls of fabric, which Leni and Tamara have painted, to ropes strung over the tops of two twenty-foot-tall extension ladders.

"I have to help out," Leni says. She feels late, and guilty. "With the banners," she half-explains.

"I'll wait over there." Cal points to an empty loading dock across the street. "Unless I can help?"

Leni promises to find him when she's finished and jogs over to Eric, who's yelling at two guys Leni doesn't know, trying to get the speakers at the right angle. It's guerrilla art. There's never enough time to set up properly. At least Eric's grapevine is long and well-established. Word definitely got out. People are filtering in from both streets.

"Whoa, whoa, whoa!" Leonard screams. One of the ladders begins to tilt, catches the banner, tearing it. "Fuck!" he yells.

Leni mends the tear in the banner, while Tamara paces in front of the ladders, sucking on a cigarette. A commotion at the corner takes their attention. Three women have appeared. Like the witches from *Macbeth*, in oversized black capes, their faces painted white, their lips black, they move as a unit. When they reach the stage, Leonard greets each with a hug.

Leni finishes her mending. The speakers are in place. The ropes finally secured over the extension ladders. Two hundred people, at least, now stand in front of the stage and more are arriving. Four drag queens float in off Broome Street. Sequin gowns and fur wraps. Platform shoes the size of cinder blocks. High hair. They seem alien, reminiscent of a cubist painting. And proud. From the ground behind the makeshift stage, Leni can't see to the loading dock where Cal was waiting. She wonders if he's been scared off yet.

Eric, connecting the last cable for the speakers, admonishes all of them to get ready. Tamara scurries to the back of the stage, stands beside Leni. Leonard does jumping jacks in place and cannonball breaths. Warming up. Then he crouches down and opens his guitar case.

At the signal from Eric, Leni and Tamara hoist the sheet of fabric, like a sail up the wall behind the stage.

"SILENCE KILLS. PRESIDENT REAGAN, LISTEN UP."

Everyone in the crowd fumbles in their pockets. As though a fuse is wending its way through the crowd, candles and lighters are lit and thrust into the air. Leni and Tamara secure the ropes holding the fabric.

Leonard throws his guitar strap over his shoulder. Eric cranks the amp. Distorted chords slice the air, slam into the brick and asphalt, and ricochet back into the crowd. The noise draws more people out from the neighboring buildings and in from the street.

Leni and Tamara grab two ten-foot poles from the ground. They step onto the back of the stage. Raise the poles high. As they walk away from each other, another banner unfurls with a likeness of Edvard Munch's *The Scream*. Two men step up, take the banner, and hold it up higher. Swaying it back and forth.

The three witches now step onto the stage. They pull drums from their capes and start an incantatory drumming beneath the throbbing guitar riffs. The vibrations travel through Leni's body. Five men emerge from the crowd and, with help, step onto the platform. Leni steps off the stage. She looks for Cal. But the crowd, getting thicker, moves in closer, blocking her view.

The five men gingerly strip off their jackets and shirts. They are as thin as stalks, ghastly thin, their bodies wasting away from AIDS. Another banner is unfurled: "25,000 DEAD. 50,000 MORE DYING."

The guitar and drumming continue. More candles held aloft. The shirtless men raise their arms and circle in place in a slow, macabre dance as two police cars pull up. Blue and red lights circle silently. Four policemen emerge and walk like gunslingers toward the crowd, which—quite remarkably—parts, opening a path to Leonard, the three swaying black-clad drummers, and the skeletal dancers on the makeshift stage. One of the shirtless dancers is handed a bullhorn.

"Your son or daughter, brother or sister, could be next," the man shouts at the police through the bullhorn, his voice quivering, but the words unmistakable. "You know it's true. Your son or daughter, brother or sister, could be next."

The police try to quiet the crowd. "This is an unlawful gathering," one of them says through a bullhorn of his own, to a roar of "Boo!"

Moments later a white van arrives. Two men get out, one shouldering a film camera. The other shadows him, cords draped over one arm, a microphone in the other. They walk into the crowd, some of whom have begun to chant, "We Are Your Sons and Daughters, Brothers and Sisters. We Are Your Sons and

Daughters, Brothers and Sisters," while others thrust themselves in front of the camera, shouting and waving their arms.

Two of the policemen retreat to their car, presumably to call for backup. Leni joins Tamara. They dip large brushes into a gallon of red paint and splatter it against the towering white sheet behind the stage. Sirens whirl closer as red paint, viscous as blood, drips down the banner. A police car pulls up on Centre Street. Then a police van on Broome.

Police emerge from the van like it's a clown car. Except they have shields and helmets and billy clubs. They line up, two men thick, around the corner, and stand. Implacable as lead.

"This is an unlawful assembly," the policeman with the bullhorn shouts again, "and a disruption of the peace." This, of course, only causes more of a disruption. The guitar screeches, the chants roar.

"You must disperse," the policeman tries again. "You must disperse."

Leni lays down her brush. She looks for Cal. The loading dock is empty.

Some in the crowd scurry like mice as the police with their shields raised and visors lowered press in. Others stand their ground. A few taunt the police. Leni stays on the stage. She sees Cal now, jogging down Broome Street toward the stage. He waves for her to come to him. She shakes her head. Waves him away. She knows getting arrested would jeopardize his work. She shouts for him to leave, knowing he can't hear her.

As some in the crowd converge toward the police, Cal slips in, coming to her.

"You go! Go!" she shouts.

He looks forlorn. Confused and worried.

She scans the lot. Some are leaving. The crowd is getting smaller. Tamara, paintbrush in hand and shouting, moves toward the police, or toward the news camera, it's hard to tell which.

Leonard and the skeletal dancers, the witches and the queens and dozens more, continue chanting. Cal reaches Leni.

"I'm not leaving you!" he shouts. "This will all be on TV." He points to the cameraman and soundman. "Getting arrested won't get you any more publicity." He looks worried, for her?

Leni scans the crowd as Tamara approaches, arms outstretched.

"We did it!" she grabs Leni in a hug, smearing red paint across Leni's T-shirt. "National TV, baby!" She totters back onto the stage in her stiletto heels.

Cal extends his hand. Leni takes it.

The crowd has thinned, but the taunting and chanting, bullhorns and drumming continue. They slip out onto Broome Street and jog, hand in hand, away from the crowd. At West Broadway, the cacophony now a rumble, they walk.

"Thank you for a most memorable evening."

"Wow," Leni chuckles. "You're welcome."

"So you do this kind of thing often?"

"'Happenings?' When I'm asked."

"Who paid for all that?"

"Who pays? Good question. It used to be grants. But that's drying up. Someone'll have extra money from selling a piece. Or a gig. Or a trust fund."

"So you're not completely opposed to the marketplace."

"Ah, well. Art and commerce is a tricky mix."

"And worlds collide," Cal says.

"We're protesting the 'establishment,' remember?" She smirks at him, eyebrows raised.

"Is your work a protest?"

"No." She lets her hand slip from Cal's.

"Did I offend you?" he asks. "I didn't mean to. I like your paintings. Very much."

"No."

But he's pricked something. She still feels an outsider. Even among all these outsiders. Except for Eric, whom she gifted one painting, these "friends" don't know the work she does at home, in her studio. The sketches, the drawings, the paintings. They know little about her. Haven't asked. And she hasn't offered. It's like she stands on a lily pad. She jumps to shore, a happening here or an obscure exhibit there, with artists pushing boundaries in every direction, then back to her lily pad where she works, alone, late into the night.

Except on this night, Cal, in some strange way, has connected these two worlds.

"Want to get a bite to eat?" she asks.

"I shouldn't."

"Right," she says quickly, jumping back to her lily pad. There's a fiancée somewhere uptown.

They walk.

"See me again," he says.

CHAPTER TWENTY-FIVE

Caleb

Cal paced back and forth in front of the side entrance to the Plaza Hotel across from Central Park. She was late. He'd been very clear. Thursday (when Darla would be at a conference in Philadelphia). Ten p.m. There was something he wanted her to see, he'd said. She was skeptical, but he was insistent and, finally, she had agreed.

He had to keep moving, trying to dodge an arrow: dejection, like he hadn't felt since the end of high school and college.

At ten-thirty, he turned to consoling himself: it was for the best; this had been a bad idea; a lapse in judgment. Running into Leni again had been a test, an opportunity to banish the nostalgia he'd been living under without even really knowing it, so he could start his life with Darla with a clean slate. It was time to acknowledge the life he'd worked hard for. So what if it didn't comport with the dreams he concocted as a teenager, so what if instead he was just amassing wealth like his father? How many boys grow up to be firemen or astronauts? He thought he had grown up. But he'd been living with one foot in his life, at work and with Darla, and one foot suspended above the ground. It was time, truly, to grow up. Be a husband. One day soon, a father.

Rounding what would be his last lap along Fifty-Ninth Street, there she was.

"Wo-ow—" She gave him the once-over. "You're a preppy."

A smile spread across his face. "You're definitely not."

Leni fanned her arms wide, looked down over her well-worn leather jacket to the tight black velvet pants and thick-soled boots, then sized up Cal's L.L. Bean duck boots, creased khakis, and sixty-forty jacket.

"I used to have this dream," she said, "that I'd be walking down the street and all of a sudden, like someone had cast a spell on me, I'd be in clothes that I'd never wear in a million years. White go-go boots with fringe and really big hair. Or a pink velour jumpsuit and aqua blue eye shadow. And I'd have to go through my day—as me—but in these clothes that belonged to another person entirely." She sized up Cal again, cocked her head. "Can I call you Biff?"

"I'd prefer not." He felt chastised.

"Let's get a drink." Leni started for the dark side entrance to the Plaza.

"No." His tone was more insistent than he intended.

"Oh, of course. I'm so sorry."

He shook his head. "There's just not time."

Hotel guests ogled her jaguar spots, the shiny velvet pants.

"Not time. Not time for what?"

"Just come with me." He took her hand, felt her resistance. "Please. I want to show you one thing and then you decide."

A clutch of babbling, brightly dressed tourists passed in front of them. A Bentley idled at the curb. And across the street, a line of horse-drawn carriages extended from the statue of General Sherman at Fifth Avenue west along Central Park South, past broken streetlights. The dark moonless night stretched above them.

"A carriage ride? Really?" She was incredulous. "Weren't you listening? You used to be such a good listener."

He walked resolutely west on Fifty-Ninth Street, ignoring her protests, his hand tight around hers, and stopped at the top of Seventh Avenue. There a pickup truck, hitched to an empty two-horse trailer, crouched across the street, beyond any streetlight's reach. Seventh Avenue ended at the park, which was closed to traffic. There shouldn't be any cars coming down Seventh, especially this time of night.

Leni stared at the trailer. "Oh, my God. You're kidding."

"It's 'a happening,'" he said.

"This is completely nuts."

He couldn't blame her for deciding that rustling carriage horses was a most foolhardy gesture and leaving. And he'd likely never see her again. He waited.

"What's our story? If we're caught." Hands to her hips, contemplating.

"We don't have one."

She nodded and looked, squinting, across Fifty-Ninth Street, then down Seventh Avenue.

"These guys don't own their horses, right? That's what I've read," Cal said.

"A few do. They won't be the ones out here this late on a weeknight."

Cal watched Leni stare at the trailer, an apology forming on his lips. Then she pushed the sleeves of her jacket to her elbows.

"OK then. What's the plan, Captain?"

Cal opened the pickup's door and grabbed two brand-new nylon halters and lead ropes he'd bought at Miller's Saddle Shop on Twenty-Fourth Street. Taking Leni's hand, he jogged with her across Fifty-Ninth Street and, staying close to the wall that borders the park where it's darkest, started back toward the traffic circle at Fifth Avenue and the line of carriages.

The night was clear and crisp. No moon (luckily), but a lovely night for a ride through the park. Eight drivers were gathered, talking, near the park entrance at Fifth Avenue, their harnessed horses strung lazily along Fifty-Ninth Street, heads low, dozing. They watched a carriage leave off the front of the line. Two of the drivers standing by the park's entrance returned to their carriages, led their horses forward, then rejoined the other drivers at the head of the line. The rest let their horses and carriages stay where they were. One driver, in a tall hat and topcoat, a good sixty feet between him and the next carriage, stayed put, under a streetlight, thumbing a tabloid.

"That's Jerry," Leni said softly. "Dumb as a post."

They approached the horse at the rear of the line, a chestnut mare with eyes half-shut, one rear leg cocked, hoof balanced on the toe. Leni approached her, one eye on the drivers. Cal circled around into the street. The mare didn't flinch as they began to unhitch her. Cal led the mare out of the harness, turned her around, and started for the trailer. Leni jogged ahead. At the trailer, she let the tailgate down and stood to the side.

"'At-a girl," Leni said softly, patting the mare's solid rump. "'At-a girl . . .'"

The mare followed Cal up the ramp and into the trailer, docile as a lamb. He hoisted a bag of hay up in front of her. She snatched a bite. Leni snapped the tail-piece into place. Piece of cake.

They jogged back across Fifty-Ninth Street. Sirens whirred in the distance, it was hard to know exactly where. The horse now at the back of the line was a big, sway-backed bay. Cal stroked his nose and started to unbuckle the girth and breeching strap.

"Wait." Leni gasped.

Cal stopped, straightened up, stuffed the halter and lead under his jacket. Footsteps approached. A group of friends passed, not paying Leni and Cal any attention. Cal resumed fumbling with the harness.

"No, wait." Leni whispered again. The sirens blasted. Closer this time, coming down Fifth Avenue. "That one," Leni pointed. "It's Herman." The next carriage down, six or seven behind Jerry (still reading his newspaper), was a huge black horse with hooves like moon boots and a forelock clipped so short it stood up straight between his ears.

"Herman Munster," she whispered, flummoxed that he hadn't put two and two together.

"No," Cal shook his head. "We've got to take this one at the end of the line."

"Please, Cal. We have to take Herman."

Against his better judgment, he redid the girth and straps on the bay's harness and started toward Herman.

Leni skipped along the sidewalk, got to Herman, and began unhitching the harness. Cal leaned his cheek against Herman's thick shoulder as he undid the breast collar. They quickly handed straps of leather back and forth and unlaced the reins through the terrets. The familiar smell of horse, sweat and grain and earth, was reassuring.

The sirens sounded again, sharper and closer still. Cal slipped the stiff halter over Herman's ears and took hold of the lead rope. The first carriage was moving forward. Some of the drivers would be returning any minute. Leni jogged ahead.

Cal turned the massive horse into the street toward the trailer, which was a good hundred feet away. Herman's hooves on the asphalt seemed to ring like gongs and Cal knew again that this was a terrible mistake. The sirens circled off Fifth Avenue and blared toward them. Cal glanced down the street. Two fire engines and an ambulance, lights whirling, sirens jabbing the air, barreled toward them. Cars heading east toward Fifth Avenue weren't pulling over. Another blast from the first engine. It was so loud, Cal felt like his head was inside a bell. Herman jerked his nose into the air.

"Whoa, steady there." Cal tried to calm the big horse. "Steady, boy," he said again.

The only person, ironically, who would have possibly understood what Cal was doing was Rob. He'd have to fire Cal anyway for a felony. And the one who would never understand was Darla. Any second Cal was going to be flattened by either a marauding fire engine or a panicking draft horse. He hoped that Herman would at least get away, even if it was just for ten minutes, into Central Park, to remember—and if he never actually had it himself, it must be somewhere in his horse subconsciousness—what it was like to stand on soft earth, with space and grass and trees around him.

A siren and air horn blasted beside Cal. Herman shook his head and broke into a trot. The siren of the second engine blared past them. They were thirty feet from the corner. The ambulance roared up. Herman was trying harder to shake Cal off. The ambulance passed. Herman was mad and scared. Cal had no idea how they'd get him in the trailer.

Leni was at the tailgate. Cal crossed the street shouting, "Go! You go!"

"What?!" she cried.

Herman was sidestepping into Seventh Avenue. Cal slapped the horse's ribs hard with the end of the lead rope. Herman took a clumsy step toward the curb. "Go. Now," Cal told Leni again. "I never should have gotten you into this."

"Are you kidding? We got this!" she stood beside the tailgate, ready to usher Herman in.

She held out her arms to keep him from stepping past the

tailgate to the sidewalk and began singing to the big horse, "That's it, big guy. That's it . . ." He took a hesitant step toward the ramp. Leni kept up her sweet patter.

Cal stood at Herman's shoulder and tickled his ribs with the lead rope. Herman lowered his head, sniffed the trailer, let out a snort, like he was thinking, "What kind of trick is this?" and threw his head in the air.

"Give him here." Leni reached for the lead rope. Cal passed it to her. She walked to the top of the ramp, clicked her tongue, luring the horse inside. He sniffed the trailer some more.

"Get up there, get up." Cal slapped the wall of horse rump. The mare poked the bag of hay with her nose. Herman snorted and lunged into the trailer. Leni gasped.

"Leni!"

"I'm fine!" She was laughing. "Let's go!"

Cal snapped the tail-piece in, raised the tailgate, slid the bolt on either side into place, and jumped in the driver's side door. Leni hopped out the front of the trailer and into the truck, smiling ear to ear.

"I'm dropping you at the subway," Cal said. "You get lost in the crowd."

"Like hell you are. We're not exactly Bonnie and Clyde. It's going to be OK. I can feel it." She slapped the dashboard. "Go!"

Her eyes burned straight ahead, blazing their trail. Cal pulled slowly from the curb, heading south as more sirens veered toward them, then away, swaying north around Columbus Circle and up Central Park West to join the others.

"Where are we going?"

"Right now, the Lincoln Tunnel," Cal answered.

It had been fourteen years since he'd driven a horse trailer and driving in east Texas wasn't much like driving in midtown Manhattan.

Approaching Tenth Avenue on Fifty-Seventh Street, the trailer suddenly jolted and swayed, tugging on the pickup. Of course, they had no idea if Herman and the mare would get along. One of them kicked the tailgate. Leni and Cal held their breath, looked at each other.

"I don't think they can get at each other," Leni said. "I tied their lead ropes pretty tight."

The trailer jerked to the right again. They listened. The horses quieted down. And in fourteen minutes, they were sandwiched between two tractor trailers, rolling into the Lincoln tunnel.

"Whoo-hoo!" Leni yelled. Then again, "Whoo-hoo! It feels good to holler." She slapped her thigh. "OK, Captain. Our final destination?"

Cal had found a small farm animal rescue center in New Jersey, near the Pennsylvania border. An older couple with thirty acres. He was a semi-retired veterinarian.

"You're amazing." Leni said.

He could feel her smile beneath his ribs. *I love you*, he wanted to say.

"I'm starving," Leni announced.

"Look in there." Cal pointed to a small insulated bag on the floor. She pulled it out and set it on the seat between them.

"You think of everything, Caleb McGrath. You always thought of everything." She began to unwrap a sandwich. "Peanut butter on Wonder bread! Mountain Dew and Fanta!" She folded her long legs on the seat, twisted toward Cal, and kissed his cheek.

Well past the sprawl of New Jersey's industrial corridor, Route 78 reached out into farmland. Cal continued to scan the mirrors and even the sky, expecting to be followed, but all was quiet. Leni gave up trying to find a decent radio station and turned it off.

"I miss space," she said, peering into the darkness. "You convince yourself when you're in New York that it's not important. That the energy from colliding with each other like neutrons or whatever they are, or we are, is worth it."

That metaphor felt like a reaching for him. He held out his hand. She took it.

"I'm not always sure, though," she said.

It was one in the morning when they reached the farm. A floodlight showed the way to a large red barn at the bottom of a hill. An old stone farmhouse at the top was dark. Cal had told the couple that he would be arriving late, which didn't concern them. He wasn't the only one to somewhat surreptitiously rescue overburdened animals. An emaciated former racehorse, an abandoned foal, and once a Dutch Belted cow with a gunshot wound to her flank had all turned up in the middle of a night. Herman and the mare were, as far as Cal could tell, just aged and weary. Proof of ownership wasn't required. They were a charity. The only money exchanged was a donation to help with the horses' upkeep.

Cal pulled up beneath the light of the barn. The wide sliding doors were open. The only sound was the occasional rustling of straw in one stall or another.

He'd been instructed to leave the horses in a small paddock to the left of the barn. Two piles of fresh hay were laid out, the water tub full. They led the horses in and slid off their halters. Heads high, they each scanned their new surroundings. Herman gave a snort. And that was that. They ambled off, without a glance of thanks, to the hay at the edge of the light.

Leni slipped her arm around Cal's waist. Her slender body against his.

"Thank you," she said.

"You're welcome." He laid his arm across her shoulders.

"Herman and the mare thank you, too," she added.

"I don't think they much care." He guessed this shouldn't have surprised him.

The horses nudged their piles of hay and munched. Leni and Cal climbed the wooden fence and sat side by side. It felt easy. Like one of them had merely been on a very long trip and they were back where they belonged, watching horses.

"They don't look much like Foggy or Flint, do they?"

"No, they don't," Cal agreed.

"I guess we look pretty different, too." She chuckled.

"Only that you're even more beautiful."

He watched her smile fade. She stared at the horses. Cal lingered on the soft angles of her face, the curve of her jaw, the little scar above her eye—all just as he remembered. He didn't regret what he'd said.

"I'm sorry," she began, looking out into the darkness still, "that I hurt you." She paused, began drawing a pattern on her velvet pants with one finger. "I'm sorry I didn't see another way to have handled it." She paused again.

"I'm sorry that you didn't think you could tell me, and that you went through all that alone." He wanted to reach for her hand, but she'd clasped them in her lap.

"We all scattered like pool balls. My dad the only one who stayed in place. Marguerite in California. Maman in France. Hank Junior wherever. You and me . . .," she trailed off.

"Both in New York."

"Yeah, how about that."

"Did you want to be found?" he asked.

"I didn't think so." She looked up to the dark sky. "But I think I was wrong." She turned to Cal.

A whisper of moonlight circled the barn and shone across her lips. He kissed her. Her soft lips, both familiar and unfamiliar.

Perched on the fence, suspended in the night air, she kissed him back.

The receptionist at the motel up the road, with two unlit letters in its sign, was dozing in an armchair. She roused herself just enough to check them in.

As Cal fumbled with the room key, Leni threaded her hands, so warm, inside his shirt. Her belly against the small of his back, cheek against his shoulder, one thigh pressed his forward, then the other. They entered the room already moving as one.

Cal switched on the overhead light. They blinked and squinted. Laughing, he took her face in his hands and kissed her.

"Wait," she pressed her fingers to his lips.

What do they say in AA, "Don't give up before the miracle"? He'd held on to his sobriety. Through college and grad school, his first job, and this one. Through moves and loneliness. He didn't remember the burst of enthusiasm that others talked about, life blooming into Technicolor once they'd shaken off their dependence on booze. For him, everywhere he went, in every room, even the outdoors, the light remained just a little dim, the voltage a little low. He'd gotten used to it, as one gets used to a low-grade fever. Grown accustomed to life under a shadow, as though some great predator bird were following, flying high above him wherever he went.

Leni slid her fingers down his chin and neck and slipped free of his arms. She went to the bathroom and returned with a towel, which she draped over the lampshade on the bedside table and turned it on. Cal switched off the overhead light. Leni sat on the bed. The light—soft now, shimmering and luminous—grazed the tiny gold hoops climbing her ear. She let her jacket drop to the floor, pried one boot off with her toes, then the other, and began to unbutton her pants.

Cal laid her back against the pillows, scooped her legs onto the bed. She opened her arms, her legs, and he lowered himself gently toward her, felt her chest rise, then melt back with each breath. Her thighs squeezed just below his ribs, her hips rising to meet him.

He sat up as she pushed his jacket off his shoulders, unbuttoned the top buttons of his shirt, and pulled it off over his head. Cal lifted her shirt. Her skin, pale and smooth, stretched across her ribs as she arched her back up, pressing into his hands. Her breasts. He remembered the feel of them in his hands. Pulling her pants off, kissing the inside of her thighs, her sighs, sharp intakes of breath. Longing and despair, rediscovery and reunion. She sidled beneath him. Her long limbs pulsed him toward her. She guided him inside her. Everything melted into touch. Time bridged. He shuddered and came.

Cal woke, Leni nestled in his arms. She slithered around to face him, her thigh sliding over his, then she was on top. They made love again.

After a shower, slippery, soapy hands over every inch of each other's body, they got dressed, closed the door on the stained carpet, scuffed baseboard, dull beige walls and bedspread, and emerged into the harsh light of the morning.

At breakfast, they denied themselves nothing. Pancakes, bacon and sausage, eggs, toast, juice, and coffee. They returned the trailer and truck to the rental company just off the highway and picked up Cal's BMW.

It was a clear day and warmer than it had been. The sky bright blue, the fields green and lush. Heading east on Route 202, Leni fished in the glove compartment for a piece of paper and a pen.

"What are you writing?"

"You'll see."

"No, really," his first thought—a slap, chest clenching—was a letter to Darla. "What are you writing?"

"Wait a minute . . ." She crossed something out, wrote some more, then read: "'To whom it may concern—and had you been more concerned, this likely would not have transpired—the two carriage horses who escaped their enslavement last night are now safely retired from their dreary lives as beasts of burden. They send their regards to their former fellow captives. Signed, The Benevolent St. Francis of Assisi Order of Equine Liberation.' What do you think?" She was very pleased with herself.

"Sounds pretty radical."

"This was pretty radical, Cal. Especially for you." She laughed. "There are a lot more animals to rescue. I can make us masks and capes."

He smiled, knowing the rescue was a one-off.

"I guess getting indicted wouldn't be such a good career move, would it?" Leni asked.

"Not so much."

He reached for Leni's hand. She took his, squeezed hard. She was real. This was real. He took in her profile, the puff of dyed white hair. The black leather. Her strong grip. How could one person be both so tough and so soft and open in his arms.

"What do you think," she began, paused, looked out the window at the passing fields, "Foy would be? If he'd lived."

Cal didn't answer right away. He slid back to a time with his friend, frozen in perfect form, the memory of him polished by time. His smile. His even temper. His refusal to let anybody down.

"I think," Cal began slowly, "whatever Foy decided to do, he would have been successful. He'd be respected. And happy. I think he would have had a good marriage and been a good father." Leni, still staring out the window, is nodding. "And I think he would have been a sports journalist."

"You do?" she seemed pleased at this.

"Yeah, I really do."

"Do you think he would have stayed in Naples?"

"Texas, for sure. He wasn't a wanderer. He wasn't restless. But I think he'd go to a bigger market than Naples."

"Dallas?" she asks.

He was surprised at the authority she seemed to be giving him.

"Fort Worth," he clarified.

"Yes. That makes more sense." She stared out the window again.

"This feels good." She turned to Cal. "I don't talk about him. Ever. I think it's that I can't risk anything about him being misunderstood. If that makes any sense."

It did. Because that was how he'd always felt about her.

"You know who else I can't talk about?"

Will it be him?

"Foggy," she said.

His disappointment was fleeting, because he understood that, too.

"Are they OK, do you know? Foggy and Flint?"

He told her all he knew. That Walter took Foggy in after his mother died. One of his granddaughters did a little barrel racing on her. That one of the Moore's cowboys bought Flint. He'd be retired now.

"It hurts to think of her, Foggy."

As they squeezed through the Holland Tunnel, Cal gripped the steering wheel of his car feeling the full constricting weight of his life. So many of their stories—his and Leni's—were stories of premature loss. Their brothers, their horses, each another. Early, unanticipated loss saturated their lives. How they navigated that, what bargains they negotiated with themselves and the world set their courses in life. Maybe Cal had driven a terrible bargain. He'd given up his dreams, punished himself for the yearning, in return for what? Money? Control? Validation? Leni seemed to stare life more squarely in the eye, with less bargaining.

They inched east on Canal Street, an eighteen-wheeler in front of them, its air brakes gasping, and an impatient taxi behind honking uselessly. Cal felt Leni's energy change. She ran her hand along the leather bucket seat.

"I don't want you. . . ." She paused, looked out on the grimy tangle of streets converging at the mouth of the tunnel. "I don't want you to look back and think this—last night, or anything of us—was a mistake."

"You've never been a mistake, Leni." He reached for her hand.

"Wait." She squeezed his hand hard. "I should have told you the truth."

They crawled forward another ten feet. "I thought you left to be with Hank. All these years, that's what I thought."

"No, no. It wasn't that." She was adamant.

"It's OK. I know that now."

She started to speak again.

He stroked her arm, then her cheek. She quieted, leaned her face into his palm. "We took our own paths," he said. "And here we are." She nodded, forehead furled, beginning to speak. But he didn't need to hear anything more. "It's all right now, Leni. It is."

"You know there's little I'd like more than to see you again," she said. "But—"

"No 'buts.'" She tried to interject. "No 'buts,'" he repeated, insisted.

C al watched Darla circle the living room, gnawing her finger-nails. He stayed in the doorway, out of her way.

Of course he knew Darla would be angry and hurt. Seeing her angry now, for the first time, was still a little startling and confirmed how limited their experience of one another had been. They'd contained themselves so neatly. He suspected this wasn't a conscious choice. It just took time and experiences, some under pressure, to know a person. In many ways, not unimportant, their days had simply rolled too smoothly forward. Until now.

"What do you mean you still love her? You were like, thirteen!" she shrieked.

"Eighteen," he corrected, retreating to facts.

Her arm flailed as she circled in front of the sofa, sending a vase of flowers on the end table crashing to the floor. They both ignored it.

"That was . . . how many years ago was that?"

"Fourteen," he answered.

"More than half my life." She glared as she passed him, bare toes clenching the new ivory carpet with each step. "So, you're going to marry *her* now. Is that it?"

"I don't know."

"You're supposed to marry me!" She stared at Cal, her hand pressed to her heart.

He was sorry. Sorry for the suddenness of it. Sorry that she was in love with him. Sorry that he was shredding her trust. He wouldn't let himself slip into rationales—that she didn't really know him, or understand him. There had been only so much he let her see. He knew that.

"This is fucking absurd." She resumed her laps around the room.

Maybe it was. Most leaps of faith were.

Rounding the coffee table one last time, Darla wrung the engagement ring off her finger, flung it at him, missed, and ran from the room.

Cal watched the ring tumble into the floor vent.

CHAPTER TWENTY-SIX

Leni

October is ushered out by a nor'easter. Fifty-mile-an-hour winds. Cold rain. Two nights after Leni and Cal's horse rescue escapade, Eric calls. At midnight. Night sweats. Trouble breathing.

Leni grabs her bike and races to his apartment on Bleecker. Her arm wraps around his waist, his ribs pressing into her, as she guides him down the stairs and hails a cab to St. Vincent's Hospital.

His head nestles against her chest as the taxi swerves up Sixth Avenue. "You're my sister," he mumbles. "Did you hear me? When they admit me, you're family."

She nods.

For the next two days, Leni stays at Eric's bedside, going home only to feed Abyssinia and get a change of clothes. Nurses come and go. IVs are administered and changed, vitals checked. She answers questions about his living situation and who will look after him. He forbids any hint of pity. Any tears. "I'm leaning on you," he tells her. At night, shades drawn, she curls up in the chair beside his bed. Early on the third morning, Eric insists she go home.

"Your brother's not going anywhere for another day or two, at least," a nurse assures her.

Leni wonders what exactly the nurse means. She retrieves her bike from in front of Eric's loft and cycles slowly home through Greenwich Village.

Abyssinia struts off, mad, when Leni comes in. She forgives her when fresh kibble cascades into her bowl.

The light on the answering machine pulses in the corner. Leni ignores it. A quick glance in the mirror by the kitchen sink. The hair—bright and spotted—has to go. She scours the cabinet. A half hour and a long shower later, towel around her neck, she looks in the mirror. Black. That's better.

At the table, pencil in hand, tea poured, she opens a sketch-book. Flips through the pages. Finds her place. Her concentration's not there. Maybe she should get back to the hospital. This, after all, is her chance, in the perverted ways of the universe, to right a wrong. To tend and comfort Eric, her make-believe brother, as she didn't have the chance to do for Foy.

The opposite in so many ways of Foy. Generous, yes. Cantankerous and arrogant. Impatient. So self-assured he willed Leni to be, too. Often she can't believe the things they've done together. Hanging art in impossible places—elevators and limousines. Happenings on street corners, in parks, Hudson River piers. Eric could coax talents from his friends they didn't know they had, and sometimes didn't have. Her sewing skills and athleticism impressed him. And when she gave him the painting—one of her favorites—almost a year ago, tears filled his eyes.

The buzzer jars Leni from her tired reverie. She flips the hood of her sweatshirt over her still damp hair, slips her feet into pink fuzzy slippers, and trots down the stairs.

Cal, with a wicker basket over his arm, stands at the door, blinking in the daylight.

"I've been trying to reach you. Don't you check your messages?"

She'd been almost glad to be too distracted to dwell on Cal. There'd been too little space in her head to untangle what had happened, too much under the hospital's bright fluorescent lights that needed her attention, and to stay in that present, with Eric, where she could help some little bit. Nothing like the clinic in De Kalb when it was too late.

And each time Cal did bloom in her mind—just let him go, she'd tell herself. He's engaged. Let him go.

Leni thrusts her hands in the pockets of the paint-stained sweatshirt. Looks down at her fuzzy slippers. Leaves flutter to the ground around them.

"Your hair!"

She nods.

"What's wrong? Something's happened."

Where to start? "A rough few days. A sick friend." She wipes the hood of the sweatshirt off her head.

"I'm sorry."

"A good friend."

"Where is he or she?"

"St. Vincent's."

Cal sets the basket down. Waits.

"AIDS," she says. Eric's admonishment ringing in her ears. No pity. "His family, good Midwestern Christians, disowned him."

"I'm so sorry." Cal opens his arms.

She steps forward, lets her cheek rest against his chest. His chin balances on the crown of her head. She inhales the scent of his freshly washed shirt, the warm spice of his aftershave. The rhythm of his breathing becomes her own.

Then with a jolt, she thinks. *Why is he there? What are they?* He gently presses her head back to his chest.

"I thought," he begins, the steady vibration of his voice humming against her cheek, "that today would be a good day for a picnic."

"A picnic?"

"Yes. A Sunday picnic."

The last thing she ate was a stale sandwich in the hospital cafeteria the day before. "Oh. What do you have there?"

"Well. I'm glad you asked. I went to Zabar's." Cal kisses the top of her head and releases her. He lifts the basket and pulls back the towel. "Smoked fish." He points. "Crackers. Green beans, pasta salad, chocolate mousse and lemon squares. And we're going to take a cruise."

"A cruise?"

"To Staten Island."

"How exotic. But Cal—"

"Leni—"

She raises her hand, palm open. Stop. "Cal, we can't do this."

"I broke off the engagement." He smooths the towel back over the food.

"You what?"

"I told Darla I can't marry her. I'm moving out. I'm staying with Rob."

"Oh, Cal."

"Leni, listen. It was the honest thing to do." He seems so resolved. "Regardless of what happens with us. It was the right thing."

She studies the plaid squares of his flannel shirt, trying to get her bearings.

"So," he steps closer, reaches for her. She takes his hand. It feels strong, assured. He pulls her toward him. "We'll take a cruise. To an island just off the coast."

She smiles. He kisses her.

"You might want different footwear."

Eyes locked on his, she leans back, opening the dented metal door. He follows her upstairs, where they make love. Slowly. Gently.

They emerge from the subway at Fulton Street, the picnic basket at Cal's side, a backpack slung over Leni's shoulder. Their jackets flap in the wind funneling through the skyscrapers as they head west, through the financial district's gray, deserted streets to the ferry terminal.

On the corner of Exchange Place and Broad Street, Leni opens her backpack, pulls out a black pen as thick as two fingers, with a wide foam nib at the tip, and begins to draw on the side of a gray granite building. Cal spins around.

"Whoa!" He scans the street for witnesses or police, as Leni swiftly, deftly, in long swooping lines from above her head to her waist, draws the rear half of a running horse. With four final quick strokes, a tail flies out behind. They haven't been seen. He regains his composure. "Half a horse?"

"I don't like frames," she caps the pen. "Never have."

"A creature," he points, "condemned to search endlessly for its severed half?"

She acknowledges the metaphor.

Eying the granite office tower at the end of the block, she sallies forth, skimming the ground. Uncaps her pen. Cal, self-appointed lookout, gives the all clear. In quick strokes—her arm flowing up and across and back and down—the chest, neck, and head of a running horse emerges on the gray granite. A block of the city now strung together by the galloping strides of a horse.

"That's amazing," Cal gasps.

At Bowling Green, they pass the old US Custom House and make their way to the ferry terminal. They board the waiting ferry, find a bench near the bow, and set out their picnic. The weekend passengers, tourists and shoppers mostly, read the paper or, arms resting on the railing, gaze across the water. The engines rumble hypnotically below them. The salty air ruffles their hair. And the ferry edges out into the harbor.

Leni spoons some of everything onto a paper plate for Cal and fixes another for herself. They share stories of their first months in New York and laugh about how nothing, not a single thing, resembles life in Naples, Texas. Not the pace or the weather, the air or the sky, the food, people's greetings, the subway, the pigeons, the rats or the miniature fluffy dogs.

They ride the ferry out and back a second time, standing at the bow, the cool, moist air washing over them as they approach the skyscrapers and canyons of the city.

She remembers craving the anonymity of New York. Believing, after Ohio, at barely eighteen, that she could build a life and make her art fresh from whole cloth. A part of her hasn't admitted, has been a little ashamed, that she couldn't let go of Naples, of her past. Something keeps her from forging headlong into a future. Maybe this is why she doesn't show her work. She doesn't want to talk about the past. She's wanted to contain it. In the sketches and drawings of horses and of Foy she keeps in notebooks and drawers. Pieces of chaparral make their way into her paintings. She doesn't set out for that to happen. She just can't get around it, despite being in a place that is the chaparral's opposite. Still, always perhaps, she'll count the strides to lampposts, and assess animals—stray cats or pet dogs—for illness or dismay, as she watched her father do.

They reach the ferry terminal. Throttles thrown, the engines grind louder as the ferry slows and sidles up to the dock. Leni watches the water churn below. Recalibrating, she turns to Cal, slides her hands inside his jacket, pulls him to her, and tastes the salty air on his lips.

Caleb

They spun toward Leni's bed, Cal's coat, her sweater, his pants in a trail on the floor. They kissed. Hungry, fervent. Peeling her shirt up and over her head, he stopped to kiss her breasts, her nipples rising beneath his mouth. She unbuttoned his shirt, pushed it off his shoulders, slipped beneath him, and pulled him toward her, inside her. They breathed, sighed, and gasped. Then lay in one another's arms a long time, damp and soft with sex.

He stroked the cleft, the soft skin, between her collarbones and kissed her there.

"I love," he said, "that you can barrel race, deliver a calf, stitch up a horse, and step into this grimy, chaotic city without missing a beat."

She rolled onto her back, arm over her face, suddenly bashful.

"And I love," he persevered, "how you move. Easy and fluid. I can see the energy flow through you."

She leaned forward, tilted her head until their lips touched.

"Tell me about your work," she said, settling back to listen.

He wondered how to make deals to turn parking lots and empty warehouse spaces into housing sound interesting.

"OK," he began. "Well, it's like the Wild West out there right now. Bankers and real-estate developers are way out ahead of the regulators. What I believe, though, is that if you want to live to see another day in this industry, which we do and our investors do, you have to run the numbers honestly, know who you're dealing with, guard your reputation. And," he raised his index finger, "something my father taught me—if you don't know who the sucker is at the table, it's probably you. I make sure we aren't the suckers at any table."

"Wow. You operate in a whole other world," Leni mused. "How much money are we talking about, for one of these deals?"

"It could be under a million to refurbish something in a smaller market, say Philadelphia. Could be seventy-five or a hundred million to convert a warehouse in a major market."

"I always knew whatever you did, you'd be playing with the big boys."

"There are a lot of boys bigger than us," he chuckled and put his arm around her.

Then: "I want to look at your paintings." He said this with sudden adamancy, then marched, naked, to the back of the long apartment, scouted for the light switch. Leni, wearing only Cal's shirt twirled around her head, followed. She switched on the clamp on work lights.

There were three paintings on the wall, acrylic on canvas. Her brushstrokes thick and wide here, delicate and precise there. Texture and depth. The images weren't representational, though some seemed recognizable. Subtle depictions of animals and leaves, twigs and bare trees, combined to make up her own iconography. One had a horizontal quality, like the flat east Texas landscape. Was that a storm coming in from the edge of this canvas, or the sun rising in that one?

"These should be seen, Leni."

"I see them." She wrinkled her nose, looked at him sideways, then came closer and cradled his thick leg between her thighs.

"Are you trying to distract me?"

"Yes." She pressed the length of her naked torso against him.

"I mean it," he said, kissing her neck. "I don't know the art world. But I know what I see in people's apartments."

"Is that right," she mumbled.

"And in offices. Don't roll your eyes. People have to work. They should have art where they work, shouldn't they?"

Leni covered her eyes with the heels of her hands.

"What's in there?" Cal went to the storage cabinet with wide, shallow drawers between the windows.

"Just more drawings." Leni followed on his heels.

He bent down, reached to open the bottom drawer.

Quickly, she pushed the drawer closed with her foot.

"Leni?"

"Not in there." She said sharply. "You can look in the other drawers, if you want."

He didn't press. "No, that's OK."

They ordered in from the Chinese restaurant on the corner and ate as Abyssinia threaded between their legs, and Cal waded through another of Leni's silences. Then, wrapped around one another, they fell asleep.

The next week, Cal began his search for an apartment. The prices for Manhattan condos and co-ops were climbing by the day. He felt some pressure to move fast.

Each apartment he entered, in addition to assessing the building's financials, the fixtures and location, he found himself gauging the light, whether there was adequate wall space to hang canvases, and imagining where Leni's work tables could go. He saw one apartment that he thought might be suitable on West End Avenue. It had only been on the market for two days, but it turned out there'd already been an accepted offer.

At the end of the week, when he went to pick Leni up for dinner, he intended to bring up the apartment search and discuss it with her. When he got to her apartment, though, she greeted him brusquely and, picking up a bucket and rag, quickly returned to scrubbing the rear windows.

Cal stroked Abyssinia, who lounged on the worktable. "Is something wrong?" he asked after several minutes.

"I need to feel like I'm doing something useful," she replied.

"I see." He didn't. He waited, knowing she would say as much as she wanted—and usually no more—when she wanted.

"It's Eric," she said, wringing a rag out in the bucket.

Cal knew the Gay Men's Health Crisis Center had helped her arrange for nursing and hospice care, and that she went by many mornings to check on him. "Did you see him this morning?"

She nodded. "He's wasting away."

Cal waited for Leni to finish her task. While she got ready to go to dinner, Cal decided the apartment conversation could wait. Besides, wouldn't it be better to find the best ones to choose from and then tell her. And if it was important for Leni to feel like she was doing something useful, there was another topic he'd been wanting to bring up.

Leni gathered her keys and turned off some lights, and they headed for the door.

"Are there any galleries you'd like to show your work at?" he asked, holding the door open for her.

She hesitated. "Maybe."

"Do you have slides?"

"Maybe." She jiggled the keys in her hand.

"Leni!"

"OK, OK. I might have a couple of galleries scoped out."

"And slides?"

Leni turned the key in the first two locks. "No." She stomped down the stairs.

"Why not?" Cal felt irritated with her. "Isn't that what artists do?"

"Maybe I'm not a real artist," she said over her shoulder.

"Leni!" Cal stopped at the top of the last flight of stairs.

Leni looked up at him like a petulant child. They stared at each other for a long moment. Never push, Cal reminded himself.

"Eric gets photographers lined up for projects and tries to get me to bring some pieces over. But I haven't done it." She shook her head and glanced back at Cal. "It takes money, you know." She pushed open the door.

She was reluctant to let him help. He didn't understand why. But he was coming to believe in time. She pouted. And, again, he waited.

"OK," she said one morning, just out of the shower, rubbing her head with a towel.

"OK what?"

"The slides."

He would have liked her to have been happier about it.

"Thank you," she muttered, and returned to the bathroom.

It was a Saturday morning in January, Cal met Leni at her apartment. He followed her to the long table at the back of her place, gingerly avoiding the clothes strewn all along the floor.

"How do I look?"

She turned, arms outstretched, and stared at him. He couldn't remember her ever asking him for an assessment of her appearance.

"You're beautiful."

Her hair was closely cropped again and white blond. Her dark eyebrows and burnished red lipstick accentuated her green eyes. She wore slim-fitting black jeans, a cream-colored turtleneck, and boots with two-inch-thick soles, which made her legs look even longer and slimmer than usual.

"No, really," she prompted. "Do I look professional? But kind of, I don't know, casual."

"Relaxed."

"Yeah. Relaxed is good. Do I look relaxed?"

"No. Not at this very moment."

Her shoulders slumped.

He wasn't accustomed to seeing her so vulnerable in this way. "It's not the outfit. You just have to . . . relax."

She scowled at him.

"You look striking," he said. "Confident and relaxed."

This sent her back to her clothes baskets.

"What did I say wrong?"

"Can you finish putting those slides in sleeves for me?" She pointed to a cardboard box on top of the metal cabinet where she stored drawings and paintings. He'd ordered, and happily paid for, five (she'd only wanted three) sets of slides.

Leni grabbed an armful of clothes and slipped behind the screen to change.

The bottom drawer of the cabinet was ajar. Very slowly, one eye on the screen behind which Leni was changing, Cal opened the drawer. Laid neatly inside was a stack of twelve or thirteen drawings, almost all on paper. Some were dreamscapes, others were very recognizable animals, landscapes with rivers, and impressionistic cityscapes, a sketch of the very apartment he was now crouching in. Each piece was dated July. Subsequent years. And on each piece at the top left was written, "For you. Always."

Before Leni could reemerge, he slid the drawer closed and carefully resumed inserting slides into the transparent sleeves.

It was close to noon when they started for SoHo. Leni was back in the cream-colored turtleneck and black pants, and armed with her slides. She had seven galleries on her list. They huddled on the sidewalk before she entered each one. Cal gave her a pep talk. Then she'd stride in, alone, head high. Three of the seven galleries asked to keep a set of slides.

Cal insisted they go to the Odeon Restaurant to celebrate. Despite Leni's insistence there was nothing to celebrate yet, he thought they'd made good headway.

"You've got to enjoy every step," he said, pulling her along behind him as snow began to fall, softening the sounds of the city as they proceeded down West Broadway.

They got a table by the window where they could watch the snow drift down. The restaurant was pleasantly crowded. Cal ordered Leni a half bottle of champagne. Amidst the buzz and thrum of conversation and the tinkling of silverware and glassware, the anxiety of the day ebbed, and Leni's mood lightened.

Looking at the snow, she asked, "Have you noticed New Yorkers always complain about the weather?" She smiled. "I find that funny since they don't depend on it. You know? They're not farming."

Cal laughed.

"If you could go anywhere, where would you like to go?" she asked, flirtatiously.

"Norway," he answered with some authority.

"Oh." Leni seemed to mull it over seriously for a moment. "A long ways from Morris County, Texas."

"We're already a long ways from Morris County, Texas."

"Not always."

Cal let that slide. "I'd like to see the fjords. And the aurora borealis."

"Let's go," Leni said, finishing her champagne with a flourish.

Her mood and enthusiasm pleased Cal. He was glad she was thinking of a future. It would have been a good moment to bring up his apartment search, had he thought of it.

I t was late when they got back to Leni's apartment and they were both tired. They hung up their coats and scarves. On his way to the toilet, Cal pointed to the answering machine blinking in the back corner of the apartment. Leni kicked off her boots and started for the machine, slipping bracelets off as she went.

When he came out, Leni was frantically putting her boots and coat back on.

"Eric," she said.

A hospital bed sat in the middle of the dimly lit loft space. The bare wood floors were scuffed. The drafty windows rattled with the evening's cold wind. Small, unframed paintings hung everywhere. Eric's and his friends', Cal guessed. Leni's painting was featured prominently above a table laden with prescription bottles, vials, and medical paraphernalia.

The nurse, a middle-aged man, was at the bedside. With a gloved hand, he dabbed ointment on Eric's parched lips. Leni slid on a pair of latex gloves. The nurse moved aside, letting Leni come in closer. She took Eric's hand in hers. Eric's eyes moved ever so slightly toward her. He knew she was there, that she had come. The nurse briefly laid a hand on Leni's shoulder, then walked from the bed toward Cal, pulling off his gloves.

"Not long now," he whispered.

Cal supposed Foy had been this close to death when he cradled his head between his knees in the back of Rabbit's pickup. Foy so young, in the peak of health not an hour before his death. Eric looked ancient. The skin pulled so taut over his cheeks and jaw, baring the hollows of his skull. His eyes open and sunken. His mouth, too. Cal reminded himself that in fact Eric was only in his forties. How much more life he could have lived.

Leni was whispering to Eric. Cal could make out some words, but more than any words, he knew, was her presence. Her voice. She would keep talking softly, evenly, until—twenty minutes, forty minutes, Cal had no idea—Eric took his last breath.

Leni stood. The nurse approached. Took Eric's wrist in his hand and noted the time.

She went to Cal. He held her tightly as the sobs moved through her. He believed he could feel the grief reach all the way back to losing Foy.

During the next two weeks, Leni allowed herself to lean on Cal. He stayed with her for several days and nights, calling into work and monitoring a few deals over the phone with Theresa's help. After that, they spent almost every night together and spoke on the phone multiple times a day. Often Leni would call about simple quotidian things, like what to have for dinner, or the size of the fur ball Abyssinia coughed up. Other times, though, she needed to express a sorrow so deep Cal felt that only he—knowing her history—could help contain it, could hold her up until she released it or reached the other side. This made him feel complete, in a way he hadn't ever felt before.

By the first week of March, birds were chirping, buds on the trees were beginning to plump up, and Leni was getting back on her feet. The day Cal resumed the apartment search, his realtor took him to the perfect place. A parlor floor apartment, with eleven-foot ceilings and lots of original detail, in a four-story, extra-wide and very deep brownstone on West Seventy-Fourth Street, near Central Park and not far from Lincoln Center. The back room had large windows and a view over the block's backyards. Plenty of light, and plenty of wall space for a perfect studio.

The market was even hotter than before. He made an offer.

CHAPTER TWENTY-SEVEN

Leni

"The Upper West Side?" Leni confirms. "That's so far."

She dabs cerulean-blue pigment on her palette and swirls it into a dollop of golden oak brown.

"It's a subway ride from wherever you want to go." Cal settles his jacket on the back of a chair, picks up an *Art in America*, and leans against the long table. "There's a perfect studio in the back. It's twice the size of this." He leans against the table, flips through the magazine.

"I like my studio," Leni mumbles, a brush in her teeth as she smudges a stroke on the canvas with her finger.

"Lots of light," he says, thumbing through the magazine, trying to be nonchalant. Knowing his desire could scare her. She mustn't feel pressured.

"There's nothing wrong with this light," she says. "I can control it." To prove the point, she adjusts one of the clip-on lights to shine less directly on the canvas.

Cal sets down the magazine.

Her eyes remain fixed on the canvas in front of her. She smears the blue and golden brown across the top of the canvas with a painter's knife. Wipes the blade clean on a rag tucked into her belt loop. Takes a brush and feathers the paint into the charcoal and deep blue already on the canvas.

"You could at least take a look at it."

"I'm comfortable here." She won't look at him.

"Change can be good," he says, talking faster. They're both skirting the real point.

"I don't go above Fourteenth Street, unless it's for a job or a museum."

"Come on, Leni," something snapping. "Grow up a little more." Immediately: "I'm sorry."

"Oh." She pulls the rag from her belt. Wipes her hands. "Living uptown and making real money is how to be a grown-up."

"That's not what I meant."

"Isn't it? Anything else is, I don't know, infantile, I guess." Now she stares at him. Those green eyes cold as jade.

"Would you stop?" He holds his hands up, surrendering.

"Long live greed and ripping off the next guy." Fist thrust in the air.

"You know that's not what I was saying."

"You're the one who said, 'Grow up.'" She returns to her painting.

"I'm sorry." He goes to her, strokes her neck and back. She shudders. He steps back. "What I want," he says carefully, "is for us to be together. To live together."

Her jaw tightens. She scrutinizes the canvas. Dabs paint here. Then there.

"I'm sorry," he repeats. "I jumped the gun."

No comment.

"Come look at places with me. For us. Please."

"You've already made an offer on a place you want."

"I'll withdraw it."

The truth is other people's desires make her feel trapped. She's had to fight so hard for what she's wanted. And sacrificed so much. She's afraid of losing what's her own.

"Leni. Talk to me."

"You set me up."

"Set you up?" his voice rising. "I love you."

She swallows, her lips pressed together. She's tumbling backward, landing in an old habit. When pressed, pull in. Hold tight. She might as well be slouched on the floor of Foy's closet, cross-legged, diary in her lap.

Cal struggles to reroute the conversation, get her back. "Let's go get a coffee."

"I need to get some work done."

"We can just go," he points, "down to the Kiev." No response. Upping the ante. "I'll get you one of those banana muffins?"

"I don't need your money."

"Leni." He clasps her arm. Not hard. "Look at me, goddammit."

She wrenches free. A reflex. "You didn't even ask me, Cal." She stands very upright. And still. Impenetrable. "You didn't even ask." She can practically see his heart thudding in his chest.

"I just want to give us a try. We've been given this second chance, Leni." Texas slipping back into the rhythm and tone of his words.

She turns back to the canvas and stands, palette in one hand, the other hanging at her side. Frozen.

"I love you, Leni. I always have."

She hesitates, says nothing. He starts toward the table.

She turns, takes a step toward him. Her foot catches on a fold in the drop cloth. The palette, then the brush, slap the rolling metal cabinet. "Dammit!" she yells.

Cal spins around. "Why are you so angry? I don't under-stand." He's shouting now. He never shouts.

"I don't know! I don't know what to say."

"Well, what do you want, Leni?"

She stares at the mess, paint and brushes on the floor.

Cal waits. Waits some more. "Well, that says it all. Right there. Because if there's one thing you always know, Leni, it's what you want. Obviously, it's not me."

He grabs his coat from the chair.

She doesn't know what to say. Words have vanished.

The door swings shut behind him. Should she follow him?

All relationships end. Isn't that so, she thinks? One way or another, at one point in time or another. They all end.

PART FIVE:

BLOOD

Love is a sacred reserve of energy;
It is like the blood of spiritual evolution.
—Teilhard de Chardin

CHAPTER TWENTY-EIGHT

August 2016

Caleb

All living organisms—Cal remembered something from the last biology class he took in eleventh grade—have a process by which they dissolve gases. Primarily oxygen and carbon dioxide are circulated in a fluid, such as sap or blood. This fluid provides the medium for the exchange, the diffusion, of gases across membranes. Viscous plasma circulates the veins, arteries, and capillaries of all vertebrates, transporting oxygen to and carbon dioxide from tissue in the brain, lungs and heart, toes, pads or fins.

This dredged up bit of knowledge has become relevant.

For two thousand years, Western physicians worked from the theory that the body is comprised of four humors. The literal translation of the Greek word "humor" is sap or juice. All disease, so this theory went, is related to an excess or deficit of one or the other humor: black and yellow bile, phlegm and blood. Blood was associated with air. Its season spring. And its accompanying temperament, sanguine. From ancient times until only two hundred years ago, bloodletting was the predominant medical procedure, used to treat acne and asthma, tuberculosis, gout or cancer. It was even—perhaps at its most appalling and misguided—a treatment for hemorrhaging and used to prepare a patient for surgery and childbirth. This reminds him that humans get a lot wrong before they get it right.

How will future generations reflect back on dripping poisons into the bloodstream as a cure?

In spite of the chemicals and tests, radiation and more tests, juices and vitamins, bee pollen and wheat grass, Cal's lymphoma has progressed to stage 4-B.

CHAPTER TWENTY-NINE

August 25, 2016

Leni

These still and humid New England heat waves make Leni feel lethargic. No breeze at all off the Housatonic River in this tony Connecticut town. The gallery's on the second floor of a mustard yellow clapboard, one in a row of historic houses set back from a brick sidewalk made uneven by the roots of hundred-year-old maple trees. The requisite bookstore and café are up the block, women's clothing and crafts stores down.

Not that Leni's complaining. Melanie, the gallery owner, gives her a one-woman show every other summer. It might have been the day Melanie appeared in her riding breeches, and she and Leni spent an hour talking about horses and Leni's volunteering with the Racehorse Retirement League, which saves thoroughbreds bound for the chopping block, that clinched it. Not to short-shrift her work. Leni's paintings do sell here. And in two days, after the opening, she'll be back on the coast of Maine to finish her summer teaching gig. Cool nights. Cold ocean waters pounding the rocks beneath the cottage she rents every summer on a slender promontory above Rockland.

Right now, though, this damn show has to be hung. Leni wipes sweat from her forehead. The gallery assistant, Chloe, an art major on summer break from Colby, twists a clump of earth-toned dreadlocks into a knot on top of her head as they start back to the van to fetch the last two paintings and carefully maneuver them up the narrow flight of stairs.

Leni and Chloe unwrap the twelve canvases. They roll up the bubble wrap to reuse, and stuff the cellophane and torn tape into large black garbage bags. Then they test possible placements for the paintings, leaning them against the wall. Eight charcoal drawings will go on the short wall by the entrance. The largest canvas in the middle of the long wall.

"I love these, Em," Chloe says, peeling a stray piece of tape off her hands.

Leni smiles. She's not sure. Never sure right before a show. Are they worthy? She's gotten more representational, not less, as the years have rolled on. Shadowy figures. In movement or contemplation. Rarely is there interaction among the sometime figures, more than one critic has noticed. "As though each in his or her own imagination, floating in proximity, never quite engaging," another said. What she likes—this incarnation of Madeleine Bonet O'Hare—is to instigate, inspire stories in the viewer's mind. Not to dictate. She's honed her technique. For the pieces destined for shows, at least. Layers of paint. Sometimes one applied before the first layer has dried. Reminiscent of the frescos she was so taken with when she studied in Italy almost forty years earlier. She'd like to get back to Europe one day. One day when, she wonders. Time's not slowing down.

Chloe leans another one of the larger paintings against the far wall. A dreamy landscape. Clouds like barrels—grays and blue, hints of maroon—over a roiling sea.

"What do you think?" Chloe asks, looking at the sequence of paintings laid up against the wall.

"Good enough for now," Leni proclaims. "Thank you."

"No problem." The ubiquitous Millennial comeback. They stand, arms crossed, surveying the gallery.

"I'm going to go get an iced coffee. Want one?" Leni asks.

"I'll take a kombucha."

In the office to get her purse, Leni glances in the mirror by the door. She sweeps stray strands of gray into a bun, and secures it with a pencil before heading out to the street.

L eni trudges back up the stairs to the gallery. Chloe's in the office gathering hooks and nails from a metal cabinet.

"So, I was in here," Chloe, not looking up, launches into a story. "Came out and a woman was in the gallery looking at the paintings."

"Oh, I'm sorry, Chloe. I figured I'd be right back. I didn't lock the door."

"No problem."

Leni pulls the sweating bottle of kombucha from a paper bag.

"Did you tell her the show opens Saturday?"

"She knew." Chloe uncaps the bottle, downs half of it. "She asked for Madeleine O'Hare. You just missed her."

"A collector?" Leni asks.

"I don't think so," Chloe murmurs, going to the window.

Leni goes to the window and stands beside Chloe. They peer through the mullions, their shoulders, moist with sweat, touching.

"Right there." Chloe points to a tall, slender woman walking away, rivulets of brown hair brushing her waist.

"You could catch her."

Leni shakes her head.

"You want me to run after her?" Chloe asks, more animated.

"No." Something inside Leni has gone cold, as though she'd seen an apparition. "She knew when the opening was?"

"Yeah. Said she wouldn't be able to make it, though."

Leni watches the young woman get into a Volvo wagon and drive off until she's out of sight.

CHAPTER THIRTY

September 12, 2016

Caleb

Sporadically over the years, after traveling a lengthy and circuitous route, a late birthday or holiday card from Hank Junior would find Cal. In February, a card with an actual return address—a small town on an island in the St. Lawrence near Montreal—arrived somewhat close to Cal's actual birthday. He put it in his contact file and forgot about it.

Until last month, when he had to fill out Advance Directives and Health Care Proxies. All of which prompted Cal to think about next of kin.

When Hank Junior got Cal's letter, with news of his illness, Hank called straight away and insisted Cal come visit.

So Cal sits, ambivalent and tired, by the plate glass windows in a baggage claim area at Montreal's Pierre Trudeau Airport. Coat, scarf, and hat draped across his lap, he scrolls through the *New York Times* on an iPad, looking up every paragraph or two to scan the tides of people, hoping to recognize his brother, who evidently still doesn't wear a watch.

There's no answer at Hank's house. Cal decides to give Hank another half hour. If he doesn't show up by then, he'll find a return flight, assured that Hank Junior remains as self-centered and unreliable as he was all those years ago. Sometimes it's just as well to have preconceptions affirmed.

Cal stands and gathers his coat and scarf when the revolving door closest to him tosses in a man, who quickly zeroes in on Cal and, hand outstretched, strides toward him, enormous rubber-soled boots squeaking with each step on the polished floor.

Hank Junior is still as solid as a post. He sports now the salt and pepper hair their father had, a full beard (mostly gray), and tortoise-rimmed glasses. His jeans are half-tucked into the thick boots, which are laced up only halfway. In a plaid flannel shirt and bulky cardigan sweater with leather patches at the elbows, he could be a professor on sabbatical.

With a formidable grasp on Cal's hand, Hank launches into an apology. "I forgot my wallet. Had to turn back. Almost missed the ferry. Then there was an accident on 40, coming into the city. Look at you," he sizes Cal up for a split second. "And I don't have a mobile phone. I had one. A phone," he rattles on. "But it drove me crazy. I chucked it in the river. Was your trip OK?"

"Fine." Cal leans down to get his cane and bag.

"You just have to tell me if there's anything at all you need." He snatches Cal's overnight bag. "I mean it. Any little fucking thing."

With Cal's bag in hand, Hank pauses, eyes cast down. Cal watches his brother take three deep breaths, like some sort of reset. "OK." He looks at Cal. "Ready?"

Windshield wipers slap side to side as Hank's pickup forges out of the city through steady rain and heavy traffic and onto the Thousand Islands Parkway. Though two men can talk about remarkably little when left alone, they do progress beyond the Montreal winters to exchange rates and trade barriers. Hank is now a woodworker, making artificially distressed furniture primarily for export to the US.

After driving forty minutes, they wait, the windows steaming up, for the ferry to Île de Carillon. On board, they get out of the truck and, heads bowed into the wind, climb the wet metal stairs, through a heavy metal door to the waiting room inside where they sit on one of a dozen orange plastic benches. Rain pelts the windows. Sour diesel fumes seep inside each time someone comes in from the deck. It's a short crossing over several hundred yards of nervous water, so dark and dense it looks as viscous as crude oil, toward an island with tall pines standing like sentries in the cold rain.

The ferry slips into a wide dock and empties the half dozen cars onto a narrow street. A few wood-framed buildings make up what there is of the village. They drive a half a mile to an outcropping of homes and stop in front of a well-kept two-story clapboard cottage, stained a brown like decomposing leaves, with two dormers in front, a porch extending the width of the house, and a bright red door. A picket fence, weathered as well, not white, circles the small lot. A copse of fir trees shiver behind it. As soon as the gate latches behind them, two large dogs lope out from under the porch, tails wagging.

"Meet Clive." Hank points to a big, shaggy black dog with a square face and enormous paws. "And Brandy." A smooth-coated red dog with a long nose and tapered waist.

Hank swings open the unlocked door, sets Cal's bag down, and goes to stoke a wood stove in the center of the open room.

It is a tidy home. Modest. Wood paneling, wide-planked wood floors, exposed ceiling beams. To the left of the stove is a large, dark green sofa and two armchairs set around an oval rag rug. To the right is a beautiful, rough-edged dining table and four chairs, which his brother made in the workshop out back. Along the back wall, behind a counter with two stools in front, is a small kitchen. A staircase skirts the back wall.

"Your room's upstairs on the right," Hank says, pointing, then pushes a log into the stove.

"Do you want something to drink? I can go get some beer, if you want. We don't keep any around."

Cal notes the "we." And the lack of alcohol. "I'd like a cup of tea, if you have any."

"We have a shitload of teas." He goes to the kitchen.

"Are you married?" Cal asks.

"No. You?"

Cal shakes his head.

"Ever?" Hank asks.

"Almost. Once." Cal pulls out one of the stools at the kitchen counter and sits.

"I live here with Mary Lynn." As Hank fills the kettle, he tells Cal a bit about her, a full-blooded Chippewa and a social worker who travels a good bit of the time.

"Will I meet her?" Cal asks.

"I imagine you will." Hank takes down a mug that says, "Life on Life's Terms," opens another cabinet and takes out some teas. "I'm sorry to have made you travel. I hope it wasn't too hard on you."

Not as hard as sitting across from a brother he hadn't seen in forty years, and had hated for most of them.

"You still can't come back into the country?" Cal asks, contemplating the motto on the mug.

"Technically I can," he says. "But I've been told the FBI doesn't really let things go."

"The FBI used to call me," Cal says.

"What'd you tell them?"

"I never had anything to tell them." Cal points to the chamomile.

"I wanted it that way. For your sake."

"And for Momma's?"

Hank pauses. "I was in touch with her when I could be."

"Not when she needed you." Why mince words?

"I ain't saying I done things perfect." Hank's Texas accent swoops into the room. "Or right." He wipes the counter down. "I'm not," he says more softly. "I'm sorry for an awful lot of things."

"That seems appropriate." Cal watches Hank drag a sponge across the counter two more times. "She wanted me to tell you she loved you."

The kettle shrieks, and Hank pours steaming water into the mug, hands it to Cal, and leans back against the sink.

Seated there, his hands around the warm mug, Cal's not sure why he made the trip in his weakened state. What did he or his brother want or expect? Two men, aging, childless. Sitting across from Hank Junior, Cal wonders if it's ever possible to live in the present with a sibling.

"I didn't do what you think I did," Hank says.

So many things come to mind. He didn't rustle a hundred thousand dollars' worth of cattle? He didn't shoot Jesus Galan?

"Can we talk about Leni or not?" Hank interrupts Cal's musing.

No statute of limitations there.

Before Cal can answer, shopping bags rustle at the door. A woman steps in, shakes off her yellow rain coat and hat, and stretches her full length to hang them on the coat rack by the door. She gives Hank a quiet smile, a nod to Cal, pulls off her boots, sets them neatly on a rubber mat and starts toward the kitchen.

"I am Mary Lynn."

"Caleb." He takes her hand.

"Yes," she says. "I hope the travel didn't tire you."

Her black hair, straight and sharp, is cut even with her jaw. Her mouth level as a pencil. A narrow nose descends between straight black eyebrows. She is short, petite, really. She wears a snug blue wool sweater and straight black skirt that comes just below her knees.

She doesn't seem unwelcoming or cold exactly, just remarkably contained, reminding Cal of photographs one sees of royalty. She and Hank stand side by side, without touching or speaking, looking at Cal.

"I will be out back," she says after a long moment. She lifts a fleece jacket from a hook on the back door, slips into another pair of boots, and heads out into the wet and cold. Through the kitchen window, Cal watches the dogs prance over and follow her to the square wood-framed workshop. The dogs wait at the closed door, their wagging tails slow, then stop, and they amble over to lie down again under the eaves.

"No," Cal says. "We can't talk about Leni."

The rain starts back up in earnest during dinner; mud blankets the incline of the small yard. Mary Lynn fetches two large towels, calls the dogs in, and wipes them off. They lie down by the wood stove.

Cal watches Hank Junior and Mary Lynn nearly wordlessly work together, feeding the dogs, setting the table, preparing dinner in the tiny kitchen: sautéed chicken, mashed potatoes and a romaine salad. She is not warm in the way that makes you want to tell your secrets. She seems, though, grounded and steadying. Cal can sense her calming effect on his brother, who used to banter ceaselessly, always keeping people at bay, staving off connection. He is grateful not to have to sit through a round robin of anecdotes and witty stories, or play the "everything's fine" card.

After dinner, Mary Lynn brings out coffee, and tea for Cal. Hank steps over the dogs and puts another log in the stove. When he sits back down, Mary Lynn gives him a long look, void of any expression Cal could recognize, before returning to the kitchen. Hank tells Cal he'll be right back. He gets up from the table, takes a coat off the hook, and goes out through the rain to his workshop. Cal goes to join Mary Lynn in the kitchen. She declines his offer to help and tells him to sit or his tea will get cold. Cal does as he's told.

Hank returns, takes a package wrapped in brown paper from under his jacket, slips off his boots, hangs up the jacket, and sets the package down in front of Cal.

Mary Lynn leashes up the dogs, gets her coat, and they jangle out the front door for a walk.

The postmark is May 20, 1987. The heavy brown packing paper has softened with age. It is addressed, in thick red ink, to someone whose name Cal doesn't recognize in Ontario. The return address, Chillicothe, Ohio.

Cal slides a knife through the tape and slowly peels back the thick paper to reveal four notebooks. Two have the black-and-white mottled covers, labeled "Composition," used by grade school and high school students everywhere. The other two are spiral notebooks, their cardboard fronts and backs covered with pencil and ink doodles and drawings. They are Leni's.

"How did you get these?"

"When we left, Leni and I, I took her to Chillicothe. To stay with the Ingrahams. That's where I went when I got back from—"

"I know." Cal interrupts his brother.

Hank sets down the plate he's drying, tosses the dish towel across his shoulder, and rounds the kitchen counter.

"After I left, I stayed in touch with them through a couple other guys from 'Nam. They'd forward a card or a letter now and again."

Cal studies the covers of the notebooks.

"When Dolly and Ham passed away," Hank goes on, "their sons went through the house and found these diaries in their brother's old room. They remembered Leni but didn't know how to find her. They got word to me. I tried to find her. Last address I found was in New York. Sent a letter, never heard back from her, though. But they got the diaries to me."

"I'm not in contact with her," Cal says, coolly.

What exactly did Hank think Cal would want with these? He stares at the journals in his lap, the doodles and drawings. Unbidden, he remembers Hank following Leni from the homecoming game, his arm draped around her waist at the Roadhouse pool table. He doesn't want to imagine Leni and Hank, plotting to escape Naples together, in the dead of night. He pushed back his doubt and believed her that there'd been nothing between them. And he had fallen in love all over again with her long-limbed grace, her irreverence, her dedication, her pain, her isolation.

The first page of the earliest composition notebook is dated June 16th, 1968. The handwriting is neat and round.

Foggy was a good girl today. Daddy promised I could register for the gymkhana at the Franklin County Fair come August if I continue with helping Maman when she asks and taking care of the barn, which I intend to do. They got a barrel race at the end . . .

The names of animals, in letters like bubbles, lined the margins. London Fog, Agatha, Roger. The permanent residents of the small O'Hare farm. On the top of one page, Cal can make out Marguerite's name above a round face with pageboy hair. There's another face next to it, Leni's presumably, with a tongue sticking out. There are simple sketches of trees and horses, desks, dogs, boots and hats.

The first thick spiral notebook begins in the fall of 1970. Cal flips the pages. More drawings, more detailed. *I hate Miss Cully*, the high school biology teacher, written neatly across the top of a page midway through. Nobody liked her. And, *I will endeavor to be patient with Maman* fills two pages, like a disciplined child made to write a coerced affirmation on the chalkboard.

The second spiral notebook begins in April 1972. It contains more detailed sketches. Some of them have been damaged along the bottom by spilled ink, or something. A running horse. A cluster of hens. A squirrel seated on a tractor eating an acorn. More complaints about Marguerite. The scores of Foy's baseball games and his stats. Her hope to work that summer with her father, accompany him on his rounds. Praise for Foggy. And some bitter complaining about her mother.

By August, she writes of running off on Foggy, wishing she could just keep going and never return. Except that she'd miss Foy, watching his games, their jokes and banter.

Cal can read on these pages, across all those years, how close Leni and Foy had been. How proud she was of him. Siblings are the witnesses to one's most crucial years. And Leni and Foy were more than witnesses, they were allies. Foy protected Leni and supported her. And she adored him.

He came to a small sketch of a horse's leg with a gash across the pastern. A description of the horse she and Foy had found, the wound on his leg and how she had tended it, and how—as

scared as she had been and with shaking hands—she sutured
him up herself.

Pressed between the next two crinkled pages, a dried white
clover and cedar sage. And this, from the morning Leni and Cal
met at the river, the day after that terrible squall when she and
Foy found Captain Flint:

August 20, 1972

*There's a quietness about him. But I can tell how smart
he is. Not like his daddy, who'll stare folks down ready to
bully them. Or his brother. Who Marguerite for some reason
thinks she can catch. She's not like any girl he'd ever be with.
I don't know why she doesn't see this. Anyway, he's not like
anyone I can think of. Foy said he's "solid," which to Foy is
like saying he could be president. He loves his horse, too. That
big pretty bay. And he's not afraid to show it . . .*

Reading this diary is like finding a little footbridge spanning
the gap between two people. Wouldn't this have been what one
dreamt of in first love, to know the other from the inside? Cal,
rapt and nervous, even all these years past, reads on.

The next pages are hard to read. Much of them blotted out
with dark smudges. Ink had bled through the thin paper. He
turns the page.

August 24, 1972.

Black.

Every inch. Drawn not with a marker or thick crayon, but
scratched, line after line, with a thin-nibbed pen until the page,
edge to edge, was black. Black as space. Black as nothingness.

Foy was dead.

There are no drawings for more than a month. Leni wrote, mostly, to Foy. Sometimes talking things out with him, other times explaining to him what had happened, how he'd died, assuring him and comforting him. Missing him.

By early October, some sketches return. Pencil drawings of Foggy. And Flint. And this:

"*OK. It's fine,*" she wrote. "*I don't know why I was thinking so much about Caleb McGrath anyway. He doesn't want to talk to me!*"

They'd had a spat, apparently.

Less writing about Maman and Marguerite. Her father relatively absent. Hank making several appearances. His swagger. His toughness. How he puts her on edge. And how he sucks up the attention wherever he is and seems to believe he can take whatever he wants.

And by the end of that month, "*I love him.*" Over and over. "*I love him. I love him.*"

Who?

A stem of dried heather pressed between the next pages, which contain the sketch of a barn to the left, a figure seated on the grass, jean jacket, long legs stretched out in the grass: Cal.

She had loved him.

She wrote about trying to understand physics. (What an ass he must have been, trying to impress her.) She wrote about Foggy and Flint and riding together. She wrote about when they first made love, her heart, she said, filled like a moon rising in her chest—and, indeed, neither had any contraception. After he was accepted to Princeton, there were pages with calculations, numbers added up in the margins. What she could save with this job or that, over months, through the summer, the fall. Meager amounts. Just hope. And faith. And fear crept in. Fear that he would forget her, that she couldn't keep up. That she'd been living in a dream.

Then:

December 20, 1972

It's been two months.
I'm sure.

The few entries from Ohio are cryptic. The drawings small, strained. And the last written page:

July 23, 1973

It's the best thing. For the baby.
> *For Heather. A name soft like the grasslands where she came from.*
>> *They wrapped her up safe and tight, then I closed my eyes.*
>> *I won't let anything in that deep ever again. Not ever.*

His memory reels back twenty-six years to their three-mile walk on the New York sidewalk from his office to her apartment.

What was it she said? Hank helped her find a doctor. For an abortion.

Did she say that? Or did he assume something? No. She said that.

"I don't know, exactly, what you knew," Hanks starts, "and I haven't seen you in—"

"Forty-two years," Cal helps him with the math and stares at the folded sheet of paper wedged in the diary. He unfolds the paper. A quick scan: "Birth Certificate" is written in bold across the top. He folds it back up, looks away.

"So you knew?" Hank seems surprised and relieved.

"I didn't know anything until I saw her again in New York. 1986." Cal pauses, takes a breath. "That's the first time I knew she was pregnant. She told me," he turns to meet his brother's eyes, "you helped her get an abortion. On your way out of town."

"No, no." Hank stands, arms crossed, each hand squeezing and releasing the opposite bicep. "We didn't tell you—"

Cal picks up the photocopied birth certificate, looks again, more closely.

Leni had a baby girl on July 13, 1973.

Mother: Madeleine Bonet O'Hare. Father: Hank C. McGrath, Jr.

"'We?'" He wedges the paper back in the diary and flings it across the table.

Fuck Hank for dragging him up there, making him go through this. Again. Now.

Breathe.

Whatever game they played, or Hank's playing, it's too long ago. Nothing to be done. He looks at his brother, looks for the swaggering, hard-drinking, irresponsible, angry young man he was when he returned from overseas. Hank is looking back at him, his eyes intent, forehead creased. Expectant.

"Hank, I can't get worked up about this all over again." He's not going to give his brother the satisfaction. But it takes great effort not to get upset. Not to give into the fury of having been duped again. Twice. For loving the same woman. He feels his weakness, his frailty. His bones. So much of him having already wasted away.

Mary Lynn returns with the wet dogs, their tags jingling, their nails clattering on the wooden floor as they trot over to Hank. He ignores them.

"So this is why you asked me here?" Cal eyes Hank, then Mary Lynn, who, reaching for the coat hook, stops, arms extended in midair. "What are you looking for from me? Forgiveness? Then ask. And I'll forgive you. I can't hold on to this kind of shit any longer."

"It shouldn't be hard to contact her," Hank says. "If you want to."

Now Cal's furious. "Leni? Why would I want to do that?"

"No." Hank looks to Mary Lynn, then back to Cal. "Your daughter."

Cal grabs the diary, waves the copy of the birth certificate in the air. "*Your* daughter, Hank! *Your* daughter."

"What? No, no, no," Hank goes to Cal, snatches the paper and studies it, shaking his head. "I swear to you there was nothing like that between me and Leni." He turns it over, as if looking for an answer on the blank page.

"Your name's right there, Hank." Cal taps the paper with his finger.

"There is no way that baby girl was mine." Hank's voice has become shaky. Mary Lynn goes to him, rests her small hand on his arm. Hank shakes his head. He taps his fingers on the table with each careful point. "Leni stayed in Ohio. With the Ingrahams. For eight months. She had the baby. And she gave it up for adoption."

Cal stares at Leni's journals on the table. "The Ingrahams."

"That's where I went when I got back from Viet Nam. Their son—"

"I know," Cal cut his brother off. He picks up the copy of the birth certificate. Reads, again, his brother listed as the father.

"I swear, Cal. There's not a chance in hell that baby girl is mine."

"Neither of you told me anything, Hank. Not a goddamned thing—"

"That's on me. Partly or mostly. I don't know." Hank jumps in.

"Do you have any idea what a difference that would have made?" He hears his own plea to be understood.

"Leni wanted, well, she wanted you to get out. To go to Princeton. I made her promise," Hank continues, "not to tell you.

You were so smart, Cal. I didn't want you minding feed prices and reworking oil wells under Dad. I wanted you to get out, too." He looks up, expectant. "You found the money, right?"

There it is again: McGrath men thinking money will clean up any spill. But Cal can see this is painful for his brother, too. He sees it in his face. His brother has changed.

He studies again the paper in his hands.

That Leni landed in a pocket of kindness, in a family that in their grief sheltered her, Cal was glad. Glad that their goodness was big enough to stop her fall. And he could understand her grief. She was too young to be a mother, and he to be a father. For all that. For the sea of misunderstandings that circled them. For their blindness, each of them. For the inability in their youth to know, much less ask, for what they truly needed of one another, Cal cried. In front of the brother he'd hated for so many years, he cried.

Cal lies down on the narrow bed, props the iPad against his knees. Armed with the name of the hospital and the date of the birth, in half an hour he has the online forms filled out to contact the adoption agency.

CHAPTER THIRTY-ONE

October 16, 2016
Wassaic, New York

Caleb

Cal scours the train schedules tacked to a tall bulletin board beneath dirty plexiglass for the next train back to Manhattan. Holding his coat closed against the wind with one hand and a cane in the other, he watches a red Volvo wagon pull in and roll slowly to a stop alongside the platform.

A young woman slides out of the driver's seat. Her light brown hair is gathered back and up loosely on her head. Slim-fitting jeans accentuate her long legs. She adjusts the purse on her shoulder, straightens her sunglasses, pulls a long gray sweater around herself, and, clamping her arms across her waist, starts toward the platform stairs, not looking up until she reaches the top step.

"Are you . . .?" She hesitates.

"Caleb McGrath. Yes." He extends his hand.

She has his mother's nose. His nose. Thin and straight. Nervously, he pats his hair, tousled by a gust of wind. "You're—"

"Heather. Watson." Her hand quivers as she takes his.

"Thank you for coming." He wants to smooth the conversation. Doesn't know what else to say.

"Of course." A half smile softens her face. "Where would you like to go?" She looks north, her hair floating off her rather delicate face in the breeze. She reminds him of a slender water bird, a willet perhaps. Still. And wired to sense predators.

"It doesn't matter," he says, trying not to stare at her.

She looks back at him briefly; her sunglasses slip down her nose just enough. Eyes the same hazel green he knew was the color of the sea before he'd ever seen the sea.

"There's a café in town a few miles up."

He follows her down the steps to her car.

A small purple boa and tiny sparkling red slippers are piled on the passenger seat, which is almost shaggy with long blond dog fur. She tosses the clothes in the back between a child's booster seat and a full car seat, gets in, and, leaning over, begins brushing the passenger seat rapidly with her hand.

"I'm sorry about this," she says.

"Don't be."

"But that's such a nice coat." She releases tufts of fur out the open car door.

It is. And black, of course.

"I like dogs," Cal says.

"Really?"

"Yes." He laughs, to assure her, and lets himself down slowly into the worn bucket seat. "What kind of dog do you have?"

"A big, dumb golden retriever. Sweet and reliable as they come."

Cal rests the cane between his legs. She starts the car. Cal tries to extrapolate from the size of those ruby red slippers the height of the child who'd wear them. He looks to the backseat. A small yellow dump truck. Multiple Care Bear books. A boy and a girl, he guesses. Grandchildren.

"When's your train back?" she asks, continuing to wipe strands of hair from her face.

"It doesn't matter," he replies. "They leave almost every hour."

Slowly, carefully, she pulls out onto the empty two-lane road. Just meeting like this, maybe she also feels they are as fragile and unformed as newborns.

"You have children?" he asks.

"Yes. A boy and a girl."

"Tell me about them."

"Well," she pauses and turns her hand over, as though words may trickle down her open palm. Cal waits. "Sophie's five. And Felix is three," she concludes. Both hands back on the steering wheel.

It feels intrusive to press for more.

They pass vast fields, huge round rolls of hay sit stranded and patient on one side, the brown stubble of harvested corn on the other.

"Where did you grow up?" he asks.

"Ohio. And you?"

"East Texas."

"Do you go back?"

"No," Cal answers, sounding more curt than he intended. "Not since my mother passed away."

"When was that?"

"A long time ago. Nineteen eighty."

"And your father?"

They slow, coming up behind a green tractor pulling a spindly contraption chugging half on the shoulder and half on the road.

"Not so long ago," he answers. "Two thousand and ten. I went back then."

The farmer, jostling with the tractor's lurching, waves them past. Heather pulls around and accelerates up the hill. At the top, the road narrows. They are suddenly hemmed in on either side by woods, orange and gold. A chipmunk, its tail pointing straight to the sky, spurts across the road.

How could he make something coherent of his life to offer someone he should have known her whole life, but didn't? He doesn't know if he'll see her again. He feels acutely the pressure of time these days.

"I never knew about you," he says.

She nods.

They pass a gas station, then a small, red brick firehouse with a sign out front announcing a shrimp fry Saturday night.

Imagining her wondering about him all these years makes his chest hurt. "Have you felt an absence?" Cal stares unabashedly at her.

She nods again.

He knows well that longing can be boundless, without perimeters.

"I know young families," he begins, "who have adopted. And those children are deeply wanted. I hope that's how you felt, growing up. That you were chosen."

She nods again, wipes a tear from her cheek.

They arrive in Millerton, a small town, a village really. Clapboard storefronts climb the small, winding main street. The musty, slightly acrid smell of burning leaves is in the air. They pass a diner with a red neon "Open" sign in the window. She slows.

"Maybe we could just drive," Heather says suddenly. "I like to drive. You could see some fall colors."

"That would be fine."

"Unless you want a coffee?" She dips her head, her green eyes catching him over the tops of her glasses.

"I don't actually drink coffee anymore."

She makes a jagged three-point turn in front of a small shop with fishing gear and Pendleton shirts in the window. Cal stretches out his legs and lays the cane down alongside the door. They head back down the hill and onto the long road north into Columbia County.

There are a hundred things he could ask her. He tries to put himself in her shoes. wonders what she might want to know of him.

Her eyes are fixed on the road. "Tell me about my mother."

CHAPTER THIRTY-TWO

December 6, 2016

Leni

She's getting a later start than she wanted, as usual. It's dusk and rush hour as Leni heads up the Westside Drive in a rental van full of paintings, drawings, monotypes, and lithographs. Every December, for the past nine years, Leni's cajoled friends and other faculty members from the School of Visual Arts, where she teaches one semester a year, to donate an item for the Racehorse Retirement League's holiday auction. Held in Millbrook, New York, home to a clutch of super-wealthy equestrians and art collectors.

For the past several years, Leni has co-chaired the event with Meredith Marburger. Meredith finds corporate sponsors and dives into her friends' deep pockets. Leni procures the art. Exposure, she reminds her friends and colleagues, and the occasional promising student.

The Thursday evening traffic on the Henry Hudson and the Taconic squeezes and stretches like a slow accordion. It's dark when she gets to the rolling pastures of Dutchess County, but she knows the roads well. She should reach the Marburgers' just in time for one of Bill's gin martinis. Tomorrow and Saturday morning, she'll hang the show, along with the volunteers Meredith has wrangled. Saturday night, she'll skirt the periphery, hobnob as required. And Sunday, before heading back to the City, she'll visit Metaphor Farm, one of the nearby thoroughbred retirement farms. She'll climb a fence, watch the horses graze lazily on the winter grass, and take out her sketchbook, if the weather complies.

"**M**adeleine Bonet." Leni sets down her bag.

"William Marburger," she replies as he wraps her in a bear hug.

"The very same. Eagerly awaiting your arrival." He is a man accustomed to wielding power and is a consummate flirt. Tall. Successful. Cocky. Baritone voice. How many affairs has he juggled in his day, she wonders. "Martini?" he inquires.

"You bet."

"Come in. Come in. You look ravishing. Meredith's a basket case."

Leni follows him into the library. A wet bar in one corner. An enormous and expensively upholstered sofa and wing-backed chairs on a Persian rug. As Leni admires the prints on the blood-red wall, nineteenth-century hunting scenes, Bill shakes the martinis and strains them into two chilled glasses.

"A toast." He hands Leni a glass. "What shall we toast to?"

She feels pinned, like a butterfly to paper. "To freedom." Leni raises her glass.

"From?" he cocks his head.

"To." She holds his gaze. "Freedom to pursue one's desires and achieve one's potential." They clink glasses.

"Thank God, you've made it." Meredith swoops in. Black pencil pants, red leather flats. Too thin. Blond hair swept back into a ponytail. Brief hug. Kiss on both cheeks.

"I'm a nervous wreck," she announces. Then, to Bill, "A Manhattan tonight, dear." Back to Leni. "A hundred and fifty guests. Mitsy wanted to use a new caterer out of Hudson. The menu's atrocious. Goat cheese tartlets for dessert." She wrinkles her nose.

"Tell her it will be fine, Madeleine," Bill says, straining Meredith's drink into a glass.

"It will be fine," Leni says.

"You're just saying that." Meredith accepts the drink.

"All you need for a good party is good music."

"Quite right," Bill chimes in.

"Do you really think so?"

Meredith sips her Manhattan. Leni admires the light flickering through the amber liquid. The maraschino cherry, brooding in the well of the glass, glistens like a gemstone as red as Meredith's shoes. Does her outfit determine her drink choice, or vice versa? Leni wonders.

"Did Bill tell you?" Meredith turns to Leni.

"That she looks ravishing? Yes, I did."

"Oh, stop it," Meredith chastises her husband. "That he's invited Jim Redmond for dinner." Meredith's eyes tip upwards to look at Leni, as she carefully sips her Manhattan. "Tonight."

It takes Leni several beats to place the name. "Ah," she sighs, as the doorbell rings.

Last year, the recently divorced Jim Redmond, a good friend of the Marburgers and a private equity investor at some firm Leni was supposed to have heard of in Manhattan, fawned over Leni. They met for a couple of dinners in the City early in the year. A nice enough guy. A little short. Smart. Mildly self-effacing. Plays bluegrass guitar. There was nothing at all to disparage about him, really. Only that he so clearly wanted someone to love. Which is why Leni put him off and didn't think it wise to sleep with him. By late spring, he stopped calling.

Bill returns to the study with Jim. He is—Leni notices as they all exchange greetings, kisses on the cheeks—cute. Something still boyish about him. Full head of hair, though streaked with gray. The body of a stocky athlete. Maybe a rugby player in his youth at some prep school.

At dinner, he is solicitous of Leni. Asking how her work is going. He knows she had a show in Kent in August. He's keeping some tabs on her, she realizes. Doing his best to start conversation with Leni, to meet her in her world. How much he enjoyed the Tomás Saraceno *Cloud City* exhibit at the Met. Asking what she thought of the controversial Marina Abramovic show at MOMA. Meredith and Bill exchange once, twice, a furtive glance. Just enough to reveal their investment in this potential match, Jim and Em.

"And your work, is it going well?" she asks, lamely. Knowing she can't follow up any reply. Investments. Private equity and real estate. Perhaps she ought to be more interested in this. But she can't get through the front page of the *New York Times* business section without yawning.

Bill picks up the ball. "Jim's starting a new fund. First round of closings in the spring, yes?" Jim nods. "Real estate fund of funds. It's done well for us." Bill nods to Meredith. "Some new managers this time around?"

"Yes, of course." He looks at Leni. She's not bored yet. "One I really wanted to reinvest in is winding down, however. Their key man isn't well. You may know him. Caleb McGrath. He's got a place up here somewhere, outside Millbrook."

Such a shock to hear his name. It takes a moment to weave

all this together. Cal? Has a place around here? She hasn't heard his name in thirty years. Real estate. Funds. Investment. She sets down her fork.

"Yes, yes." Bill's sawing into his steak.

"Do we know him?" Meredith slides her fork beneath several peas.

"He keeps a pretty low profile around here," Bill says, chewing, appetite undiminished. "I know him from a deal I worked on with you." He points his knife at Jim.

"Right," Jim says. "Anyway, quite ill apparently. So that fund may be winding down. But the pipeline's full."

"Can we please, for the sake of our guest, not fall too far down the rabbit hole of private real estate deals?"

Leni remembers that Meredith and Bill met through work. She was an analyst at some big bank involved with taking over some company or taking another public. She can't keep it straight.

"Apologies," Jim says, smiling at Leni. "No more shop talk. Let's talk about the gala. How's it—"

"Caleb McGrath," Leni interrupts, looking at Jim.

Meredith looks startled.

"I know him," Leni explains.

"Really? How?"

"We're from the same hometown."

"No!" Meredith looks to Bill, to confirm how utterly surprising this is.

"He's not well?" Leni looks again to Jim.

"Um-hum." Jim nods and prepares another bite. "Apparently. He's stopped working. Cancer, I heard."

Leni says she's sorry to hear this, and the conversation turns to Saturday night's event. The dinner menu, Meredith's preoccupation. The auction. The number of guests and paintings. Bill's the auctioneer, again. Like a classy, witty barker, he picks people in the crowd, lures and good-heartedly shames them into bidding. It works.

"And you have a painting in the mix?" Jim asks Leni.

"She'd better," Meredith, perhaps one glass of wine too many, is adamant.

Leni smiles. "Yes, I do."

The conversation winds down. "You seem tired, Em." Meredith frowns. "Madeleine lugged all the paintings up here today."

"Happy to do it." Leni folds her napkin and lays it on the table. "It's a long day tomorrow."

"A working day for us all," Bill agrees. With that, he pushes his chair from the table. The glasses shimmy.

"Indeed," Jim affably agrees, and stands.

A t the door, saying goodbye, Jim holds Leni's hand a little too long before leaving.

"Nice to see Jim again, isn't it?" Bill says.

"Bill." Meredith nudges him, a barely perceptible shake of the head.

Leni wouldn't have picked Bill for a matchmaker.

After thanking them for dinner and going over the next day's schedule with Meredith, Leni excuses herself to the guest room.

When she was younger, there were men, of course. Fewer now. Lovers were never muses for Leni. They were distractions. And at some point, it might be a few months, or a couple of years, she would want to return to her work and her teaching unencumbered. The two longest relationships she'd had over the years were with men who lived elsewhere. Wyoming and London. Wyoming, whom she met while at an artists' residency, is married now. But they keep in touch, there's still deep affection. And London she met through friends while he was in New

York installing a show at the New Museum. This ended less amicably, though she can't remember exactly the circumstances. She does remember his calling her remote. She's accepted this about herself.

If a deep fissure opens early in one's life, there are—as Leni sees it—two choices one can make, consciously or unconsciously. One can carry into every relationship a need and a hope that it will suture up the hole left long ago. Or one can suture up the wound oneself and go on from there. Hold onto one's own strength, follow one's own pursuits, and—consciously or unconsciously—not risk opening up any new clefts, another loss. Leni chose the latter. Attaching herself to her work and to teaching, which have taken her around the country. To Ireland, Paris, Berlin, and Rome, as well. Not that she doesn't have some regrets. Some longings. Like she knows the daughter she gave birth to is forty-three and five months. That she has forty-three drawings for her. And she knows that in fifteen days, it will be forty-four years since she last laid eyes on Foggy. And forty-four years, three months, and eighteen days since she lost her brother.

Her aversion to self-pity keeps her from dwelling on these dates. But she cannot help knowing them. They are seared into her, like brands. And Cal? There's no one date for Cal. He may have been, though, the last person she really let see her. Her pain, her aspirations. And the last person she'd wanted to get lost in.

CHAPTER THIRTY-THREE

New York, New York
January 26, 2017

Caleb

Cal is in his favorite armchair by the window, a cashmere throw over his legs. It's hard to stay warm. Heather lifts the tray from his lap.

"Do you want to rest?" she asks. Her hair swings over her shoulder as she straightens up.

"In a bit." He is content to linger in his perch, shelves of his books behind him, West Seventy-Fourth Street with its row of wide brownstones leading to its glimpse of Central Park in front of him.

The fatigue is unrelenting now. He no longer fights it. Cyclophosphamide is not as discriminating as one would hope. The treatments left him nauseated, bruised, and exhausted to his bones. Crossing his legs takes forethought and will. Like most, he started this journey committed to beating back the disease. Mustering all the usual battle metaphors: he'd fight it, whip it, gather an arsenal of treatments and doctors, etc. He traveled the parallel paths of hope and denial. The disease, though, continued to run alongside, outpacing him now. He finished the last round of treatments two months ago and has surrendered. They tell him the pain in his abdomen, neck, and groin is lymph nodes, swollen and pressing on nerves. The painkillers help.

"You remind me of her, you know." He reaches for the oxygen tube.

"So you've said." Heather sets the tray on the coffee table, rolls the oxygen tank closer. "You're all I can handle right now," she says over her shoulder, heading to the kitchen.

Cal doesn't want to press; it's not his place. She did tell him that seven years earlier, when she and her husband, Gary, were getting ready to start a family, she tried to find her birth parents. She lost the trail to her mother after Leni's stint at the University of Ohio and the scholarship to study in Europe. Almost by accident (or maybe not really), she may have found the trail again last summer, flipping through an art magazine. But, Heather told Cal, if it was her mother, she was quite a successful artist who traveled the world, was unmarried, and had no children—at least none that appeared in any bio—leading Heather to determine that it was unlikely this particular woman wanted to be a mother. And the father—or the one on the birth certificate—left Texas with the law on his tail, which rather discouraged her from looking for him again.

Cal, though, has done some quiet reconnaissance of his own, for his own reasons, and in case Heather were to change her mind. Leni—or M. Bonet—teaches regularly at the School of Visual Arts in New York and has taught from Rockland, Maine to Savannah, Georgia and overseas. She shows in the City and elsewhere, including in a gallery barely twenty miles from his house upstate. When he told Rob this, they chuckled to think that he, Leni, and Heather had landed in such prox-imity. He also discovered that Leni donates paintings regularly to auction fundraisers for an upstate New York horse rescue association. Bingo.

Through the fall, when Cal could still go upstate, he and Heather met a half dozen times, for lengthy breakfasts or lunches. She opened up more each time they met, talking about her parents in Ohio, her two brothers, one adopted. Solid middle class. College at Ohio State. She's a graphic designer, works mostly from home for clients in Manhattan. She got her talent, he assures her, from her mother.

In November, two days before Cal went in for his last treatment, Heather brought the kids into the City. Felix, three, and Sophie, who had just turned six. He was introduced as a friend of the family. They went to the Central Park Zoo and watched the monkeys and big cats, then watched the polar bear flop back and forth in his too small pool until Heather said it made her sad and they moved over to the seal pond.

Felix is a solid little guy. For the trip to the zoo, he wore a homemade black cape with a red letter *F* embroidered on the back. It stands for "phantom," he told Cal proudly.

"I see," Cal said, nodding.

"Do you like phantom ninjas?" Felix asked.

"You bet I do," Cal told him, hoping he wouldn't ask for any specifics. Sophie wore a pink corduroy jumper over paisley leggings and her ruby red slippers. Cal complimented her style. She nodded seriously. Sophie started off the afternoon very shy. But by the end, after they'd stood together and watched the red pandas climb their trees, and the African pygmy goats buck and romp, and she'd ridden the merry-go-round three times, she took Cal's hand and confessed that she loved horses. He told her he did, too, and that he used to have horses. She wanted to know their names. "Captain Flint, Reverie, Lady Belle, and Buck," he told her. "Captain Flint was very special." And he told her how he had trained Flint to follow him like a big dog by putting carrots in his back pocket, which Flint would snatch, thinking he was being sneaky. Still holding onto Cal's hand, Sophie told him all about their big dog, Harold. "He snatches things, too," she told him.

For many years, Cal had counted himself lucky that he didn't have children. Not because he didn't like them. He actually liked the few he's known. One or two enormously, including Rob's son, Lucas, who Cal met when he was just four days old. Holding him, a silent nearly boneless thing, Cal felt that infant like an explosion in the present, particles extending back through time and shooting forward, both. It was then he understood that children are both one's past and future. He also knew that having a child would make him confront his own incompetence in ways he didn't necessarily want to confront. And he couldn't protect them from pain. From the disappointment of lost love, failed ambition, pride, or insecurity. He couldn't prevent their sense of wonder and style—like ruby red slippers and paisley leggings—their art and brilliance, from being squelched or diverted. So, he consoled himself, those times when the loss from being barren crossed his mind, by conjuring some gratitude for having avoided all that pain.

He knows now, though, that he had it all wrong. Because even one's pain is precious. Our striving and yearning are the manifestation of hope. And hope is the essence of all goodness. This is what he's come to understand. A slow learner, perhaps. But he learned it. Learned a lot near the end. And he is grateful for the lesson and for those who taught it to him along the way.

Heather returns, an extra sweater in hand. She straightens the magazines and newspaper on the coffee table, refills a pitcher of water, and places it on the side table beside his chair.

"What can I do for you before I leave?" she asks.

"I think I'll watch a movie. What DVDs are there?" he asks.

She checks the stack. "*Lord of the Rings. Avatar.*"

He shakes his head.

"*The Bourne Legacy.*"

Those he likes. "When can you come again?" he asks.

"I can come down Thursday." She slips a DVD out from the stack. "Gary's mom can watch the kids."

He makes a mental note that today is Sunday. That ought to be all right, he thinks.

"In two weeks Sophie's out of school for February break."

He had wanted to take them all, Heather, Sophie, and Felix, to the Metropolitan Museum to see the Temple of Dendur and the medieval armor exhibit. They'll get there sometime, of course, without him.

"Do you want any more of this?" Heather holds up a large, sweating wax paper cup. "Did Rob bring this?" she asks.

"Yes. He came by this morning."

Since Cal got sick, a year and a half ago, he and Rob—college roommate and former business partner—have had dinner every week. He comes by most mornings now. If Cal doesn't feel like eating, Rob'll bring a chocolate milkshake and—fighting his own weight and cholesterol for the past six years—watch every sip Cal takes. Cal always offers him some, even though he knows he shouldn't. When Cal was in the midst of treatments, Rob would send food— puddings, pies, anything to try to keep Cal's weight up—and DVDs of blockbuster movies and sporting events, including the Oklahoma State Rodeo, which Cal watched from beginning to end four times. Last week, the depths of winter settling in, Rob and his third wife, Ingrid, brought him the cashmere throw, soft as air and as warm as sitting by a fire. Cal thinks the third time's the charm on the marriage front. Ingrid is every bit Rob's match. Cal's glad for that.

Felix and Sophie have made drawings for Cal. He watches Heather tape them on the wall by the TV. He still can't help sometimes searching when he looks at her. There's Leni's silky brown hair. That's obvious. But there are other things, odd things you'd never think genes would replicate. Like he hears Leni in the way Heather clears her throat, twice in very short succession, and the way she cocks her head when thinking. Heather presses one last time on the corners of each of the children's drawings, making sure the phantom ninja, the pink horse, their completely out of scale house, and Harold are all securely affixed.

She plumps the pillow behind Cal's back one last time and kisses him on the forehead.

CHAPTER THIRTY-FOUR

March 4, 2017
New York, New York

Caleb

Cal scans his desiccated body. The morphine drips into what had been a body of water, mostly. Bodies of water and tides. Rivers of time. The enormity of the sea and memory.

He hovers. Between the gray linoleum floor and the ceiling's bright lights. His body barely makes an imprint on the white sheets beneath the white blanket. Red Jell-O beside a clear plastic pitcher on the beige side table. A milkshake melts in a waxed paper cup. His thoughts are at once muddled and vast.

Cal arrived at the hospital's hospice wing during the night, he doesn't recall how many nights ago, by ambulance. He remembers its insistent swirling lights, the gurney clanking.

His room, he's told, has a view across the East River to Brooklyn and Queens. He prefers, though, to keep the thin shades drawn. Day or night, it makes no difference. Routines, the scaffolding for climbing over time, aren't necessary any longer. He tumbles between sleeping and waking, dozes over the soft beeps and hums of machines and monitors and floats, languid, in the penumbral light of dawn or dusk, across water and prairie, seascapes and landscapes, an occasional cluster of people. Consciousness, as he's often suspected, has fewer sharp edges than we imagine.

He feels no hunger. Thirst, though, still. The sensation of liquids, cool or warm, in his mouth is still good.

Rob and Ingrid alternate visiting. One of them came by when he was asleep. A milkshake is in a bowl of ice by his bed. But he can no longer summon up the memory of cream and vanilla. Chemicals have seeped even into his tongue and turned the taste to something more like chrome.

His eyelids slide shut.

A silhouette of a figure seated before the thin shade. A woman. Her hair pushed back behind her ears. Her face cast down. Perhaps she is reading. He doesn't want to disturb her. Though quite likely she is not really there at all. There have been other visions. His eyes close, he slips back into the stream of half-sleep, half-consciousness. Waits for the image or vision to move on.

Paper rustles next to him.

He lifts his eyelids. The figure is there still. It moves closer.

"Can I get you anything?"

He stares. Imagines shaking his head. Cannot stop staring. It is more than enough that she has come. In whatever form.

"Are you in pain?"

"No." He's not sure the word slid out. His mouth is so dry. Lips parched. His eyes flicker toward the clear morphine solution dangling beside the headboard and dripping through a narrow tube to his forearm.

He closes his eyes.

If he were honest, and could count the hours over the years, it would be days upon days, weeks, spent in imaginary conversation with her. First angry and self-righteous, occasionally clever. Then resigned, sad, yearning to understand. Accepting. Maybe it's not odd that she would appear. Like this. Maybe, finally, he has summoned her, across time. And she's just arriving now, very late. But not too late. That's the thing. He wonders if specters, or phantoms, age. Would she be as he last saw her in New York? In her prime. Strong and alluring.

He waits for the vision to speak or move on.

He feels the blanket pulled up and smoothed across his chest.

He lifts his hand. Touches flesh.

Open eyes again. He searches her face.

Gray hair, cut to her shoulders. Beautiful to him still.

Still holding his feeble hand, she pulls the chair closer to the bed.

"Is it all right that I've come?" she asks.

He nods.

"Is there anything I can do for you?" she asks.

He is not able to stop looking at her face. "How . . ." he whispers.

She leans closer.

He is becoming only air. He tries again. "How did you find . . .?"

"How did I find you?"

He nods.

"Your friend, Rob, found me." She smiles.

Rob. Quite the fairy godmother: a sixty-two-year-old recovering alcoholic, venture capitalist with a paunch. You just never know.

"Talk. Talk to me. About you."

"That'll put you back to sleep." She smiles.

His eyes close. He shakes his head.

She strokes his hand. He can feel her touch. Something of him is solid still.

"I paint," she says softly. "And teach. Wherever I'm offered a job. Painting and thinking about painting. That's what I do, mostly."

"Married," he whispers.

"No. Never married. You?"

He shakes his head.

A nurse comes in. Checks the bag with the morphine solution, presses a button on the monitor by the bed and waits as it groans and ejects a printed page, which she scans quickly.

"Is there anything I can do for him?" Leni asks the nurse.

"There's Biotene there on the table. For dry mouth. And some ointment." The nurse mimes putting ointment on her lips.

Leni lets go of his hand. Smooths ointment across his lips. A spray of Biotene into his open mouth.

"Are you happy?" Those words came out. *Stupid question*, he thinks. As if life were static. "Have you been happy?"

"Yes. At times." She smiles. "I try to do what I love and share it." She shrugs. "Have you been happy?"

"Not sure," he answers.

"Ever?"

He tries to smile at her.

She has not changed. Not really. Something in her truly never wavered. This is how it seems to him. She had always been strong and forthright. Lonely in high school, even though she had all the makings of a popular girl. She was pretty and athletic and artistic. He thought even back then that she frightened some people. She didn't need them in the way other teenagers needed their friends. Most people want to flow along with the currents of their family, their town. To fit in. And it can be good to have a current to step back into when life pulls you off course. Leni, though, followed something inside herself.

He can see something else now, too. How he built a life around an absence. Plastering over the negative space with well-paying jobs, nice homes, pretty girlfriends. He's been very fortunate. This, though, is not the same as authentic. And the absence wasn't Leni. He'd lost himself. All that he had yearned for, all that seemed possible, when he was on the wide open Texas plains with her.

"You didn't tell me," he whispers. Finally. "Why?"

"Tell you what?"

He waits.

"I didn't know how," she says.

"How doesn't matter."

She nods. "When did you find out?"

"Hank. Canada. Your diaries."

"My diaries. I figured they'd have been thrown out ages ago." She's still holding, gently, his hand.

"You didn't throw them out." It's hard to get this out. His breaths are so shallow.

"No. I didn't."

She rests her forehead on his hand, which she holds now in both of hers. "You know Hank wasn't the father." She lifts her head, studies him.

Eyes closed, Cal nods.

"I didn't want to entangle you. Maybe that was wrong. I don't know. But I wanted the world to know she had a father. To send her out with 'Father Unknown' seemed even more of a lie."

He feels his hand in hers. Feels his body on the sheets. Takes in her words.

"Afterwards, I wanted to die."

He nods again, knows this from her diary.

"Once I came through that, I couldn't look back," she says. "Can you understand that? I had to believe what I did was right. That I was letting you have your life. And me mine, too."

Cal looks at her. We all close doors and have doors closed on us. Sometimes it takes a lifetime to love again, to wait for the forgiveness required.

His eyes slide closed again.

"Is it all right if I stay?"

He nods. She settles back into the armchair at his bedside.

Sensation. Thirst. Again. Dim light. Cal looks toward the window. Rob is there, reading glasses on the end of his nose. A folded paper in his hand.

Breathe. "Calculating returns?"

"Sudoku." Rob lays the paper in his lap. "What can I get you?"

Cal reaches for the water on the stand by his bed.

"Wait a minute there, champ." Rob stands, slips an arm beneath Cal's head and upper back, lifts him, and lays a pillow behind his head and neck. "Comfortable?"

Rob holds the cup of water, steadies the straw.

"Lucas finishes his midterms tomorrow. He's catching a train Friday morning to come see you."

Cal doesn't know when Friday is.

Rob sets the cup down on the side table. Cal lifts his hand. Rob takes it.

His eyes close.

Leni is there. Still or again. A sketchpad on her lap and a char-coal pencil in her hand. The shade behind her is opaque now.

Seeing his eyes open, she goes to him. Again smooths oint-ment on his lips.

"Rob came by." She holds the cup with a straw to his mouth. He sips.

Whatever it is that has tethered him here—light, breath, sound—is fraying.

He slips back into time on her voice.

"He loves you," she says.

He knows this. Closes his eyes, drifts. Words require such effort. He's not certain he can still muster them.

"Drawing," he whispers. "What are you drawing?"

"What I see."

He sees, too, the gaunt, bald, barely there figure before her. The white blanket, white sheets. The machines with a ghostly glow.

"Do you want to look?"

She stands, takes the pad, and turns it so he can see. It is a young man, standing in a field of tall grass. The collar of his jacket turned up slightly at his neck. His hair swept to the side. He looks up, to the sky.

"Recognize him?"

"Flint."

"What?" Leni presses the pad to her chest, leans closer.

A breath. Gathering again memory and words. "Flint."

She sits, turns the page on her pad. Begins drawing.

He drifts.

Gratitude.

For Leni. For Rob. Spreads through his body like a light. Gratitude for the care he's receiving. The cleanliness. The mor-phine. The cool liquids.

He feels suddenly very large.

He sees the fields in East Texas. The barn with the tall fence. Horses grazing. Captain Flint. And Foggy. Together, head to tail, dozing in the sun. And himself. A younger self, standing in the field.

He blinks.

Taped to the railing surrounding the narrow hospital bed, and to the walls around him, are charcoal and pastel sketches.

Fields, horses, cows.

He lifts his hand. Someone—flesh, warmth—takes it.

It is Leni.

Still.

Always.

He lets go.

CHAPTER THIRTY-FIVE

Saint-Brieuc, France
August 26, 2017

Ludevigne

She settles into her beach chair, pulls a thin sweater over her thick arms, and adjusts her hat against the sun, the new summer one she just finished, with goldcrest and willow warbler feathers, like a very small open fan, tucked in the shiny gossamer ribbon. She watches the little girl, thin as a wisp, and her younger brother, sturdy as a pony, gallop to the water's edge, shriek when the cold sea licks their toes, and run back toward their mother and grandmother.

She had long ago relinquished imagining any of her own children, with their children in tow, taking the place of the young families she'd see. Now, though, here is her daughter walking the wide beach with the granddaughter and great-grandchildren she has only recently come to know existed. She used to think it is only death that is inexorable. But it is life, too, of course. How could she have neglected this, she thinks, as the little girl, her blond ponytail in a tangle, stands before her, her small palm open wide to display an assortment of tiny scallop and Trochidae shells. The boy barrels up, plunging one hand in front of his sister's, to reveal a fistful of stones and a small strand of kelp, as he rubs his eyes hard with his other fist.

Ludevigne's daughter is gray-haired now herself. She and her daughter approach, not breaking their stride or conversation until they arrive before her. The boy clings to his mother, rolling his face back and forth on her thigh. "Salt," he whines. "In my eye."

This is their last day. Tomorrow they will take the train back to Paris and a plane back to New York. Madeleine has promised to come again next summer, and to do her best to bring Marguerite, and her daughters, both well into their twenties now.

Over these days, Ludevigne watched her daughter and "new" granddaughter melt into conversation every chance they got. She has been content merely to sit in their company, all of them. There is too much past to retrace, and it is too heavy to conjure up. They have spoken, of course, something of their lives. But the present is too precious to waste.

The night before there was a dinner with cousins to say goodbye to "*les Américains.*" The children stood slack-jawed as the adults conversed in French, their heads swinging back and forth between speakers, trying to make out what was being said. When laughter broke out, the boy would tug on his mother, "What'd they say, Momma? What'd they say?"

After dinner, Madeleine retrieved the narrow, rectangular box she'd lugged across the ocean. She opened it in the kitchen and when dessert was finished, coffee cups and empty plates scattered over the table, she emerged holding a painting, its back exposed to the group, as she explained in her now broken French that she hoped they would allow her this intrusion. She turned the painting around in her arms to reveal a portrait of her brother, the son lost so many years ago. His likeness peering out to them, deep brown eyes, a modest smile, hands in the pockets of his jeans. There were gasps. Ludevigne reached both hands out to her daughter.

"Why are they crying, Momma? Why are they crying?" the children want to know.

"Just remember," she told them. "One day you'll understand."

APPENDIX

THE LAST WILL & TESTAMENT OF
CALEB D. McGRATH of
22 West Seventy-fourth Street, New York, NY
and Sugar Hill Road, Millbrook, NY.

I, **CALEB B. MCGRATH**, residing at 22 West 74th Street, New York, New York and Sugar Hill Road, Millbrook, New York, and being of sound mind, do hereby make, publish and declare this to be my LAST WILL and TESTAMENT, and do hereby revoke any and all former Wills and Codicils heretofore made by me.

....

I do hereby appoint **ROBERT J. MILSTON, III** as my Executor and Trustee.

.....

ARTICLE V. As of the date of my death, I give, bequeath and devise to my Trustee, named herein, the real property, consisting of 36.8 acres located on Sugar Hill Road, Millbrook, New York to be held in trust for **F & F EQUINE RETIREMENT**

FARM, a recognized 501(c)(3) organization under the applicable statutes of the State of New York, pursuant to the terms set forth herein.

....

It is further my wish that **MADELEINE O'HARE, aka M. BONET**, currently of 725 Nevins Street, Brooklyn, NY be executive director of the **F & F Equine Retirement Farm**, and that the residence located at Sugar Hill Road, Millbrook, New York be at her disposal.

Should for any reason, **MADELEINE O'HARE** decline or fail to serve, my Trustee and Executor shall select a willing and capable successor Executor Director.

It is further my wish that the real property located at 22 West 74th Street, New York, New York be sold and that said proceeds, less any applicable taxes and encumbrances, if any, be transferred to the **F & F Equine Retirement Fund Endowment** for the benefit of **F & F Equine Retirement Farm**, and managed pursuant to the terms set forth therein.

......

ARTICLE VIII. The residuary of my estate I leave in the following proportion:

A. Half to endow the Trust, dated November 2, 2016, for the benefit of the **F & F Equine Retirement Farm**, Sugar Hill Road, Millbrook, NY.

B. And the remaining half of my residuary estate shall pass outright in equal shares to my brother, **HANK MCGRATH, JR.** of Ile de Carillon, Quebec, Canada; **MADELEINE O'HARE aka M. BONNET** of Brooklyn, NY; and **HEATHER WATSON** of Millerton, New York. In the event that Hank McGrath, Jr. or Madeleine O'Hare shall not survive me, their share shall pass to Heather Watson. In the event that Heather Watson does not survive me, her share shall pass to her then living issue in trust until they reach the age of twenty-four (24) years.....

.....

Signed this 12th day of February, 2017

New York, New York

_____

Caleb D. McGrath

ACKNOWLEDGMENTS

To begin at the beginning, a girl—galloping hard across the Texas chaparral, running from or to something—emerged in a workshop with the generous and wise Christy Walker. From there, Leni and Caleb, their families and their worlds, were born. Thank you, Christy.

I'm grateful beyond words for the friendship and graciousness of those who read early drafts and continued (perhaps undeservedly) to encourage me. Among them: Alex Enders, Sarah French, Polly Johnson, Claudia Barron, Jodi Rothe, S. Kirk Walsh, Kiffer Sikes, and my sister, Lorrie Brown. Also Bill Roorbach, Diane Cohen Schneider and the Spurwinker clan. I thank also Kate Moses for her unflagging support. My sincere apologies to any who I've forgotten.

The beautiful paintings of my friend, Shawn Dulaney, helped to inform Leni's art.

A whole cadre of people contributed their expertise and time to the production of this book and deserve thanks, including: Peggy Naut, for her careful copyediting; Julie Metz and her team for the cover design and layout; Lauren Wise, who ushered the whole thing to print; and Brooke Warner, a tireless champion of women writers (I honestly don't know when she sleeps). I hope this book is worthy of the time and attention these women shared.

I'm grateful, too, for the winter residency at the Virginia Center for the Creative Arts that allowed me to complete the first draft, and for the Brooklyn Writers Space—founded by Scott Adkins and Erin Courtney—where I spent many hours, most of them in silence, among its wonderful community of committed writers.

And who would I be without the horses who taught me patience, grace and grit, most especially Baldy and Reverie; the Texas chaparral whose subtle beauty is etched in my core; and the artists who when I first landed in New York City, lonely and insecure, startled and enlivened me—Michael, the handsome painter and craftsman with a southern drawl, who married me and stood steadfast through all the twists and turns that would lead (eventually) to this book, most of all . . . I miss you so.

ABOUT THE AUTHOR

D onnaldson Brown grew up riding horses across the Texas
plains. An attorney and former screenwriter, she's performed
her spoken word pieces in and around New York, including for
the Berkshire Theatre Festival and the Deep Listening Institute.
Her personal essay "Spell Breaking" was published in the
anthology *Spell Breaking: Listening to the Dreaming Heart*. She
is a current fellow of Craigardan Arts Colony and past fellow of
the Virginia Center for the Creative Arts and the Squaw Valley
Community of Writers. She divides her time between Brooklyn,
New York, and the Berkshires in western Massachusetts.

Author photo © Kate Burton

SELECTED TITLES FROM SHE WRITES PRESS

She Writes Press is an independent publishing
company founded to serve women writers everywhere.
Visit us at www.shewritespress.com.

The Best Part of Us by Sally Cole-Misch. $16.95, 978-1-63152-741-8. Beth cherished her childhood summers on her family's beautiful northern Canadian island—until their ownership was questioned and a horrible storm forced them to leave. Fourteen years later, after she's created a new life in urban Chicago, far from the natural world, her grandfather asks her to return to the island to see if what was lost still remains.

Mt. Moriah's Wake by Melissa Norton Carro. $16.95, 978-1-64742-138-0. A young woman returning home to her small southern town must face her past and the skeletons in her small community—and come to terms with her present life.

School Tales by Sharon Myrick. $16.95, 978-1-63152-423-3. A lively rendering of what's wrong, and what could be right, about high school—told through the voices of teenagers living in a small town of the southern Shenandoah Valley in Virginia who are desperate to become self-directed.

The Wiregrass by Pam Webber. $16.95, 978-1-63152-943-6. A story about a summer of discontent, change, and dangerous mysteries in a small Southern Wiregrass town.

Valeria Vose by Alice Bingham Gorman. $16.95, 978-1-63152-409-7. When privileged Southern woman Valeria Vose discovers her husband's infidelity through his lover's attempted suicide, she turns to an Episcopal priest for direction and solace—and spins into a clandestine, ill-fated love affair that forces her to confront all her preconceived values and expectations.